D0296639

THE
HUNDRED YEARS
WAR

by

EDOUARD PERROY
Professor of Medieval History at the Sorbonne

with an introduction to the English edition by
DAVID C. DOUGLAS
Professor of History in the University of Bristol

1951
EYRE & SPOTTISWOODE
LONDON

La Guerre de Cent Ans was first
published in Paris in 1945
This, the first authorized English edition,
has been translated by W. B. WELLS

*This book is printed in Great Britain for
Eyre & Spottiswoode (Publishers) Ltd.,
15 Bedford Street, London, W.C.2, by
Butler & Tanner Ltd., Frome and London*

CONTENTS

CONTENTS

MAPS

TABLES

INTRODUCTION

To INTRODUCE to English readers an historical work written by a distinguished Professor of History at the Sorbonne is a high privilege, and in exercising it a writer must inevitably be conscious of attempting a task which might seem otiose or even impertinent. Yet there is reason why another voice should be raised to call attention to the important volume – and that an English one – since Monsieur Perroy's book goes some considerable way towards filling a gap in English historical literature. The Hundred Years War provides some of the best known episodes in our national story, but as a unity it probably looms less largely than it should in our national consciousness. Sluys and Crécy, Poitiers and Agincourt are, as battles, familiar names; the treaties of Brétigny and Troyes are famous; but the political background of diplomacy and war against which they must be considered remains for most of us somewhat nebulous. The elaborate and successful investigations of English history in the later Middle Ages with which the names of Stubbs and Tout are particularly associated, have in the main been concerned with constitutional development and ecclesiastical controversy. Less progress has however perhaps been made in the elucidation of the diplomatic history of the period, and of the problems relating to Anglo-French relations in this age. It would not be difficult to defend the opinion that the best general history of the reign of Edward III is that which Joshua Barnes produced in 1688. The Hundred Years War, as a whole, still awaits its English historian.

None the less, it is impossible to dissociate the social and constitutional growth of England during this age from the military history of the period. The development of Parliament at this time was by no means unconnected with the demands made upon the royal revenue by the needs of the war in France. The machinery of the royal administration was likewise affected. The preliminaries to the Hundred Years War thus saw established in England an office of diplomacy directed by an official styled 'Keeper of the Processes' who has been described as a 'sort of under-secretary of state for foreign affairs', and a major factor in the English successes has been held to be 'an administrative system at home singularly elastic, and capable of expansion and adaptation to war needs'. Again, the anti-papal legislations of fourteenth-century England was stimulated by the conflict, being fostered by the belief, perhaps unjustified, that the Popes at Avignon were less anxious to promote peace than to further French interests. It has been alleged that Henry V's revival of the struggle was not unconnected with a desire to use the enthusiasm generated by a foreign war to allay discontent at home, and more certainly during the period of the Wars of the Roses the position of the Lancastrian dynasty in England was weakened by the defeats of the English armies in France.

If, however, the Hundred Years War forms an essential part of the History of England, it cannot of course be considered merely from an English standpoint. To write the story of that war, a man must be in possession of an intimate knowledge of both the countries chiefly affected, and he must also have a first-hand acquaintance with the trend of recent historical studies in each of them. The author of the present book may be numbered among the few individuals who can claim such qualifications. While his major preoccupations have always been with medieval France, his long residences in England, and his long service in a Scottish university, have brought him into close and sympathetic contact with our own life and our own past. In this book the Hundred Years War is described in relation to its results on two contrasted communities with both of which the author is familiar.

During the period with which this book is concerned, four generations of Englishmen and Frenchmen conducted their domestic affairs against the background of a continental struggle in which they all found themselves directly or indirectly involved. It is true that there were pauses in the war, and in particular there was the long truce between 1380 and 1415. But the campaigns of Edward III, the Lancastrian attack under Henry V, and the French recovery, form part of a single story which stretches from 1328 to after 1445; and that fact alone gives to a work on the Hundred Years War a special and a topical significance to-day when Anglo-French relations are patently of such importance to the western world. The circumstances in which this book was produced add moreover additional weight to this consideration. It was compiled, says the author, in such intervals of leisure as were afforded to him during the winter of 1943–44 in the midst of 'an exciting game of hide-and-seek with the Gestapo'. For this reason, it may be suspected, the work has gained an actuality which it would never otherwise have possessed. Comparison between distinct ages is both dangerous and misleading if it be pushed too far. But an account of a period when France was largely occupied by a foreign power surely gains in force when written by a Frenchman who experienced to the full the consequences of another, and a very different, occupation. There is of course no suggestion by this careful and scholarly writer that the examples of the fourteenth century can offer any detailed guidance for the political action of our own days. But few will be found to dispute his claim that 'when a nation reaches the depth of the abyss, as was the case at that time and in our own, certain ways of behaviour in misfortune, certain reactions against fate, throw mutual light upon one another'. Here, certainly, is food for reflection. In no exact sense does 'History repeat itself'. But the flux of human affairs is constant, and as the spiral uncoils, so are similar problems posed to different men with different capacities and desires. 'The great and exemplary wheels of heaven' revolve, and we who watch them are brought to contemplate the marriage between Time and the Hour.

More superficially, there might easily be sought other more direct points of connexion between the military history of that remote age and our own. The Normandy beach-head which allied troops made familiar to the world in recent years played its important part in the Hundred Years War. In 1346 Edward III landed at Barfleur in the neighbourhood of the American landings of 1944, and in his subsequent campaign he took in succession Saint-Lô and Caen before proceeding eastwards through Crécy to Calais. Again in 1417 Henry V (like General Eisenhower) decided that the mastery of Lower Normandy was the best preparation for the conquest of the Seine valley, and the Treaty of Troyes of 1420 has recently been compared with the abortive Act of Union proposed by the British Government on 16 June 1940. Such comparisons are, however, more facile than illuminating. The circumstances of the invasions were so widely different, and as Professor Jacob has recently pointed out the Treaty of Troyes foreshadowed a union which was much less close than that suggested in 1940. The fifteenth-century arrangement implied 'not a rigid administrative unity but a dynastic superiority binding two peoples each governing itself under its own laws and customs'.

Nevertheless, if the circumstances of the Hundred Years War must be placed in their medieval setting, it remains true that the history of that war is of primary interest as a chapter in the history of two peoples whose destinies have become inextricably intertwined. The fact that a Duke of Normandy in the eleventh century made himself King of England, that in the twelfth century the descendants of that Duke won for themselves a large empire in France, produced conditions which were exactly calculated to promote an uneasy alternation between projects of union and periods of acute conflict. The destruction of the Angevin Empire as an effective political unit in the thirteenth century and the later centralization effected respectively by Edward I and Philip IV might seem to have weakened the connexion between the two countries, but sentiments deriving from the earlier age none the less persisted even into the fifteenth century. It was not merely arid legalism, it was not simply astute propaganda, which inspired Henry V to claim as his own inheritance Normandy, Maine, Anjou and Touraine, or to assert that his ancestors had been unjustly deprived of these provinces by Philip Augustus. To modern students conscious that the early Renaissance was even then beginning to brighten in Italy, and that the age of nationalism was about to dawn, such sentiments may well seem anachronistic. But to Henry V, and to many of his advisers, they were a reality. Normandy was always 'his own' duchy, and Rouen 'his own' city. Passion is always a stronger element in politics than the cool assessment of contemporary circumstance, and one of the prime causes of the Hundred Years War must be sought in traditions from a past that was already remote at the time of Agincourt. Before ever Edward III resolved on his French enterprise, before Philip VI, the first Valois, succeeded to his uneasy inheritance, France and England had been brought into an intimate historical relationship from which neither could escape. Of this relationship, close, embarrassing and enduring, the Hundred Years War was at once a symptom and a solvent.

This was a feudal world, and in its complicated meshes both countries were involved. It is easy – and it is just – to discover the immediate cause of the outbreak of the Hundred Years War in the impossible situation created by the position of an English king who was also Duke of Gascony. An independent prince, he was also a French vassal, subject in France to a monarch whose interests were frequently directly opposed to his own. Here indeed was a reason for war much more important than Edward III's much advertised claim to the French throne. The dynastic argument advanced in connexion with this claim may indeed be regarded primarily as a move in propaganda calculated to appeal to possible allies. It takes its place, however, in that tradition of Angevin aspirations which was a legacy from the past, and it was partly for that reason that it was developed later by Henry V. More significantly was it designed to appeal to feudal sentiment. It gave a spurious excuse of legality to any vassals of the French king who desired to revolt. Such men could thus while pursuing a self-regarding policy argue that they were but transferring their allegiance to another and more legitimate overlord.

Such feudal relationships were of the first importance at the beginning of the Hundred Years War, and they influenced most of its course. Even as the contemporary Papacy could still assert, though with waning success, obligations which over-rode the boundaries of modern national states, so also were these divisions blurred by the interests of feudal families with connexions on both sides of the Channel. Only very gradually, and never completely, did the Hundred Years War come to be in the modern sense a war between 'France' and 'England'. In the first phase of the war, Edward III received support from Robert of Artois, brother-in-law to Philip VI, and sixty years later the whole character of the conflict was modified by the strife in France between the Burgundian and Armagnac factions. The assassination in 1407 of Louis of Orleans by Burgundian partisans, and the consequent enmity between John the Fearless, Duke of Burgundy, and Bernard, Count of Armagnac, were symptoms of a deep-seated political malaise. The more notorious murder in 1419 of John the Fearless on the bridge of Montereau by Armagnac nobles under the eyes of the future Charles VII opened the way to much more serious consequences. Such events made possible for a time a real alliance between the English and the Burgundians so that the conflict was for long (within France) of the nature of a Civil War. Henry V might conquer 'his own' duchy of Normandy and reorganize its administration, but it was the Burgundians who in 1418 seized Paris, and when in 1422 the infant son of the victor of Agincourt was recognized and crowned as King of France, he was acknowledged as their natural lord by the citizens, and the University, of the French capital.

Amid these events it is difficult to explain the development of the Hundred Years War by close reference to more modern notions of politics. Yet underlying them it might be possible to discern a manifestation of those permanent problems relating to the opposed ideals of political order and political liberty. In the first quarter of the fifteenth century there were two regimes in France: in the north a France 'occupied by a foreign prince whose power rested to a large extent upon the support of a French party'; towards the south, a France weaker in strength, but perhaps stronger in integrity, under the jurisdiction of the Dauphin reigning at Bourges. Here was certainly an opportunity for statesmanship, for the cleavage stretched further than political divisions. The war had disorganized French society; suffering had spread; and contemporaries had watched what a modern historian has described as 'the desolation of the church'. Simple folk yearned after security. But who could supply it? It is hardly surprising that Henry V saw the possibilities latent in the situation. Not the least potent factor in his success was his offer of a new order which might re-establish justice, reform the administration, and put an end to civil disturbance. It was good propaganda, and effective against a young Dauphin weak in himself and surrounded by venal counsellors.

To-day, it is fashionable to explain the causes of all wars by reference to economic rather than political factors, and the Hundred Years War is certainly to be considered in relation to this general question. The relations between Edward III and the Flemish towns at the outbreak of hostilities were undoubtedly influenced by the ramifications of the English wool trade. Flanders at the beginning of the Hundred Years War was a French fief; its aristocracy were French in sympathy but the burgesses of its important towns were dependent for their prosperity on the wool from the backs of English sheep. It was natural, therefore, that strong support for the claims of Edward III should come from Flemish burgesses who were threatened by an interruption of a commerce which was essential to their well-being, and it is similarly significant that the first battles of the war were fought in Flanders. Similarly, when in 1411 John the Fearless, Duke of Burgundy, sought English help against the Armagnacs he offered to hand over four Flemish towns to English control, and posed as being able to ensure the safety of Calais where was stationed the English wool staple. Later, after John's murder at Montereau, his young successor Philip received the support of the burgesses of Flanders in his efforts to sustain and develop the same alliance. The fluctuating effects of the Hundred Years War on the development and organization of the English wool trade have been described for English readers by Eileen Power, and during the struggle the English war effort was in fact substantially financed by English wool merchants. The desperate expedients to which both Edward III and Philip VI were reduced in order to obtain money for war purposes compelled them, and their successors, to pay some attention, however unwillingly, to the rival commercial interests in their respective countries.

Nevertheless, it would be easy to emphasize unduly the influence of the commercial classes in England and France on either the outbreak or the continuance of the war. The hostilities certainly did more harm than good to the English wool trade, and Edward III's alliance with the Flemish towns had little appreciable effect on the course of the conflict. Again, in the early years of the fifteenth century the English crown was for a time as ready to enter into an alliance with the Armagnacs as with the Burgundians, and when after the advent of Henry V as king, the English fortunes in France became linked with those of the Burgundians, this was due more to political than to economic reasons. Commercial rivalry undoubtedly played its part in stimulating a conflict of interests, just as the destructive effects of the war fostered social unrest both in France and England. But outbreaks such as the Peasant Revolt in England, the Jacqueries in France, the Harelle at Rouen, and the Cabochian uprising in Paris might well have occurred even if there had never been a struggle between the French and English monarchies. An exclusively economic interpretation of human history – and of human conflict – will in short find little support from a study of the Hundred Years War.

Indeed, if attention were to be concentrated solely on economic considerations it might be difficult to provide an adequate explanation of the English successes in the war. At the outbreak of hostilities the resources of the two countries seemed so disproportionate. M. Perroy's interesting statistics show that when the war started the population of France was about three times that of England. Her countryside supported a peasantry comparable in numbers to that of the present day, and while the towns were not of course of the same relative importance then as now, they too were rapidly increasing in size and prosperity. Paris during this period was rapidly expanding. Moreover, the profound changes in international trade and commerce which were characteristic of the thirteenth century had not as yet appreciably affected the prosperity of France, and the prestige of France was without rival in Europe. The Empire was divided. The Papacy was in the throes of schism. France was the acknowledged leader in western Christendom. Yet it was on this country, thriving and respected, that there fell the initial disasters of the war. Even so, such was the French strength that it only needed the single reign of Charles V for France to make a rapid recovery, and by 1380 France could once again be considered the predominant power in the West. Against such an adversary England might well seem to be unevenly matched. She was relatively poor and relatively under-populated, and at the time when hostilities began she had but recently emerged from a period of civil strife. But it was England and not France, that until after the time of Henry V dominated the war in Europe.

An explanation of this apparent paradox may probably best be sought not in the economic but in the more strictly military sphere. France during the early decades of the struggle refused to adapt herself to new developments in the art of war. Her feudal army, although strong and respected, had few ideas of tactics save the unsupported cavalry charge. The English on the other hand during the Scottish war had learnt at Stirling Bridge and Falkirk that in favourable circumstances infantry could be more than a match for the mounted knight. Their leaders had moreover comprehended the only conditions upon which such success might be obtained. The footmen must be equipped with a long-range weapon, trained in its use, and themselves confident in its power. At Crécy the decision was obtained because the expert bowmen in the English force were able to stand on the defensive against a cavalry charge, in the sure knowledge that if they kept their line, and controlled the rapid delivery of their weapons, the cavalry charge would be broken up before it ever got home. At Poitiers the French had so far learnt this lesson that they fought on foot, but even so the device proved ineffective against the ordered use of the long-range weapon of the archers. At Agincourt, once again, victory was due to the disciplined action of a new type of specially trained foot soldiers ignorant alike of feudal traditions and feudal courtesies.

Here, and not in any comparison of the fighting capacity of individuals, is to be found the explanation of the English victories in the Hundred Years War. Too much emphasis has been given to the fact that the defeated French armies in the great battles were more numerous than those of the victors. An army fighting on its own territory against an expeditionary force will always have a large following of untrained and relatively ineffective supporters. It was the earlier recognition of the importance of a long-range weapon in the hands of a disciplined foot-soldier that gave the English their first successes. As soon as it was realized that the cavalry charge by itself could do little against such tactics, the advantage of the English in France began to dwindle. Charles V taught his commanders – and particularly Du Guesclin – to avoid large set battles – to suffer pillage rather than to court defeat, and the futility of the later expeditions of Edward III in France testified to the success of this policy. Agincourt illustrated the disastrous results of a reversal to an outworn tactical method, and the wisdom of Charles V was later to be demonstrated afresh. In truth, while the English kingdom could afford large scale raiding expeditions, it could not afford the men or the money to hold down a hostile countryside. Henry V himself was only successful in this because he could rely on the support of a large French party, and confine his own attention primarily to the difficult task of occupying

Normandy. When after 1435 the Burgundian faction had left the English alliance, the task of the English in France became impossible. The end was then in sight, and was hastened by the decline of the long bow as the dominant long-range weapon. Before the close of the war, the tactical advantage had passed to the French. Formigny, though on a smaller scale, may in this sense be regarded as Crécy in reverse. There, too, a small disciplined force of infantry relying this time on the controlled fire of primitive artillery succeeded in overcoming a much larger force. The supreme tactical factor in the Hundred Years War was thus from a new angle demonstrated afresh.

The chief weakness of the French kingdom throughout the war lay in its recurrent disunion. The strength of its opponent was to be found in a centralized system of administrative control. During the fourteenth century earlier feudal conditions in France were giving place to a social order in which the magnates of the land, having established quasi-independent princedoms for themselves, were seeking to control the royal administration in their own interests. In particular the power of various members of the royal house, – close relatives of the reigning kings – and the disputes between them, were a perpetual source of disturbance which reached its climax in the Burgundian-Armagnac feud. The careers of the Louis, Duke of Anjou, of Louis, Duke of Orleans, of John, Duke of Berry, and of the Burgundian dukes are sufficient to illustrate the disastrous effects of such divisions. The administrative machine was in its turn dislocated in that for long periods the monarchy found itself served by a crowd of competing officials whose chief concern was not to give effect to the policy of the king, but rather to aid the patrons to whom they looked for advancement. Between 1328 and 1422 only one French king, namely Charles V, was able to control the situation. His 'Marmosets' may have been venal, and they certainly were unpopular, but they fostered the interests of the monarchy, and strengthened its policy. Generally speaking, however, the French monarchy throughout this period suffered from an inherent weakness caused by competing interests within the royal administration itself.

Such conditions were of course not peculiar to France. A constant feature of English history during this age was likewise a struggle within the royal administration between the professional servants of the king and the great magnates of the land who as the king's 'natural counsellors' sought to obtain control over the household administration. That struggle in fact goes far to explain the disturbances at the end of the reign of Edward III and the failure of Richard II to build up the royal power afresh on more autocratic foundations. Generally speaking, however, the 'overmighty subject' was kept in check in England before the end of the reign of Henry V, or at least made to co-operate to a reasonable extent with the king. Not until the time of Henry VI did the rivalry of aristocratic factions reproduce in England some of the conditions associated with the struggle between the Burgundians and Armagnacs in France. Then indeed did the English war-effort become weakened at the same time as defeats abroad lowered the prestige of the monarchy at home. Before the last phase of the Hundred Years War, however, the administrative machine, established by Henry II and developed by Edward I, served the English monarchy reasonably well. Despite the development of a 'bastard Feudalism' which contributed to a disastrous 'lack of governance', there remained in England during the whole of the foureenth century a far more intimate relationship between Westminster and the shires, than was to be found between the French royal administration and the French provinces. There was also a closer connexion between the English baronage and the royal court. And down to the end of the first quarter of the fifteenth century there persisted in England an enduring consciousness of the 'community of the realm'.

In part this was due to previous history: to the absence in England of anything corresponding to the greater French fiefs; to the previous absence in England of such political divisions as had been created for instance by the Angevin empire. But in part also was it due to the fact that between 1328 and 1422 France was far less fortunate than was England in the persons of her kings. On both private and public grounds it is possible for many different reasons to criticize Edward III and Richard II, Henry IV and Henry V. But taken together, and viewed in respect of their contrasted characteristics, they represent a succession of more than average ability. Very different was the case in France. Philip VI was, it is true, faced by exceptional difficulties, but he showed himself irresolute and reckless, neither exciting respect nor deserving it. John the Good was imbued with the sentiments of chivalric honour, but having obtained royalty he showed himself unworthy of it, and temperamentally he was a natural defeatist. Charles VI, with a taint in his blood, was still immature at the age of twenty-four, and though he never grew up, it was his tragedy to grow old. After his lapse into imbecility in 1392, the great French monarchy remained for thirty years in gilded disgrace under the charge of a madman. Even Charles VII, under whom delivery was to come, was personally unimpressive: lethargic, ill-natured and morose he displayed few qualities of leadership, and the successes of his later years were due far more to others than to himself. From this melancholy sequence one man alone stands out. Charles V has perhaps been overpraised by some of his admirers, but if he was not great, he was certainly not negligible. An intellectual rather than a warrior he was introspective, given to petty device, something of a quibbler and not guiltless of bad faith. But he did possess both a sense of royal dignity, and a consciousness of the duties it implied. In his self-questioning and legal subtleties he may sometimes seem to have 'doubted his present if not his future', but his sense of duty, and his resourceful tenacity, served his country well, and he was 'the right king for a France weakened and temporarily dismembered'. Yet even Charles V cannot by himself reverse the adverse judgement which must be passed upon the kings of the House of Valois during this age. It is significant that while on the English side the popular hero of the Hundred Years War remains a Lancastrian king, the acclaim of France is still, and properly, given, not to a monarch, but to a girl from Lorraine.

Students of this book may indeed be tempted to consider the validity of those current interpretations of history which are based upon purely mechanistic principles. If economic factors will not by themselves explain the causes of the Hundred Years War, it will be found equally difficult to discount the influence of individual character upon its course. Subsequent legend and popular sentiment have, as is always the case in respect of any prolonged conflict, tended to enhance unduly the importance of certain figures in the war. It is probable for instance that too much has been made to depend upon the personality of Du Guesclin who was less the *preux chevalier* of tradition, than a subaltern commander whose devotion was greater than his ability, and whose successes depended more upon the sagacity of his master than upon his own obstinate valour. Nor is it surprising that fortuitous association with the Maid has irradiated beyond historic reality the exploits of such as Dunois and La Hire. Many of the minor personalities in the battles of the Hundred Years War, and indeed some of the more spectacular mediocrities such as John of Bohemia, who took part in it, may certainly be allowed to pass into oblivion by the student of historical causation. None the less the personal factor remains of importance. The prestige of Edward III in the middle of his reign was an asset to his cause, and Charles V made his individual contribution to the recovery of France after the Treaty of Brétigny. With the fifteenth century, moreover, personal influences can be more clearly discerned. When all due allowances have been made for the exaggerations of contemporaries and the panegyrics of posterity, it would be hard to gainsay the opinion that the story of the Hundred Years War would have been other than it was apart from the personal qualities and the individual characters of Henry V and Joan of Arc.

Henry V is known to most Englishmen through the medium of Shakespeare's dramatic pageant. It is therefore notable that the king's latest English biographer, Professor Jacob, should conclude that 'a critical estimate, while it may have many reservations, is likely to support the Henry of Shakespeare as a true figure of history'. Here, of course, is a portrait illuminated by Elizabethan sentiment, in respect particularly of the relations between the Crown and the Church, and of the national aspirations of sixteenth century England. At the same time, dramatic necessities lead to overemphasis. But if some of the glowing tints need to be toned down, the final summary leaves essentially unimpaired the notion of a dominant king strong in the enthusiasms he evoked and fortified by the support of the people over whom he ruled. Slight of build, diseased, unlovable, Henry V was, in fact, at once calculating and courageous, superstitious and sincere. He was revoltingly cruel. He adhered unflinchingly to his purposes through the manifold chicaneries which he did not scruple to employ. A politician of outstanding ability, a military commander of considerable capacity, Henry V had above all the qualities of a great leader in that he could present to those he led a picture of himself very different from the private reality it masked.

> The King's a bawcock, and a heart of gold
> A lad of life, an imp of fame,
> Of parents good, of fist right valiant
> I kiss his dirty shoe, and from my heartstrings
> I love the lovely bully.

The real man was very different from the popular conception of him, but Henry V knew how to exploit the crude appeal voiced by Fluellen. He had a personal magnetism, and he displayed a wide humanity even if he did not feel it. The magnificent and familiar speeches which Shakespeare puts into his mouth – the harangue at Harfleur, the exhortation before Agincourt – are authentic in spirit if fictitious in fact. They reflect, and in part explain, the conscious influence exercised by this king over his English contemporaries in order to persuade them of the justice of his cause, and to excite their devoted service to make it prevail. Only thus was he enabled, in truth, to persuade many of his subjects 'to sell the pasture to provide the horse', and to impart confidence to tired troops by 'a little touch of Harry in the night'.

The infectious authenticity latent in Shakespeare's portraiture of Henry V makes it the more necessary to recall that this was a medieval, not a Tudor, sovereign. Henry V was far less a prophet of modern nationalism than the embodiment of an older theory of royalty which exalted the position of the king at the same time as it emphasized the special obligations attaching to the royal office: duties involving the maintenance of secular order; duties relating especially to the protection of the Church. Even as he clung to Angevin claims over his French dominions trying thereby to restore the conditions of the twelfth century, so also was he inspired by an earlier notion of kingship which would have been understood by St. Louis.

> Upon the King! let us our lives, our souls,
> Our debts, our careful wives, our children, and
> Our sins lay on the king; – we must bear all.
> O hard condition! twin-born with greatness,
> Subjected to the breath of every fool
> Whose sense no more can feel but his own wringing!
> What infinite heart's ease must kings neglect
> That private men enjoy!

The picture is of course unduly heightened, but many of the king's known utterances would in part support it. For this was the man who, in the fifteenth century, harboured as his greatest desire the wish to lead a united Europe in a crusade to Palestine, and who, morbidly conscious both of his duties and his sins, despairingly held up as an ideal to himself and his subjects to be 'the mirror of all Christian kings'. Probably he was fortunate not to survive his successes: he was barely thirty-five when he died.

To pass from Henry V to Joan of Arc – from the English hero of the Hundred Years War to the French heroine – involves an abrupt transition. But here too it is necessary to distinguish sharply between the contemporary influence and the posthumous fame of a dominant figure. The character of the Maid, the full reports which have survived of both her trials, have produced a modern literature which is astonishing both in its diversity and in its bulk, and one of M. Perroy's most difficult tasks has been to pass judgement upon it. He is inclined to the view that it was only Joan's immediate circle which felt the full force of her personality, and that elsewhere in France, during her life time, her fame spread fitfully and slowly. Many of those who in fact were most in her debt seem at the time to have been scarcely aware of her wonderful adventure, and her final sacrifice was certainly received with deplorable indifference both by the king she exalted and by many of his subjects in the provinces he ruled. Even the rehabilitation of 1456 takes on the character of a political manœuvre designed to buttress the title of Charles VII, and it may be doubted whether if she had not suffered martyrdom, and if that martyrdom had not been copiously recorded, much would have been known about her, or much written about her personal contribution to the strictly military history of the Hundred Years War.

None the less, when all such considerations have been weighed, the essential and traditional importance of Joan remains unscathed. In her case, as in the case of every martyr, it is impossible to separate the story of her life from the passion of her death, and her posthumous influence was an integral part of her achievement. It is given to few thus to fire the imagination of men, and if the French recovery for which she served as a signal did not for a time assume, after its first success, 'the surging sweep of a storm', nevertheless her sacrifice 'heralded decisive victory'. The many who owed so much to her were indifferent to her fate, but some among her enemies seem already to have been conscious of what she wrought. 'The Burgundian chroniclers by the venomous violence of their attacks, by the calumnies which they circulated to sully Joan's memory proved that in government circles the Maid's early successes created such dismay that (as they thought) only the stake at Rouen could efface its memory.' And if the contemporary public was, as if inevitably, scarcely affected by something which did not immediately affect its own comfort, that memory remained ineffacable. Joan left behind her acts: for the first time the Lancastrian arms had been halted on the road to victory, and the King of Bourges had been given the prestige of a unique coronation. In this way, concludes M. Perroy, 'Joan of Arc's intervention was decisive, and the page she wrote, contrary to all expectation, in the history of France deserves to be remembered as one of her finest.'

Beyond that, Joan's influence on her posterity depended upon considerations with which this book is not concerned. It should not however be minimized. Her final victory is, in the ultimate assessment, to be judged as a triumph of character, and she had a root of authority in her. It is a fact of history, and not an unimportant one, that the flames surrounding her scaffold at Rouen have shone through five centuries in the European memory, and for that reason alone it would be true to say that the history of the War in which she engaged would, both in its course and in its results, have been very different had she never lived and died. She escapes classification: she remains unique. To-day, for both French and English, the most enduring figure in the Hundred Years War is Joan the Maid.

The posthumous fame of both Henry V and Joan of Arc may prompt the question how far the Hundred Years War is to be considered as a national conflict. Certainly it was not so at its beginning when the feudality in the two kingdoms went to battle against each other according to the set courtesies of chivalric custom, and often chose their side with little regard to the demands of any national feeling. Undoubtedly the devastations of the English in France, and the ravagings by Norman sailors of the south coast of England, introduced a sterner element into the struggle, but throughout the fifteenth century the war can hardly be compared with a modern national struggle in which whole populations are engaged. In the time of Edward III, for example, the English peasant for long knew little of the wars of the princes, and during the long truce which marked the reign of Richard II there could exist in the highest circles a cordial relation between the two powers. Western Christendom still existed in the sentiment of both peoples, and the English were still content to learn from Gallic culture. Chaucer, for example, served under Edward III in the French wars, and he had been himself a prisoner. Yet throughout his works it is difficult to detect any trace of dislike for Frenchmen as such, and indeed he introduced into the language he helped to form, a large mixture of romance idioms which he brought from overseas. As the years passed he drew more on Italian than Gallic inspiration, but he none the less gave vivid expression to the sense of belonging to a common civilization in which both England and France were partners.

With the progress of the war, however, its character slowly changed, and its results were to produce an altered relationship between France and England. It is significant that even from the start many men in England were suspicious that a Pope born within the kingdom of the French king could not be trusted to be impartial in the struggle, and the conflict could hardly have been continued so long had there not been some popular support for it in both countries. As the decades passed, Englishmen began to take a patriotic pride in the exploits of the armies in France whilst Frenchmen began to look for a deliverer who might rid them of an intolerable foreign oppression. There is thus already a different temper to be detected in the fifteenth century from what there had been in the time of Edward III, and the war was at once its cause and its consequence. Henry V cannot, as has been seen, be regarded without distortion, as an apostle of nationalism, but his career none the less fostered the growth of national feeling. Joan the Maid was inspired by an inspiration different from those which are kindled by modern nationalistic states, but her life and death were made to give a sanction to much that was soon to come. By the middle of the fifteenth century such phrases as 'good Frenchmen' and 'true French men' appear in the chronicles as opposed to 'Français reniés' and 'Français anglais'. It was a new sentiment and one that was pregnant with future consequence.

For those reasons it is legitimate to regard the Hundred Years War as one among the many solvents of the medieval political order, and as marking the beginning of a new era in the history of Anglo-French relations. Indeed, it might almost be suggested that in this respect its most notable results were the sphere of political sentiments and ideas. Both countries, of course, felt the consequences of the prolonged strain. In England the final failure involved the downfall of the house of Lancaster and precipitated the Wars of the Roses. In France the countryside of several provinces long bore terrible witness to the ferocity of the savage campaigns. But the dynasty of York lost little time in reconstituting the royal authority, and France soon started on the road to recovery. Nevertheless, after the Hundred Years War neither French nor English ever thought about each other in quite the same way as they had done before it began, and never again were they to be conscious in quite the former manner as belonging to the same overriding political system. Feudalism as a cohesive force within and between the two peoples had been destroyed. Passing also were those ideas of political and social solidarity among the western peoples which the men of an earlier generation had respected though never realized. A new wind was beginning to blow from across the Alps. Less than half a century separated the death of Joan the Maid from the birth of Machiavelli, but the distance between them is not to be measured in years.

It is thus that in both France and England the real beneficiaries of the Hundred Years War were to be the monarchy and the middle class who united together to destroy the older aristocracies, and who built for their own advantage a new sovereignty upon the ruins of the older order. The transformation in the art of war implied the end of feudalism, and in its place there arose a monarchy of a new type, strongly centralized and omnipotent, claiming an absolute jurisdiction over all in the land and recognizing no limits, secular or ecclesiastical, to its authority. Francis I and Henry VIII are already foreshadowed in the acts, and in the diplomacy, of Edward IV and Louis XI. The modern absolute state, built upon nationalism, omnipotent and a-moral, was arising; and it held the future in its keeping. But perhaps those who in our own days have watched some of the consequences of its acts may be tempted to re-consider the circumstances of its origin. The twentieth century has twice seen the armies of France and England joined together in a common cause, and the future of that civilization from which they both sprang may well now depend in great measure upon a mutual understanding between the two participants in the Hundred Years War. M. Perroy is in himself, and for his work, a worthy ambassador in such a cause, and his remarkable book is as important for the history of this country as for that of his own.

DAVID DOUGLAS

THE HUNDRED YEARS WAR

AUTHOR'S PREFACE

THE GREATER part of this book was written uninterruptedly, during the winter of 1943-4, thanks to the precarious leisure granted to me during an exciting game of hide-and-seek with the Gestapo. It was a roving life, but a fine one, and all of us who lived and worked 'underground' now look back upon it with regret. Suddenly flung into outlawry, abruptly parted from my familiar environment of students and books, I seemed, in contact with this present so harshly real, to gain a better understanding of the past, even though I had hitherto devoted most of my time to it.

I had contemplated this book for a long time; but it would not have been quite the same if it had appeared before 1939, or even if I had written it during the early months of the German occupation. Not that one should press too far the theory that history repeats itself, or delude oneself about the lessons that one may draw from it. It would be naïve to suppose that the tragic ups-and-downs of the Hundred Years' War can guide our action in the present or enable us to foresee our future nor can one even seek ground for hope in this story of failure, downfall and recovery in the past. But when a nation reaches the depths of the abyss, as was the case at that time and in our own, certain ways of behaviour in misfortune, certain reactions against fate, throw mutual light upon one another. Though I have never – at least consciously – transposed our present preoccupations into the past, or lost sight of the fact that it is the historical atmosphere which illuminates a period, nevertheless certain actions have become more comprehensible; one is better placed to explain a surrender, or to excuse a revolt.

At the time of the Hundred Years' War, only two countries in Western Christendom counted as political forces: England and France. Their kings flung them heedlessly into a feudal struggle, to which a dynastic conflict was soon added; but the war did not look like going beyond the customary lines of these confirmed inveterate squabbles. Contrary to all expectation, however, it went on and on, broke out again in fresh places and involved one generation after another. Indifferent to these quarrels which they did not understand, the two peoples tried, so far as they could, to evade the growing burden which it was sought to thrust on them. All they did was to prolong the conflict, which was waged on either side with slender resources. Meanwhile they toiled and suffered. Once the war was brought home to them, they reached the point of hating each other and so making any peace impossible or impracticable. Around them the world became transformed;

and within the two countries, as always happens in troubled times, the change was even more swift. Out of their wounds, out of their blood, the modern monarchies were born, and the transition from a feudal society to a State bureaucracy was hastened, since it was imposed by the necessities of war and buttressed by the nationalisms that the war itself developed.

From the French point of view there was a more poignant tragedy. It would be idle to try and list all that the Capetian kingdom lost in the course of this endless, exhausting conflict. Its material prosperity, so great at the beginning of the war, was impaired for centuries, and did not recover fully until the eve of the Revolution. Ended, too, was its hegemony, intellectual and political, over a Europe submissive to its teaching. It had to await the age of Louis XIV before its influence in this respect made itself felt again. It is easier to summarize what France gained from the storm: the framework of a modern State; the greater cohesion of her disparate provinces; the respect for the royal authority, based upon the beginning of national sentiment. But the birth of these advantages was achieved at the price of bitter pangs. Twice France all but foundered. Beneath the blows of the Plantagenets, she suffered the dismemberment of her provinces, the formation of a great independent Aquitaine, the loss of sovereignty over a good third of the kingdom. The attack of the Lancastrians, half a century later, was still more sinister for her, since it almost united the two crowns of France and England on one and the same head. Indeed, some saw in this solution the sole escape from the war, civil disorder and economic ruin. Rightly or wrongly, events willed otherwise. The collaboration of the two peoples under the aegis of the Lancastrians proved to be impossible. Victory was finally granted to the Valois, because they symbolized the independence of a nation which had at last become conscious of itself.

While I was engaged on this book I had at my disposal only a small stock of notes, gathered in the course of years from books and archives. I had to recall many facts and episodes, solely with the aid of memory, which is always imperfect. This led inevitably to some details of omission, some mistakes in names, some small errors of chronology. Many of these I have been able to correct in the course of a close revision; but some I may have missed. For this I make my apologies to my readers, though without seeking to excuse my mistakes. I think that they in no way affect the main outlines of my narrative, the ideas which guide it, the interpretations, sometimes unconventional, which it presents, and the conclusions to which it leads.

EDOUARD PERROY

AUTHOR'S PREFACE

POSTSCRIPT FOR ENGLISH EDITION

The present English translation was made possible through the kindness of Professor D. C. Douglas and was competently achieved by Mr. Warre Bradley Wells, who was most patient with an over-punctilious author. I took the opportunity for a thorough revision of the text, trying to incorporate in this new edition the result of recent research on the period, while correcting many factual errors. I am particularly indebted to Professors Helen M. Cam, Hilda Johnstone, R. Fawtier and R. Boutruche, and to Mr. R. H. Hilton, who have offered helpful criticism and suggestions.

Paris, 1951.   E. P.

Part I

THE ADVERSARIES

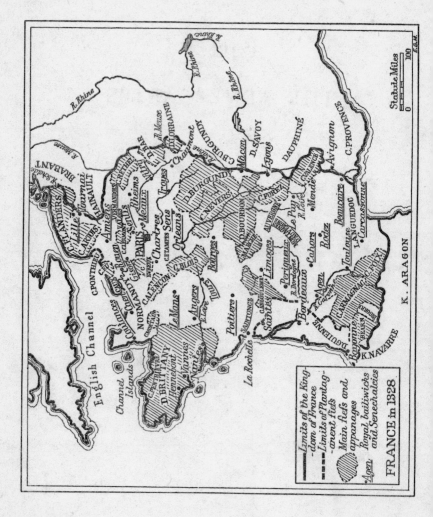

FRANCE in 1328

Limits of the King-
dom of France
Limits of Planting-
enet fiefs
Main fiefs and
appanages
Agen Royal bailiwicks
and Seneschalcies

Statute Miles
0   100

Part I

THE ADVERSARIES

IN January 1327, the throne of England, from which the unpopular Edward II had just been driven by his rebellious barons, was given to his son, a boy of fourteen, Edward Plantagenet III. Less than thirteen months later, the last of the three sons of Philip the Fair, the Capetian Charles IV, died in Paris. In the absence of a male heir, the barons of France chose as his successor his first cousin, Philip VI of Valois (April 1328). These two almost coincident events opened for the two Western kingdoms a fresh phase in their history, marked by a desperate struggle between the two dynasties which went on for more than a century and has been given the name of the Hundred Years' War.

An impartial observer trying to estimate the opposing forces in 1328 is immediately struck by the crushing disproportion – though it was doubtless more apparent than real – between the fame and wealth of the glorious kingdom of France and the weakness and poverty of the little kingdom of England. Among the two adversaries about to engage in a conflict of such unforeseen duration, no one could have predicted the reversal of strength which, to the great astonishment of contemporaries, put the heirs of Saint Louis in peril and raised those of the Plantagenets to the heights of power.

1. FRANCE IN 1328

THE KINGDOM of France on the death of the last direct Capetian had not yet extended its boundaries to anything like the area of modern France. Indeed, its land frontiers scarcely differed from those which, in the Carolingian period, marked the boundaries of Western France, the share allotted to Charles the Bald by the Treaty of Verdun. It was separated from its neighbour, the Empire whose territory bordered it from the North Sea to the Mediterranean, by an artificial frontier, imperfectly known even by contemporaries and full of enclaves and contested territories.

Roughly, however, this frontier followed the course of the Scheldt from its mouth to the south of Cambrai, reached the Meuse to the north-east of Rethel, followed the upper course of this river, and finally the courses of the Saône and the Rhône. Recent encroachments had enabled the frontier to reach these rivers at certain places although it had for centuries stopped short of them. For example, Ostrevant, the part of Hainault to the west of the Scheldt between Valenciennes and Douai, had come under Capetian jurisdiction in the reign of Philip the Fair. The same applied to the part of Barrois lying on the left bank of the Meuse, to the city and county of Lyons, and to the bishopric of Viviers, to the west of the Saône and the Rhône, all of which had placed themselves under royal protection. In the south-west, the French frontier did not everywhere attain the line of the Pyrenees. The kingdom of Navarre – though it is true that between 1274 and 1328 it was administered by Capetian officials – stretched north of the mountains over what was later called Lower Navarre. In addition, in 1258 Saint Louis had renounced what had for centuries been a purely nominal suzerainty over Roussillon and the county of Catalonia, which were possessions of the Aragonese monarchy.

On the other hand, it should not be assumed that this frontier set a rigid limit to French influence in Western Europe. Taking advantage of the decay of the Empire, which had not had a holder worthy of its glorious past since the death of Frederick II (1250), the Capetian monarchy had had no difficulty in extending its protectorate over almost all the territories of the former Lotharingia, from the Low Countries to the kingdom of Arles, in regions where common language had inevitably brought about a certain amount of identity of political views. Most of the princes of the Empire with possessions beyond the eastern marches of the kingdom had become protégés of the King of France. They received *fiefs de bourse* – or, as we should now say, pensions – from him and supported his policy. This applied to Brabant and Hainault, Barrois and Lorraine, Savoy and

Dauphiné. Moreover, the county palatine of Burgundy (the present Franche-Comté) had become a Capetian possession since the marriage of its heiress to Philip V the Tall; and Provence, since the time of Saint Louis, was in the hands of the King of Sicily, a descendant of the Capetian Charles of Anjou.

The Papacy had taken up its abode in this region. John XXII, elected in 1316, the second of a long line of French Popes, had been Bishop of Avignon before his elevation to the throne of Saint Peter. He continued to reside in his former episcopal palace, which his successor, Benedict XII, turned into an imposing fortress. Avignon was at the gates of the kingdom of France. It was a quasi-independent city, under the joint lordship of the Sovereign Pontiff and the Count of Provence. An increase of material strength and moral prestige accrued to the Capetian dynasty from the establishment, in principle provisional though it might be, of the Court of Rome on the banks of the Rhône.

If we consider only the geographical limits of the kingdom of France, the Capetian monarchy, in the course of the century which had just elapsed, had reached a degree of power which could be explained only by unprecedented demographic development and economic prosperity. The whole of Europe, it should be added, had shared in this upward movement, whose first signs became apparent at the end of the tenth century and the beginning of the eleventh. But it was faster and more marked in France than anywhere else, and, when it attained its climax, round about 1300, it might be said that France had a lead over the rest of Western Christendom which put her in a position to exert a political and cultural hegemony and indeed made it inevitable that she should.

It was, above all, in the sphere of rural economy, which was still the basis of all medieval society, that the superiority of France over the rest of Europe made itself manifest. The great processes of clearing and developing marshy or forest land, creating new villages and towns, had reached their culmination. Their development had been controlled on the one hand by the need to keep enough forest land for the provision of fuel and timber, for the grazing of roving live-stock, and for the preservation of game; and, on the other hand, through the need to provide agriculture, whose methods still remained rudimentary, with paying products. Even with the primitive technique available, much marginal land had been tilled, though the first ravages of the Hundred Years' War were to throw them back permanently into fallow and heath. The wretched harvests it produced would never have paid its tillers, had it not been a question of providing at all costs a really heavy population with the food necessary for its maintenance.

The upward demographic movement also explains the almost complete disappearance, on the great lay and ecclesiastical estates, of the manorial system of cultivation, maintained by serf man-power and day-labourers without settled homes. Apart from the forests, the heaths, and some meadow land and vineyards, all the manorial demesnes had gradually been split up into long-term peasant holdings, which yielded their lords only modest cash rents. Even on the Cistercian estates, long managed through 'granges', with the work of lay brothers supervised by a monk-farmer, farming leases or peasant holdings had gradually nibbled away the monastic demesne. The coincident disappearance of serfdom, in the few provinces where it had prevailed, and of labour services, which weighed heavily on tenants, had turned the peasant into a regular owner of his holding, burdened only by modest charges. Though in more developed districts, such as Normandy, short-term farming was already familiar, there prevailed almost everywhere perpetual hereditary tenure, against payment of a small rent, to which were added transfer and succession duties and the rendering of some manorial services which were troublesome rather than arduous, the whole being infinitely less burdensome than the taxes with which a modern treasury encumbers the land and its holders.

It would be useful at this point to introduce some figures, present some statistics, and state the average density of population or its total for the kingdom. Unfortunately this is impossible. All the demographic conjectures which historians have made rest, in the absence of conclusive texts, only on fragile foundations. Nevertheless one valuable document, unique of its kind, enables us to make some reasonably substantiated estimates precisely for the date with which we are concerned. It is a return of parishes and households, by bailiwicks and seneschalships, which Philip VI probably caused to be drawn up on the morrow of his accession for a purely fiscal purpose: that of preparing the basis of the subsidy which would cover the expenses of the levying of troops for the Flanders campaign in July 1328. It enumerates the parishes, and estimates the number of households, homes, or 'hearths' which they contain, and upon which the tax known as hearth-tax would fall. But it limited its inquiry solely to the royal domain, in other words the territory which the sovereign controlled directly, leaving aside the few great fiefs still subsisting, where hearth-tax was not levied, at least by royal officials. As we shall see later, these great fiefs represented only a little more than a quarter of the extent of the kingdom.

We shall not be very far from the truth in estimating that France in 1328, with her some 32,000 parishes, sheltered an approximate total of 3,300,000 households, which would carry her total population to a minimum of 10 or 12 million souls. It was a remarkable density for the period, and it was probably not reached or surpassed except by some favoured regions of Italy, and it left the territories of Spain, Central Germany, and the British Isles, still thinly populated, very far behind. At the same time, as the great bulk of this population remained rural, one is inevitably driven to conclude that some regions of France possessed rural dwellings as numerous as, or perhaps more numerous than, those which were to be counted at the end of the eighteenth century or under the July monarchy, both periods at which the peasant population reached its maximum.

Rural prosperity was matched by the development of the towns, essential for the maintenance of a thriving trade, of which the end of the thirteenth century, here again, marked the apogee. France had unique luck in possessing, in Paris, the sole great city in Christian Europe which could already be called a metropolis, in the modern sense of the word. The city's rise is scarcely to be explained except on political and cultural grounds, for it had no specialized industry. But it had a multitude of crafts brought into existence by the government services, the presence of the court, which rarely left the city or its nearby residences, and also the presence, at the University, of a cosmopolitan crowd of students. Its population, including the suburbs, must have been in the region of 150,000 souls. Nor did its rise stop, at least until the cumulative misfortunes of the war made themselves harshly felt, towards the end of the fourteenth century. While many a provincial town, including the most prosperous, believing in the continued rise of its wealth, built about this time vast walls which for centuries were to prove too large for it, Paris burst out of the girdle of its walls, spacious though they were, which dated from Philip Augustus. Charles V found himself forced to annex to Paris a whole new quarter, to the north and east of the old fortifications, between the Temple and the Bastille Saint-Antoine, built by himself: the Marais, which then became for two generations the favourite residence of the monarchy.

The other towns of the kingdom had not reached anything like this size. Even the great cloth-making centres of Flanders, swarming with artisans and humming with looms, were no more than overgrown villages, whose population often reached 10,000 inhabitants, but rarely seems to have exceeded 20,000. Still, it was the cloth-making industry which, throughout the Middle Ages, remained the sole great industry working for export and creating an intensive movement of international trade in the countries of the West. Flanders, an integral part of the kingdom, profited by this to such a degree that, until the end of the thirteenth century, it exercised a regular monopoly of sale in the markets of Europe. Leaving it to the other towns of France and to the small Flemish centres of rural industry to make ordinary cloth, or small-cloth, as it was called, which satisfied the needs of local customers, the big northern towns, first Arras, then Douai, then Ypres, Bruges and Ghent, and, to a smaller extent, Lille and Tournai, specialized in fine products, which were readily exported to all the countries of Europe and even beyond. Italian merchants came across the mountains in search of high-quality cloth, for which they exchanged the luxury products of the Moslem world: silks, spices, arms, leather, jewels. The opulent fairs of Champagne, on the land route between Flanders and Italy, for long served as the natural meeting-point for these international transactions, coupled with banking operations, with whose complex technique only the Italians were as yet familiar. Troyes, Provins, Bar-sur-Aube, and

Lagny – the last three quite small towns – thus made the acquaintance, at fixed times of the year, of a cosmopolitan crowd of merchants gathered from all Northern France, Italian bankers, debtors of every kind or their agents, who here settled their debts and made their payments.

But, towards the end of the thirteenth century, profound changes imperilled the balance of international trade, from which some favoured provinces of the kingdom had hitherto profited. First, Flanders lost its industrial hegemony. The social struggles which brought the poverty-stricken workers and the patrician capitalists to grips, together with the wars which the King of France waged to punish rebels and recall the count to the strict observance of his duties as a vassal, suffice to explain the slowing-down of cloth production. Simultaneously, for reasons much more obscure, the fairs of Champagne fell into decay. It has been suggested that the tax exactions of Philip the Fair's officials, who administered the county of Champagne in the name of the king's wife, had much to do with the progressive desertion of the fairs, up to that time so prosperous. Other causes seem to have been more potent in hastening the decline of the fairs of Champagne: the opening of a direct land route from Milan to the Rhine through the Central Alps; the growing practice, for Italian merchants, of carrying on their business through resident factors in the main trade centres of the West; and lastly, towards the end of the thirteenth century, the annual sailing of the Genoese galleys round the coasts of Spain towards the docks of Damme, Bruges's outer harbour.

But – this is the essential point – these recent changes did not affect the economic prosperity of the kingdom of France taken as a whole. Though the big towns of Brabant, such as Brussels and Malines, and of Hainault, such as Valenciennes, all centres situated in Imperial territory, had been the first to compete effectively with the Flanders cloth-trade, looms elsewhere inside the kingdom were already beginning to produce fine cloth which was valued by wealthy customers, notably by the royal Court. Normandy with Rouen, Picardy with Amiens, Champagne with Rheims and Châlons, and the capital itself vied with one another in winning markets. Big business, though it deserted the fairs of Champagne, transferred itself elsewhere. Bruges became the most prosperous centre of international exchanges, being the point of contact between the trade of the Mediterranean, carried on by the Italians, and that of the Baltic, in the hands of the Hanseatic towns. On the land routes, fairs, old and new, experienced a revival of prosperity. One need mention only the fair of Le Lendit, near Paris, and those of Chalon-sur-Saône in Burgundy and Beaucaire in Languedoc. On the sea-coast of the kingdom, some ports were making rapid strides, such as La Rochelle, the centre of the salt and wine trade, and Calais, where English wool was landed.

This prosperity, whose outstanding features I have sketched very summarily, was hastened by the period of peace which the kingdom had enjoyed almost without interruption, since the middle of the thirteenth century. Apart from the disastrous but short escapade in Aragon, upon which Philip III had rashly embarked (1285); the very easy campaigns in Guienne, to which I shall return; and also the harder wars in Flanders, where Philip the Fair and his sons encountered considerable difficulty, but which affected only a strictly limited area, France had known a tranquillity but little troubled by 'private' wars between vassals, which were becoming less and less frequent.

Peace and prosperity, in their turn, allowed a progressive strengthening of the royal authority, which showed itself in the creation, doubtless belated and slow, but continuous, of the instruments of government essential to the life of a State. In the central services, more and more specialized, one would no longer recognize, though it still existed in theory, the old feudal *curia regis*, made up of the whole of the sovereign's entourage, high officials, courtiers, barons, and prelates. One must make an exception of the king's household, which, from the reign of Saint Louis, had become detached from the *curia* and in fact, with its six departments, amounted only to the sovereign's personal staff, to whom the tasks of government were not entrusted. Of its two financial services, the *Chambre aux deniers*, whose name first appeared in 1303, and the *Argenterie*, created in 1315, a kind of warehouse and jewel-house, the first was supplied only by transfers from the treasury, and the second acquired some importance only from the fact that, by pawning its wealth, it could provide an ever hard-up monarchy with liquid assets at moments of need. All this would not have meant much if the king's household, with its chamberlains and, soon afterwards, its 'Masters of Requests', had not included the sovereign's closest friends and formed a nursery of officials. But, out of some 500 members who made up this household, whose ever-growing numbers provoked protests from the Estates from the reign of Philip of Valois, very few were officials and administrators in the modern sense of the word, very few penetrated into the government services.

Of all these, the king's Council was the one that remained the most fluid, the most vague. It might, on occasion, be identical with the court, and include all the officials and the barons, lay and ecclesiastical, or consist of a limited delegation of these barons, or comprise only the king's close advisers. There were, however, some appointed councillors, heads of services or privileged favourites, who were paid fixed salaries and were under oath not to reveal the secrets of the deliberations. At one point, under Philip the Fair's sons, the barons, copying what had just happened in England, tried to control this Council by giving it a fixed composition. Documents of the period mention the existence of a Close Council, limited to twenty-four members, which was also called the Great Council or Council of the Month, since the barons had demanded that it should hold at least one sitting a month. But Philip V's craft seems to have had no difficulty in neutralizing the tutelage under which it was sought to place his power. After him, there was no further question of this baronial control.

During the reign of Philip of Valois, the Council had resumed its flexibility and fluidity, which were the expression of the liberty left to the sovereign to take only such advice as he deemed fit. The Council had not only a consultative role, but indeed an executive one, since it transmitted to other authorities the decisions taken. It also had judicial functions, re-serving for its examination the most thorny cases which only the king, as sovereign judge, could decide, and receiving the pleas laid before it by the 'Masters of Requests' of the king's household. The clerics, the knights, and the minor barons who made up its fixed personnel, had not yet divided among themselves the examination of various types of questions submitted to the Council.

Quite different were the four or five great services at the centre of the government which looked after administration and dispensed justice. The Treasury, controlled by two or three treasurers and a changer, collected the revenues of the crown lands which were not spent locally, made pay-ments and transfers on the orders of the Council, kept complicated accounts, and dealt with disputes relating to the king's domain. The Mint, with a supreme master, and the Forests, with masters and surveyors, each had a separate administration and they too exercised judicial powers. The Chancery, through its notaries and secretaries, forwarded all the royal decrees, which were sealed with the great seal or the 'seal of secrecy': hence the name of secretaries given to the handful of clerks entrusted with the sovereign's private correspondence.

I must deal separately with two essential organisms, the *Parlement* and the *Chambre des comptes*, which by 1328 had barely achieved a really autonomous character. The *Cour en Parlement*, which was definitely organ-ized by Philip V's decrees in 1319 and 1320, but had to await the ordinance of March 1345 to be called *Cour de Parlement*, possessed a fixed personnel of presidents, councillors, clerical or lay, and 'Masters of Requests', divided into four chambers: the grand chamber, the criminal chamber, the chamber of inquests, and the chamber of requests, with the addition on occasion, for southern cases, of a tribunal of Roman law. As profes-sional lawyers, its judges were ardent supporters not only of the common law, but also of the royal majesty, whose authority they were bent on making respected throughout the kingdom. They received and called for all appeals, from wherever they came: not merely from the lower royal courts of the bailiwicks and seneschalships, but also the seigniorial courts of the greatest vassals. Appeal to the *Parlement* was the most powerful weapon in the hands of the monarchy for interfering in the administration of the great fiefs. During the vacations of the supreme court, some favoured provinces were visited by delegations of councillors, which dealt with local appeals on the spot, and were given the name of *Échiquier* in Normandy and *Grands Jours* in Champagne.

The *Chambre des comptes*, whose autonomous existence went back to 1304, but which did not receive its constituent charter until the ordinance of Vivier-en-Brie in January 1320, formed the corner-stone of this royal administration. All those who handled money, from the treasurers down to the humblest provosts, were accountable to it. As guardian of the crown lands, it searched for usurpations and fraudulent alienations, received the extents of fiefs, and watched over the good running of all the services. It opposed prodigality on the part of the king just as it sought out and prosecuted swindling or negligent officials.

Despite continually increasing specialization, this central administration had as yet only a very small personnel, which it was easy to keep in hand. The *Parlement* by itself comprised more than 100 judges. But in the Chancery, the Treasury, the *Chambre des Comptes*, and the Forestry administration there were in all, not counting junior personnel, only 80 or 85 officials. The government civil service did not number as many as 200 officials, all in all.

Local administration needed a more numerous personnel, and its recent multiplication, at the beginning of the fourteenth century, was keenly resented by those subject to it. It was divided into bailiwicks and seneschalships – the latter limited to the former domains of Aquitaine and Toulouse – whose boundaries were uncertain and whose scope was ill-defined. But, through the medium of bailiffs, seneschals, and their subordinates, it enabled the king's authority to make itself felt not only by the subjects of the crown lands, but also by those of the vassals, great and small. The return of households of 1328 lists 24 bailiwicks and 10 seneschalships, which may be grouped as follows: (1) bailiwicks of the original royal domain: the viscounty of Paris, administered by a provost possessing the powers of a bailiff, Orleans, Senlis, Vermandois, Amiens, Sens, Tours, Bourges, and Mâcon, whose bailiff also had the title of seneschal of Lyons since the annexation of that town, to which may be added Lille, acquired by Philip the Fair; (2) the five bailiwicks of Normandy (Caux, Rouen, Caen, Coutances, Gisors); (3) the four bailiwicks of Champagne (Troyes, Meaux-Provins, Vitry, Chaumont); (4) the bailiwicks of the Valois appanage, Valois, Anjou, and Maine; (5) those of the appanage of Alphonse of Poitiers: Auvergne and the mountains of Auvergne, and the seneschalships of Poitou and Saintonge; (6) the former domains of the Saint-Gilles family: Rouergue, Toulouse, Carcassonne, and Beaucaire; (7) Bigorre; (8) the seneschalships recently recovered in Aquitaine: Limousin, Périgord, and Agenais.

This domain proper, that is to say the territory which the king controlled directly or through the medium of minor vassals, comprised at this period 23,800 parishes with a total of 2,470,000 households. Here bailiffs and seneschals, usually chosen from the gentry and frequently changed, represented the king in the fullness of his power. In the sphere of finance, they farmed out the domain to provosts, *bayles* or *viguiers*, and supervised the district tax-collectors, the forestry officials, and the commissioners entrusted with temporary fiscal duties. In the sphere of justice, they presided personally over the bailiwick courts, or, through the medium of *juges-mages*, those of the southern seneschalships, and heard appeals from the seigniorial courts, subject to a possible appeal to the *Parlement*. Bailiff or seneschal had under his orders a chancellor or a keeper of the seal, a procurator, and a ceaselessly increasing number of sergeants, ushers, and beadles.

Earning only modest salaries, but usually honest, except in the very lowest ranks, these officials of humble origin, puffed up with pride at acting in the king's name, served his interests devotedly, and were imbued, especially since the death of Saint Louis, with an almost religious belief in monarchy. Thus they regarded all seigniorial rights and jurisdictions and town franchises, in short everything that stood in the way of their passion for levelling, as slighting to the royal majesty. The king, indeed, put up with these limitations to his power better than they did. Their encroachments did not stop at the boundaries of the royal domain. They blithely crossed those of the great fiefs and the appanage territories, which still extended over a good quarter of the area of the kingdom.

For, whatever may be suggested by a superficial study of the 'annexations' by which the royal domain had been enormously enriched since the time of Philip Augustus, it was no part of the policy of the Capetians, who were essentially feudal sovereigns, to absorb, whether by conquest, purchase, or inheritance, the whole of the territories which made up the kingdom. Their policy in this respect had been dictated by chance. Though they had overthrown the most powerful of their vassals, they did not want to control directly more land than sufficed to meet their increasing need of money. Usually they had granted their most recent acquisitions to their cadets in the form of appanages, being satisfied to replace a fallen dynasty by a younger branch of their family, from which they expected stronger fidelity as vassals.

But, by a freak of chance, most of these appanages so carelessly conceded had reverted to the royal domain, either because their possessors inherited the crown, or because they died without issue. The result was that, on the morrow of the accession of the Valois to the throne, there remained only five appanages of very small size, which were incapable of opposing the royal will. These were, from north to south: Artois, ruled by Countess Matilda, grand-niece of Saint Louis and mother-in-law of the late Philip V; Beaumont-le-Roger, recently granted to Robert of Artois, nephew of Matilda, but soon to be confiscated owing to his disloyalty as a vassal, though his children received the county of Eu as compensation; Évreux, in the hands of a nephew of Philip the Fair, also named Philip, who, through his marriage to Louis X's daughter, acquired in addition the counties of Angoulême and Mortain; Alençon and Perche, granted by Philip VI to his brother Charles, founder of a dynasty which did not disappear until the reign of Louis XI; and finally Bourbon, which, though its principal seigneury was not originally an appanage, had in

1327 exchanged its tiny county of Clermont, in Beauvaisis, for that of Marche, and had been given a peerage and a ducal title for Bourbonnais. These princes holding appanages were on a level with the little dynasties of counts which still maintained themselves here and there, for example in Blois, Rethel, Bar, Nevers, and Forez.

There remained, face to face with the king, only four great feudatories, all of them peers of France. But Brittany, raised to a duchy in 1297, and Burgundy, where old branches of the Capetian tree still maintained themselves, were principalities still sketchily organized. Their dukes exercised only limited authority over powerful and indocile barons, and they were therefore little danger to the monarchy. It was different with the county of Flanders and the duchy of Guienne, of which the first was powerful through the prosperity of its industry and trade and the long standing of its administrative organization, and the second because its duke was at the same time King of England.

The case of Flanders admirably illustrates the Capetian policy towards the great fiefs: to establish the ascendancy of the royal administration over them, but without annexing them to the king's domain. True, the crown's officials, through activities whose initiative came more from themselves than their master, imposed their authority harshly. Yet, despite appearances, it was no part of their policy, either in Flanders or Guienne, to expel a recalcitrant vassal by force. From the reign of Philip the Fair, they more and more frequently summoned before the royal courts cases in which the king could claim to have an interest, accepted and encouraged appeals from the count's courts to that of the *Parlement*, placed under their protection appellants whom they removed from the count's jurisdiction, interfered in urban quarrels, took a hand in the administration of the towns, caused the royal banner to be flown there, and enforced the use of the French language in the cases in which they were concerned.

In Flanders this policy encountered unexpected resistance. Knowing nothing about the social struggles which divided the industrial towns, the royal officials powerfully aided the patricians in enslaving the working masses. They provoked a revolt of Count Guy of Dampierre, exasperated by all their encroachments, followed by a revolt of the wretched artisans against the intolerable dictatorship of the capitalist *leliaerts*, partisans of the *fleurs-de-lys*. A fierce but indecisive war ended in 1305, by the treaty of Athis-sur-Orge, with the restitution of the fief to the son of the rebellious vassal, Robert of Béthune. The King of France confined himself to demanding the destruction of the walls of the big Flemish towns, an oath of fidelity from all the inhabitants of the county, and the payment of a heavy war indemnity, guaranteed by the temporary occupation of the castellanies of Lille, Douai, and Béthune. In 1312 the count chose to free himself from the indemnity by ceding the pledged territories to his suzerain. Finally, in 1320, Béthune was reassigned to Artois and replaced by the castellany of Orchies. This completed the 'transfer of Flanders', the

43

sole territorial annexation which the Capetians obtained at the end of long, costly, and hard punitive campaigns. For the rest, it was enough for them that the new count had returned to his obedience and no longer opposed the activity of the royal officials.

Still thoroughly imbued with the feudal spirit, indeed quite patriarchal even half a century earlier, the French monarchy, impelled by the bold initiative of its agents and spurred on by its southern lawyers, who were stuffed with Roman law and inclined towards the tyrannical absolutism of the Byzantine empire, tended perhaps unconsciously, but surely, to transform the kingdom into a modern State, in which the will of the sovereign, as the supreme law of the nation, must be obeyed without a murmur. But the French monarchy, like all the other kingdoms of Europe, lacked two essential implements for the consummation of its ambitions: a regular army and stable finances.

For centuries the feudal monarchies had known no armies other than the 'hosting' of vassals, summoned only in case of war. It was made up firstly and above all by the contingent of knights, horsemen heavily armed at their own expense, reinforced by the untrained mass of infantry provided by the towns and the rural communities. In theory every vassal, indeed every subject, owed the service of hosting to his suzerain king. But custom had soon reduced this obligation to very little. To the royal hosting the vassals of the crown were now bound to bring only a small contingent of knights, which represented scarcely more than a tenth of the forces they had at their own disposal for their private wars. The towns sent only a given number of infantry. Moreover, in accordance with almost all local customs, the service of the knights, when they fought outside their own provinces, was limited to forty days, and that of the infantry to three months.

These factors affected the character of the military operations conducted by the most powerful sovereigns in Europe, and made themselves felt during almost the whole of the Hundred Years' War. In the first place, there was an extremely small number of effectives, much below the grossly swollen figures quoted by the chroniclers. In their frequently severe campaigns, the last Capetian kings could put only ridiculously small contingents into the field. The knights, whose number sometimes fell as low as 600, never exceeded 2,500. The sergeants—more lightly armed horsemen – did not amount to twice as many. The infantry, whose services were not highly considered, rarely exceeded 5,000 men. With these scanty effectives, 10,000 to 15,000 men all told, the King of France was regarded, and rightly, as the strongest sovereign in Christendom. The Valois managed slightly to augment the number of their soldiers; but they did not succeed in doubling it.

In addition, the short term of military service forbade any large-scale operations. The hosting was summoned at the last moment, and always assembled more slowly than had been foreseen. The campaign was begun only late in the summer, and was soon overtaken by the winter, which meant disbandment. Until the introduction of artillery, which had barely begun, there could be no question of undertaking a siege, which the progress of military architecture had made a long-term operation. A pitched battle, whose result was always uncertain, was rarely risked. As a rule, everything was limited to a short destructive raid against the enemy. Then a truce, badly kept on either side, postponed operations until the following summer.

To offset these inconveniences the later Capetians could find only palliatives. More than their predecessors, they called upon foreign mercenaries, knights of the Empire, and Genoese cross-bowmen. But the high rate of pay and the danger of these undisciplined and plundering mercenaries led them to recruit only a small number, a mere reinforcement. Above all, in order to enable the hosting to continue operations beyond the customary six weeks, they were driven to offer them pay. So the whole army, whatever the source of its recruitment, feudal or foreign, was now paid. Pay, fixed by royal decree from 1274, amounted to 20 *sous* of Tours [1] a day for knights banneret, 10 *sous* for knights bachelor, 6 to 7 *sous* for squires, 15 *deniers* for cross-bowmen, and 1 *sou* for foot-sergeants. A special administration dealt with recruiting, supervised numbers, and took charge of payment. While the Constable or commander-in-chief had general direction of operations and encampment, two marshals for the cavalry and the master of cross-bowmen for the infantry made contracts with captains and held musters to ensure that the promised number of effectives was really reached. Two or three 'war treasurers' and the clerk of the master of cross-bowmen were entrusted with making payments in accordance with the roll-calls provided by the musters.

In theory, the system permitted the raising of a large army. For, from the end of the thirteenth century, the almost complete disappearance of private wars had deprived the nobility of their favourite pastime and induced them readily to sell their services to the king. There were formed at this time regular companies of professional men-at-arms, grouped in '*routes*' under the leadership of experienced captains. Acting on their own account, or in response to the call of the great vassals summoned to the hosting, these *routiers*, whose talent for rapine France was soon to know to her cost, succumbed in large numbers to the lure of pay. In 1337 we find the Count of Foix alone bringing to the hosting of Guienne a thousand soldiers and servants, including more than 300 horsemen. But, in actual practice, the king never had at his disposal more than a limited number of effectives, because he had not the money to pay for a large army.

The deeply rooted tradition still ruled, at the beginning of the fourteenth century, that the king should 'live of his own', in other words

---

[1] The two moneys of account most used in France were the *livre* of Tours (*tournois*), which, by the end of the thirteenth century, was worth a fourth of the pound sterling, and the *livre* of Paris (*parisis*), the ratio between them being: £1 *parisis* = £1 5s. *tournois*. In other terms, £1 sterling = £3 4s. *parisis* = £4 *tournois*.

on the products of his domain and the casual revenue which he might expect from the exercise of his rights as suzerain. Doubtless these revenues were very large. We cannot be more exact, since the almost complete disappearance of French financial archives makes any statistical statement, even approximate, out of the question. But, even so, they seem to have been inadequate for the maintenance of an ever more complex administration and for the diplomatic and political needs of the first kingdom of Europe. In time of war, things were much worse. Then the monarchy found itself driven to demand an exceptional contribution from its vassals and subjects, in the form of a tax in place of military service, which it did its best to extend to the whole kingdom.

In this indirect way, the idea of taxation, unknown to the medieval world, was enabled, though not without opposition, to reappear in the political theory of the State. But it was far from being accepted by all, and as yet there could be no question of permanent taxation. Still, the wars in Guienne and Flanders under Philip the Fair and his sons contributed powerfully towards acclimatizing the royal tax. Twice over, from 1294 to 1304, and then from 1313 to 1324, the king had to call almost yearly upon his extremely reluctant taxpayers. Despite everything, the tax remained an 'extraordinary' resort – it retained this epithet until the end of the *ancien régime* – with an uncertain yield, only too often below the royal needs. It had not yet emerged from a period of experiment, in which miscalculations were more numerous than successes. Various kinds of tax were tried turn about by the ingenuity of the royal officials; indirect taxes, in the form of taxes on merchandise, to which public opinion gave the offensive name of *maltôte*, or 'bad tax'; quota taxes, a levy of one-fiftieth or one-hundredth on fortunes, which, however, were estimated so roughly that the experiment proved disastrous; and finally assessment taxes, calculated by households or hearths, hence their name of *fouage*, which was gradually replaced by that of *taille*.

In order to be accepted by the people, taxation could not be decreed until the last moment, when war was already declared and operations were imminent; conditions which excluded the possibility of long-term preparations. It met with strong opposition from the taxpayers, and required difficult negotiations, reductions, payment by lump sums, and exemptions. Its collection, which was poorly organized, proceeded slowly. Once the campaign was over, the king's subjects, thinking the danger passed, paid up still worse, while the king's debts were increased. In the end, a very small part of his expenses was covered by taxation. So, willy-nilly, the needy monarchy was reduced to expedients which, while they did not take care of the morrow, enabled it to plug the most gaping holes.

Of all these expedients, the most famous, though not the most fruitful, begun by Philip the Fair and abused, in their financial straits, by the Valois kings, was the 'mutation' of the currency. There was no question, as a badly informed posterity has accused the enemy of Boniface VIII and the persecutor of the Templars, of making counterfeit coinage. The king always announced the conversion or 'mutation' which he proposed to introduce into the monetary system, and kept scrupulously to the terms of his decrees, whether he arbitrarily increased the value of gold and silver coins (*gros, moutons, écus, agnels*) in relation to money of account (*livres, sous, deniers*) in which payments were stipulated, or depreciated the currency by enacting less weight or fineness for the new coinage, while maintaining the same value for it in money of account. In short, the Capetians and the Valois practised devaluation, partial and disguised bankruptcy, towards which the similar manipulations, though on a larger scale, undertaken by our modern States should make us indulgent. Its financial advantage was as obvious as it was fleeting. In addition to the profit of minting, which was often considerable, the king lightened his debts, contracted in strong currency by paying them off in weak currency, until the time came when his own debtors, by returning depreciated coinage to the royal coffers, annulled the benefit to the treasury.

Later in the fourteenth century, these currency manipulations were to be prompted also by economic stress. In the absence of any considerable mining, the stock of precious metal kept on declining slowly. As soon as a recession of trade set in – this was to happen after 1335 – the circulation of coins slowed down and merchants found themselves with not enough cash to carry on their business; this involved the minting of more coins, but of less value. Nearly all the currencies of Europe, even the English sterling, then underwent weakening on a larger or smaller scale. But the extensive devaluations practised by the kings of France, often at very close intervals, and despite a public opinion which constantly demanded and often obtained a return to stable currency, were primarily fiscal expedients.

That these financial difficulties were a source of weakness to the monarchy, and that the fiscal experiments of the later Capetian kings aroused discontent, is not to be denied. Still, the opposition which was shown here and there to the encroachments of the royal officials and their fiscal demands did not succeed in shaking the royal edifice, patiently and carefully built. There was no one to unite the malcontents, stimulate the opposition, put a brake on government despotism. The clergy, despite their apparent autonomy in relation to the lay power and the strong monarchical concentration displayed in the pontifical *Curia*, were entirely in the hands of the king. Their servility was displayed in the struggle which Philip the Fair boldly waged against the Papacy. No doubt it was with an ill grace that they paid the tenths demanded by the sovereign on various grounds, with or without the assent of the Holy See. No doubt they registered impatience at the ceaseless encroachments which the king's agents made on their extravagant judicial privileges. But they were content to obtain from the king, at various times, charters which guaranteed the full exercise of ecclesiastical jurisdiction. To these charters, of course, the royal officials paid no attention. So, in the assembly at the Bois de Vincennes in 1329, Philip of Valois's lawyers were able to uphold, against the cleverest canonists in France, the royal thesis which limited ecclesiastical jurisdiction over person and property and allowed appeal from the ecclesiastical courts to that of the king, by the procedure which soon came to be called 'as abuse'. Henceforth the benefit of clergy, so long formidable, ceased to impose any restraint on the supreme authority of the sovereign lawgiver.

The nobility, who, with the clergy, held the main part of landed wealth in the kingdom, and remained the faithful trustees of the feudal spirit, might have proved more dangerous. It was their interests which were most deeply touched by the recent transformation of the monarchy and the innovations of its agents. The king demanded of them a more strict fulfilment of their duties as vassals at the very moment when their impoverishment, through the interplay of economic circumstances, made this additional burden harder for them to bear. Like the clergy, they found their jurisdiction continually nibbled away by the activity of the royal judges. The prohibition of private wars, still not very effective under Saint Louis, but more strictly enforced since the time of Philip the Fair, meant the loss of their favourite occupation.

Nevertheless the nobility proved incapable of grasping their opportunity when, on Philip the Fair's death, they might have taken combined action with all the discontented taxpayers. In the leagues which they formed in most of the provinces, at the end of 1314, they gave no thought, except in the south of Languedoc, and even there in a purely fleeting fashion, to alliances with the townsmen, whose support would have been valuable. Except in Brittany, where the duke undertook to present their claims to the king, the territorial princes remained prudently neutral. In 1315 the nobility secured from the young Louis X, but only province by province, charters confirming their ancient privileges. As soon as the movement died down, however, these became a dead letter, except in Normandy, where the Charter to the Normans long enjoyed successive confirmations.

The lack of political sense on the part of the nobility, perhaps more marked in France than elsewhere, and their increasing spirit of caste explain why, at their moments of revolt, they always neglected to unite their forces with those of the burgesses, whose low birth they despised while they envied their wealth. The close co-operation which, on the contrary, united the knights of the shires and the representatives of the boroughs in the English House of Commons partly explains the different constitutional evolution of the two monarchies.

Finally this opposition, which neither the clergy nor the nobility were capable of guiding, had no organization through which to express itself. It is true that on occasion, notably in 1308, at the height of the scandal over the Templars, Philip the Fair called together barons, prelates, and proxies of the religious houses and the urban communities, and invited them to support his policy. In these assemblies some historians, at the cost of an audacious anticipation, have seen the first Estates General of the French monarchy. But these exceptional sittings of representatives of the nation had no purpose except to approve, without discussing, the speeches which were made to them. As they put forward no grievances, discussed no demand for taxes, and expressed no political views, they could not claim to exercise any control over a monarchy which knew no law except the common law. We are told, indeed, that on several occasions the last two Capetians summoned assemblies, local or general, of barons and prominent persons, and asked them to settle the succession to the throne, to approve certain important decisions, or even, at times, to grant subsidies. But we have next to no information about either their composition or their deliberations. It does not appear that, under Philip V or Charles IV, they showed the least opposition or expressed the least desire to control the royal government. If their complaints had been violent, the echo of them would certainly have reached the ears of the chroniclers, who did not deem it useful to say much about these assemblies. Before they could dream of demanding reforms, it would have been necessary that the principle of no taxation without the consent of the taxed should be solidly established. Things had not yet reached this point, since taxation still remained but a novel experiment, as uncertain as it was disliked by the nation.

So, despite some defects in its political and administrative framework, which would have been dangerous only if the other Christian States had not also suffered from them, it was a powerful kingdom and a strongly based monarchy that Philip VI of Valois inherited in 1328.

2. ENGLAND IN 1328

IN MANY features of her social and political organization and her monarchical institutions, England in the fourteenth century resembled France. To avoid tiresome repetition, I shall confine my examination to points of difference rather than resemblance in the two kingdoms.

The country over which reigned a dynasty French in origin, by marriage, and in taste, the Plantagenets, was neither as large nor as rich as that whose destiny the Capetian sovereigns had hitherto guided. Despite their recent, but very imperfectly fulfilled attempts, the Plantagenets were still far from controlling the whole of the British Isles. Over the kingdom of Scotland the kings of England had for centuries exercised a nominal suzerainty, which Edward I had been bent upon making effective, by methods very like those that the Capetians had used in Guienne and Flanders. First he supported a sovereign of his own choice. Then he confiscated the little northern kingdom. But ten years of almost ceaseless struggle (1296–1307) gave the Plantagenets only fleeting success. When the knighthood of Edward II was crushed by the Scottish Highlanders in June 1314 – just as the Flanders militia, twelve years earlier, cut the nobility of France to pieces at Courtrai – Scottish independence was registered by the facts. The border counties, Cumberland, Northumberland, Durham, got nothing out of the war but ruin, constantly repeated by the raids of hostile troops.

Ireland, conquered in theory since the reign of Henry II, periodically reverted to independence. The king's lieutenants made themselves obeyed only in some areas in the east, around Dublin, and in the south, in the region of Cork and Waterford. Everywhere else the chiefs of the Celtic clans, powerful especially in Connaught and Ulster, and a handful of great English families, long settled in the country – hence their name of Anglo-Irish – set their authority at defiance. Alone of all the island territories, outside England properly speaking, Wales had been subjected under Edward I, as the result of hard campaigns, and erected into a principality whose destiny had been directed by the king's eldest son. Welsh revolts, though still to be feared, no longer imperilled the implacable English administration which had been imposed on the country.

Within these rather restricted boundaries, England remained relatively poor and underpeopled. Her development, belatedly begun under the Anglo-Norman sovereigns, and made still slower by periodical relapses into political anarchy, had not enabled her to attain the degree of prosperity which some favoured regions of the continent had reached. For her sparse population a small number of dioceses, which it was not found necessary to increase until the sixteenth century, still sufficed: 14 for the province of Canterbury, 3 for that of York, plus the 4 Welsh bishoprics, which were of small size. In the absence of any intense urban development, the population, within its 8,600 parishes, can scarcely have exceeded three and a half million inhabitants, barely a third of that of France.

Agriculture was also more backward in England. The great manors, cultivated for the lord by the labour services of his tenants, had been more resistant than in France to the upward curve of population. No large clearances were undertaken until the thirteenth century, and then mostly on the initiative of the lords who had naturally reaped the advantage, so that instead of increasing the division of waste land among new tenants, there was on the contrary, at least for a time, an increase in labour services and an intensification of the servile condition, or villeinage, of the peasants, especially on the monastic, capitular or episcopal estates. Elsewhere, on the contrary, there was a reduction in the performance of labour, which was commuted for rents in cash.

In any case, only the richest soils had been tapped. Wide areas, on the chalk hills of Kent and Sussex and the great heaths of the Pennine Chain, which were unpromising for tillage, were utilized for the extensive rearing of sheep, which gave the English countryside an aspect all its own and provided the country with its richest exportable product, wool, a raw material much to the liking of the Low Countries' looms. On the Cistercian estates in Yorkshire sheep-farming achieved such a degree of perfection that English wool was rightly regarded in the continental markets as the finest in Europe.

In the absence of any export industry – it was not until fairly late in the fourteenth century that certain products of English craftsmanship, such as alabaster reliefs, came into circulation on the continent – the towns remained small, even the ports on the south and east coasts. No crowd of European students flocked to the Universities of Oxford and Cambridge as they did to Paris, though Oxford was famous for the learning of its Franciscan teachers. There was only one large centre, London, still confined, as it was to be for centuries, solely to the City north of the Thames. The recent growth of the nearby borough of Westminster, a kind of administrative capital, and the construction along the Strand, the road linking the two towns, of fine seigniorial mansions, gave it a population of about 40,000, much below that of the French capital. Its powerful and quarrelsome craft-guilds confined their activity to internal trade. In all other commercial spheres, foreigners were the masters, and they remained so fairly far into the century, until the time came when growing xenophobia dispossessed them of their monopoly, to the advantage of English sailors and merchants. As everywhere else, the Italians handled money. The Gascons, almost on their own, carried on Atlantic trade. The Flemings, the Brabançons, and the Hanseatic towns, above all, enjoyed extensive privileges in London, and had prosperous colonies there, which were envied by the populace.

Political organization presented, as in France, a mixture of archaic features, expressing the still predominant feudal spirit, and strong monarchical institutions, prefiguring the modern State. These institutions, however, had been organized earlier than in the Capetian kingdom, were more developed, and consequently stronger and better accepted by the people, and this gave the royal authority and the agents charged with enforcing it a self-confidence and a security perhaps unique at that time in Europe. Yet by a curious contrast, this kingdom with so strong an administrative framework was periodically plunged into political struggles of unparalleled violence, in which a baronage coherent and united, though less wealthy than the French, opposed the king's person and demanded for itself control of his officials and direction of the country's affairs.

England properly speaking was divided into thirty-nine shires, very unequal in size. These were only administrative areas, not, as in France, feudal entities. The title of earl which was borne by the higher barons did not imply territorial possession of the counties from which they derived their names. Powerful though they were, from as far back as the Norman conquest the upper aristocracy had had their fiefs, manors, and honours scattered in different shires, and never forming vast estates all in one place. Into these disjointed possessions the king's agents insinuated themselves everywhere without meeting effective opposition. The sole exception to the rule was the palatine counties, favoured territories where the king's writ did not run, into which the royal officials did not penetrate, and which possessed quasi-independent chanceries and courts of justice. Of the two palatinates still surviving, one, the county of Chester, near the Welsh frontier, had reverted to the royal estate on the extinction of its family of earls; the other, in the north, was in the hands of the Bishop of Durham. In 1351, Edward III raised the county of Lancaster into a palatinate, with the life title of duke, in favour of his cousin Henry of Lancaster. On the death of this baron, he renewed the grant for Henry's son-in-law, a younger son of the sovereign, John of Gaunt.

Outside the palatinates there were, to be sure, a number of manorial jurisdictions, lay and ecclesiastical, called franchises, to which their holders were jealously attached. But for long since they had been reduced to impotence by the activities of the royal officials, who called to their own jurisdiction cases in which the king claimed to be interested and laid down without dispute the rule of appeal to the royal courts. The pettifogging spirit of the Anglo-Normans and their marked taste for juridical theories had created a formalist, complex system of law which exalted the king as the supreme lawgiver. The least disturbance of order, being regarded as a breach of the king's peace, led to a suit in which the king, as the injured party, could demand from his judges exemplary punishment of offenders. From this expedient, it was an easy step to the notion, strange to the men of the Middle Ages, of a Public Prosecutor acting apart from any complaint made by private individuals.

In the shires a host of officials ensured the monarchical administration: reeves, or estate agents; foresters and verderers, charged with applying the strict, but already disregarded, laws relating to the great areas known as forest, an enormous game preserve; escheators, or administrators of the properties of the king's vassals, before their transfer to heirs or during their minority; coroners, who presided over inquiries relating to violent deaths; collectors, charged with levying regular or temporary taxes. The sheriff, analogous with the Capetian bailiff, a person of modest birth who held office only for a short time, ensured contact between the king and his subjects. He collected the king's revenues, for part of which he owed a fixed farm, paid out local expenses, and presented his accounts annually to the Exchequer. He returned all royal writs to their issuing authorities, with a note on the measures taken for their enforcement. Finally he presided every month over the county court, to which free men were summoned, where justice was rendered and the grand juries so characteristic of medieval England were chosen, and where also the knights of the shire to represent the county in Parliament were elected.

Departmentalism of the central organs of government, long since separated from the *curia regis*, was older and more advanced than in France. Three services, under the direction respectively of the chancellor, the treasurer, and the chief justices, formed regular ministries, in the modern sense of the word. The chancery, orderly and fond of red tape – it has left us extensive archives – dispatched the innumerable letters, orders, and writs under the great seal which carried the king's will everywhere. The exchequer, already more than two centuries old, was the centre of the financial administration. The lower exchequer, or exchequer of receipt, played the part of a treasury; the upper exchequer, or exchequer of accounts, that of an audit office. We do not know much about its working in the fourteenth century, since the formidable mass of its archives has hitherto discouraged research. There is no doubt, however, that its large staff, directed by the chamberlains and barons of the exchequer, exercised a partially effective control over expenditure and the accountable officers.

Finally, supreme justice was rendered by two fixed courts, sitting in Westminster, in addition to the periodical circuits of itinerant judges whose 'general eyres' were being gradually replaced by shorter circuits of assizes. The two courts were the Common Bench and the King's Bench, of which originally the first remained fixed and the second followed the king wherever he went. The two of them now sat side by side, and some degree of specialization was already beginning to exist between them, the Common Bench for choice judging civil cases between private individuals and the King's Bench criminal cases and those in which the Crown was concerned.

In detaching themselves from the court, these great services acquired an autonomy which sometimes made their direct control by the sovereign difficult, especially at moments when the baronage, masters of the council, put officials of its own choice at their head. Hence arose the political role, much greater than in France, which was played by the king's household, whose members, close friends of the sovereign, could better interpret his will and make it known more rapidly. Under the direction of the keeper of the privy seal, a regular private secretariat existed within the household, whose essential role was to order, on the directions of the king and the council, the issue by the chancellor of letters under the great seal; but it made no bones about giving direct orders to the Exchequer or to local officials. Two financial departments, the Wardrobe and the Chamber, in theory supplied by assignments from the Treasury, often caused the product of certain royal revenues to be paid directly to them, thus acquiring an autonomy which asserted itself above all in time of war, when any campaign in which the sovereign took part was directly financed by the Wardrobe. In the household the King of England possessed a kind of duplicate government, which he used to the full when he wanted to shake off the tutelage of a baronial council. It also rendered great services to Edward III during his lengthy stays on the continent.

We must consider separately the unique institution of Parliament. It was already the fruit of a long process of evolution; but in no way did it give England the character of a controlled or constitutional monarchy, which she did not acquire until very much later. At the beginning of the fourteenth century, the quasi-periodical assemblies of the king's court, yearly or twice yearly according to circumstances, still presented the appearance of an enlarged Great Council, in which the sovereign's habitual councillors were reinforced, for a brief session of some days or some weeks, by a certain number of barons and prelates, summoned individually by reason of their feudal tenure. They made up the Council in Parliament, a particularly solemn form of the king's court.

For the past two generations, the habit had taken root of consulting also the representatives of other classes of the nation, merchants, clerics, burgesses, knights of the shires. The merchants, as an 'estate', were rarely represented. The lower clergy had ceased to come to Parliament under Edward II: their prelates summoned them to convocations, generally held at the same time. So the two knights from every shire and the two burgesses from every town – four for London – alone remained to make up what was later to be called the House of Commons. Their role was still episodic, and they took no part in the proceedings of the Council. Only one of their members, the Speaker, was later charged with presenting the wishes and complaints of the Commons to the king.

So Parliament, thus constituted, was far from an essentially political or legislative assembly. In fact, it possessed indiscriminately all the attributes of the *curia regis*, and in the first place that of dispensing justice. By means of petition, discontented subjects could ask it for the redress of grievances.

This procedure was so popular that, at the beginning of every session, it was necessary to appoint several commissions (analogous with the chambers of inquiry and requests of the *Parlement* of Paris, but essentially temporary) charged with sifting and examining the mass of petitions and preparing the Council's decisions. By retaining such petitions as possessed general interest and adding their personal complaints to them, the members could present 'common petitions' to the Council, and in this way exercise a political influence, which was especially noticeable when the monarchy was in difficulties. Their power was further increased by the fact that it was to them, more often than they wished, that requests for the granting of subsidies were addressed. Nevertheless, the Council remained sole judge of the legislative measures to be promulgated in Parliament. These solemn decrees were then given the name of statutes, were transmitted to the judges, and ranked as equal and supplementary to the customary or common law in the courts of justice.

The troubles which marked the reign of Edward II did something to increase the prestige of Parliament, notably in the legislative sphere. In 1322, at its meeting in York, the king, by solemn statute, annulled all the legislative acts passed during the last eleven years by the 'Lords Ordainers' and, seeking to avoid a similar annulment of royalist legislation in the future, proclaimed aloud that any decree promulgated in Parliament could not be rescinded except by a new Parliament. It was probably about this same date – though some historians postdate its writing until the end of the century – that a clerk interested in constitutional law wrote the *Modus tenendi Parliamentum*, an ideal description, brazenly placed under the aegis of William the Conqueror, of the role which should be played in the feudal monarchy by the hierarchy of Estates and their representatives: it was from their agreement with the king that the supreme law proceeded.

In short, Parliament, an integral part of English monarchical institutions, but the latest in date and therefore playing the least well defined role, could be for the sovereign either the best aid to his policy or the worst obstacle to his will. To a popular king, a strict lawgiver and a good administrator, it offered the priceless support of public opinion and enabled him to take a lofty tone towards foreign sovereigns and the head of the Church in the name of the nation. If the sovereign was maladroit and aroused against him a baronage always ready to denounce his mistakes, Parliament served as an instrument for the opposition and imposed the tutelage of his adversaries upon the king. This alternation of strength and weakness made a rhythm for the history of medieval England.

In the financial sphere, the Plantagenets had the advantage of possessing resources which, though relatively modest, were more or less stable. Edward I had obtained from the merchants the grant of a tax or custom on the export of wool and hides. Without soliciting its renewal, his successors continued to levy it. In times of need, they obtained from assemblies of merchants the grant of an extra duty, the *maltôte* of 40 shillings a sack, which successive Parliaments tried in vain to abolish. Its yield was increased by an institution for which the credit belonged to Edward II's councillors, the 'staple of wool'. The king named either a continental port (this was the foreign staple) or several English ports (the home staple) which alone were empowered to handle the export of wool. Here this valuable raw material was bonded in public warehouses where it paid the tax before being shipped or sold to foreign buyers.

To this fruitful indirect tax were added the subsidies voted by the Commons, usually a tax on personal property, at the rate of one-tenth for the towns and one-fifteenth for the country. The difficulties of assessment and the ingenuity of the taxpayers, who at all times practised fiscal evasion, did not enable it to yield more than a modest revenue. But these subsidies, frequently solicited from Parliament, as well as the tenths granted by the clergy in their convocations, had acquired a certain regularity. They were paid without much murmuring, since the members were elected with full power to pledge their constituents.

The whole of these resources, sufficient in normal times – at the utmost £80,000 – did not permit the financing of great enterprises. Like the Valois, the Plantagenets lived on expedients, dunned by usurers, ceaselessly driven towards bankruptcy. They had at least the merit of not adopting drastic monetary changes. The pound sterling, already stronger than the Tours or the Paris *livre*, soon gained a premium over the French currency, and at the end of a century of exhausting war it had not been devalued by more than 20 per cent.

A few words will suffice to describe the military forces which the king had at his disposal. The English army, like the French, was recruited on the basis of the feudal hosting. The hard campaigns in Wales and Scotland under Edward I had inured it to war, but not to the point of making it invincible. The defeat at Bannockburn, inflicted on the English cavalry by the charge of the Scottish pikemen, was a proof that the mounted nobility had not yet changed their age-old tactics. The whole army was paid, to enable longer campaigns to be undertaken. The contracts made with the captains, called indentures (these were charter-parties of which the two copies, written on the same piece of parchment, were detached along an indented line), enabled the strength provided to be verified at any moment and ensured payment. The infantry, whose services were as yet scarcely appreciated, were recruited among the highland populations of the West, especially in Wales. Their cohesion was stronger than that of the mediocre militia which the King of France had at his disposal. Finally, in the continental wars, the Plantagenets had the valuable reinforcement of the Gascon contingents, keen fighters, and also that of imperial mercenaries, recruited at very high cost in the Low Countries.

The remaining problem was to transport overseas the forces raised in the kingdom. This duty was entrusted to the two admirals, that of the North and that of the West, each in charge of a stretch of coast. In normal times they were only judges in the sphere of maritime law, but, in case of war, they organized the impressment of ships in all the mercantile ports; for the ancient corporation of the Cinque Ports, on the coasts of Kent and Sussex (Dover, Rye, Winchelsea, etc.), was no longer powerful enough, as it had been at the time of the Anglo-Norman dynasty, to provide all the ships necessary for the transport of an expeditionary corps, though it rarely exceeded twelve thousand men.

England, in short, conveyed the impression of a kingdom which, though small, was coherent, while its modest strength, within the strong framework of an experienced administration, was wholly in the sovereign's hands. But he had to reckon with the periodical and fierce outbreaks of political passion, which perhaps no other country in Europe experienced with such violence. From the dawn of the thirteenth century to the end of the seventeenth, the history of England was marked by cruel civil wars, directed less against the monarchy than against the person of the sovereign, and these, from the accession of John Lackland to the fall of the Stuarts, periodically left behind them trails of blood and seeds of hate. The accession of Edward III, in January 1327, was only an episode, and by no means the climax, in one of these desperate struggles, which had almost entirely filled the twenty years of Edward II's reign. It does not come within my scope to recall its main events, even summarily. At the same time, a balance-sheet is necessary. It does not redound to the credit of the island kingdom.

Edward II had inherited from his father, in 1307, a situation heavy with menace. The wars of this unlucky conqueror, especially his exhausting Scottish campaigns, the demands of his tax-collectors, the encroachments of his administration, had for some years past revived the opposition of the baronage. To appease their discontent would have taken a clever politician coupled with a statesman. Edward II was neither the one nor the other. Moderately intelligent, addicted to physical exercises such as swimming, and such pursuits as thatching and digging ditches, he liked neither war nor the exercise of power: a twofold cause of scandal to his vassals. But he clung jealously to his authority, which he used for the benefit of unworthy favourites, whose mastery over his mind gave rise to unfortunate though slanderous rumours. It did not take more to revive the resentment of the baronage, hereditarily hungry for power. It is true that they were not primarily concerned, like their predecessors of the previous century, with putting a brake on the monarchical power, lightening the weight of their feudal duties, and protecting their jurisdictions against the encroachments of the royal officials. The administrative framework was too strongly established for them to dream of destroying it. But, against the royalist doctrine of sovereign power exercised without control, they revived the old feudal theory according to which the barons, as the king's natural councillors, were entitled to collaborate in the government and if necessary control it. To do this they must in the first place lay hands on the

Council, expel the favourites, appoint men they could trust to administrative posts, and exercise effective power in the king's name.

In the absence of a capable leader, this plan, not difficult in its execution, but in its maintenance against a sovereign resolved to shake off tutelage, could only end in disaster. The fine impulse of the 'Lords Ordainers',
in league against the Bearnese favourite Piers Gaveston, and the two
dictatorships of the most ardent of them, the king's first cousin, Thomas
of Lancaster, came to grief at the end of a few months. An alliance
between the moderate barons and the king might have saved the situation, as it did under Henry III. But this was reckoning without the
selfish blindness of the former and the obstinate hatred of the latter. In
the very ranks of the baronage, Edward found a new favourite, Hugh
Despenser the younger, and imposed his greed and incompetence on a
country exhausted by ten years of civil war. England sank further and
further into political anarchy.

The last act of the tragedy, which cost the detested sovereign his life,
did not raise the prestige of the Plantagenets. Despenser, a baron of the
west, tried to carve out a principality for himself in the Welsh marches,
where the royal authority collided with powerful feudal families, enriched with the spoils of the Celtic princelings in Monmouthshire, Glam-
organ, and the nearby counties. His rivals made war upon him. He drove
the most powerful of them, Roger Mortimer of Wigmore, into exile. At
the same time, Edward quarrelled with his wife, Isabella of France, a
daughter of Philip the Fair, whose wickedness was matched by her misconduct, and banished her from his court. The King of France, Charles IV,
had just attacked Guienne, and Isabella managed to persuade her husband
that, if she negotiated directly with her brother, she could restore peace
more easily. She set off in 1325, taking her eldest son, whom she wanted
to make Duke of Aquitaine, with her. Peace was made. But in Paris
Isabella met Mortimer again, and became his mistress, if she was not
already. Their parade of this liaison shocked Charles IV, who drove them
from his court. Still accompanied by the heir to the English throne, they
found refuge with the Count of Hainault, arranged the betrothal of
young Edward to his daughter Philippa, and engaged mercenaries.

At the head of these foreign troops, towards the end of 1326 they landed
in England, which was badly guarded, marched on London, incited a
general revolt of the barons against Despenser and his clique, defeated
them after a savage war, and finally laid hands on the king's person.
Parliament, in obedience to the will of the conspirators, proclaimed his
deposition. Sir William Trussell, in the name of the whole baronage,
solemnly renounced the allegiance they owed him. Then, pending the
time when Isabella could get rid of the fallen sovereign by assassination,
his son Edward, who was only fourteen, was raised to the throne. In fact it
was Mortimer who ruled, prolonging anarchy for another three years.
Created Earl of March – he had married the last descendant of the

Lusignans of Poitou, holders of the French counties of Marche and Angoulême – and gorged with the spoils of the Despenser faction, he maintained himself only by terror. Meanwhile a posthumous popularity, such as Thomas of Lancaster had already enjoyed on the morrow of his fall, attached itself to the memory of the sovereign who had died so tragically. Miracles were said to take place at his tomb, which is still to be seen in the choir of the cathedral, then the abbey church, of Gloucester. The baronage combined once more against Mortimer. Their first plot, which was easily frustrated, led to the execution of the Earl of Kent. This situation lasted until November 1330, when Edward III shook off Mortimer's tutelage.

It is important to bear in mind that, at the moment when a change of dynasty took place in France, England, which had barely emerged from civil war, was politically powerless, though, thanks to the resources which the monarchy had at its disposal, she was capable of rapid recovery.

3. THE QUESTION OF GUIENNE

THESE TWO countries, separated only by a narrow sea, paid next to no attention to each other. In England the nobility, of Norman or Angevin origin, had ceased for more than a century to take any interest in the affairs of the continent, where they had lost their ancestral possessions for ever. They were becoming more and more anglicized. The French language, or rather a peculiarly bastard dialect of that language, Anglo-Norman, full of English words and queer twists, was scarcely spoken now except by the court and the cultured upper classes. It still remained the language of the administration and that of the lawyers, though cases in the law courts, for the convenience of the parties, were increasingly heard in English. As it was written by English clerks, Anglo-Norman conveys the impression of being painfully translated from the national tongue and becoming a language of culture like Latin. While the nobility, through their marriages, and the higher clergy, inclined by their training towards international contacts, still maintained some relations between the two countries, the other social classes came into touch only to clash in the sphere of maritime trade. These sometimes harsh contacts affected in France only the coastal provinces and the merchants and tradesmen of Flanders, Picardy, Normandy, Brittany, and La Rochelle.

It was different in the case of the two dynasties, bound together by frequent intermarriage, and by a link still more powerful, the feudal relationship. The King of England, the Plantagenet sovereign, was at the same time Duke of Aquitaine or Guienne and a peer of France. In addition, since the reign of Edward I, who had acquired it from his first wife, Eleanor of Castille, he held the little county of Ponthieu in northern France, at the mouth of the Somme. Sovereign in his island, for his continental possessions he was the vassal of the King of France.

This ambiguous situation had long existed. We need not go so far as the distant day when William the Bastard, Duke of Normandy, set off to conquer the Anglo-Saxon kingdom (1066). Relations between vassal and suzerain had suddenly worsened when Henry II Plantagenet, already Count of Anjou, Touraine and Maine, husband of Eleanor of Aquitaine, in whose name he administered a great duchy extending from the Loire to the Pyrenees, holder of Normandy by means of conquest, finally succeeded to the English throne (1154). Then a long struggle ensued between Plantagenets and Capetians, which some modern historians, at the risk of confusion, have proposed to call 'the first Hundred Years' War', and in which the suzerain strove to overthrow a vassal ten times more powerful than himself.

It led in the end to the break-up of the Plantagenets' continental empire. But by the treaty of Paris, signed in May 1258 and ratified in December 1259, Saint Louis surrendered to his brother-in-law Henry III possession of Guienne, from which the Capetian forces had never managed to dislodge him, and even added to it some territories occupied by his predecessors, which, immediately or later, went to swell the southern duchy. In return, the Plantagenet renounced all the lost provinces, from Normandy to Poitou, and, above all, he consented to do homage to the King of France for his peerage-duchy. It has been rightly said that the Treaty of Paris, which replaced the two sovereigns in a most delicate feudal position, was at the very root of the Hundred Years' War. Its application, which immediately raised overwhelming difficulties, provoked ceaseless conflicts for the next seventy years. The one that brought Edward III and Philip VI to grips was only their inevitable end.

Other causes, which we must not neglect, contributed obscurely to strain the relations between the two dynasties, and even the two countries. Expanding trade brought the sailors of Gascony, representing English interests, into contact with increasingly wider areas of the kingdom of France. They carried the wines of Guienne to England, where they were better liked by the upper classes than the native wines and beers. From La Rochelle, the outlet for Poitou and Saintonge, and from Nantes they brought the salt of the Poitevin marshes and the bay of Bourgneuf which was essential to the English fishermen for their salting. Their ships, which rarely ventured far out to sea, needed a favourable reception in the Breton ports where they sheltered. Finally, we know how much sheep-farming and the English treasury depended on the Flemish market, where the raw wool was sold. Poitou, Brittany and Flanders were all provinces which Edward III, in some degree, exerted himself to control.

We should not, however, suppose that in intervening at these precise points, the Plantagenets deliberately sought to favour the commercial expansion of England. Unlike our modern imperialisms, the medieval monarchies did not go to war to create outlets for their trade or to gain markets. We cannot speak, before the second half of the fifteenth century, of any economic policy on the part of the sovereigns which took precedence over their dynastic dreams and their projects of conquest. Very much on the contrary, the economic weapon was to be employed by Edward III to satisfy his political ambitions. When he adopted measures of confiscation against enemy merchants, or, as he did in the case of Flanders, stopped the exports of wool, the most tangible result of these measures was to ruin his subjects and dry up the resources of the very man who had ordered them.

All the same, the commercial contacts which have just been noted largely contributed towards worsening Anglo-French relations, already so apt to be strained. Between the sailors of the two allegiances they created a rivalry, soon turned into hatred, which brought about acts of pillage and piracy, destruction of ships, sometimes even regular privateering wars. Particularly serious brawls, which broke out between sailors of Bayonne and Normandy in 1293, first in Bayonne and then in La Rochelle, served as a pretext chosen by Philip the Fair to declare war on Edward I and confiscate the fief of Aquitaine.

So we come back to this question of Guienne, the eternal apple of discord between the two dynasties. I need not recount its whole history from 1259 to 1328; but it is impossible to say nothing about it, lest we fail to understand the great conflict which lay ahead.

Not the least acute difficulties between suzerain and vassal were those in the territorial sphere. Almost wantonly, the Treaty of Paris had created a complex situation by promising the contingent restitution to the duchy of Aquitaine of certain territories (Saintonge 'beyond the Charente' and that part of Quercy and Agenais which had belonged to the counts of Toulouse), if Alphonse of Poitiers and his wife Joan of Toulouse, to whom they belonged, should leave no children. This happened in 1271, but neither Philip III nor his son showed themselves in any hurry to hand over the promised territories. It was not until the convention of Paris, concluded in November 1286, that the matter was settled without leaving too much resentment behind it. But this did not affect the fact that the boundaries of the Aquitaine fief, as usual at this period, remained vague and undefined. Interwoven rights and privileged enclaves were the source of wrangles and disputes. The officials of the King of France, always more ardent than their master in embittering quarrels, made no bones about nibbling away ducal rights beyond the frontier.

A matter still more serious was that the two adversaries, each afraid of the other's intentions in these marches with their uncertain frontiers, had begun to build castles and fortified new towns (*bastides*). From the coast of Saintonge to the mid-Garonne, across Périgord, Quercy, and Agenais, and again from the Garonne to Béarn, the countryside bristled with their double line of menacing walls. On the Capetian side Alphonse of Poitiers took the lead. Edward I brought the experience acquired in the Holy Land, which he had already applied in Wales, to his building, notably in the case of the castle of La Réole. These preparations continued on either side during the first quarter of the fourteenth century, maintaining a dangerous state of armed peace. In 1323, when a vassal of the King of France began to build a *bastide* at Saint-Sardos, near Agen, Gascon bands took it by surprise and burned it down. This was the signal for a new war and a fresh confiscation of the fief of Aquitaine by King Charles IV.

In the sphere of feudal relations, the causes of conflict were graver, because they were constantly renewed. Pursuing the policy of intervention which they applied with success in the other fiefs of the crown, the Capetian officials, the seneschals of Poitou, Périgord, and Saintonge and their subordinates, whose zeal far surpassed their master's intentions, kept on acting in Guienne, proclaiming the king's rights and inciting the people to appeal against the verdicts of the English seneschals. This policy, disquieting enough in the reign of Philip III, was provisionally halted by an agreement between the sovereigns, according to which the king's court would return all the appeals it received to the seneschal of Aquitaine, and would take them up again only if the ducal court had not done justice to the appellants within three months.

But encroachments multiplied during the reign of Philip the Fair, and especially appeals to the *Parlement*, to such an extent that Edward I found himself compelled permanently to employ attorneys and advocates at the Paris court to defend his interests in the 'Guienne cases' which became ever more numerous. Then the complaints of the officials of Aquitaine became more bitter. They declared that they were no longer capable of making the ducal authority respected owing to the constant interference of the royal agents. The appeals which these agents incited brought the judicial powers of the English seneschal to nothing, and placed under royal protection appellants who, in the eyes of the Bordeaux authorities, were simply rebels against their duke. The execution of the sentences passed by the royal courts was carried out brutally. Sergeants and ushers set up escutcheons bearing the *fleurs-de-lys* everywhere, made arbitrary arrests and seizures and proclaimed confiscations.

Subjects of the Capetians, insolently taking advantage of the protection of the royal officials, behaved in Guienne as though they were in a conquered country. An early case was quoted in which a body of Norman merchants, disliking their reception by the Gascons, gathered in arms under the walls of Saintes, insulted the English seneschal, and threatened to sack the town. If we are to believe the files of complaints lodged from time to time by the Plantagenet sovereign, exasperated by all this truculence, French sergeants penetrated into Aquitainian Agenais and asked the people: 'To whom do you owe allegiance, the King of France or the King of England?' Those who replied 'the King of England', as their duty to the Duke of Aquitaine demanded, found themselves haled before a Capetian court, charged with treason, and severely punished. In 1317, when the administration of the English seneschal of Saintonge gave rise to complaint, Philip V summoned him to his court and instituted an inquiry by his own seneschal of Périgord. Edward II forbade the seneschal of Saintonge to obey Philip's summons. To do so would have meant flouting his own authority in Guienne. On the other hand, the French officials loudly complained about the hindrances which the King of England's men put in the way of the exercise of their legitimate functions and the enforcement of their master's sovereign rights. If they were to be believed, the seneschal of Guienne, by threats, blackmail and even torture, forced his Gascon subjects to renounce their appeals to the *Parlement*.

Sometimes, scared by all this animosity and entangled in these obscure feudal affairs, the two sovereigns decided to clear up the arrears of complaints and entrusted mixed commissions of inquiry with the duty of passing final judgment on the questions in dispute. But neither the 'process' of Montreuil, begun in 1311, nor that of Périgueux, ordered in 1316, led to an amicable settlement. They compiled records which provided no solution, because the very basis of the problem remained at issue. The French officials believed that they were entitled to act in Guienne as they did in the other fiefs of the crown. In doing so, they gave the Plantagenet's subjects the impression, partly justified, that they aimed at dispossessing their master not only of all real authority in his duchy, but even of the fief itself, by a slow process of incessant encroachment.

A graver mistake on the part of the French officials was that they forgot that the King of England could not be treated as a mere duke and peer, incapable of freeing himself from the vice in which he was clasped. Sovereign in his island, the Plantagenet did not admit that he should be bullied in his French fiefs. As King of England, he could conclude foreign alliances directed against France, without in any way contravening his duty as a vassal towards the Capetian. This was what happened in 1297, when, to obviate the confiscation of Guienne, Edward I, sure of the support of Flanders, concluded an alliance with the German sovereign Adolf of Nassau and landed in the Low Countries, ready to transform a feudal conflict into an international war.

The vassal's irritation was also shown in the calculated slowness with which he performed his duty as a vassal and the reservations with which he deliberately surrounded his homage. As early as June 1286, in paying homage to Philip the Fair, Edward I expressly reserved his rights over the Gascon territories which the King of France still held. In 1303, on the pretext that he was held up by Scottish affairs, he failed to accept an invitation to investiture when his fief was restored to him. Belatedly, in September 1304, he thought of sending the Prince of Wales to accomplish this formality. On his accession, Edward II certainly paid homage again, when he went to Boulogne to fetch his bride Isabella of France (1308); but his struggle with his barons prevented him, or so he said, from paying his homage to Louis X. When Philip V succeeded his brother, it took repeated summonses and two and a half years of waiting before he sent his proxies, in June 1319, to convey his homage in his name. Though he repeated the ceremony in person a year later, it was only because his suzerain, legitimately exasperated, made this a condition of the restitution of Ponthieu, which had been occupied by Capetian agents for the past three years as a pledge for damages claimed by Norman merchants from their English and Gascon rivals. There was the same comedy on the accession of Charles IV. After eighteen months of waiting, a French embassy came to the Plantagenet's court to demand his homage. Edward II dodged the demand, first claiming that the summons should have been addressed to him in his Gascon fief and not in London, where his suzerain had no right, and then pleading difficulties at home and illness, real or feigned, in order to put off paying his homage, which he had not yet done when a breach came.

For the conflict, always latent, sometimes degenerated into open war. This was not the doing of the outraged vassal, though he might have used his suzerain's bullying as a pretext to defy him with every appearance of right. It came from the side of the King of France, who claimed that the Duke of Aquitaine's disobedience was established by his court and pronounced against him a sentence of confiscation in due and proper form, which his troops proceeded to execute on the spot. In the first of these conflicts Philip the Fair's bad faith was flagrant. French and Gascons had brawled at Bayonne. By way of reprisal, Bayonne sailors went and attacked La Rochelle. Immediately the King of France called upon the Plantagenet's lieutenant in Bordeaux to hand over the guilty parties to him, 'in order to punish them as reason required and justice demanded'. When this order was not executed quickly or fully enough to suit the suzerain, he ordered the seneschal of Périgord to seize the whole of the fief. He was repelled by force of arms. Then Philip summoned Edward I before his court. In vain did Edward get his friends to intervene and suggest the surrender of the chief fortresses on the Gascon frontier as a pledge of his good will. Philip accepted the fortresses, and then continued the campaign, which now became easy. What was his motive? It is hard to say. If he wanted to avoid an Anglo-Flemish alliance, which was already being planned against him, his sudden action served only to precipitate it. If he wished to make his Gascon vassal return to his allegiance, the mere threat of intervention would have sufficed. He committed himself deeply to the affair, as though he wanted to expel the Plantagenets from their French fiefs; but his later conduct proved that he meant nothing of the kind.

Thirty years later, his son Charles IV displayed a similar brutality as a sequel to the incident at Saint-Sardos (November 1323). In reprisal for the destruction of the French *bastide*, he sent troops to attack the English castle of Montpezat. They were defeated and held to ransom. In vain did Edward II disavow his Gascon subjects, who were too zealous for his liking, propose negotiations and promise reparations. Refusing to listen to reason, in July 1324 Charles IV confiscated his brother-in-law's fief.

It should be noted that on both occasions the conquest proved easy. Three short summer campaigns, in 1294, 1295, and 1296, sufficed to enable Charles of Valois to occupy the whole of Aquitaine. In 1324, it was again Charles of Valois, now growing old, who undertook to execute the sentence. The fall of La Réole brought about the submission of almost all the duchy, with the Anglo-Gascons maintaining themselves only in Bordeaux, Bayonne, Saint-Sever, and a few castles of less importance. But each time, just as he was within sight of his goal, the King of France relinquished it. In 1297, Philip the Fair, doubtless anxious about the Flemish revolt, accepted papal mediation from Boniface VIII, whose arbitration he endorsed without discussion. It was ratified by the treaty of Montreuil (June 1299), which provided for the restitution of his fiefs to Edward I. It is doubtful if Philip would have consented to this had he really contemplated annexing these fiefs to his own domain. Charles IV acted similarly when, in May 1325, at the request of Pope John XXII and of the Queen of England, his sister, he agreed to a fresh restitution.

So, in both cases, confiscation was only a means of pressure, brutal but effective, for bringing back a recalcitrant vassal to his allegiance. The King of France sought only to affirm, by resort to force, his suzerain rights over the duchy. Disinheritance of the vassal did not enter into his plans. But these conflicts presented dangers which neither Philip the Fair nor Charles IV clearly perceived. They gave the Capetian councillors the false impression that confiscation would always be easy and could be repeated indefinitely in order to tighten their grasp on Guienne. But, if Edward I's reaction was slow and belated, this was because all his energy was turned towards the conquest of Scotland. The inaction of his son Edward II was easily explained by the anarchy into which his rash policy had plunged his kingdom. Things were not always to be like this. The time was soon to come when the Plantagenets, convinced that the King of France had no other object but to deprive them of their fief, would bring all the strength of their island kingdom to the defence of threatened Guienne. They were all the more ready to do so because they could now count on the ardent support of their Gascon subjects. Impatient of all authority, the Gascons had favoured the encroachment of the Capetian officers in order to embarrass Edward I's agents, whose meddlesome demands they detested. But experience of French occupation, twice repeated, had introduced them to a master much more tyrannical than the distant King of England. Henceforth, for a century and a half, Gascon sentiment was unshakeably hostile to everything that came from Paris. In the struggles to come, its bellicose nobility and its plundering adventurers were to be the Plantagenets' best helpers and surest allies in their continental enterprises.

Reabsorption of the fief into the royal domain would have put an end to the Gascon problem. If they did not wish, or did not dare, to adopt this solution, how did the kings of France conceive a return to normal and enduring relations between themselves and their English vassals? Two solutions presented themselves, which they considered sufficient, without seeing their weakness. The first was the tightening of family links, a method uniformly employed at the time to appease dynastic quarrels. The arbitration of Boniface VIII in 1298 provided for a double marriage, which Edward I had already proposed before the breach, and which Philip the Fair accepted with alacrity. In 1299 the King of England, widower of Eleanor of Castille, married the sister of the King of France, of whom he was first cousin once removed. At the same time his eldest son became engaged to the daughter of the Capetian sovereign, Isabella, who became Edward II's wife in 1308. It would be idle to reproach the promoters of this latter marriage with being the cause of the future Edward III's dynastic claims to the crown of France. Philip had three fine, upstanding sons, and it could not be foreseen that they would leave no male heirs. In any case, when he became the brother-in-law of the later Capetian kings, Edward II did not get on any the better with them as the affair of Saint-Sardos showed.

The difficulty arose, in short, from the fact that the King of England could not tolerate being at the same time vassal of the King of France, with all the humiliations that this dependence involved since Capetian policy had increased the burdens and duties of vassals to its own advantage. He could circumvent this difficulty by making Aquitaine the appanage of one of his sons, who, being less powerful, would accept the condition of a vassal more easily. Edward I, who had himself administered Aquitaine during his father's lifetime, did not dare to give it to his son, whom he distrusted, until the last months of his reign. But in 1325, in response to the self-interested proposal of Queen Isabella, Edward II consented to relinquish it in favour of his heir. Charles IV gladly accepted the transfer, against payment of a conveyance fee of 60,000 *livres*, and, on September 10th, invested the young prince of Aquitaine and Ponthieu. The solution might have been definitive if it had been a question of a younger son, who might have founded a family and established at Bordeaux a dynasty independent of the English crown. In the case of the heir to the throne, the sole solution which was considered, it was merely provisional. In fact, it lasted only a few months.

When, early in 1326, Edward II, to punish his adulterous and fugitive wife, confiscated her English possessions and declared her guilty of treason, he included in the same disgrace the young prince whom Isabella had kept with her. His officials took the administration of Aquitaine in hand, until the newly invested duke should return to his allegiance. Charles IV, who had begun the evacuation of Guienne by his troops, ordered its reoccupation. A year later, Edward III became king. On March 31st 1327, he concluded a 'final peace' with his uncle of France. The Capetian sovereign would restore the duchy. He would amnesty all the Gascon 'rebels', with the exception of eight barons who would be banished and whose castles would be razed to the ground. In return, his vassal, in addition to the transfer fee of 60,000 *livres* promised in 1325, would pay a war indemnity of 50,000 marks. But, pending these payments, he postponed the evacuation. The Capetians, who had long since reinstalled themselves in Limousin, Périgord, and Quercy, also kept Agenais and, beyond the Garonne, Bazadais. The sphere of English domination was reduced to the maritime strip, without any deep hinterland, between the mouth of the Charente and the Pyrenees. This was the position when Charles IV died in his turn. Despite the official conclusion of peace, the maintenance of the French occupation, the brutality of the French officers, who continued to take reprisals against the amnestied rebels, the humiliations heaped upon a vassal who, though reconciled, was not re-established in his rights – all this kept up a spirit of hatred out of which war might emerge, and did emerge.

4. THE SUCCESSION TO THE THRONE OF FRANCE

ALMOST all text-books still repeat that the Hundred Years' War broke out because, on the accession of the dynasty of the Valois, Edward III, by virtue of the rights which he held from his mother, assumed the position of claimant to the crown of France. According to this version, the long conflict which set the two monarchies at grips was, in its origin as well as in its development, a quarrel essentially dynastic. Nothing is further from the truth. Still repeated though it is, the mistake has long since been exposed by the best historians who have tackled this thorny problem.

Nowadays it is established that the primary cause of the conflict is to be sought in the disturbing question of Guienne, whose data I have just described. It was because Philip of Valois succeeded no better than his predecessors in allaying the anxiety and resentment of his Gascon vassal that the breach took place; and it was by the confiscation of Guienne, the third in a little more than forty years, that the King of France, in May 1337, gave the signal for war.

The Hundred Years' War was a conflict feudal in its origin, and it remained so throughout the whole of the fourteenth century, until the accession of the Lancastrians to the throne of England. The dynastic question, which arose at the same time, long remained in the background. What happened was that, by way of reply to the confiscation of his fief, the outraged vassal bethought himself of claiming the crown of France and thus having a sound reason on his side. But he readily abandoned these dynastic ambitions when the Valois, beaten on the field of battle, gave him territorial compensations in the region of Aquitaine and assurances of sovereignty which made the Plantagenet the equal, and no longer the vassal, of the King of France. The fact remains that, though it arose indirectly, the dynastic question envenomed and complicated the conflict and in the long run, under Henry V of Lancaster, took precedence over the feudal question, the legacy of a distant and now outdated past. It is therefore essential to understand how, in the first third of the fourteenth century, the problem of the succession to the throne of France arose and was solved.

When, on June 5th 1316, the eldest son of Philip the Fair died young after a short reign of eighteen months, no law of succession enabled the person upon whom the crown of France should devolve to be named without argument. That the succession was hereditary no one denied. During two centuries, the first Capetians had succeeded in making it hereditary *de facto*, by arranging, during their lifetime, that their eldest

69

THE FRENCH SUCCESSION IN THE FOURTEENTH CENTURY

Isabella of Aragon = PHILIP III †1285 = Mary of Brabant

- **PHILIP IV THE FAIR, 1285–1314** = Joan of Champagne, Q. of Navarre
  - **LOUIS X 1314–16**
    - Joan, Q. of Navarre
  - **PHILIP V 1316–22**
    - daughters
  - **CHARLES IV 1322–28**
    - daughters
  - Isabella, †1358 = Edward II
    - Edward III 1327–78
      - Edward, P. of Wales †1376
        - Richard II 1377–99
      - Lionel, D. of Clarence †1368
        - daughter
      - John, D. of Lancaster †1399
        - Henry IV 1399–1413
      - Edmund, D. of York †1403
        - Edward, D. of York †1405
      - Thomas, D. of Gloucester †1397
- Charles, C. of Valois, Anjou, and Maine †1325
  - **PHILIP VI OF VALOIS 1328–50**
    - **JOHN THE GOOD 1350–64**
      - **CHARLES V 1364–80**
        - **CHARLES VI 1380–1422**
        - Louis, D. Orleans †1407
      - Louis, D. Anjou †1384
        - Louis II, D. Anjou †1416
      - John, D. Berry †1416
      - Philip the Bold, D. Burgundy †1404
        - John the Fearless, D. Burgundy †1419
    - Philip, D. of Orleans †1370
- Louis, C. of Evreux
  - Philip, C. of Evreux †1336 = Joan, Q. of Navarre
    - Charles II the Bad, K. of Navarre †1387
      - Charles III the Noble, K. of Navarre †1425

sons should be chosen and crowned kings. They then succeeded without further intervention on the part of the barons. Thanks to this expedient, the hereditary principle had so far insinuated itself into custom – that custom which, to the men of the Middle Ages, was the supreme rule of law – that, at the beginning of the thirteenth century, Philip Augustus no longer deemed it desirable to associate his heir, whom incidentally he distrusted, with him before his death. Louis VIII, and after him Saint Louis, then Philip III, then Philip the Fair, then again Louis X all assumed power on the death of the preceding sovereign without their claim being contested by anyone. This was particularly notable on the death of Louis VIII, who left only a little boy as his heir.

It so happened that, by a stroke of luck unique in history, this long line of kings, from Hugh Capet at the close of the tenth century to Philip the Fair at the dawn of the fourteenth, always left, at every generation, one or more sons capable of succeeding them. Hereditary succession in the male line was on record in fact. It did not exist in law, since no precedent had as yet enabled it to be formulated explicitly as a rule. The kings themselves consistently recoiled from the task, quite simple though it was, of decreeing how their inheritance was to devolve in future.

On the other hand, should the occasion arise, everything seemed to point in favour of succession in the female line, in default of a male heir. The much-heralded Salic law, whose long-forgotten clauses were to be unearthed by the lawyers of the Valois, very belatedly to be sure – not until the time of Charles V – in order to strengthen their masters' legal position, was by this time only a museum piece of no compelling value, which deceived no one. In all the provincial customs of the kingdom of France, the rule of female succession, in default of a direct male heir, was so well established that all kinds of ingenious systems had had to be evolved to enable fiefs fallen to the distaff side to provide their suzerain with the military service required by feudal law. Nor did it ever enter the legal minds of the feudal period to make any distinction whatever between the rules of private law and those of public law. In the eyes of most subjects, and of the kings themselves, a kingdom was just an inheritance like any other, subject to the same laws and the same customs.

In claiming the contrary, the jurists of the crown, steeped in Roman law, were breaking new ground in custom, to the great scandal of their contemporaries. In doing so, moreover, they were placing the glorious French monarchy higher than any other kingdom, exalting it above temporal crowns. Since it was, according to them, a dignity too eminent, a power too great, to devolve upon a mere woman, it resembled the Empire, which remained elective and, like the papacy, also elective, could be entrusted only to a man. Everywhere else, as crowns had become hereditary, they were subject to the same rules of devolution as private inheritances, in other words transmissible to women. This was the case in England, Scotland, Portugal, Navarre, Castille, Aragon, Sicily, Poland,

and Hungary. If a different law was to be admitted in France, it was not enough that such pre-eminence of the kingdom over all others, affirmed only in the restricted circle of paid lawyers, should be accepted. It was necessary that a combination of circumstances should occur. It remains for us to examine this combination.

For the first time in the long line of the Capetians, Louis X left no son. By his first wife, Margaret of Burgundy, who had met a tragic death in the frightful scandal which overtook Philip the Fair's three daughters-in-law in 1314, he had had a daughter, Joan, still a minor in 1316. But from the very fact of the misconduct of which her mother had been convicted, her legitimacy might be disputed. Louis's second wife, Clemence of Hungary, was pregnant at the time of her early widowhood. If she gave birth to a son, the child would be king. No one had any doubt about that. If the child was a daughter, there was no telling what solution would be found in the end.

Pending the event, a regency was necessary. This might be claimed either by Charles of Valois, paternal uncle of the last king and doyen of the princes of the blood, or Duke Eudes IV of Burgundy, maternal uncle and guardian-elect of the young Joan of France. But these two candidates let themselves be outmanoeuvred by Philip the Fair's second son, the brother of the dead king, Philip, Count of Poitiers, the only one of these last Capetians who seems to have had a strong character and an outstanding personality. Philip seized the regency of the two kingdoms of France and Navarre, the paternal and maternal heritages of his dead brother, bought off needy Charles of Valois by the promise of financial compensation, and finally calmed the anxiety of Eudes of Burgundy by an agreement which safeguarded, until her still remote coming of age, the rights of his ward to both successions.

Master of power in fact, the Count of Poitiers had now more than half won the game. After five months of his uncontested regency, on November 13th 1316, the queen gave birth to a son. The child would have been king – and indeed many genealogists, to keep the record straight, insert him in the list of the sovereigns of France under the name of John I the Posthumous – if he had not died five days after his birth. This unforeseen event took Joan's partisans aback. Still, many of them felt that the daughter should now succeed her father, though they were not ready to oppose the ambitious regent's designs by force of arms.

So, when Philip claimed the crown, opposition broke out among the barons, including the greatest, who were scandalized to find that he wanted to treat the kingdom contrary to the customs which governed their fiefs. By obscure bargains, whose details are not known to us, the regent succeeded in surmounting all obstacles one after the other. First Charles of Valois and, above all, the regent's younger brother, Charles, Count of La Marche, who had made himself a zealous and clamorous defender of his niece's rights, were in turn reduced to silence. Finally, on January 9th

1317, Philip V had himself crowned at Rheims. But most of the temporal peers, the dukes of Brittany, Guienne, and Burgundy and the Count of Flanders, abstained from attending the traditional ceremony, as though they grudged acceptance of the accomplished fact. Only two lay peers of France were to be seen in attendance on the new king, and these were the most recent, his uncle Charles of Valois and his mother-in-law Matilda of Artois.

To strengthen a power obviously shaky and of dubious legitimacy, the new king asked for the assent of an assembly of notables, summoned in Paris at the following Candlemas (February 2nd). These prelates and barons, to whom were added burgesses from the chief towns and doctors of the University of Paris, could not with decency set themselves up against a crowned king. With what arguments did he convince them? We have never been told. In any case, in order to legitimatize the Count of Poitiers's patent usurpation, they proclaimed that 'a woman cannot succeed to the kingdom of France'. A rule of law was thus defined, and there was no going back on it.

It should be added that Philip, a decidedly ungrateful uncle, bitterly disputed with his niece the inheritance which should have come to her from her grandmother Joan of Champagne, namely the kingdom of Navarre and the counties of Champagne and Brie. He recognized, it is true, her claim to Navarre; but, pending her coming of age – she was only seven – he assumed, and retained throughout his reign, the title of King of Navarre and the administration of the Pyrenean kingdom. As for Champagne, he kept it for himself, promising territorial or financial compensation. This was the occasion of a 'commotion' by the Champagne barons, who, exasperated by the spoliation of which their legitimate countess had been the victim, sought to shake off the usurper's tutelage, but in vain.

In all this, let us note carefully, the struggle was confined to Joan and her uncle Philip. At no time was there any intervention by other pretenders, whose claims, in the circumstances, would have been very flimsy. There is no doubt that the King of England's council thought for a moment about putting forward the possible rights of Queen Isabella, sister of Louis X and Philip V; but it went no further in this direction, and Edward II recognized the new king, though he apologized for being unable to attend his coronation.

The precedent of 1316–17 had so far acquired the force of law that when, after a reign of five years, Philip V the Tall died in his turn (January 2nd 1322), leaving only five daughters by his wife Joan, daughter of the Count of Burgundy, his younger brother, Charles of La Marche – the very man who had formerly protested so violently against the disinheritance of Louis X's daughter – brusquely put aside all his nieces and became King Charles IV the Fair. No one seems to have protested, this time.

But the reign of Charles IV was no more than the two preceding reigns destined to have a long and brilliant future. On February 1st 1328, at the age of thirty-three, the last Capetian died in his turn. He had been married three times, first to Blanche of Burgundy, whom he divorced and shut up in a convent after the scandal which I have mentioned; then to Mary of Luxemburg, who had left him a daughter, still a minor; and finally to his first cousin, Joan of Évreux, who was pregnant at the time when the king's early death made her a widow. Eleven and a half years afterwards, a situation was reproduced identical with that which had enabled Philip V to assume the regency, and then the crown.

This time, three candidates seemed to be in a position to claim the regency. First of all there was the young Philip of Évreux, who combined in himself the triple qualification of being first cousin of the last three kings, since he descended from Louis of Évreux, Philip the Fair's younger half-brother; of having married Joan of France, Louis X's daughter, thrust aside from the throne eleven years earlier; and finally of being the brother-in-law of the last king, and consequently the natural councillor of his sister, Joan, and the guardian-designate of the child with whom she was pregnant. But his youth, his political inexperience, and his weakness of character, not unlike that of his father, led to his failure to put forward his claim and promote his candidature.

Next in consideration came the King of England, Edward III, the nearest relation in blood of the last three sovereigns, since he was the son of their sister Isabella. But he was far away, and unable to make the most of his claim in time. He was young, too. Could one seriously contemplate entrusting the great kingdom of France to a youth of sixteen, who, in his island of England, endured without a murmur the close and humiliating tutelage of his mother, that virago detested in France? Finally there remained Philip of Valois. As first cousin of the dead sovereigns, his claim took precedence of that of Philip of Évreux. Something of the prestige of his father was reflected upon him, that Charles of Valois of whom it was to be said that he had been 'son of a king, brother of a king, uncle of three kings and father of a king, but never king himself'. Until his quite recent death, in December 1325, Charles of Valois had exercised considerable influence over the policy of his nephews.

To be sure, his son Philip, though a man of experience – he was nearly thirty-five – had not yet shown the measure of his worth. He was first Count of Maine, in other words of the part of his maternal inheritance which had been granted him as an appanage, and he had become, since 1326, Count of Anjou and Valois. He was known to be adventurous, like his father, and fond of distant expeditions. But the only one which he had yet undertaken, in Italy, to help the Lombard cities in revolt against the Visconti, had ended somewhat ingloriously. The chivalrous prince had simply let himself be bought off and had beaten a profitable but dishonouring retreat. However, this was not held against him; for an assembly of barons, to which, this time, neither burgesses from the towns nor doctors

74

from the University were summoned, entrusted Charles of Valois's son with the regency of the kingdom of France, and, into the bargain, that of Navarre, to which he had no right.

Two months later, on April 1st 1328, Queen Joan of Évreux gave birth to a daughter. There was no question of keeping the crown for this child, since, in similar circumstances, Louis X's daughter and then those of Philip V had in turn been thrust aside. But, out of the former candidates for the regency, two could now lay claim to the throne with a semblance of good reason and dispute over the kingdom as heirs male of the Capetians. As nephew of the last kings of the line and their relation thrice removed, Edward III of England was closer to them than the Count of Valois, who was only their first cousin and consequently a relation four times removed.

In favour of Philip it could be argued that his relationship was entirely through males. That of the Plantagenet, on the contrary, included a woman, his mother Isabella of France. Thrust aside from the succession at the same time as her nieces by reason of her sex, could the Queen of England claim to transmit to her son a right which she herself could not enjoy? The lawyers of the crown of France, not without logic, said that she could not. Less consistently, those of England said that she could. The question of law, raised for the first time, could not be decided one way or the other by an appeal to precedent.

One would like to have details of the discussion – doubtless it was very brief – of the assembly of barons which the regent summoned at the Bois de Vincennes on the morrow of Joan of Évreux's deliverance. It is probable that the legal arguments put forward on either side by the defenders of the two theses were less decisive than considerations of expediency, all of which told in favour of the Count of Valois. For nearly two months Philip had held effective power to everyone's satisfaction. In his capacity as regent, he presided in person over the deliberations of this enlarged Great Council, entrusted with nominating a sovereign. Could his candidature be set aside and an absentee be preferred to him without danger?

Against Edward III stood the fact, not, as is too often repeated, that he was a foreigner – for he could hardly be called a 'foreigner', in the modern sense of the word, since he was French in speech and education, son of a princess of France, himself a peer of France, Duke of Guienne and Count of Ponthieu, husband of a daughter of Hainault who was herself Philip of Valois's niece – but that he was a Plantagenet, in other words King of England and a disobedient vassal, traditionally in conflict with his sovereign. His only too frequent 'rebellions' had necessitated, within the past thirty years, two confiscations of the Gascon fief, followed by two armed conflicts and the last of these wars, barely over, remained fresh in everyone's mind. In 1325, Edward had stayed at the Court of France, a boy dragged at his mother's heels. The manners of this wicked and shameless woman, her slanders, her parade of her liaison with Mortimer, had been found detestable. It was recalled that Charles IV had banished her from his court. As she was known to be still all-powerful in the government of England, the French baronage feared that, if they chose her son, they would be installing this haughty princess and her foreign clique in Paris for an indefinite period.

Like that of February 1317, the assembly in April 1328 created law rather than found it ready to hand. But while, in 1317, the forceful exclusion of Louis X's daughter struck many as an act of injustice contrary to custom, the verdict of 1328, by which the Count of Valois was chosen in preference to the too young and too distant King of England, was accepted without a murmur in the kingdom of France. It was the logical sequel to the precedents twice created by Philip V and Charles IV. It raised to the throne a prince who, if not as yet very popular, was at least no stranger at court and was liked by the nobility. Much later the Flemings, who cherished an inveterate hatred towards Philip VI because he had rudely chastised them, nicknamed him the 'foundling king'. This contemptuous name has too often been taken up by modern historians; but it could not be applied, in this spring of 1328, to the unanimously chosen successor to the last Capetian.

The new reign began under the happiest auspices. It reunited the considerable strength of the kingdom with the resources of the appanage of Valois and Anjou. Internally no opposition was recorded. Externally, for the time being, no serious danger was to be feared, since the troubles of the young Edward III in England prevented him from giving free rein to his disappointment as a rejected candidate. The dynastic change took place smoothly. All the vassals came to pay homage to Philip at his coronation. Without anxiety about the future, he could impose upon the daughters of the late kings a settlement of their rights fruitful to himself, and then set off for war against the Flemish communes. Though the accession of the Valois constituted, so to speak, its prelude, conflict between the two dynasties did not as yet seem close at hand.

Part II
THE START OF THE STRUGGLE
1328–1340

Part II

THE START OF THE STRUGGLE
(1328-1340)

IMPROBABLE though it was, a breach still remained possible. Was Philip VI's accession to the throne of France to give rise to a dynastic conflict between Plantagenet and Valois which, coupled with the irritating feudal question of Aquitaine, might lead to war between the two great monarchies of Western Christendom, still scarcely recovered from a quite recent quarrel? Conscious of the gravity of the problem, Philip's councillors stated it in all its stark simplicity. If Edward, Duke of Guienne and Count of Ponthieu, agreed to pay homage to their master for his continental fiefs, it would mean that he recognized the legitimacy of the new dynasty and renounced his own claim to the throne of France. To compel the Plantagenet to pay homage was the goal which they set themselves to attain, if necessary by the use of that policy of intimidation, still quite recent, which they had not forgotten. When they succeeded, in 1331, it seemed that the new king of France had nothing more to fear from an enemy too weak for him.

1. EDWARD III'S HOMAGE

PHILIP's election by the barons and peers of France was not welcomed, as may be imagined, at the court of London. In the eyes of haughty Isabella and her lover Mortimer, Philip was, as the Flemings were to nickname him, a 'foundling king', the usurper of a throne which by right should have come to the young Edward III. The Plantagenet's council refused to accept the accomplished fact, and decided to put forward their master's rights. But they lacked the strength to risk an armed conflict lightly. So they adopted, of necessity, a temporizing policy which enabled the 'usurper' to establish himself without fear. Faced with the change of dynasty, Edward counted on opposition and disturbance in France. He would wait until they happened and then try to take advantage of them. The English officials in Guienne received orders to watch the trend of public opinion, stir it up against the new king if possible, and hold themselves ready to take action at the least alert.

In fact, nothing happened. Philip, who had held the regency for more than two months, found no one to contest his right to the throne. With entire impunity, he was able to gratify public opinion by sacrificing a few particularly hated financial officials – a procedure which had become, so to speak, the necessary accompaniment of a new reign – and summon all his vassals to his coronation. The ceremony, which took place at Rheims on May 29th 1328, marked the peaceful strength of his power. All the holders of fiefs, great and small, came to pay him homage. The daughters of the last Capetians, ousted from the royal succession, received but meagre compensation. The most dangerous of them was Joan, daughter of Louis X and wife of his cousin, Philip of Évreux. Since the death of her father, she claimed Navarre and Champagne, the inheritance of Philip the Fair's wife, where succession in the female line was well established. In the first place, Philip V had set aside his niece, by an agreement reached in 1318 with the young princess's guardian, Duke Eudes IV of Burgundy. He had kept the whole inheritance, in return for a promise of an income of 15,000 *livres* to be assessed on the counties of Angoulême, Mortain, and Coutances and 50,000 *livres* cash. Charles IV, despite the stipulations of this agreement, had done the same. Very belatedly, in the last months of his reign, he promised a supplementary indemnity of 20,000 *livres*.

Philip VI, though he had no right to this inheritance, retained the main part of it. On the morrow of his coronation, he let Joan and her husband have the kingdom of Navarre, so that a younger branch of the house of France thus became established there for more than a century;

but he kept Champagne and Brie for himself, ceding in return the counties of Angoulême and Mortain, which, however, were of less value. Philip V's daughters were expected to receive the county of Burgundy, which came to them from their mother. Charles IV's heiress and his widow, the young Joan of Évreux – who lived on as a widow for nearly half a century – received illusory compensations still less substantial. No one protested against these settlements, which benefited the crown of France.

Much more important, the beginning of Philip VI's reign was marked by a striking military success. For several years past the great fief of Flanders, so harshly treated by the policy of the later Capetians, had been seething with discontent. To be sure, the fidelity of the count was not this time in question. Guy of Dampierre and Robert of Béthune had learnt to their cost what it meant to revolt against too powerful a suzerain. But the Flemish population, especially in the Flemish-speaking and industrial districts of the north and west, exasperated by the heavy war indemnities which they had had to pay the king, and further threatened in the prosperity of their weaving industry, had again risen against both the royal authority and that of the count, the king's ally. From 1322 the revolt of the countryside had assumed alarming proportions. It was probably stirred up by the little cloth-making centres' hatred of the draconian regulation by which the big towns bound them. Soon the artisans of the towns, who had borne the patricians' re-establishment with ill grace, joined in the movement.

In response to an appeal from his vassal, Philip decided to go and punish the rebels and, at the same time, wipe out the affront which the communes' contingents had inflicted in 1302 when they crushed the chivalry of France at Courtrai. The last of the 'hostings' of Flanders proved the most glorious of all and worthily crowned a policy pursued without weakening for more than thirty years. In July 1328, on the battlefield of Cassel, a fitting sequel to that on which the 'golden spurs' had been defeated, the charge of Philip VI's vassals routed the Flemish artisans and ruthlessly restored them to their obedience.

Against a king whose reign began under such happy auspices, what could the weak Edward III do? On the morrow of Philip's coronation at Rheims, two English bishops arrived in Paris to set before his councillors the rights of their master to the crown of France and protest against Philip's usurpation. It was a protest 'through diplomatic channels', as we should say nowadays, and we know what speech is worth when there is no strength to support it. No one took the protest seriously. But, on his return from the campaign in Flanders, Philip felt strong enough to act in his turn. Of all his vassals, only the Duke of Guienne had hitherto failed to pay him homage. He must be forced to do so. The Abbot of Fécamp, Pierre Roger (later Pope under the name of Clement VI), was sent to London to summon the recalcitrant vassal.

He found an embarrassed adversary, too weak to refuse point-blank and run the risk of war, yet at the same time disinclined to yield to the ultimatum, which would be equivalent to destroying beyond redemption the rights which he could not defend by force of arms. Isabella, whose looseness of tongue was as well known as that of her conduct, would have replied insolently to the ambassador that never would her son pay homage to the Valois, for Edward was the son of a king, and Philip only the son of a count. The Plantagenet sovereign's other councillors preferred to give a more evasive and temporising answer. Then Philip VI decided upon strong measures. Faithful to the tradition of the last Capetians, he informed the King of England, through a fresh embassy, that, if he failed to take the oath of fealty and reply to a second summons, he would proceed against the defaulter 'by force and by right'. The threat of confiscation of the fief was clear and precise. Edward yielded. On April 14th 1329, he wrote to the King of France:

> My most serene prince and lord, to whom I wish every success and every happiness, I desire to inform your magnificence that I have long since had the desire to pay you a visit in France, in order to fulfil my duties as was fitting; but, as a result of the hindrances and difficulties which beset me in my kingdom, as you must be aware, I have not been able up to now to accomplish the project which I had formed. As soon as I am free, and God willing, I shall come in person to pay you the homage which I owe you.

It remained only for Edward to keep this promise. Less than two months later, at the beginning of June, in the midst of tourneys and feasts attended by the flower of French chivalry and several sovereigns, the ceremony of homage took place in the choir of the cathedral at Amiens. The formula of the oath, on which the two kings' councillors had finally agreed, was left rather vague, to be sure. The chamberlain of France, addressing the crowned vassal, asked him: 'Sire, do you become the King of France's man for the duchy of Guienne and its appurtenances, which you recognize that you hold from him as Duke of Guienne and peer of France, as you and your ancestors, kings of England and dukes of Guienne, have done for the same duchy to his predecessors as kings of France?' The young King of England replied: *'Voire'* – that is, 'Yes' – and then placed his hands in those of Philip. The homage was paid: first victory for the diplomacy of the Valois.

It was true that other subjects of quarrel remained intact; but they did not present grave danger from the point of view of France, now that they were again reduced to the level of a feudal dispute. There were territorial conflicts: what were the exact frontiers of the duchy of Aquitaine, whose restitution to the pardoned vassal had been promised by the recent treaty of 1327? There were commercial conflicts: how were the merchants of the two kingdoms who had suffered from measures of marque and reprisal since the start of the war in 1324 to be indemnified? Finally, there were financial conflicts: how were the war indemnities provided for by the latest treaties to be calculated and paid? At Amiens the suzerain and his vassal undertook to set up conferences of experts without delay in order to settle these irritating questions. Faithful once again to the Capetian policy whose inheritance he had accepted, the new King of France could not conceive of peace between the two kingdoms except in terms of a closer tightening of the family links between the two dynasties. Once material questions were settled, he contemplated that a double marriage should unite Edward's brother to his daughter and his eldest son to a sister of the King of England. It would seem that nothing had changed in what had been the relationship between Capetians and Plantagenets for the past half-century: homage paid with ill grace and according to an ambiguous formula; endless quarrels about the frontiers of the duchy, over which hung the ever-presen tthreat of confiscation; matrimonial arrangements to tighten the links between the two reigning houses – everything was still there.

In the negotiations which were soon opened, there was not much more progress than in the previous years. The English asked for the restitution of the castles and territories within Aquitaine improperly occupied by French garrisons, and a complete amnesty for the Gascon nobles who had remained faithful to their duke during the last conflict. On their side the delegates of the King of France required payment of the indemnity of 50,000 marks promised in 1327 by Edward III and the 'relief' of 60,000 livres demanded in 1325, together with the destruction of the castles of those banished nobles whom Charles IV had excepted from his pardon. On May 8th 1330, however, the convention of the Bois de Vincennes, ratified by both parties, provided for the constitution of mixed commissions of inquiry, which should examine documents and witnesses and reach a final settlement of every point in dispute. All this again was in accord with tradition.

Matters were at this point when a fresh step by the French lawyers suddenly increased the tension. It struck them that the formula of the homage paid by Edward III a year earlier lacked precision. Yet it repeated, more or less, the very terms of the oath taken by Henry III in 1259, Edward I in 1274 and 1286, Edward II in 1308 and 1320, and his son again in 1325. From its ambiguity the kings of England might argue that they owed the suzerain of the fief of Aquitaine no more than 'simple' homage, a rather vague oath of fealty which implied no precise obligation on the part of the vassal. On the contrary, the other great vassals of the crown, notably the peers of France, owed 'liege' homage, by which the vassal swore to defend his lord 'before any other man' and 'against all men living and dead', and was bound, in addition, to provide the service of hosting at his own expense.

Apparently without any previous discussion of the question, the Plantagenet was summoned to appear before the king's court on July 28th 1330, to define the terms of his homage and to declare that it implied 'liege' homage. Just what did Philip VI's councillors mean by this brusque demand? Having won the first round in a close contest in the ceremony at Amiens, and thinking the young Duke of Guienne to be incapable of effective resistance to the threats implicit in their legal arguments, did they hope to provoke a fresh refusal by their adversary and then proceed to a third confiscation of his Gascon fief? Their intentions were not revealed but that this was what they meant seemed probable to the English. The machination brought to a climax their exasperation against a suzerain at once pettifogging and unfair.

Edward was not in a position to resist the demands of the Valois any more than in 1329. In his island a fresh political upheaval was under way. The young sovereign, now eighteen years old, found his mother's tutelage vexatious and burdensome. Roger Mortimer's flaunting of his recently acquired wealth, combined with three years of inglorious government, had turned the baronage against the coterie which held power. A plot was hatched among the malcontents, and the king put himself at its head. In November 1330 Mortimer was arrested and put to death, and Isabella was banished to a remote castle. Meanwhile Edward, absorbed in preparations for this *coup d'état* and the establishment of his personal power, was badly placed to answer the summons of the Valois's officials. His default might provoke the most perfidious steps and he feared the worst for his territorial possessions. His instructions to his officials in Guienne advised desperate resistance, if the King of France should seek to seize the duchy by force of arms. But if he contented himself with sending officers and sergeants to execute the decisions of his court, Edward's officials were to be on their guard against provoking the least incident and should 'endure with good humour and fair words, without much argument or resistance, to tide over the wickedness of the times'.

The submissiveness of the Gascon officials, the humble attitude of the English ambassadors who went to plead their master's cause, and above all the mediation of Pope John XXII, which King Edward had invoked, ended by softening his touchy suzerain. If Philip had ever intended to confiscate Aquitaine, he did not proceed with his plan. He contented himself with an agreement concluded in Paris on March 9th 1331, which excused the King of England from a fresh rendering of homage, but only on a written undertaking that the ceremony at Amiens was regarded by either side as implying liege homage. Some weeks later, in April, Edward and Philip had a secret meeting at Pont-Sainte-Maxence, the last before the opening of armed conflict. Once more they affirmed their common desire to remove the endless difficulties in Aquitaine and settle the disagreements about frontiers, banishments, and war indemnities.

So it had taken no more than three years for the diplomacy of the Valois, again, employing all the methods used by the last Capetians and covering all the tracks already beaten by them, to win a victory of the highest importance over their Gascon vassal. Edward's homage at Amiens, and his subsequent declaration which put it on the same footing as liege homage, would seem to have set aside the dynastic pretensions of the Plantagenets for ever. Beaten in every round of this close conflict, Edward was back in a position more humiliating than ever in relation to his suzerain. Aquitaine remained diminished by a partial occupation and weakened by the greater subjection of its duke to the French monarchy. The threat which had hung over it for two generations seemed more definite than ever. Decidedly the reign of the Valois had begun well.

2. TOWARDS THE BREACH

SIX YEARS later, nothing was left of this first victory. Not only had Edward gone back on his oath at Amiens and again put forward his claim to the crown of France, but also, to ward off a fresh confiscation of Guienne, he had grouped against his rival the most formidable continental coalition of which England had had the support since Bouvines. So sudden a change of fortune needs explaining. We now know the remote causes of the war; the question of Aquitaine constituted the constant and commercial and financial quarrels the variables. But it is only by an examination of those crucial and confused years, 1331–7, that we may define the immediate causes, those which dictated decisive actions and involved irrevocable measures. No conflict in history can be called inevitable: it is the will of men which makes it so. Who were these men in this case?

The most recent historians of the Anglo-French conflict, struck by the disastrous series of mistakes and blunders which, within the space of a dozen years, reduced the French monarchy from the front rank which it occupied to that of an attacked and soon defeated power, have explained this very rapid decline by the incapacity of its king. They delight in putting two characters in complete contrast: Edward III, a political genius fertile in ever fresh ideas, but at the same time a cold calculator who drew up long-term plans, knew where he was going and what he wanted, and surpassed his adversary in the diplomatic sphere just as he crushed him on the field of battle; Philip VI, on the contrary, visionary and vain, versatile when continuity of view was wanted, obstinate when he should have been adaptable, fooled by a rival too clever for him, incapable of pressing his advantage while there was yet time, and letting himself be beaten in a struggle for which he had failed to prepare.

Each of these portraits needs some touching-up. There is no question, of course, of whitewashing the first Valois king. His contemporaries themselves, like the chronicler John le Bel, felt puzzled, not knowing what to make of this brave and chivalrous prince, bent on making the royal authority which he had inherited respected without demur, even if this meant the implacable execution of a 'stern justice'; but, at the same time, heedless of his own interests once a passion – revenge or vainglory – was aroused. His diplomacy proceeded by fits and starts, sometimes too trusting and sometimes more wily than it need have been.

But did the fault lie in the king alone? Was he not badly advised, and by the very people who had guided the policy of his predecessors? With

86

regard to England and the Gascon fief, it is striking to note the continuity of policy and the identity of method between Charles IV and Philip of Valois: intimidation, ruses, threats, endless quibbles, all with the object of making the indocile vassal yield and of humiliating him. Up to a point, the game had succeeded. This was because, for nearly twenty years, the England of Edward II, and still more that of Isabella and Mortimer, sunk in the anarchy in which she was kept by the struggles of the baronage against the king's power, could carry on only a policy which inevitably lacked grandeur, since it had no strength. Charles IV took advantage of this to launch the war of Saint-Sardos and keep part of Aquitaine for himself. Philip VI, in his turn, played upon his adversary's weakness to humble him to the point of liege homage. What the advisers of the King of France did not understand was that these easy times were gone, and that, with Edward III firmly seated on his throne, the French monarchy had found an adversary of its own weight.

Still, it can truthfully be said that it took time for the character of this enemy to reveal itself fully. After 1340, when he had turned thirty, Edward III might be called the born enemy of the Valois, sworn to wrest Aquitaine and the whole of the former Plantagenet empire from the hands of the hated dynasty. He was then revealed as an opportunist of genius, who used his adversary's difficulties to the full, and constantly modified the detail of his plans in order to adapt them to changing circumstances. But in 1330, on the morrow of the *coup d'état* which gave him power, these qualities of the mature man had not yet appeared. Already, however, in this elegant knight, imbued with French civilization, one could perceive unusual abilities. It is tempting to compare him with his grandfather Edward I when he assumed power after the unhappy reign of Henry III. In Edward III, however, we find less harshness, less passion for legislature and increasing bureaucracy. The taste of Edward III was for diplomacy and war; he asked nothing from his subjects except that they should pay the bill. More even than Edward I, he managed to interest his people, and especially the nobility, in his projects of conquest and his foreign campaigns. This was a new factor, and its consequences were most important. For the first time for two centuries, the English baronage supported the continental policy of their master, when he decided to wage war overseas.

But no one as yet dreamed of this, in this year 1331. The Plantagenet's resentment against the rival who had supplanted him, the suzerain who had humiliated him, lasting though it might be, remained hidden for the time being. French and English diplomats continued to meet, in Paris, in London, sometimes even in Avignon, and have endless discussions about the conclusion of a 'good peace'. Not that they felt themselves to be at war, far from it. But, despite the sovereigns' promises, despite agreements in principle, the ever increasing back-log of detailed quarrels, almost all about Aquitaine, remained to be settled. Discussions about them had been going on for generations, without any worsening of relations on this account. When, after the two kings' meeting at Pont-Saints-Maxence, negotiations were resumed between their councillors, much less ready than their masters to talk about understanding and mutual concessions, they followed a slow, sinuous but familiar course, in which neither Philip nor Edward scented any danger.

Far from thinking about making war on each other, the two sovereigns let themselves be lured into grandiose projects of glory and distant conquest, in which their rivalry might be changed into chivalrous emulation. First of all, there was the question of the crusade. The progress of Seljukid piracy in the Aegean sea and the attacks of the Mamelukes of Syria on Cyprus and Little Armenia had set John XXII's entourage talking once more about a general crusade. Zealous propagandists, mostly Italian, addressed themselves to the sovereigns, such as Marino Sanudo, who dedicated to Philip VI a Latin treatise on the necessity and methods of a crusade, the *Secreta fidelium crucis*, or Roger of Stavegny, whose memorandum, entitled *Le Conquest de Terre Sainte*, was written in London. Both sovereigns let themselves be tempted. In the spring of 1332, Edward suggested to Philip, in addition to a marriage which would tighten the links between the two dynasties, a fresh meeting at which they would draw up plans for the crusade. Then he gave his agreement in principle and promised to take the cross. More enthusiastic still, Philip VI soon volunteered as the prime mover of the project.

In July, assured of the King of France's support, the Pope granted him a tenth, valid for six years, to be levied on the clergy of his kingdom. This would feed the funds of the 'treasurers of the passage to the Holy Land', and enable the 'holy voyage' to be set on foot as soon as possible. A year later, Philip was appointed leader of the projected expedition. The crusade was preached throughout Europe: the Archbishop of Rouen, Pierre Roger, assumed the spiritual direction of the preaching. Slowly, as suited a time when plans always outran the means available, the crusade was organized. When Pope John XXII, a native of Cahors, was succeeded, in December 1334, by the Cistercian Jacques Fournier, a native of the county of Foix, who assumed the name of Benedict XII, a fresh impulse was given to the expedition. Under the high command of the King of France, Duke Louis I of Bourbon was appointed captain-general. Finally the departure was fixed for May 1st 1335, by which date all the crusaders were to reach the embarkation ports on the Mediterranean coast. The Hospitallers and Venice promised to provide vessels. The Pope himself chartered four galleys at his own expense and concentrated stores at Marseilles.

The King of England, who had at first talked about taking part in the expedition, had quickly withdrawn from the affair, leaving all the glory of preparation and command to Philip. Edward III had found nearer to hand a sphere of action more propitious for his feats of arms. This was the defeat and conquest of Scotland: a task apparently easy, given the exiguity and poverty of the little northern kingdom, but one that for two generations had meant bitter disappointments for the Plantagenets. More than once, in the early years of the century, Edward I had almost succeeded in it. Left incomplete, his work had collapsed after him, when the Scottish highlanders had inflicted the humiliating defeat of Bannockburn on Edward II's army (1314). With still more doggedness than in the past, the third Edward took up these plans of conquest, almost as chimerical, I may point out, as the Valois's project of a crusade.

At first he did not intervene directly, but contented himself with supporting with money and men the efforts of his protégé Edward Balliol, the son of John of Bailleul or Balliol who for some years, under Edward I, had sat on the throne of Scotland under the tutelage of England. In the summer of 1332, Edward Balliol opened his campaign against the national king, David Bruce, conquered part of the Lowlands, and had himself crowned king. Henceforth there was no further question, in London at least, of the crusade. The King of England settled permanently in the north of the country, in order to keep a closer watch on events on the Scottish border and prepare for his coming campaigns. The administrative and judicial services, Chancery, Exchequer, Common Bench, deserted the banks of the Thames and moved to York, which thus became a kind of war capital, close to the king and his army. In 1333, Edward III took the offensive. The first English campaign ended with the recapture of Berwick, on the east coast, a powerful citadel whose fall opened to the victor the way to Edinburgh and Perth and the conquest of the whole country south of the Forth, which Balliol had ceded to him in full sovereignty.

But, even in the hills of Scotland, Edward III once more found the hand of the King of France, which seemed to bar his way. Ever since, in 1295, the Scots had forced their king, John Balliol, to seek an alliance with Philip the Fair in order to shake off the English tutelage, the Franco-Scottish alliance had become an established tradition, one might almost say a diplomatic dogma, in Western Christendom. Philip of Valois felt that it lay neither within his interest nor his duty to abandon his Scottish ally. He needed peace with the Plantagenet if he wanted finally to set off on the projected crusade; but he was not going to buy it by the abandonment of a little country whose armed diversions, in case of an Anglo-French conflict, might so usefully embarrass his adversary. On the other hand Edward III, doubtful about the Valois's good faith, was already afraid lest, thanks to his campaigns in Scotland, his suzerain should attempt some new stroke on the frontier of Aquitaine. He ordered his plenipotentiaries to sacrifice as much as possible to the French demands, with the result that in May 1334 agreement seemed to be reached on all the questions relating to the fief of Aquitaine. In Paris it was promptly rumoured that peace was made.

But rejoicing did not last long. 'It was no time before things went otherwise,' a chronicler tells us, 'for the English messengers were barely back in their lodgings when the King of France summoned them again and told them that it was his intention that King David of Scotland and all the Scots should be included in this peace.' No peace in Aquitaine without Edward's abandonment of the conquest of Scotland: such was the Valois's latest demand. If Edward persisted – and he had no intention of stopping half-way – he had everything to fear from French 'perfidy': the confiscation of Aquitaine; the dispatch, without any need for a declaration of war, of help for David Bruce's forces in the form of men, money, and supplies.

So to Edward's persisting resentment of past humiliations there was now added mutual distrust between the two kings. They watched each other, they were afraid of each other, they accused each other of dark designs. Slowly and inexorably, so to speak, their relations worsened, even though it was not always possible to fix the blame. In 1331, it was simply a question of completing and consolidating, by detailed agreements, the understanding in principle which had emerged from their meetings. Three or four years later, though nothing definite had changed the data of the problem, hope of achieving the 'final peace' had been abandoned. All that the two kings asked was that the war should not become general. Neither Philip, too much preoccupied by his dreams of the crusade, nor Edward, absorbed in Scotland, wanted a general war. But they had got to the point of fearing it, and that was enough to make it possible.

From December 1334 onwards, the policy of Benedict XII ended by precipitating the conflict which it aimed at avoiding. More firmly resolved than his predecessor to achieve the crusade, the new pontiff kept Valois and Plantagenet on the slippery slope down which they were sliding and devoted himself, as we should say in our diplomatic jargon, to 'localizing the conflict'. But, after refusing to come to an agreement with Edward if he continued to attack his Scottish ally, Philip, faithful to that policy of gradual encroachment which we have noted, now bethought himself to propose, and indeed to impose, his own mediation between England and Scotland. It would have been a self-interested, biased mediation, with a foregone result, and could only have led to a general war.

Benedict hastened with all speed to ward off the danger. He managed to thrust Philip aside and take the Scottish affair in hand. His legates hurried to England, and, in November 1335, succeeded in getting Edward and David Bruce to conclude a short truce. But this was only a postponement. More patient and more prolonged efforts would be needed to impose peace on enemies who no longer had much desire to reach an understanding. Benedict XII devoted himself whole-heartedly to this task, so much so that he put the necessity of Anglo-French peace before the start of the crusade, already much behind its schedule. In March 1336, Philip went to Avignon, thinking that his docility would earn him the reward of an early departure of the 'holy passage'. He was told by the Pope that, since peace was still not made, the crusade had become impossible and had better be adjourned *sine die*. The preparations were cancelled, the privileges suspended, the levying of the tenth stopped. In this way Benedict hoped to hasten the Anglo-French reconciliation of which he never lost sight.

What happened was the contrary. In the first place, he infuriated Philip, hitherto amenable to his exhortations, so long as the mirage of the crusade gleamed on the horizon. With some reason, the King of France felt that he had been fooled, since he had agreed not to pursue the Scottish affair for the sake of the crusade, which was now denied him. In his disappointment, he showed himself arrogant, and rashly led Edward to imagine that he was bent on a general war. Henceforth events hastened towards the inexorable breach. The Pope lost control of them more and more. All he could do was to slow down their pace by endless and futile negotiations, which served only to add to the exasperation of the adversaries, mutually suspicious of each other's good faith. Secret negotiations, conferences, correspondence, a criss-cross of messengers – all this ended in beating the air, without any influence on the outburst of their hatred.

A rash action on Philip's part, in the spring of 1336, opened this last phase of the tragedy and hurried it towards its climax. The Scots, against whom England was preparing a final campaign, seemed to be at the end of their strength. The French ambassadors in England had secret interviews with the Scottish nobles who continued the struggle. At the same time, the fleet which had been concentrated at Marseilles with a view to the voyage to the Holy Land was transferred to the ports of Normandy, as though it were intended for a mass intervention in favour of Scotland. In fact, only slight help was dispatched, which enabled the gallant little kingdom to prolong its resistance for a short time. Henceforth Edward regarded war as inevitable. Just as Benedict had countermanded the crusade, so Edward abandoned the conquest of Scotland in order to devote himself entirely to preparations for a struggle on a larger scale.

At the end of September 1336, a meeting of Parliament at Nottingham denounced the perfidious manœuvres of the King of France in Guienne and Scotland, and voted subsidies which would enable Edward to face war. There may also have been discussion in Parliament about a fresh affirmation of his rights to the throne of the Capetians, a powerful weapon in the struggle which was foreseen to be near at hand. Then the administration left the northern provinces, where it had stayed for four years, returned to Westminster, zealously began military preparations, put the coasts in a state of alert, sent war material to Aquitaine, and concentrated troops and a fleet on the shores of the English Channel. Meanwhile, Philip divided his fleet between the Norman and Flemish ports and manned the frontier of Guienne with troops.

While each king made preparations and sought with feverish haste to find allies – I shall return to this point later – each tried also to get right on its side and provide itself with a legal pretext for a breach. Philip had no trouble in finding one. It sufficed for him to follow the example already twice set, in 1294 by Philip the Fair, in 1324 by Charles IV. Against his disloyal vassal, whose failures in feudal duty it was easy to denounce, he ordered, on May 24th 1337, confiscation of his Gascon fief. It was Philip's own way of declaring war on the King of England, without removing the conflict from the feudal sphere in which it had slowly been prepared. In fact, hostilities began at once on the frontier of Aquitaine, where the King of France's troops laid siege to several forts, and at sea, where the Norman fleet attacked Jersey and even made some successful descents on the English coast. But military preparations were incomplete in both countries, and did not as yet permit more than these unimportant skirmishes.

Benedict XII still struggled to recapture peace. In the hope of setting illusory talks on foot, he persuaded Philip to postpone the occupation of Guienne until the end of the year. But Edward was not deceived by this truce. No sooner had the confiscation of Guienne been pronounced by the court of France than he indirectly assumed the position of claimant to the throne of the Capetians. Though he did not yet take a title which in his view belonged to him of right, henceforth, in the documents of his chancery, he named his Valois enemy only by the contemptuous term of 'Philip, who calls himself King of France'. In this serious step he was influenced, so it is said, by a personage whose eventful career must now be mentioned.

Robert of Artois, grandson of Robert II, himself a nephew of Saint Louis, had been set aside from the succession to the county of Artois by his aunt Matilda. The custom of the northern provinces took no account of successional representation and made a younger daughter heiress at the expense of a grandson, if her elder brother was already dead. Twice already Robert had claimed Artois before the court of peers, first under Philip the Fair, and then under his sons. Respectful of local customs, the judges dismissed his claim. But, in order to keep him quiet, the King of France, by way of compensation, promised him a Norman appanage, with the title of Count of Beaumont-le-Roger and peer of France. This did not stop Robert pursuing his resentment against the aunt who had despoiled him. He maintained contacts among the nobility of Artois and fomented opposition to the countess and her chief councillor, Thierry of Hireçon. In 1324, when the Count of Flanders, Robert of Béthune, disregarding local custom, left his inheritance to his grandson Louis of Nevers and secured the withdrawal of his surviving children, Robert took up hope again. In 1330 he reopened the case which had already been twice decided, producing false documents inspired by the recent events in Flanders. The forger and his accomplices were ruthlessly exposed by the King of France, who henceforth developed a lasting hostility to his cousin and brother-in-law, coupled with an insurmountable repulsion. In the midst of all this Matilda died in mysterious circumstances (1332). Robert was accused of poisoning her. The king demanded exemplary punishment.

Robert's property was confiscated, and he was stripped of all his dignities, condemned as a traitor, and owed his life only to his flight. At first he took refuge with the Count of Hainault. Then Philip let it be known that he would take up arms against anyone who gave him asylum. Towards the end of 1336, Robert came to England to take refuge with Edward III, who was glad to welcome such a distinguished recruit. Contemporary opinion did not doubt that the exiled prince influenced the Plantagenet to claim the throne of France and promised to help him to overthrow the Valois dynasty.

But the King of England would certainly have come to this decision without Robert's advice. To the sentence of confiscation pronounced against him by his suzerain's court, the Duke of Aquitaine could reply, legally speaking, only by a defiance, in other words the breaking of the feudal link which bound him to an unjust lord. This left him, like all his predecessors, in a humiliating position. To establish his right, he must produce proof of the 'denial of justice' of which the King of France had been guilty. To transform the feudal conflict, in which he was an inferior, into a dynastic struggle, which would make him his adversary's equal, was a clever, indeed an essential reply, and he would have decided on it in any case.

About All Saints' Day in 1337, the Bishop of Lincoln, Henry of Burghersh, arrived in Paris to present his master's defiance. It was not addressed to the sovereign of the French kingdom, but to 'Philip of Valois, who calls himself King of France'. Edward could find no better way of denying his homage at Amiens, which had been imposed upon him by trickery and force, and, as it was paid to a usurper, had no binding value. He still hesitated, however, to take the final step and himself assume the title of King of France. For that he waited to be recognized by better men than an outlaw like Robert of Artois.

So it was in the spring of 1337 that the Hundred Years' War officially began. The conflict, as we have seen, had been simmering for several years. But, until 1336, though they feared the increasing possibility of a breach, neither of the adversaries had considered war inevitable or wanted it to break out. Neither Philip, launched upon his plans for a crusade, nor Edward, involved in the affairs of Scotland, had anything to gain by starting it. All at once, the postponement of the crusade and the untimely aid given to the Scots by Philip led Edward to believe that a breach could no longer be avoided. Faced with the Plantagenet's preparations, the Valois in his turn hurried forward the moment when he could precipitate matters. The misunderstanding was beyond remedy. Only the virtuous pontiff at Avignon tried to clear it up, and sought to place himself above the quarrel and reconcile the rival dynasties at all costs.

Did Benedict XII's dogged but ill-fated efforts, as some modern historians claim, in the end only damage the cause of the Valois? On the view of these historians, Philip was the plaything and the victim of the French Pope, who was thus unfaithful to his country's interests. Wishing to prevent war, but possessing the strength only to postpone it, Benedict held Philip back when the advantage was all on his side, and left Edward time to prepare his counterstroke. But it is in no way certain that, if the Valois had made war in 1335 or 1336, in connection with Scottish affairs, he would have been better prepared than in 1337 for offensive action, or that he would have been faced with an adversary beaten in advance. Nor is it proved that, in his mediation, Benedict was thinking only about expediting the start of a possible crusade. He was not the only man in France to cast doubt on the stability of the Valois dynasty and the real strength of a kingdom the prestige of which stood so high. Perhaps he foresaw the sorrow, the ruin, the disaster which a conflict rashly revived over the Gascon question might mean. His sole fault – at least the only one that history can hold against him – is that he failed.

3. THE FINAL PREPARATIONS

FROM THE moment when the danger seemed imminent, the activity of Edward III, that impetuous sovereign and leader of men, assumed a scope in which his gifts for fertile contrivance and organization could find free play. This was especially remarkable in the diplomatic sphere. Like his grandfather Edward I in 1297, he conceived the bold plan of turning the danger from the Valois away from Aquitaine by attacking France through the Low Countries. But he was able to adapt this policy, so to speak traditional, to the necessities of the moment by modifying its details to suit present conditions. There could now be no question of alliance with Flanders, the corner-stone of his grandfather's coalition. Louis of Nevers, who had become Count of Flanders on the death of his grandfather Robert of Béthune, knew what it cost to revolt against the touchy suzerainty of the court of Paris. A prince French by birth and education, he would be a vassal as faithful as Guy of Dampierre had been disloyal, in order to avoid any further French interference in his domains. The memory of Cassel was still very fresh in the minds of the Flemings.

To punish Louis's attachment to the King of France, Edward decided to cut off supplies from his cloth-making industry, at the risk of upsetting the balance of his own budget. A royal decree, promulgated in August 1336, and confirmed by Parliament in February 1337, henceforth forbade any export of wool outside the kingdom. In theory, this valuable raw material was in future to feed only English looms, which were still to be created. Many historians have praised Edward for this bold step and assumed that he seriously intended to organize a cloth-making industry in his kingdom, and so secure England's economic independence. This is imaginative nonsense. In fact, the measure was directed only against Flanders. The merchants of Brabant were soon granted the right to import the wool they needed, on the sole condition that they should not re-export it to Flanders. If the looms of Ghent and Ypres were to be in a bad way, it was to the advantage of those of Brussels and Malines. Furthermore, in July 1337, Edward ordered the requisition of 30,000 sacks of English wool and allowed a syndicate of merchants to sell it at his profit on the Dordrecht market, pending the establishment of the wool 'staple' at Antwerp.

By this clever move, Edward III recognized the growing influence, economic and political, which, since the beginning of the century, had been assumed amid the Dutch principalities by the great duchy of Brabant, whose destiny was directed with a masterly hand by Duke John III.

To Philip VI's attempts, begun in 1332, to bring Brabant into his sphere of influence, the Plantagenet replied by the grant of commercial privileges which made the young cloth-making industry of Brabant and the growing prosperity of the port of Antwerp dependent upon England's friendship. He had other friends in his region: William of Hainault, at the same time Count of Holland and Zeeland, who, to be sure, was vassal to his brother-in-law the King of France for Ostrevant, but whose daughter Philippa was Queen of England; further to the east, the Duke of Gelderland, traditionally attached to alliance with England. Edward was to rekindle these friendships and create new ones.

From the end of 1336, he addressed fervent messages to the Dutch princes. He presented himself as victimized and forecast an injust aggression by the King of France. 'I have made him advantageous offers,' he wrote, 'but so far he has refused my most reasonable proposals. Not content with unjustly retaining my hereditary property' (a reference to the parts of Aquitaine occupied since 1324) 'he is secretly hatching a great plot against me, and he contemplates appropriating what is left of my Gascon fief.' Fortified by these arguments, but fortified above all by the money which they freely borrowed from merchants and bankers, the Bishop of Lincoln, Henry of Burghersh, and the earls of Huntingdon and Salisbury travelled through the Low Countries and the Rhineland during the winter. In May 1337, they set up at Valenciennes a regular market for alliances, which were bought for hard cash. It cost a great deal, for the princes of the Empire were grasping. 'It is well known', a chronicler says about them, 'that the Germans are extremely covetous, and do nothing except for money.' But the English envoys built up a strong network of alliances. The dukes of Brabant and Gelderland, the counts of Hainault, Berg, Juliers, Limburg, Cleves and Marck came into the anti-French coalition.

The Plantagenet king was obviously determined to begin the struggle with the most disciplined and the strongest military forces possible. But there was not much room for innovation in the organization which I have described and which had proved itself, still quite recently, in the hard Scottish campaigns. The sovereign's orders dealt only with questions of detail, and were not perhaps quite as effective as some writers have elected to think. Still, they revealed his definitely bellicose intentions. Edward advised his nobility to learn French, the language of the court, of administration, and of the enemy. He forbade tourneys, fond though he was of them, so that his knights should devote all their time and wealth only to war. He required the people to perfect themselves in archery, and subject themselves to exercises which would make their bodies supple and strong. Much has been made of his use of commissions of 'array', regular recruiting boards set up in the counties to enlist the strongest of the peasants and workmen and so swell the ranks of the infantry. But this organization met with many disappointments, and did not succeed in forming large and disciplined contingents. The armed forces at the King of England's disposal could not quite equal, so far as numbers went, those which his adversary put into line.

The men of the Middle Ages, muddled in their figures, have given us numerical statements about the English campaigns which are frankly incredible and are contradicted by all the administrative documents brought to light by modern scholars. They speak constantly of invasion forces of twenty or thirty thousand men, if not more. For the siege of Tournai (1340) they suggest a strength reaching a hundred thousand men, including the Flemish contingents. This is sheer fantasy. Even if we admit that the kingdom's meagre resources could have provided pay for such large armies, it would have been impossible to transport them to the continent. The impressment of merchant ships, which were of very small tonnage, did not enable more than five to eight thousand cavalry and a few thousand infantry to be embarked at any one time.

Armament and discipline were a little better than the French. I am not speaking of the heavily equipped cavalry, who still formed the essential part of the armed forces, and upon whom, as a rule, rested the whole weight of the battle. Their armament and their methods of combat were identical throughout Christendom. There was little difference, on this point, between the English and the French armies. For though the English knights, during the Scottish campaign, had taken to dismounting for combat, their new tactics were soon to be copied on the continent. The English superiority was shown only in the secondary formations; in the infantry whom knights in both camps despised; the pikemen, the formidable Welsh knifemen, and above all the archers. The fire of their long bows was not very accurate, but they sprayed the enemy at long range with flights of arrows, whereas the Genoese cross-bow, adopted by the infantry of the Valois, was a heavier and slower weapon. For three flights of the English archers it fired only one. But no one at this time had any idea of the capital and decisive role which this despised infantry was to play in the pitched battles of the war.

To recruit and maintain these forces, limited though they were, called for large and continuous resources. But, even before she engaged in hostilities, England had already taxed herself beyond her strength. The campaigns in Scotland had been costly and had swollen the amount of debt. A great deal of money and many dubious expedients had been necessary to raise the sums required to buy the German alliances. At the same time, the measures taken against the Flemings, as well as the failure of the merchants, who had requisitioned and tried to sell abroad too large a quantity of wool, disorganized the foreign markets, which meant that the royal treasury no longer received so regularly the custom paid on the sacks of wool exported. It was for lack of money that the first English landing in France, contemplated for the autumn of 1337, had to be cancelled.

It was for lack of money that Edward accepted a truce for the first six months of 1338, proposed by the Pope.

In July 1338, when he finally thought it essential to cross to the continent, the treasury had been emptied by his military and diplomatic preparations. With trade at a standstill, the taxpayers had not enough ready money to pay direct taxes. Edward obtained from Parliament a 'loan' of 20,000 sacks of wool to the profit of the crown. The producers or owners would be indemnified, at a fairly low rate, by treasury assignments. The king, on his side, undertook to sell the wool on the continent, and to support his army and his diplomacy out of the large profit which he hoped to make on it. It was a bold project, which sufficiently showed to what straits the needy Plantagenet was reduced.

On his side, Philip VI, despite his larger and richer kingdom, was not much better off. His military preparations too suffered from the lack of stable and sufficient resources. Thanks to the complicity of the Avignon Popes, he had been able, more or less regularly, to levy tenths on the clergy of the kingdom, which went mostly to the profit of the royal treasury. On the accession of the Valois dynasty, John XXII had promised him to make the ecclesiastical revenues contribute 'towards the heavy charges of the kingdom' for two years, and this concession was renewed in 1330. Despite some opposition from the taxpayers, the money came in, producing an annual net revenue which sometimes exceeded 250,000 *livres*. Then, in 1332, the preaching of the crusade, through all the privileges conceded to the king, swelled these resources of clerical origin. To be sure, at this time they should have found their way to a special treasury, strictly reserved for the expenses of the 'holy voyage'. But in 1336, when the crusade was abandoned, it so happened that Philip had spent most of them on the needs of his government. Benedict XII from 1338 and Clement VI later granted fresh tenths, which were regularly renewed every two years. This aroused the jealousy of Edward III, who did not enjoy such favour from the court of Avignon.

The laity as a whole showed less docility in letting themselves be taxed. The imposition of an 'aid' – whether it took the form, according to the province or the circumstances concerned, of an income tax, a hearth tax, or a tax on merchandise – encountered any amount of local opposition, from the nobles, from the towns, from the villages. The subsidy imposed on the whole kingdom in 1328 to finance the campaign in Flanders brought in only 230,000 *livres*, less than the tenth levied on the clergy alone. In the following years it was even less easy to obtain money. The feudal aid demanded in 1332 for the knighting of the crown prince John was refused by the men of the vassals. It had to be limited solely to direct subjects of the royal domain, and then, in the face of fresh disappointments over its levy, to be dropped altogether. An aid for the crusade, which was similarly provided for by feudal custom, was ordered in 1335. Most taxpayers refused to pay, and the king received only a few small gifts. How, in these conditions, could he lay preparations for an ever possible conflict with the Plantagenet?

After the breach in 1337, the king's officials were forced to make a fresh effort. The levying of a subsidy still provoked tenacious opposition. It involved parleying with the taxpayers, reducing demands, accepting the method of imposition which a community or a region preferred. In Languedoc the tax of a *livre* per hearth, which the government wanted, was reduced by one-fifth for commoners and one-third for nobles. The towns and certain groups of inhabitants bought themselves off for a lump sum much below the yield of the hearth-tax. There were similar disappointments in Languedoïl. Some towns preferred a tax on merchandise, which was harder to levy and slower in its yield. Normandy got off cheaply with a promise to maintain for ten weeks only one thousand of the four thousand men-at-arms whom it was proposed to raise in the province. Most of the vassals, pleading their personal service to the king, demanded that the aid should not be levied on their men or that they themselves should collect it for their own profit. The lands of some religious establishments obtained complete exemption. The subsidy brought in so little that, before the end of the year 1337, the monarchy was unable to pay its officials. The salaries of judges and lawyers were withheld for a year; those of sergeants were reduced by a quarter and of other officials by a fifth.

What was more serious was that, in order to obtain meagre subsidies, the monarchy had to turn suppliant, or even beggar. The grant of an aid involved in return the confirmation of old privileges, the concession of new ones, letters of non-prejudice, often mass exemptions. The king's commissioners had to haggle with the people. They were recommended to be pleasant, gentle, meek. In these difficult negotiations the principle became established, *de facto* rather than *de jure*, of taxation by consent of the taxpayers and their representatives. It was at this time that those local assemblies, numerous and frequent, but with no fixity of composition or procedure, which began to be called Estates came into the full light of day.

The necessity of obtaining money at all costs meant that recourse to the Estates became almost an obligation which no one felt that the king had a right to avoid. We do not know much about the working of these assemblies or their composition, except that the large towns played a leading role in them. It appears that they were mostly convened locally. It was not until 1343 that the first Estates made their appearance which historians, rather prematurely, called general. They brought together members from all the north and centre of the kingdom: that part of it which was soon named Languedoïl, in contrast to Languedoc, always consulted separately. Emboldened in proportion as they felt that the government to be in greater difficulties, the assemblies demanded ruinous compensations. In 1337 the Norman Estates, assembled at Pont-Audemer, invoked the Charter to the Normans of 1315 in order to refuse any subsidy. They finally voted a meagre gift *ex gratia* only on the condition that their liberties were confirmed and that they were granted letters of non-prejudice. Two years later, the Norman members united against Prince John's repeated demands, debated a long time, and finally got their financial privileges defined, to the great disadvantage of the royal treasury. In 1340, the nobles of the bailiwick of Vermandois laid down still harder conditions. The lords themselves were to choose the tax-collectors; the money would be used solely to pay the armed forces of the province; the levy would stop from the day of the royal army's disbandment. When the contributor happened to agree to make an effort, he confined it to the short duration of a summer campaign, without realizing that the war had henceforth assumed a new character.

This uncertainty about the morrow partly explains the slowness and the inefficacy of the military preparations in this year 1337-8, which was, so to speak, a vigil of arms. It can hardly be held, however, to excuse some slackness, in the diplomatic sphere, about counterbalancing the pro-English coalition by a closer union of the friends of France. Without completely neglecting this task, Philip did not put exemplary ardour into it. His counter-coalition proved definitely inferior to the compact group of his adversaries. Yet he had old friends in the Low Countries: Louis of Nevers, Count of Flanders; John of Luxemburg, who was also King of Bohemia. Since he could no longer count either on Hainault or on Brabant, he bought the alliance of the Bishop of Liège, the Count of Zweibrücken, Henry of Bavaria, and the town of Cambrai. The group, imposing as it might appear, was sparse and scattered in face of the pro-English coalition. Luckier on his southern frontier, Philip opened negotiations with Castille and, in December 1336, concluded a treaty of alliance with Alfonso XI, and could thus count on the support of the Castilian fleet in the coming war.

Finally, in order to demonstrate his newly acquired independence towards the court of Avignon, Philip began talks with a prince who, for more than ten years, had shown himself the sworn enemy of John XXII and Benedict XII. This was the Emperor Ludwig of Bavaria, a hardened schismatic, who was excommunicated and anathematized. Did the Valois really intend to ally himself with the head of the Empire, promise him his own aid against Avignon and solicit the Emperor's aid against the Plantagenet? It is doubtful. In any case, the negotiations, slackly conducted, led to no result, because Edward III, more prompt and more practical, had offered the necessary price to the impecunious Bavarian. Succumbing to the lure of sterling, on August 26th 1337, the Emperor allied himself with the King of England, and supported with all his authority the Dutch and Rhenish coalition, whose strength seemed dangerously to threaten the kingdom of France.

4. ENGLAND'S DISAPPOINTMENTS

The year 1338 witnessed the completion of the great English preparations on the northern frontiers of France. For their success, it was necessary to lull the suspicions of the adversary, whether he called himself
Benedict XII or Philip VI. The Pope was indignant at the clandestine
alliance concluded by the Plantagenet with the schismatic Emperor, a
secret which had been badly kept. To appease him, the King of England
readily agreed to prolong the truce until April 1st, and then until July 1st.
He protested his attachment to peace to the Holy See, and even sent plenipotentiaries to the court of Avignon, where, under the simple-minded
Benedict XII, they still sought unsuccessfully to prevent the war. As for
the Valois, it was essential to mislead him about the plots which were being
hatched. So Edward loudly proclaimed his intention, if peace could not
be preserved, to go in person to defend his duchy of Guienne against the
perfidious proceedings of the French officers.

Meanwhile bargaining continued without pause in the Low Countries
and the Rhineland. It was not enough for Edward to have bought the
alliance of the princes of the Empire at a very high price. To attach them
to his service and use them for the accomplishment of his plans of conquest, he needed to exercise a legitimate authority over them, which
would hold them back from desertion, always a possibility. He negotiated
the purchase from the needy Emperor of the title of deputy or Vicar of
the Empire in Lower Germany, thanks to which the Emperor's sovereign
powers could be delegated to him in all the territory of the former
Lotharingia. Finding himself so near his goal, he was in a hurry to start
his campaigning. In April he announced his intention of breaking the
truce and embarking on May 1st for the continent. Financial difficulties
prevented him from being ready on that date, but on July 16th an imposing fleet left the port of Orwell, at the mouth of the Thames, and set sail
for Antwerp. As guest of the Duke of Brabant, who had been bound more
closely in his alliance by new commercial privileges, Edward threw off the
mask and, on July 22nd, recalled the ambassadors who, to keep up appearances, had continued to negotiate at the Papal court. Then he set off for
the Rhineland to meet his imperial friend.

Amid splendid festivities at which almost all the electors of the Empire
were present, the meeting between Edward III and Ludwig of Bavaria
took place at Coblenz on September 5th 1338. The Emperor sent a
solemn defiance to the King of France and his adherents, swore to help
his new ally against the Valois for seven years, and made the German

princes promise to serve the Plantagenet faithfully in his wars. Then he invested Edward with the insignia of deputy of the Empire, a distinction which both flattered the recipient's vanity and subserved his ambition. For the King of England did not regard it simply as a bauble. He proposed to derive from it all possible extension of power. While a mint at Antwerp began striking eagled *écus*, stamped with the arms of the Empire, but in Edward III's name, on three occasions, at Herck in Brabant on October 12th, at Malines on November 2nd, and at Binche in Hainault on December 18th, he summoned the vassals within his deputyship, in order to receive their homage. Except for the Bishop of Liège, who refused to take a step which would repudiate his alliance with the Valois, all the princes of the Low Countries answered his summons, with Brabant, Gelderland, and Hainault at their head. Louis of Nevers himself did not dare to avoid the duty as a vassal which he owed for imperial Flanders, in other words his territory beyond the Scheldt. From these splendid ceremonies Edward derived a prestige which soon surpassed the limits of Lotharingia. His envoys got in touch with the counts of Burgundy, Geneva, and Savoy. The encirclement of France seemed to be continuing along her eastern frontier, as far south as the kingdom of Arles.

These pompous ceremonies and fruitful negotiations had occupied the Plantagenet until the bad weather set in, so that he could not begin hostilities, which were put off until the spring of 1339. Fresh financial difficulties further delayed the dispatch of essential reinforcements. Festivities and alliances cost dear. To dazzle his starveling allies, Edward borrowed recklessly from merchants, from burgesses of the Low Countries, from Italian bankers. He hoped to recoup himself from the sale of the wool which he had confiscated or 'borrowed' before his departure. But the transaction, entrusted to the Florentine firms of Bardi and Peruzzi, proved disappointing. Edward counted on a preliminary delivery of 20,000 sacks. Precisely 2,500 arrived. While awaiting the remainder, he pledged his jewels to money-lenders. The magnificent crown which he had had made in anticipation of his coronation as King of France was pawned to the Archbishop of Trêves for a meagre loan. As though to add to his troubles, Benedict XII, still tirelessly intent on re-establishing peace, took advantage of the slowness of the war to seek the opening of fresh negotiations. Edward had no further interest in playing with him. He informed the Pope that he would agree to no further talks so long as Philip had not, as a preliminary condition, abandoned the Scottish alliance and restored Aquitaine. In addition, in a long memorandum he set forth to the court of Avignon the reasons which had impelled him to claim the crown of France.

Edward's impatience increased from week to week. He was irritated by all the obstacles which delayed the campaign of 1339, on which he had set his hopes. At the cost of endless difficulties, English reinforcements, disembarked at Antwerp, began to concentrate round Brussels at the end of July. Edward still awaited the contingents of the German princes, promised in exchange for substantial subsidies. August and September passed without the arrival of more than a few thousand mercenaries, undisciplined and untrustworthy. At sea the French redoubled their activity, intercepted transports, delayed navigation, and sacked the Isle of Wight and other points on the English coast. At the end of September Edward lost all patience, and, without awaiting aid from his defaulting allies any longer, set out towards the French frontier. His forces seized Cambrai and ravaged Thiérache, shadowed from a distance by Philip's army. Edward challenged his enemy to fight, but the Valois did not reply. After a month of useless manœuvres, Edward fell back on Brabant. The Anglo-Imperial alliance had proved abortive and ended in lamentable failure. Fifteen months' continuous stay on the soil of the Low Countries, intense diplomatic activity, the title of deputy of the Empire, the homage and alliance of so many princes, crushing expenses—all this had produced only a futile military demonstration on the frontier of an enemy whose forces remained intact.

Anyone except Edward III would have been discouraged. But, disappointed by the princes of the Empire, he felt that he was saved when he achieved alliance with the Flemings, whose communal militia he had missed so sorely in the course of the campaign of Thiérache. With the entrance of Flanders on the scene, the second act of the drama began.

Tamed but not submissive since the campaign of Cassel, the population of maritime Flanders remained fundamentally hostile to their Valois suzerain and to the young count who supported his views. With their usual truculence, the officials of the King of France interfered in their municipal affairs and enforced circulation of the royal currency. In order to forestall their probable defection, Philip VI had vainly given official permission to his Flemish subjects to remain neutral in the coming conflict and to continue their trade with the enemy across the Channel. The closing of the wool route, which Edward had decreed almost at the same time, in order to punish Louis of Nevers's attachment to the cause of the Valois, had destroyed the beneficial effects of Philip's attempt to ease the tension. The stoppage of all arrivals of raw material in the industrial towns caused an unemployment crisis among the humbler classes of artisans, and its effects were not slow in making themselves felt. Reduced to poverty, the workers blamed the King of France. They attacked the count and his nobility, overweening in their wealth, and the well-off burgesses, whose substantial capital enabled them to face the crisis cheerfully, and whom they suspected of being still *leliaerts* at heart. The year 1337 witnessed the usual forerunners to a social crisis, disorders in the streets, demonstrations to the accompaniment of shouts of 'work and liberty'. From Valenciennes, whence they 'worked' the Low Countries, English agents got into touch with the agitators and encouraged a rebellion from which they meant to draw a good profit.

A leader soon gathered all the malcontents together and dominated them by his strong personality. Despite his wealth, and also despite his links with the nobility, James van Artevelde took the popular demands under his wing. To reopen the wool route, a reconciliation with the Plantagenet was needed. So, if we are to believe the chroniclers of the other side, Artevelde demanded that the Flemings 'should take the side of the English against the French'. In any case, on January 3rd 1338, at Ghent, the chief centre of the working-class agitation, the people elected him by acclamation as *hooftman* or captain of the city. Clever propaganda enabled him to rally the rival towns of Bruges and Ypres to the movement, together with the little rural centres of the cloth-making industry, harshly treated though they had been by the strict rules of the big cloth-making towns. Everywhere a truce was imposed on factions, and a union against the count and the king was created, in the form of a commission of government on which delegates from the chief towns sat under Artevelde's presidency. From Bailleul in the south to Termonde in the north the whole country recognized his authority. In vain did Louis of Nevers try to master this rebellion of his subjects by force. An armed attack on Ghent and another on Bruges failed against the resistance of the communal militia. In February 1339 the count had to flee to the court of the King of France, leaving the whole of Flanders in the hands of the rebels.

No sooner had Artevelde assumed power than Edward III believed he had Flanders at his disposal. He was then preparing his great Dutch and Imperial coalition against the Valois. The support of the county of Flanders, which he counted upon as imminent, would secure him a crushing superiority over his adversary. But it took him nearly two years of difficult negotiation to reach his end. This was because Artevelde was in no hurry to throw himself without profit into the English alliance. He had led a revolt against the bad administration of an inexperienced count. To repudiate the suzerain, hated though he was, would be a graver act to which he was not yet ready to consent. It would mean risking an alliance between the count and the king, a new punitive expedition by the French cavalry, a new Cassel. The memory of the disaster of 1328 was still fresh in everyone's mind. Prudently, Artevelde offered Edward only the assurance of his benevolent neutrality. In return for this limited promise, he obtained, in July 1338, an equally limited consignment of English wool, which enabled some looms to start work again. Incessantly solicited to commit himself more deeply, he refused for eighteen months to make any further concession. Edward, who valued the alliance of Brabant, could not on his side offer any economic advantages which would injure the interests at Antwerp and Brussels. Thus matters remained for the moment, and Edward had to start his belated campaign of 1339 without the support of the Flemish militia.

On the morrow of the campaign of Thiérache, Artevelde found himself constrained to take sides more openly with England. The French army, which remained intact not far from the Flemish frontiers, might turn against him at Count Louis's appeal. To ward off this new threat, the Flemings needed money and men-at-arms from the Plantagenet. So they reopened negotiations. Artevelde and Edward had a number of meetings, which ended, on December 3rd 1339, in the conclusion of an agreement, at which the Flemish alliance was bought at a high price. The Flemings would henceforth have free access to English wool, and the 'staple' was to be transferred from Antwerp to Bruges. They were promised the restoration of the castellanies of Lille, Douai, and Orchies, which had been in the hands of the King of France since the reign of Philip the Fair. They were to receive, in four instalments, a subsidy of 140,000 *livres* for military equipment and putting the county in a state of defence. Finally, in the event of an attack by the Valois, the English fleet and contingents of troop were to be placed at Artevelde's disposal. In return, the Flemings promised their military aid and – an essential point – recognized the Plantagenet as the lawful King of France.

In consequence, on February 6th 1340, Edward was able to hold his court at Ghent, at a '*parlement*' to which his new vassals were summoned. As successor of Saint Louis and Philip the Fair, he received the oath of the towns and the homage of those nobles who had not taken the count's side. Henceforth he assumed the title of 'King of England and France', had his great seal remodelled, quartered his arms with the fleur-de-lys, and dated his documents 'in the fourteenth year of our reign in England and in the first in France'. Even before operations of any scope had been undertaken, he had reached the first of his goals: the transformation of the feudal conflict into a dynastic war. Deputy of the Empire, King of France, the sovereign of the little island kingdom enjoyed a prestige which dazzled others as well as himself. On the following March 29th, the Parliament at Westminster ratified the Anglo-Flemish alliance. At the same time, the Count of Hainault, who had managed to maintain an insecure neutrality between his French suzerain and his English son-in-law, sent his defiance to the Valois. With him Philip lost his last friend in the Low Countries.

But, in the military sphere, the Flemish alliance proved as disappointing as had been the Imperial alliance. Edward had become the prey of his Dutch creditors. In February 1340 he received their permission to return to England in order to hold a Parliament and seek money and reinforcements. But he had to promise to be back before the month of June. By way of security, he had to leave his wife and his young children as hostages in Ghent, under the supervision of the unpaid bankers. So it was in Ghent that his third son, the future Duke of Lancaster, was born. In England, too, the Commons revolted against the fresh financial sacrifices which were demanded of them. It was only in return for ruinous concessions that they agreed to vote a heavy tax of one-ninth on farming income and on the personal property of the burgesses. The administration itself, and especially the departments of the Chancery and the Exchequer, had had enough of being controlled from the continent by officials of the royal household. They hampered the military preparations by their ill will, some of them even by their open opposition. Finally, the King of France made ready to repel the new army of invasion at sea. To this end, the French fleet, reinforced by Castilian squadrons and a few Genoese galleys, cruised off the Flemish coast or anchored at Sluys, the only good port of the county.

With bold persistence, Edward overcame all difficulties, broke down all opposition, and disregarded the French threat. On June 22nd he set sail for Flanders with his whole fleet. The next day but one, off the port of Sluys, he engaged the enemy. Thanks to their poor leadership and the lack of liaison between French and Castilians, the fleet of the Valois was annihilated, either sunk or burnt, in a few hours. It was a great success, which secured to the victor the command of the sea, for some years at least. But it was a success without decisive effect. The kingdom of France was intact, and had still to be conquered. Edward, as we shall see, had not the means to do it.

The English army, reinforced by the Flemish militia – in all perhaps from twenty to thirty thousand combatants – started its campaign at the end of July. It marched straight on Tournai, the first outpost of the royal domain on the banks of the Scheldt. But it had not the siege equipment essential for the assault of so strong a fortress, and was immobilized for weeks under the walls. Meanwhile Philip's army, concentrated in the hills of Artois, reached the region of Lille, harried the enemy foragers and surprised their isolated detachments, but once more refused the pitched battle which Edward seemed anxious to fight. About the middle of September the position of the two armies worsened rapidly with the approach of winter and through lack of fodder. The English, who had already suffered the far-reaching defection of Brabant, whose interests were affected by their reconciliation with Flanders, now witnessed the reconciliation of the Count of Hainault with the Valois. To avoid worse, they accepted the proposal for a truce from the envoys of Benedict XII. The truce, concluded at Esplechin, a little village near Tournai, on September 25th 1340, was to last till June 1341, with a possibility of extending it for a longer period.

The balance-sheet of the first years of the war, in fact, was scarcely favourable to the Plantagenet's cause. His campaigns had not touched the vital strength of the kingdom of France, whose cohesion seemed indeed to be increased by the approach of danger. Philip VI's growing authority was shown, above all, in the financial sphere. Disregarding the taxpayers' feelings, he went so far as to impose increased charges, part of which at least enabled him to raise sufficient troops. In 1340 he summoned the representatives of his subjects by bailiwicks and demanded from them the levying of one-fiftieth on incomes and a *maltôte* on merchandise. We are told that in Vermandois the Estates voted a reply 'little agreeable to the king'. But Philip overrode opposition and imposed his will. In 1341 he levied a *maltôte* of 4 *deniers* to the *livre* on commercial transactions almost throughout the kingdom. In 1342 the whole kingdom contributed to a hearth-tax of 20 *sous* a hearth, and we know that it produced 73,000 *livres* for the seneschalship of Carcassonne alone and 33,000 *livres* for Périgord and Quercy. Whatever the difficulties and disappointments of collection may have been, the fact remains that the Valois had managed materially to increase his extraordinary resources.

At the same time, moreover, he succeeded in making a new tax general and permanent: the salt tax (*gabelle*). Hitherto the crown had worked the salt-pans of Carcassonne and Agen, which formed part of its domainial wealth, on its own account. In the nearby districts it enjoyed an exclusive privilege of working and sale. An ordinance of March 16th 1341, for which the assent of the Estates had not been asked, extended the salt tax to the whole kingdom. Commissioners confiscated or bought all the existing stock, and established warehouses where the people were bound to buy their salt. It was not long before the monopoly of sale was maintained only in Languedoc. Everywhere else the royal stores (*greniers*) became simply warehouses where the salt in bulk had to be brought on its arrival in the town, and could be withdrawn by the merchants only against payment of the tax, in accordance with a system of assessment similar to that of the wool 'staple' from which the King of England profited. Unpopular in the highest degree though it was, this tax nevertheless lasted until the end of the *ancien régime*.

Finally – a symptomatic fact which it would be wrong to pass over in silence – the cares of the English war did not deter Philip and his councillors from a fruitful policy of enlarging the royal domain, thus continuing and extending the policy of his Capetian predecessors. In 1341 he took advantage of a 'rebellion' of King James III of Majorca, who held half of the town and lordship of Montpellier from the French crown, to confiscate and occupy his fief. James was soon pardoned; but, hard pressed by the King of Aragon, who deprived him of his little island and Pyrenean kingdom, he ended by selling his fief to Philip for 120,000 *écus* (1349). So the last rights which, for the past century and a half, the royal house of Aragon had held in Languedoc were reunited to the royal domain of France. Simultaneously, complex negotiations sought to bring under the domination of a Valois prince a province which, though outside the kingdom of France, was comprised in that 'kingdom of Arles' where, since the time of Saint Louis, undivided French influence had been exercised. Humbert, the last heir to the counts or *Dauphins* of Vienne, himself had no heir. Anxious to go and seek adventure and glory in the crusade, he was ready to sell his inheritance to the highest bidder. Successive treaties ensured its devolution to a French prince. In 1343, there was no question of giving it to anyone except a younger son of the King of France, Philip of Orleans, who would found a local dynasty there, on the understanding that any later annexation to the royal domain was forbidden. The following year, Philip VI substituted his eldest son, John of Normandy, for the younger son. Finally in 1349, by a new treaty, this time definitive, Humbert sold the Dauphiné to John's eldest son, the future Charles V, who thus became the first French prince to bear the title of Dauphin.

Part III

THE FRENCH DISASTERS
1340–1364

Part III

THE FRENCH DISASTERS

(1340–1364)

THE truce of Esplechin clearly marked the failure of the grandiose plans by which, in his megalomania, Edward III had imagined that he could rapidly overthrow the dynasty of the Valois. Some modern historians, especially in France, have been pleased to depict this Plantagenet king as a realist in spite of his vaulting ambition, quick to grasp every opportunity, a man who knew what he wanted, what he could do, and where he was going. Nothing could be less characteristic of this young sovereign in his late twenties who was, in these latter months of the year 1340, reduced to the last extremity. Once it was a question of continental conquest, Edward had shown himself quite as visionary as his enemy. The hard school of experience was to sober him, to teach him to limit his ambitions to the measure of his means. For the moment, he had just received the most bitter lesson of his long career.

Little remained of that structure of alliances, so laboriously erected, so dearly bought. The encirclement of France by the Low Countries and Germany had failed pitiably. The structure was based only on English gold. When that was lacking, everything collapsed. Ludwig of Bavaria gave the signal of defection. As early as January 1341, French diplomacy induced him to abandon the English alliance and promise friendship to the Valois. Then he revoked the deputyship of the Empire which he had granted to Edward, and led into neutrality all the princes whom English sterling had previously thrust into the field. In May 1342, when a new pontiff, Clement VI, donned the tiara at Avignon, Ludwig's policy of intervention to the west of the Empire, to which, in any case, he had committed himself only half-heartedly, had to be abandoned. The struggle between the Empire and the Papacy was renewed more bitterly than ever; Ludwig's last resources were engaged in it, and henceforth he took no interest in the Anglo-French duel.

Flanders, too, where Edward had acted for the first time as King of France, was slipping out of his grasp. Here again Philip's diplomacy, less clumsy than it has been reputed, managed to pave the way for the fall of Artevelde and the English party. In revolt against French interference, the Flemish towns had at the same time rebelled against their count, Louis of Nevers, that too faithful vassal of Philip VI. At the request of the court of Paris, the Pope excommunicated the rebels as false to their oath of allegiance towards their lawful lord. It was a sentence which had not yet lost all effectiveness. From 1342 onwards the count began to regain a footing in French-speaking Flanders. Meanwhile Artevelde could maintain his authority in the cloth-making towns only if the looms kept on working and the different social classes lived on good terms. The upstart dictator, prodigiously enriched, insolently flaunted his luxury, and displeased the working class which had raised him to power. Soon – to anticipate events a little – the weavers quarrelled bitterly with the fullers, and the little industrial centres rebelled against the economic tyranny of Ghent, Bruges, and Ypres.

For these internal dangers, for the threat of unemployment which had reappeared in Flanders, Artevelde could see only one remedy, desperate though it was: to involve himself deeper than ever in the English alliance. Since all his enemies were rallying around Louis of Nevers, he rejected the authority of the lawful count, and offered the county's coronet to Edward III's eldest son, now Duke of Cornwall and soon to be Prince of Wales. Tempted by this offer, believing himself back in the fine days of 1340, the King of England hastened to Flanders at the head of a large fleet, and, in July 1345, anchored in the port of Sluys. Artevelde's treachery was too flagrant for the people of Ghent to accept. A riot, provoked just at the right moment, led to the dictator's assassination, as he was returning from his last meeting with the King of England. Disappointed once again, Edward could do nothing but sail for home with no hope of return.

No one, admittedly, could have foreseen these events in 1340. A shrewd observer, however, as he witnessed the defection of Brabant, that of Hainault, and the inaction of the Empire, might have predicted the English failure in Flanders. In any case, the truce of Esplechin in no way improved the Plantagenet's position. Unable to pay his mercenaries, driven into bankruptcy, beset by his pack of Italian and Dutch creditors, Edward III could escape them only by flight. On November 27th 1340 he left Ghent in secret, embarked in Zeeland, and, covered with mortification, returned to his kingdom, which had been bled white by two great military campaigns, all to no purpose. In his wounded vanity, he turned upon his own officials, whom he accused of governing as they chose during his absence, ignoring his orders from overseas, and neglecting to send money to prosecute the war. The Archbishop of Canterbury, John Stratford, was in Edward's eyes the chief culprit: in the *de facto* regency which he had exercised since 1339, he had failed to take the administrative measures which the situation demanded. Stratford owed his safety only to the ecclesiastical sanctuary of the monastery of Christ-church. Other officials, judges included, were dismissed and sentenced to heavy fines. The collectors of taxes and the sheriffs, held responsible for the poor yield, were punished indiscriminately, whether they were inno-cent or guilty. These strokes of blind revenge provoked indignation on the part of the barons and the Parliament, and they imposed measures of clemency.

All this was scarcely calculated to restore a bankrupt economy. Edward had borrowed recklessly. The Italian banks, in particular that of the Bardi, and, to a smaller extent, that of the Peruzzi, had granted him enormous loans, secured on the yield of the wool tax. But the tax brought them in only a small part of their outlay. In 1343 this meant bankruptcy for them, with repercussions on all the banking houses in Europe. Then a group of English merchants came forward to take their place. They leased the customs and paid Edward a large loan: too much for their resources, too little for the needs of the crown. In their turn, bankruptcy lay in wait for them, on the morrow of the plague of 1348. Meanwhile, Edward had to live on his wits. The period of great enterprises seemed over.

If he were to conquer the Valois, whose inaction was in itself promising, Edward must find favourable ground at the least expense. Chance had it that such ground presented itself, almost at once, in Brittany.

1. THE QUARREL OVER BRITTANY

ONCE AGAIN, it was a dynastic quarrel which enabled the Plantagenets to intervene on the continent. On the death of Duke John III (April 30th 1341), two candidates disputed the inheritance of Brittany: Joan of Penthièvre, nicknamed the Lame, daughter of his younger brother Guy, long since dead, and his still younger half-brother, John, Count of Montfort. The niece descended from the elder of the brothers; the younger brother was the nearest relation of the dead duke. Did the custom of Brittany admit representation, as Joan declared and as John III had sought to establish? Or, on the contrary, should the peerage-duchy adopt the rules recently laid down for the crown and exclude women from the succession, as Montfort argued? It was a nice problem, suited to fire lawyers with enthusiasm.

As suzerain of the duchy, it was for the King of France to decide the point of law. But Joan had married a nephew of Philip, Charles of Blois, son of his sister Margaret. Fearing that Philip would be partial, Montfort thought it best to confront his adversaries with an accomplished fact. No sooner was his brother dead than he seized Nantes, his capital, laid hands by a daring raid on the ducal treasure, though it had been placed in Limoges for safety, summoned the Breton vassals and demanded their homage. The results were disappointing. All the prelates and almost all the nobles refused to ratify his *coup de force.* Then he went to war and took one after the other the strongholds of Quimper and Brest in the west, Saint-Brieuc and Dinan in the north, Rennes, Vannes, Auray, and Hennebont in the east. He was, *de facto*, master of Brittany. But he could no longer count upon the decision of the King of France, whose authority he had set at defiance by taking possession of his fief before being invested with it. So he turned towards Edward III. It was a fatal step, which was to plunge Brittany in blood for twenty-three years, weaken the Valois kingdom, and restore to the Plantagenets, in the nick of time, the prestige which they needed.

So we find John of Montfort, in July 1341, hastening to England and seeking aid. It was promised him with enthusiasm, in return for the assurance that the new duke would pay his homage to Edward III as the lawful King of France. To bind John to him more closely, Edward promised him the restitution of the earldom of Richmond, in the north of England, which his ancestors had once held. The French king, warned by Joan of Penthièvre's partisans, summoned Montfort to appear, reproached him for his dealings with England and forbade him to leave Paris, on pain of stern punishment. Fearing for his life, Montfort fled. On September 7th, the peers of France recognized the justice of Joan's claim, dismissed the objections of her contumacious rival, proclaimed Charles of Blois sole Duke of Brittany and admitted him to homage. To enforce this decision, a majestic royal army, under the command of the crown prince, John, appeared before Nantes, forced the fortress to surrender, and took Montfort prisoner. The matter seemed settled.

But this was counting without the indomitable energy of Montfort's wife, Joan of Flanders, who took up the struggle again for her young son, just as Joan of Penthièvre was the soul of the opposite party. The 'war of the two Joans' aroused the enthusiasm of the court chroniclers, since it was full of fine feats of arms, heroic escapes, and remarkable reversals of fortune. But it was a murderous and endless war, for Brittany was soon torn in half between the rivals. For Montfort were the gentry, most of the towns, the peasants of the Breton-speaking west; for Blois, the clergy, almost all the nobility, the French-speaking countryside. But it was the weight of outside support which was to decide the fate of Brittany. Behind Joan of Flanders there was Edward III, and behind Joan of Penthièvre there was Philip VI. The war between the two kings, halted for the time being at Esplechin, started again, despite the truce, on the battlefields of Brittany. We need not follow its confused ups-and-downs. Only the English intervention and its lasting results concern us.

At the outset, only a weak force, in which Robert of Artois played the last part in his adventurous life, disembarked in response to Montfort's appeal and raised the blockade of Hennebont, where Blois had besieged his rival, Joan of Flanders. Then, in October 1342, Edward himself landed with 12,000 men, conscientiously pillaged the countryside, and marched on Vannes. Before the French army, again led by the Duke of Normandy, could catch up with him, the papal legates imposed the truce of Malestroit (January 1343). The knights of the two camps, for the third time in five years, found themselves robbed of the great pitched battle for which they longed. Meanwhile, truce or no truce, the Plantagenet kept his hand on Brittany, left some garrisons there, and dispatched others to occupy the ports, castles, and strategic points in Montfort's name.

Despite the stipulations of the truce, the war soon started again. Montfort, who had promised never to return to Brittany, went back there and died at Hennebont. Then Edward took upon himself the guardianship of the young duke John IV. He shut up Joan of Flanders, who had gone mad. The King of England now controlled Breton affairs. This was at the end of 1345. How far had he travelled in the past five years; and what a compensation for the loss of Flanders, just on the point of being completed, were those new disembarkation points, the Breton ports! Two men were developing in Edward III: the ambitious man, who ran after chimeras; and the opportunist, who never missed the chance to make good the faults of the first. The Breton interlude had given England time to recover. She could now resume the direct struggle against the Valois dynasty.

A final attempt at peace, made by Clement VI, was bound to fail, now that Edward felt himself ready to go to war again. The pontiff, however, spared nothing to make his mediation a success. He remembered that he had already worked for the reconciliation of the two kingdoms, at the time when he was only Pierre Roger, Cardinal of Rouen. He had long been familiar with the subjects of the quarrel, the sensitive points, the few grounds of understanding. If he failed, it was because Valois and Plantagenet, taught by their experience of the first hostilities, now knew where they stood, had defined their war aims, and understood the lowest terms on which they would agree to lay down arms. Their points of view were more than ever irreconcilable. If we accompany their plenipotentiaries to the conferences at Avignon (October–December 1344), we shall grasp the principles from which the two adversaries – apart from momentary weakenings – were not to depart for more than half a century.

Edward began by claiming his due, in other words the kingdom of France, the 'inheritance' which came to him from his mother Isabella. This was a mere feint. Taught by bitter disappointments, he no longer hoped, he was never again to hope, to wear a crown too hard for him to win. His dynastic pretensions were only a bargaining counter. They were immediately followed by his real demand: the restitution of Guienne, within the widest possible frontiers. For the moment, he spoke only of the duchy's frontiers at the time of good King Saint Louis; but his appetite was to grow with the success of his arms. Further, he must demand this greater Guienne in full sovereignty: no more link of vassalage, no more intervention by the king's officials, no more appeals to the *Parlement*, no more threats of confiscation. If Guienne ceased to form part of the kingdom of France, the Plantagenets would at last be masters there. The very cause of the war would disappear.

Philip's councillors stood equally firm on their principles. They began by claiming that Aquitaine was well and truly confiscated. There could be no going back on this sentence, even though it had not yet been enforced. Then they sought to propose illusory compensations, which might be found in Scotland or other spheres. Finally, they agreed to the 'restitution' of the fief – which was purely symbolical, since the Plantagenets had never been effectively driven out of it – and even consented to give it the wide frontiers demanded by Edward. But sovereignty over it could not be surrendered. The King of France had the right to cede part of his domain as a fief, but not to dismember the kingdom. If the King of England was reluctant to pay his homage, because his independent crown did not lend itself to a feudal link, he had only to cede the duchy of Aquitaine to one of his sons as an appanage. This cadet would become vassal to the crown of France for it, and everyone would remain master on his own soil. These were proud words spoken by Philip VI's councillors. They were to be repeated by Charles V and by the councillors of Charles VI. Only John the Good, beneath the weight of defeat, was to forget them. But we must not anticipate; our intention here is only to define the constants of a conflict which, until the end of the century and even beyond, remained essentially feudal.

2. CRÉCY AND CALAIS

THE TRUCE, several times extended, expired at the beginning of March 1345. After the failure of the talks at Avignon, it was not renewed. Immediately the English took the offensive in Brittany, where contingents led by that formidable captain, Thomas Dagworth, captured strongholds in John IV's name, and above all in Aquitaine, where an eager Anglo-Gascon army, under the command of the Earl of Derby, went into action again, pushed forward, raiding and taking the badly defended castles by surprise, and penetrated with impunity into Poitou. Against it the King of France decided to make his strongest effort. A large and well equipped, though too slowly concentrated army was entrusted, in May 1346, to the Duke of Normandy, the king's lieutenant in Languedoc. It stopped, for weeks and weeks, under the walls of a well-garrisoned stronghold, Aiguillon, at the confluence of the Lot and the Garonne, the key to the Gascon plain, which the French had feebly allowed to fall some months earlier. Normandy's army would have stayed there much longer – the heir to the throne was known as an obstinate man – if almost incredible news from the north of France had not decided him to raise the siege, on August 20th 1346. Six days later the king suffered, in pitched battle, the greatest defeat of the war.

The attacks of his troops in Brittany and Guienne had meant nothing more for Edward III than skirmishes intended to test the ground and pin down the enemy, or diversions without a morrow. He was preparing to disembark, at a favourable time and place, having made up his mind to carry through to the end that great raid whose first attempts, in 1339, 1340, and 1342, had prematurely died away in Thiérache, Tournaisis, and Brittany. While he concentrated arms, men, and ships, he hesitated about his objective. In 1345, through Artevelde's murder, Flanders had escaped him just as he contemplated landing there. The next year unexpected help came to him, and determined his point of landing. Philip, too brutal in his 'justice', which he was incapable of offsetting by a rapid pardon, in the manner of the time, had just struck a hard blow, by a sentence of confiscation and exile, at a powerful Norman family, strongly established in Cotentin and holding in particular the important fortress of Saint-Sauveur-le-Vicomte. Disgraced and deprived of his property, Geoffrey of Harcourt came to offer his homage to the Plantagenet. So it was in Cotentin, at Saint-Vaast-la-Hougue, on July 11th 1346, that the King of England landed.

The army he led was not large. Never had the English, limited by the small tonnage of their ships, been able to put into line more than 8,000 cavalry, reinforced by a few thousand infantry. But surprise had its effect, since there was no system of coastal defence and the fortresses were lightly held. Amid general panic, the invader debouched without opposition into Lower Normandy, took Caen without striking a blow, crossed the district of Évreux, reached the Seine near Poissy, and thrust forward right into the heart of the homeland of the Capets. Would he march on Paris? A royal army, to which the vassals flocked in haste, had at length concentrated round Philip. Edward did not dream of measuring himself against this imposing enemy, too numerous for him. He slipped away northwards, hoping to reach the coast in the region of Boulogne before he was overtaken. But the French, by forced marches, came up with him. Edward had lost precious time in forcing the passage of the Somme. Willy-nilly, he had to accept battle.

At Crécy, on the plateau of Ponthieu, the improbable happened (August 26th). Why did Edward come out victorious in this unequal battle, in which in normal circumstances he should have been crushed? Chroniclers have blamed the rashness of the French knights, who dashed forward to attack with foundered horses, and charged blindly without waiting to regroup. In fact, Edward owed his triumph, strange as it may seem, to his numerical inferiority. To have awaited the enemy in the open, to have sought a hand-to-hand fight between the knights, that is, to have waged war according to the rules which he himself respected and his vassals certainly wanted to observe, would have been unpardonable folly. He had to resort to improvised ruses, of which, in his heart of hearts, he was somewhat ashamed. He had chosen favourable ground, which enabled him to follow the enemy's movements. His cavalry, impatient to join battle, were held back by his orders. Fences and hedges concealed the despised infantry. First the Welsh archers were ordered, by very rapid fire, to decimate the horses and unhorse the knights. Even a few cannon, still reserved solely for siege warfare, were perhaps used to create panic at the right moment. When the mêlée began, it was a frightful butchery. All the flower of the French nobility, the Count of Flanders, Louis de Nevers; the old King of Bohemia, John the Blind, and many another strewed the battlefield with their bodies. Prisoners of rank were numerous. The King of France fled wildly the evening after the battle, riding almost alone to seek shelter for the night in a nearby castle.

Victor against all expectation, Edward had not sufficient strength to exploit his success. He persisted in his intention to re-embark. First he must reach a port. He chose Calais, a fortress belonging to the county of Boulogne, neighbour of Flanders, which he thought he could carry without delay. But siege warfare was at this time so badly equipped that, in the case of a town with stout walls, only treachery or starvation could get the better of resolute defenders. The siege went on and on. It took all

Edward's bold tenacity not to abandon it. His soldiers regarded this winter campaign, which was contrary to custom, as a scandal, and desertions from their ranks multiplied. In the spring, the people of Calais, running short of food and witnessing the arrival of fresh English reinforcements, probably hoped to come to an agreement of a type common at the period, according to which, if they were not relieved before the beginning of August, they would surrender unconditionally. They certainly hoped that the King of France would arrive before the date fixed.

But Philip, prostrated by his first defeat, seemed to have lost all energy. He got together an army again, but it was less numerous and less eager. Its leader no longer had confidence in it, or it in him. In the month of July he advanced into the county of Boulogne. The English advance-guard harassed him and barred his way. Philip called a halt, hesitated for a few days, and then withdrew. Calais surrendered on August 4th 1347. History has popularized the wrath of the victor, which well depicts the character of this knight at once brutal and refined. It has told how he wanted to exterminate the whole population as a punishment for their over-long resistance; how he then decided to execute only the mayor and the leading burgesses; and how finally the supplications of his wife, Philippa of Hainault, appeased his anger and induced him to grant an amnesty. The scene has become a page in a picture-book.

Victor at Crécy, master of Calais, Edward had stretched his forces to the limit. He had shot his bolt and could only go home, full of glory, but almost empty-handed. But, though he concluded a fresh truce, at least he took care to leave a garrison in Calais capable of foiling any surprise. Some of the burgesses were expelled from their homes and replaced to advantage by English colonists. Philip, on his side, felt the weight of the unpopularity which attaches to the vanquished.

He might have turned on his subjects and blamed their indifference to the danger, their reluctance to pay taxes. No one had believed in a victory for the Plantagenet, no one had dreamed of a long and costly war. As early as 1343 the Estates had made difficulties about the continuance of the salt tax and the imposition for a year of a new *maltôte* on all the merchandise sold in the kingdom. In return, Philip had to promise them a return to stable currency. During the following years he had obtained only meagre grants from local assemblies, which were always recalcitrant. A few months before Crécy, there was a complaint from the Estates of Languedoïl. They demanded the same things as usual: abolition of forced loans by the king or his relations, restriction of the right of purveyance, cash payment for requisitioned goods, the elimination of useless officials, limitation of the judicial rights of bailiffs and seneschals, masters of requests of the household, and masters of water and forests. Though they accepted the maintenance of existing taxes, it was in return for a promise to abolish them as soon as possible. They believed this could be done by better administration of the king's domain, which would enable him to live off his own, without taxes. In Languedoc the Estates were more malleable. John of Normandy got a grant out of them, though a limited one, which enabled him to finance the siege of Aiguillon. But, when it came to the relief of Calais, the coffers were empty.

New Estates were summoned in Paris, on November 30th 1347. It was essential with all speed to rebuild the fleet, recruit an army, and so ward off a fresh invasion. There was a general outcry of indignation. Addressing himself to the defeated king, the Estates' spokesman said: 'You should know how and by what counsel you have conducted your wars, and how you, by bad counsel, have lost all and gained nothing, though there was no man or prince living in the world who, if you had had good counsel, should have been able to do ill to you or your subjects.' Recalling Crécy and Calais, the spokesman reminded the king 'how you went to these places honoured and in great company, at great cost and at great expense, and how you were treated shamefully and sent back scurvily and made to grant all manner of truces, even while the enemy were in your kingdom and upon it . . . And by such counsels have you been dishonoured.' The needy king had to bow to the remonstrances of his burgesses. He pocketed the insult, and became a humble beggar. The Estates were mollified, and admitted that, to make an end, it was necessary to attack the enemy at home, and therefore to reassemble an army and rebuild a fleet. The members promised to help the king 'with their bodies and their goods': nothing more definite. After that, the king had to send commissioners to negotiate locally, with the towns, the nobles, and the clergy. They obtained meagre grants, which were quickly spent on the spot.

The contemplated offensive against the island of England did not take place. At this moment a fresh disaster paralysed France, and then spread to England and Central Europe. It was the Black Death, that awful epidemic which left behind it nothing but death and desolation. It made its appearance, in the last months of 1347, in Languedoc, having been carried there, according to the chroniclers, by a ship coming from the Levant. Reading between the lines of the chroniclers' terrified description, it seems in the main that we can identify the disease as bubonic plague, recently still endemic among the peoples of the Far East, but then coupled also with the more deadly pneumonic plague. It struck an exhausted Europe unable to fight it, and found favourable ground for its diffusion in a society in which hygiene was still primitive. It made its way along the trade routes, as leprosy had done before it, and ravaged the towns, in which the population, crowded together without proper sanitation, fell an easy prey. It seems to have been less severe in rural areas, at least in some regions. No one knew how to treat it, still less to check it.

Some people, especially the wealthy, and notably the higher clergy, fled to places more remote and less unhealthy. Others accused sorcerers of having cast spells, or the Jews of having poisoned the wells. This was the pretext, in some towns in the Mediterranean south and in the Rhineland, for whole-hearted massacres of Jews, which added more dead to the victims of the plague. Almost the whole of the year 1348 was taken up by the tale of its ravages. Then the epidemic gradually died away, having reached more distant regions, though it did not disappear altogether. Its periodical revivals, in the following half-century, proved that it persisted in a low, larval condition, ready to attack the enfeebled.

If we confine ourselves solely to the hecatomb of 1348, we are scarcely in a position to count the victims and estimate the death-rate. Contemporaries have given us fantastic and incredible figures, killing off nine-tenths of the population at a stroke. If this had been the case, Europe would have been turned into a desert. We possess some definite information, but it is fragmentary and makes any generalization hazardous. One place in Burgundy, a prosperous village of 1,200 to 1,500 souls, lost more than 600 inhabitants within four months. In some rural lordships in the centre of France, the proportion of fallow land soon exceeded 20 per cent. The English rural clergy lost about 40 per cent. of their strength, and so on. If we fix the death-rate between one-fifth and one-third of the total population, in England and France alike, we shall probably keep within the limits of accuracy.

Life was very soon resumed, but at a slower pace and within a reduced framework. As after all great calamities, there were many marriages, and an excess of births, though not enough to offset the losses. The results of this terrible hecatomb made themselves felt for a long time, especially in France, which through periodical returns of the epidemic and the ravages of men-at-arms was kept in a permanent state of under-population. It is easy to understand the dislocation of rural life, which was still predominant in medieval economy. The sparse population let a large part of the land lie fallow. Rents remained unpaid, thus impoverishing the land-owning lords, noble and ecclesiastical. To ward off the worst, the big landlords – the case of the ecclesiastical manors in England has been especially studied – systematically abandoned the hill farms, with their poor soil, or turned them over to the roving grazing of sheep, which demanded less labour. They concentrated all the available hands on the more prosperous farmlands in the plains. It must have been the same with the small farmers, on a reduced scale. Almost everywhere moorland reclaimed the poor soil, with a mediocre yield and barely rentable, which had been brought into cultivation only to satisfy the needs of an abundant population.

These sacrifices, of course, did not suffice to free the agricultural labour essential for the farms which were retained. Hence, in the regions where it was possible, efforts may have been made to strengthen serfdom, or at least to impose increased services, week-works, and boon-works upon the surviving tenants. But landlords were not in a position, by themselves alone, to keep under the yoke a depleted labour force which, faced with a soaring rise in prices, demanded very high wages, increased by at least

50 per cent. They turned towards the public authorities and sought their intervention.

For the first time in the history of the western monarchies, severe legislative measures tried to regulate the system of labour, but to the benefit of the employers. It was in England that they seem to have been most effective. The first ordinance issued in 1349, and then completed and promulgated in the form of the 'Statute of Labourers', as soon as Parliament could be summoned in 1351, declared illegal all wages higher than those in force before 1348, and established penalties against masters who offered more and against labourers or artisans who left their work in the hope of finding better pay elsewhere. The farm labourer and the town artisan thus found themselves riveted to their work without being able to improve their lot. Any offence was punishable by special judicial commissions, whose circuits, later merged with those of the justices of peace, showered fines and sentences of imprisonment upon delinquents.

It was, in the last resort, the State which suffered most from the crisis, since taxable material melted like snow in the sun. Hard hit, the possessing classes, the nobility and the clergy, could neither meet their obligations as vassals nor ensure the maintenance of order. They let their castles fall into decay, an easy prey for the invader; or else they sought in brigandage an increase of their incomes which their tenants could no longer pay them. Crime increased in France well before the ravages of the *routiers*. It also troubled England, where, however, the 'free companies' were never rife. The impoverished clergy were no longer equal to their task. As it was necessary to fill the gaps, the new priests, consecrated by the batch, were inferior in learning and zeal to their predecessors. The shrinkage of revenues hit the hospitals and dried up charity. It accelerated the growth of pluralism for highly placed beneficiaries, and that of absenteeism for all. It placed the clergy as a whole in a difficult position between the simultaneous fiscal demands of the papacy and the monarchy. It was no matter of chance that the first rigorous measures decreed in England against the provision of benefices and the abuses of papal taxation were taken in 1351 and 1353, in other words on the morrow of the Black Death.

Peasants, artisans, and burgesses still made up the solid phalanx of taxpayers. But, whether it was a question of indirect taxes, always variable in terms of economic prosperity, or direct taxes, generally based on a census of hearths, the crisis of 1348 lowered their yield in an alarming degree. If the old return of hearths were maintained, as a fictitious measure of valuation, the bitterest disappointment would be experienced in its collection. To revise the return of hearths and adapt it to the present situation meant exposing the impoverishment of the country, and therefore of the State, to the light of day. So we find the three seneschalships of Languedoc, originally taxed on 210,000 hearths, reduced to 83,000 in 1370, and to only 30,000 in 1378.

For generations both the French and the English monarchies, at the best poorly endowed with revenue, since they had no permanently assured resources and no organized systems of collection, found themselves reduced to short commons. They should have recognized the impoverishment of their resources, and cut their ambitions to match their meagre means. But neither Valois nor Plantagenet had learned the hard lesson of facts. They continued to think big, to build up the most costly plans: alliances, invasions, crusades, conquests. The results could no longer correspond to their hopes. They succeeded, in fact, only in impoverishing their countries a little more, in drying up one by one the sources of future revenue. Nothing is more striking in the whole of Anglo-French policy, from 1350 to 1400 and even beyond, than this enormous disproportion between the weakness of means and the boldness of enterprises. It easily explains the inordinate length of the conflict.

3. KING JOHN'S PANIC

THE DEATH of Philip VI, in August 1350, brought to the throne his son John, whom posterity has nicknamed the Good. The new king had as yet given proof of nothing but gallantry and military incompetence, during his lieutenancy in Languedoc and at the siege of Aiguillon. Laden with honours by his father, created successively Duke of Normandy, then Count of Anjou and Maine, then again Count of Poitiers – Philip thus handed over to him all that the crown had recovered from the former Angevin empire – he was known to be dashing and deeply imbued with the ideal of chivalry: qualities which, at least at the beginning of his reign, had made Philip popular. Lavish and luxury-loving, like all the Valois, he was a man who might have been to the taste of a nobility eager for raids, fine feats of arms, and festivities.

The disasters into which he plunged, head down, were to modify his contemporaries' opinion of him. He was reproached with surrounding himself with councillors of low birth, who were incompetent, greedy, mindful only of their own fortunes, such as Robert of Lorris, Nicholas Braque, Simon of Bucy. Yet some of them had already been his father's councillors, and others were to surround his son. If his reign had been fortunate, he would have been congratulated on his choice. Froissart, always prejudiced in favour of the Plantagenets, explains John's failure by his defects of character. These were doubtless real, but they do not tell the whole story. John was quick to take offence, and subject to terrible rages which were provoked by the vaguest suspicions. He struck without rhyme or reason at those whom he distrusted, and was incapable of letting these irrational hatreds subside. His harsh justice was to the taste of the men of his time, but it was not balanced by pardons generously granted. If this caused indignation, it was because the king was not lucky in his enterprises. People went so far as to mutter the strangest accusations against him. The favour he showed some upstarts, notably the Constable Charles of Spain, was put down to moral obliquity. Posterity has not yet done justice to all these calumnies.

The misfortune was that, at a tragic moment in its history, the crown of France was worn, not by an incapable man – the epithet would be too strong – but by a mediocrity. John was conscious, to be sure, of the dangers he ran, but he lacked sufficient strength of mind to face them. He lived in a state of permanent panic, in an atmosphere of treachery, which we must bear in mind if we are to understand his brutal acts of revenge. Yet, despite the blows of fate, despite the drain of the 'pestilence', the kingdom remained rich and powerful. Sluys and Crécy had been but short-lived defeats. The capture of Calais might seem graver, militarily speaking; but it did not touch the royal domain, since it was made at the expense of the Count of Boulogne. As a base for invasion, the town presented less advantages than Bordeaux, where the English were sure of finding the useful support of Gascon contingents on the spot, or Brest, the citadel of Montfort's partisans.

So these preliminary defeats did not seem to have touched the country in its vitals. Accordingly John's court remained the meeting-place of the knights of Europe in quest of tourneys and feasts. It carried on the life of festivity which it had spent under Philip VI. To Edward III, the creator of the feasts of the Round Table and the Order of the Garter, John retorted by the foundation of the *Chevaliers de l'Étoile*, which served as a pretext for sumptuous, dazzling festivities in the 'noble mansion' of Saint-Ouen near Paris. Who could oppose the knightly king? The nobility were still the only class that counted, the only class with the power to establish reputations. They should have made common cause with the sovereign.

But this brilliant façade hid deep cracks. The social and economic crisis produced by the plague of 1348 had lasting repercussions which no one knew just how to check. It was thought advisable to enact legislation about wages, restore them to the pre-plague level, prevent the workers from leaving their masters, compel slackers to take work at low rates, on pain of being branded with a red-hot iron. All this was of no avail. The ordinance of 1351, unlike the English statutes on the same subject, does not appear to have been vigorously enforced. In the countryside, the lords witnessed the flight of their depleted labour from their lands and accused the government of ruining them. No one knew how to face renewal of the war, which John seemed fearfully to anticipate with terror. It was essential in the first place to discipline the army. An ordinance, also issued in 1351, established a new scale of pay for knights banneret, knights bachelor, and squires, fixed at twenty-five the minimum number of men-at-arms marching in 'route' under the banner of any captain, and ordered bi-monthly reviews, held without previous notice by the marshals' clerks, in order to avoid frauds in connexion with the strength and armament of the companies.

All this led to next to nothing, because the government was unable to provide regular pay, and as a result the captains disbanded their men in excess of the legal minimum and all of them lived on the country. The royal coffers remained empty, and the people, more than decimated by war and epidemics, refused to pay taxes. At every meeting of the Estates, in Languedoc and Paris alike, there was nothing but jeremiads over the exactions of the king's officials and refusals of grants by the members, who pleaded the impoverishment of their provinces or claimed that they had no mandate to pledge their constituents. The economic crisis and the financial crisis drove the government to fresh monetary 'mutations', which, in less than six years, devalued the royal currency, already very weak, by 70 per cent.

So it was essential, at all costs, to prevent the war from flaring up again in such unfavourable conditions. It was necessary to deal pitilessly with all those who, directly or indirectly, seemed to favour the enemy's cause. Into this policy of panic John flung himself recklessly and clumsily, with no resources other than his own mediocre brain, influenced by an entourage which sponged on him. The years 1350-6 were among the most incoherent in a century sufficiently fertile in delusions.

Edward III was not unaware of the weaknesses and the panic fear of the new King of France. He took pleasure in prolonging the threat, continually postponed, of a fresh landing. Since the conclusion of a truce on the morrow of the capture of Calais, the papacy was once more negotiating peace. This did not suit Edward, since he was not in a position to turn his initial advantages to profitable account. He resorted to manœuvres. In the first place, he demanded the absolution of his former Flemish allies as a condition preliminary to any negotiation. Then he questioned the impartiality of the Holy See, which he accused of opening its coffers too liberally to the King of France. He sent troops to Gascony. The death of Philip, followed by that of Clement VI (December 1352), served him merely as pretexts for putting off any discussion. The new Pope, Innocent VI, took the question in hand. Finally, in the spring of 1353, the two adversaries' ambassadors met at Guines, under the presidency of the Cardinal of Boulogne, known to possess a predominant influence over John – who had recently married his niece – and to be eager for a diplomatic success.

This was the moment chosen by the Plantagenet to provoke panic in the camp of the Valois. Ever since 1347, Edward had held prisoner Charles of Blois, the French claimant to the duchy of Brittany. The war there, which Joan of Penthièvre carried on without weakening, had resulted only in fleeting successes for her cause, such as the defeat and death of Dagworth, or the famous fight of the Thirty, a magnificent but murderous kind of tourney, well suited to provide 'copy' for the chroniclers of chivalry. In London Edward was able to obtain anything he liked from his Breton prisoner. In return for a promise of provisional freedom, he undertook to pay ransom, to hold Brittany as a fief from the King of England, to marry his children to Edward's. It was a clever feint. While he did not wish to abandon Montfort's son, who was his ward, the King of England was taking out a reinsurance. Whatever happened, Brittany would remain within his sphere of influence, and each of the claimants would seek his help.

Then an ally more dangerous for the Valois presented himself to Edward. This was Charles of Navarre, son of Joan of France and Philip of Évreux, 'prince of the lilies on all sides', and soon to become the mortal enemy of the dynasty which reigned in Paris. When he came on the scene, he was still only a youth, but an attractive one, a glib talker, intelligent and madly ambitious. As grandson, through his mother, of the last direct Capetians, his rights to the throne of France took precedence of those of the Plantagenets. One day he was to regret that he had not been born earlier. In 1328, he would doubtless have been preferred to the lack-lustre Valois. It was difficult now to go back on a past decision and raise himself to the throne of France, disputed by powerful rivals. But at least he could demand from the King of France the inheritance of which he had been despoiled. Thrust aside from the throne in 1316, Joan of France should have received the entire inheritance of her mother, Navarre and Champagne. She had been left Navarre, but Philip VI, like his Capetian predecessors, had refused to let go of rich Champagne, so near Paris. He had exchanged for it the counties of Mortain and Angoulême, which were of less value, and then he had even taken back Angoumois and promised an illusory compensation. Charles knew that his mother had been fooled. Nevertheless, in 1352 he agreed to marry King John's daughter. The fact that the young princess's dowry had not been paid provided him with one grievance more against a dynasty of usurpers.

But what could he do against the powerful French monarchy? What was the little kingdom of Navarre and a few Norman fiefs in comparison with France? He could derive strength only from intrigue. To get in touch with the King of England, promise to help the Plantagenet's cause, talk if need be about a partition of France with the English pretender, and then, when surprise and fear had taken effect, become reconciled with the Valois and wrest fresh territorial concessions from him – such was the policy of this perpetual conspirator. It was a policy lacking in grandeur or frankness, the policy of a man who doubted his own strength and played someone else's game without winning his own.

But what a wonderful instrument for Edward III! It so happened that John the Good, not content with entrusting Charles of Spain – a cadet of the royal family of Castille, of the house of La Cerda – with the Constable's sword which had fallen from the hand of Raoul of Brienne, executed for 'treason', also gave him the county of Angoulême, which Charles of Navarre regarded as his own. Early in 1354, Charles – his Spanish subjects were later to call him *el Malo*, the Bad – and his younger brothers lured the favourite into an ambush. As he was passing through Laigle, in their Norman lands, they had him savagely murdered. The king, in his grief and fury, swore revenge on the Navarrese brothers. But Charles secured the interest in his cause of his aunt and his sister, the widows of Charles IV and Philip VI, and got the Pope and others to intervene. Making plenty of noise about it, he got into touch with the English, and sought the armed aid of Henry, Duke of Lancaster, Edward III's cousin and his lieutenant for French affairs. 'Know that it was I,' he confessed insolently, 'who, with the help of God, had Charles of Spain killed.' Faced with the formidable collusion of rebel and enemy, the King of France swallowed his pride, and allowed the Cardinal of Boulogne, that self-seeking courtier, to arrange a reconciliation. Charles was restored to favour. As the price of his submission, he was given a good part of Cotentin. The Treaty of Mantes (March 1354) humiliated the King of France without appeasing his insatiable son-in-law.

Shaken by the Breton defection, aghast at the Navarrese intrigue, the French diplomats who were still negotiating at Guines with the papal legates and the English were now ready for the worst of surrenders. In April 1354 they accepted peace preliminaries. But what a price did they pay for the ending of the war and the Plantagenets' renunciation of the crown of France! They finally abandoned sovereignty over Aquitaine. To it they added Poitou, Touraine, Anjou, and Maine – the whole former Angevin empire of the twelfth century, of Henry II and Richard Cœur de Lion – and even Normandy. Edward might well triumph. He was exchanging the crown of France, of which he had never seriously dreamed, for almost half the kingdom, and, for these territorial annexations, he would be freed for ever from the link of vassalage. The surrender was so flagrant, indeed so gratuitous, that those who made it were bound to be soon disavowed. It casts a harsh light on a sad reign.

It had been agreed that the preliminaries should be ratified in the autumn, in the presence of the Pope. But at Avignon the French pulled themselves together, furious at witnessing the truce once more violated in Brittany, where English reinforcements flowed continuously, and at learning about fresh Navarrese intrigues woven on the spot with the complicity of Innocent VI. This same pontiff, however, seems belatedly to have realized the dangers which his fatherland was running. Consequently the French went back on their word and now refused to abandon the sovereignty of the ceded territories. The policy of peace had gone bankrupt. Despite all the humiliations to which he had agreed, John the Good found himself driven to war.

But nothing was ready for this war, for which Edward III once more threw the responsibility on his rival as the presumed originator of the breach. Edward of Woodstock, Prince of Wales – the Black Prince of legend – had arrived in Aquitaine to prepare for the renewal of hostilities. The first Anglo-Gascon raid, started from Bordeaux in the autumn of 1355, was able with impunity to ravage Languedoc as far as the gates of Montpellier. Operations of greater scope might be expected in 1356. Too late, John wanted money and soldiers. The Estates of Languedoïl, meeting in Paris in October, did not deny the necessity of taxation. But, distrusting the royal officials, they parleyed for a month and finally obtained what the local assemblies of Normandy and Vermandois had already demanded ten years earlier. The tax, sufficient to maintain one man-at-arms for a year *per* one hundred hearths, would be levied by the Estates themselves, and its use would be controlled by their representatives or *élus*. These representatives would collect the receipts by dioceses. The representatives-general or *Généraux élus* (three nobles, three prelates, and three burgesses) would pay the troops directly. The rendering of accounts would be made before the Estates, which implied that they would meet periodically. But all this ignored the exhaustion of the taxpayers, who were no longer ready to pay for more than local defence. While the monarchy lost control of the tax, the Estates were no more fortunate in their attempts to collect it. When the army of the vassals had to be assembled, in the spring of 1356, there was no money to pay it.

A last drama heralded final disaster. Charles of Navarre, still dissatisfied with his lot, had resumed his intrigues. In the autumn of 1355, when he was in his domain in Cotentin, he planned to cross over to England. Once more the king managed to appease him by the Treaty of Valognes. Then he established himself in Rouen and struck up a dangerous friendship with the Dauphin Charles, who had recently been created Duke of Normandy. Rumour had it that the two young men were plotting to overthrow the king. John's stored-up hatred and suspicion could stand things no longer. Suddenly, on April 5th 1356, galloping up still breathless from a long and secret ride, the King of France burst into the room in Rouen where his son, his son-in-law, and their suite were feasting. Charles the Bad's friends were seized and executed on the spot, and he himself was thrown into a dungeon. The whole past record of its victims invited this lightning stroke, yet it created a scandal, because it came too late, after too many surrenders and feigned reconciliations and because Charles enjoyed secret and mysterious sympathizers among a nobility who were frivolous, carping, fond of intrigue, and, as usual, devoid of any political sense.

After this, events moved fast. It was learned that an English raiding force, several thousand horsemen strong and led by Henry of Lancaster, had left Brittany and was advancing upon Normandy, rightly counting on the rising of all Charles's partisans. The Black Prince's Anglo-Gascon army, five or six thousand men in all, had regrouped and invaded Poitou, burning and pillaging on its way, seeking to reach and cross the Loire, with the obvious intention of linking up with the Duke of Lancaster in his operations in Normandy. Neither of the English armies, in view of their small strength, could await a pitched battle, still less seek one. Lancaster, by clever manœuvring, managed to dodge his adversary. But when the Black Prince, who was then in Berry, learned that King John's army was making ready to pursue him, he fell back slowly towards Guienne, heavily encumbered with his booty.

About the middle of September, near Maupertuis, to the west of Poitiers on the River Miosson, he was overtaken by the French army, whose strength of perhaps 9,000 was sufficient to crush him. But two cardinals, sent by Pope Innocent VI, obtained a truce for twenty-four hours, in order to attempt, at the last minute, fruitless negotiations for peace. This providential respite was employed by the English and the

Gascons to organize themselves in stronger positions. When battle was finally joined, their numerical inferiority forced them, as at Crécy, to resort to stratagems unworthy of knights: concealment along hedges, ambushes in woodland, fire of the Welsh archers which decimated the enemy's horses, feints to lure on their various 'battles' one by one. Before the combat, the Black Prince would have asked nothing better than to withdraw into his own domain, even promising not to take up arms again for seven years, so much did he fear disaster in face of his enemy. But, when the three days' struggle was over, on September 19th, those of the French who had not fallen or fled found themselves prisoners of a smaller Anglo-Gascon army. Its Gascon leaders, such as the lord (*captal*) of Buch, and Chandos, much more than the Prince of Wales, had been the architects of victory. Among the prisoners thrust along the road to Bordeaux was the King of France, who had persistently refused to flee.

4. THE FRENCH MONARCHY'S ABASEMENT

THE KING a captive: the whole tragedy for France was summed up in those words. Such a situation had not been witnessed for more than a century. But, on the morrow of Mansurah, Saint Louis had enjoyed such prestige in Europe that no one dreamed of attacking his kingdom; he had fallen into the hands of an enemy who was easily satisfied with a good ransom; and finally his subjects had not suffered from this distant and glorious war into which his faith had led him. John's position was quite different, though, of course, the safety of his person was not in question.

The remotest corners of all the provinces were moved to pity for the chivalrous sovereign's misfortune: proof of a loyalty to the monarchy which no mistake, no defeat could shake. But the suffering people wanted scapegoats. They turned on the nobility, heedless and reckless, who had spoiled for a fight and let themselves be crushed on the battlefields. They blamed the incompetence of the royal officials and the king's councillors, whose useless exactions from an over-taxed nation had not prevented disaster. Their hatred, though latent everywhere, did not break out everywhere. Through the interplay of circumstances, revolt found voice only in two strictly defined centres: the burgesses of Paris and the towns of Ile-de-France, on the one hand; the peasantry of Beauvaisis, on the other. But the audacity of a small number often gets the better of the apathy of the masses. For nearly two years, this unrelenting opposition was to put in peril the whole royal administration, the fruit of centuries of patient effort, and perhaps even the future of the dynasty.

There was indeed a constitutional crisis. It seemed all the more dangerous because the ship was without a pilot. On the battlefield of Poitiers the king's eldest son had taken to flight. Upon this youth of eighteen, after the disaster, the lieutenancy of the kingdom now devolved. His physical weakness was patent to all eyes. A sickly youth of unpleasing appearance, married too young to his cousin Joan of Bourbon, lacking in real political experience and worthless as a soldier, Charles had hitherto been nothing but the plaything of a dubious entourage. He bore the title of Dauphin, but it was the king's officials who governed Dauphiné in his name. He had been made Duke of Normandy, but he had spent only a few months in his appanage, leading a life of careless pleasure. He had let himself be beguiled by his brother-in-law of Navarre, and perhaps had plotted with him against his father. Nothing about him foreshadowed the man of long matured plans, clever at getting out of tight corners and gambling with fate. The youth who, stiffened by misfortune, was to become Charles V seemed as yet only a pitiful puppet. He surrounded himself with King John's most decried councillors, and learned from them to become underhand. He defied unpopularity and seemed to mock the misery of the people.

Their retort was not slow in coming. A month after Poitiers, Charles had to summon the Estates of Languedoïl in Paris, in order to deal with the growing financial straits. At once, in this numerous assembly, two oppositions made their appearance. In the first place, there was that of the burgesses, eager to defend their interests in the name of the common weal, anxious about the disturbance caused to trade, and believing themselves to be in a position to demand much, since they were the chief creditors of the State. Then there was the opposition, more disquieting and more hypocritical, of a small group of ambitious men, friends of the King of Navarre, whom they wanted to raise to the first place in the abandoned kingdom. From their alliance the Dauphin might fear the worst. Two men personified these two oppositions: Étienne Marcel, provost of the merchants (the equivalent of mayor) and a rich cloth-merchant of the capital, whose parents had made a fortune as purveyors to the court, a sincere soul and an ardent reformer, convinced of the justice of his cause and his own capacity as a leader; and Robert le Coq, Bishop of Laon, a glib talker who worked on behalf of the King of Navarre, and whose intentions were less pure.

What did the burgesses want? Before all else, they wanted to reform the government and the administration, restrain the greed of the officials, and eliminate abuses in the great departments of State, long denounced by the members for the towns. These reforms, they believed in their simplicity, would enable the king to live solely on the resources of his domain and do away with unpopular taxation. At the same time they demanded the dismissal and impeachment of the king's most compromised councillors. Other exceptional measures were essential. Beside the weak Dauphin must be placed a council elected by the Estates, a regular instrument of tutelage, on which, side by side with four bishops and twelve knights, would sit a round dozen of burgesses. Finally the burgesses imperiously demanded the release of the King of Navarre, whose popularity increased in proportion to the kingdom's misfortunes.

Faced with these stern demands, the Dauphin thought he could resort to evasions and gain time. He left Paris and went to Metz, where he met his uncle Charles of Luxemburg, who had been Emperor for the past ten years. He got nothing out of him beyond fine words of encouragement. After his return to Paris, on March 3rd 1357, a fresh session of the Estates imposed upon him a great reforming ordinance, which was a curious attempt at a controlled monarchy. A purging commission was set up, which dismissed, arrested and sentenced offending officials and confiscated their property, rather at random. Half a dozen representatives of the Estates were henceforth to sit on the Council – the Estates gave up their plan to nominate the whole of it – and the administration of the great departments of State, of the royal domain and of local agents was to be closely supervised. In spite of everything, the conduct of the war necessitated the levy of extraordinary taxes; but they were to be entirely controlled by the Estates, despite the unhappy experiment of 1355. Finally, regular meetings of the members of the three orders for the auditing of accounts were contemplated.

Was the monarchy to be put in tutelage? If we look at the matter closely, we have here only a caricature of constitutional reform. The Estates had no political tradition. They were heteroclite assemblies, summoned only in case of necessity, and they could not create the instruments of a permanent control. The purge satisfied immediate hatreds: it offered no guarantee for the future. The desire for administrative reform led to no practical result, for lack of sincerely devoted agents to carry it out. More might have been expected from the entrance of members of the Estates into the Council. But they were in a minority there. As soon as the danger was past, the old councillors raised their heads again or resumed their places. The Estates dare not dispense with the Dauphin, the depositary of the royal authority. All the efforts of the reformers broke against his obstinate ill will. Very soon the movement, begun with such enthusiasm, ran on the rocks, and thus made a resort to force inevitable on one side or the other.

Despite appearances, the last word remained with the monarchy, represented by the feeble Dauphin. He had on his side the officials, tradition, administrative continuity. The representatives of the Estates, entrusted with levying and administering the subsidies, collided with the inertia of the taxpayers, wretched peasants and artisans, who faced the improvised collectors with a tax strike. The proud provost of the merchants himself, driven to the worst expedients just like the king's officials, decreed a fresh devaluation, although a return to stable currency formed part of the reform programme. The Estates, taken for all in all, lacked prestige. Too frequent meetings tired the members, who were also concerned about the dangers and expense of travelling. Soon the meetings were more or less limited to the Parisian burgesses.

There still remained the test of force, which the Dauphin, who had neither troops nor money, could not consider lightly. In the summer of 1357 Charles tried to resume power. He did not enforce the reforming ordinance, and restored his bad councillors to favour. Étienne Marcel soon took steps to bring him to heel. In November, with the help of numerous accomplices, the King of Navarre escaped from prison, to the great delight of the Estates, who were again in session. Robert le Coq, after a brief exile, returned to Paris. The Dauphin must be terrorized in order to keep him in tutelage. No bones were made about this. In February 1358, a parody of the Estates decreed that henceforth no meetings should be held outside Paris. Charles of Navarre was summoned to Paris, and a reconciliation was imposed on the brothers-in-law. The Dauphin humiliated himself to the point of ordering expiatory ceremonies for the victims of the Rouen tragedy. Finally the provost of the merchants organized a riot. In the Dauphin's own bedroom and before his eyes, the rioters massacred his close friends, the marshals of Champagne and Normandy, and made the heir to the throne don a hood of blue and red, the colours of the Parisian burgesses.

All this inept brutality hastened a breach. On March 14th, Charles assumed the title of Regent, which gave him greater authority than that of lieutenant of the king. On the 25th he fled from Paris, reached Senlis, summoned opposition Estates, and consulted the nobles and the towns of Vermandois and then of Champagne. He placed his family in safety in the fortress known as the " Market " of Meaux. He raised troops and fell upon the Navarrese bands which were ravaging the countryside. Under the influence of danger, Étienne Marcel's state of exaltation became inflamed. He believed himself to be summoned to a lofty purpose, as defender of the liberties of the burgesses against an incompetent and oppressive monarchy. He wrote to the Flemish towns and reminded them of Artevelde, setting himself up as his spiritual heir. But he got no help except from the most compromising of allies. On May 28th came the peasant rising.

It was a mysterious revolt, this rising of the peasants of Beauvaisis and Soissonnais: one of those terrible awakenings of misery, so frequent in the Middle Ages, in which the possessing class could see nothing but a sudden throwing-off of the reins by the riff-raff. The ruination wrought by the *routiers*, who for the past year had been scouring and pillaging the country either in the name of the English or on behalf of Charles of Navarre, and the ill-timed insistence of the tax-collectors suffice to explain it. Perhaps, too, the demands of the lords, many of whom, taken prisoners at Poitiers, needed money for their ransoms, added the last straw to the people's wrath; but we lack textual proof of this.

At first surprise brought the peasants success. Their rebellious bands, under unknown but formidable leaders, such as Guillaume Karle, massacred the nobles, pillaged and burned their castles, and spread in all directions, like a patch of oil. *Jacquerie* has become a synonym for a peasant rising, destructive but with no aim and no morrow. What did the Jacques want? They never said. What could they do? Not much, once the first effect of surprise had passed. Badly armed, badly led, they fell an easy prey to the heavy squadrons of the knights. Moreover the nobility, confused for the moment, found a leader. Putting his class interests above political intrigue, Charles of Navarre placed himself at the head of the resistance, even though he was relieving the Dauphin of a very grave anxiety. His energy got the better of the peasants near Mello and order was soon restored. Among the nobility whose saviour he had become, Charles of Navarre thus cheaply acquired an almost incredible popularity, which he contemplated turning to account without delay.

The more politically minded, but less clever, Étienne Marcel thought he could make use of the peasants against the regent. The burgesses' militia, sent to their help, arrived too late and turned against Meaux, but was unable to carry off the Dauphine. This was the beginning of the collapse. The Dauphin held aloof from the capital, and governed without it and against it; but he still had partisans there, who incited the moderates against Marcel's dictatorship. Faced with these elusive conspirators, Marcel had only one course left open: to appeal to the King of Navarre, whose eloquence was still recruiting partisans, and to the English bands which were operating on his pay. But nothing did him any good: neither the entrance of Anglo-Navarrese troops into Paris on July 22nd, nor his offer of the post of captain of the city to Charles the Bad. After a week of confused discussions and secret movements, on the 31st Étienne Marcel was struck down in the street on his way back from an inspection of the ramparts. Charles of Navarre resumed the campaign. The Dauphin returned to Paris, cheered by the very people who had driven him out. There was no need for prolonged reprisals or many executions. The Parisian revolution was over. The monarchy, though materially exhausted, emerged from it morally enhanced.

Now there was time to think about the king. In Bordeaux, where the Black Prince had made much of his distinguished prisoner, and then in London, where he arrived on May 24th 1357 and where the sumptuous manor of Savoy, on the road which led from the City to Westminster, was placed at his disposal, John the Good was tasting with pleasure the bitter wine of defeat. He had no reason to feel ashamed. He was a brave soldier and he had fought well. If, in spite of that, he had been beaten, it was because 'the events of battles are doubtful'. A defeat in due form did not humiliate a true soldier. Edward III gave him a good reception, and even felt attracted towards this empty-headed man, punctilious about honour, faithful to the chivalrous ritual which Edward himself so much respected.

In the midst of festivities, John thought about his subjects; but it was in order that they should think about him. A fairly large number of letters from the prisoner have been preserved, and one could make a fine selection from them, at once pathetic and puerile. On the field of Poitiers, the French had lost their father. It was for this that he pitied them most, not for their wretchedness or the threats that hung over them. Only one thing mattered: his prompt deliverance, for which all of them must work. He counted upon their utmost generosity when it came to paying his ransom. As for the political conditions which the enemy might impose, such as territorial amputations or surrenders of sovereignty, they must not be rejected straight away; they were 'some other things which are very much lighter to do' than to suffer prolonged captivity. The worthy sovereign looked like being no very clever negotiator when the time came; he would be likely to sell the interests of the crown cheaply to recover this freedom.

Yet at the outset everything seemed to go well. A two years' truce had been concluded at Bordeaux, again under the aegis of the Holy See. In September 1357 Edward's councillors, those of John, three cardinals sent by the Pope, and representatives of the Dauphin met in London. As it was a matter not only of freeing John, but also of making a 'good and lasting peace', a high price for Edward's renunciation of the throne of France seemed likely. Contrary to all expectation, the English demands were less than at Guines. In January 1358 a draft treaty (known as the first Treaty of London) fixed the royal ransom at four million gold *écus*, and demanded the cession of Guienne in full sovereignty, together with Saintonge, Poitou, Limousin, Quercy, Rouerge, and Bigorre, which, with the addition of Ponthieu and Calais, made up a good third of the kingdom. In view of the circumstances, the Dauphin himself found the terms acceptable. He had feared worse.

He was quite right. Edward III soon repented of his comparative generosity. As he wanted to obtain some personal advantages from the Pope, with whom he was in dispute over the harsh treatment of the Bishop of Ely by the king's judges, and knew that the Pontiff desired peace, he deliberately delayed ratification of the treaty. Meanwhile the Parisian revolution, the peasant rising, and the war which the King of Navarre had been waging against the Dauphin from August onwards in Normandy and almost to the gates of Paris aroused Edward's covetousness anew. He could exact more from an enemy who was brought to bay. The commissioners whom John the Good had sent into the provinces to raise a first instalment of his ransom had returned empty-handed. Only Languedoc, less ravaged by the war, had provided some money. Edward made a good pretence of being enraged. Since he had not been paid, he would break the treaty.

Six months earlier, at the time of the jousts on St. George's day, he had embraced John in sign of peace. Now he kept him under close watch and threatened to send him to a castle for safer keeping. The Dauphin remained entangled in the Navarrese war and was unable to pursue negotiations. The papal legates, believing peace to be made, had not returned to London. A *tête-à-tête* between the victor and the vanquished, who was very anxious about the fresh severity with which he was threatened and frightened of a harsher captivity, turned to the Plantagenet's advantage. Edward prided himself on the fact that 'great treaties and fine proposals' were 'offered him from day to day by the French'. So, on March 24th 1359, came the second Treaty of London, much more severe than the first. It settled the payment of John's ransom, still fixed at four million *écus*, by close instalments, guaranteed by the taking of hostages of royal blood or men of distinction. Freed or not, John would remain technically a prisoner until complete fulfilment of the treaty. The territorial cessions were made worse. To them was now added the territory between the Loire and the Channel, Touraine, Anjou, Maine, and Normandy, plus the coastal regions between the Somme and Calais, plus again the homage of Brittany. The western half of the kingdom of France was taken off, with the whole of its coast, along a line running from Calais to the Pyrenees. Never, even in the days of the weak Louis VII, had the Plantagenets known such continental power. All this of course – an essential concession in Edward III's eyes – came to him in full sovereignty, without any obligation of vassaldom.

The King of England soon found that he had been too greedy. It so happened that the Navarrese war turned to the Dauphin's advantage. Charles the Bad, feeling himself abandoned, made his peace at Pontoise, thus relieving the capital of grave concern. Could France now dream of accepting John the Good's surrenders? A meeting of the Estates, this time amenable to the Dauphin's suggestions, declared that the treaty was 'neither tolerable nor practical'. Another meeting voted some taxes with a view to the renewal of hostilities. So matters had now reached this point: Edward III was constrained to go in person and bring France to reason, although the sovereign of this battered country was already his prisoner. But, in order to beat the enemy, it was necessary that he should give battle. Charles, however, knew his weakness. Taught by experience, and influenced by his unwarlike nature, he went on a war-strike. It was clever tactics, which were later attributed to Duguesclin's contrivance; but they were in fact those of the Dauphin. In default of a pitched battle, a raid by a few thousand men could only pillage the country, not conquer it, still less occupy it. In the long run, its strength would exhaust itself, when it had nothing left to devastate. The 'poor people' would suffer from its ravages, but the monarchy would not risk its meagre forces, which it could not vainly sacrifice.

So, at the end of October 1359, Edward and his sons landed at Calais without opposition. They slowly ravaged Artois, Thiérache, and Champagne. They failed to capture Rheims, whose stout walls excluded the possibility of scaling. They turned away from Burgundy, whose duke escaped the scourge by buying the troopers' retreat at a high price. They lit camp-fires for a fortnight in the Parisian countryside. Finally they ravaged the region of Beauce. Meanwhile the Norman sailors made an appearance with all impunity off Winchelsea, provoking panic among the English, who feared a landing, which since 1340 they had thought impossible. At length the weather took a hand in the game. A sudden tornado disorganized the invaders in the region of Chartres. It was time to wind up this lamentable escapade. On May 8th 1360, after scarcely a week of discussion, the Dauphin and the Prince of Wales agreed on peace preliminaries in the little village of Brétigny in Beauce. Immediately afterwards, the King of England left France, where he was never to be seen again at the head of an army.

The failure for the Plantagenet was obvious. His great raid brought him back behind the first Treaty of London, which he had scorned eighteen months earlier. What he accepted now was a treaty serious enough for France, but still less grave than the surrenders to which she had previously agreed. Territorially it reverted to the conditions defined in London in 1358: the formation of a great sovereign Aquitaine, extending from the lower Loire to the Central Plateau and the Pyrenees; and the cession of bridgeheads in the north, with Ponthieu, Calais, and the county of Guines. But the financial clauses were lightened. John's ransom was reduced to three million *écus* (£500,000) instead of four. A first instalment of 600,000 *écus*, the heaviest, would free the King of France, who would await its payment in Calais. The ceded territories – except La Rochelle, which would pass into English hands at once – would be handed over to Edward in the year following John's liberation. Six annual payments of 400,000 *écus* would then extinguish the Valois' debt and progressively free the hostages: princes of the blood, great feudatories, barons, burgesses from eighteen towns, who would meanwhile reside in London at their own expense. Provision was also made for definitive ratification of the treaty at Calais, on payment of the first instalment of the royal prisoner's ransom and before his setting at liberty.

Since there was no hoping for better terms, the Dauphin, this time in agreement with his father, made desperate efforts to satisfy the English demands. The king must be freed: after that, one would see. John arrived in Calais on July 8th. Meanwhile every town and every province were taxed to the limit of their capacity, and begged to pay their contributions 'nimbly'. Once again, northern France, hard hit by the recent devastations, could not give much; but Languedoc contributed freely. About the middle of October 400,000 *écus*, two-thirds of the sum demanded, had been gathered together in the abbey of Saint-Bertin near Saint-Omer. A good sportsman if it cost him little, Edward declared himself satisfied with this sum. Gradually, one by one, the King of England, his sons, the Dauphin, and the princes' councillors reached Calais. There was further negotiation and then, on October 24th, the Brétigny preliminaries, with slight modifications, were solemnly ratified. It was more than an agreement between Plantagenet and Valois: it was believed to be a general peace. Edward III made his peace with the Count of Flanders. John was once more reconciled with Charles of Navarre. The two kings, now linked by pacts of friendship and perpetual alliance, promised to work together for the appeasement of the quarrel over Brittany. With the West pacified, the papacy could once more set on foot its visionary plan for a crusade.

On one important point alone, the Treaty of Calais differed from the Brétigny preliminaries. In the original text, the two kings immediately renounced their claims which, though reciprocal, were of unequal value: Edward his claim to the title of King of France, a vain bauble, since he had never been able to secure its recognition; John his claim to sovereignty over the ceded territories, which meant the amputation of his kingdom by one-third and the closing of all the south-west of France to his judges, his tax-collectors, and his armies. At Calais, on the contrary, the 'renunciations' were the subject of a special agreement. Their exchange was put off until later, after the transfer of territory. It was provided for by November 30th 1361 at the latest. In appearance, this modification was small. In fact, it was to have incalculable consequences. Here some historians have fancied they could see the hand of the Dauphin and his councillors, who, with the consummate cleverness of which they had already given proof during the previous years, foresaw the future, felt that the date would be deferred, and therefore reserved the crown's sovereign rights over the provinces provisionally lost. The thing seems hard to believe. Could anyone foresee the slowness, the stratagems, the delays of an enemy never satisfied? The Dauphin's mentality was not such as to possess this foreknowledge of the future. Nevertheless events were to prove that he might have foreseen it.

I shall not follow the king on his path of freedom across his recovered – or rather partly recovered – kingdom. The story of his steps would serve only to let us penetrate further into the mind of a prince who, having only three more years to live, achieved none of his visionary plans. Once again, misfortune failed to humble him. He might at least have known that, after four years of absence, he would find France bruised, diminished, mutilated. He might have tried to dress her wounds, to restore internal order, to rebuild her strength by a wise economy. But to believe him capable of such patient calculation would be to mistake the man. Without lifting a hand, he witnessed the excesses of the *routiers* as they pillaged his richest provinces. The peace so dearly bought, at the cost of so much bloodshed, so much suffering, meant to him merely an unexpected opportunity of achieving at last his father's ambition and his own: the crusade. As soon as he could, he hastened to Avignon. To be sure, the roads of his kingdom were not safe, and he had to take a roundabout route by way of Burgundy, Bresse, and Dauphiné through Empire territory. But the saintly Pope Urban V found in him a more valuable, more zealous collaborator than Philip VI had ever been for Benedict XII. The man vanquished at Poitiers already imagined himself captain-general of the crusade, at the head of a European army, marching to meet the Ottoman menace.

This plan went the way of many others. Hard facts took care to put it on the shelf of dreams. More pressing tasks kept John in his kingdom, of which not the least was the execution of the terms of the Treaty of Calais; to which we must return.

The territorial clauses were by far the easiest to apply, even though with considerable delay. The King of France's councillors did not want to complete the surrender until the King of England, by way of return, had cleared the French provinces of the *routiers* who pillaged them in his name. The Plantagenet stated that he had stopped these troopers' pay; if they went on pillaging on their own account, that was none of his business. So John gave way once more. But the English commissioners, entrusted with the formalities of annexation, did not arrive until August 1361. In every region ceded they assumed the powers of the Valois's officials and received the homage of his vassals and the oath of the towns.

There was opposition here and there, about which we do not know much. Perhaps the populations would not have shrunk from changing masters, if the king had remained their supreme suzerain. Their loyalty to the crown made them grieve over being henceforth completely separated from the kingdom of France. But the expression of these feelings was sporadic and discreet. Perhaps indeed in some cases it was the result of calculation. When a town delayed its submission, it was in order to obtain confirmation and extension of its privileges. When a vassal refused to pay homage except to the King of England in person, it was in order to create a precedent from which his autonomy would profit. It was to be the same until 1789, in other words until budding patriotism swept away the selfish vanity of local privileges. By the spring of 1362 the painful operation was approaching its end. To complete this great transfer of territory only a few districts remained in dispute, such as Belleville in Poitou and Montreuil in Ponthieu. Edward III was in a position to set up his new continental possessions as a vast principality of Aquitaine, and the victor of Poitiers, the Black Prince, was appointed to control its destiny.

The payment of John's ransom was subject to longer delay. This was because it was not easy to raise such a sum from a continually impoverished country, which had recently lost a third of its territory. This time, as it was a question of freeing the captive king, a case provided for by feudal custom, there was no need to consult the Estates. A royal ordinance of December 6th 1360 brought into force for six years – the first example of taxation both general and continuous – a triple tax on merchandise, salt, and wine. These consumer taxes were difficult to levy, unpopular and, into the bargain, strictly dependent upon economic prosperity, while this was a period of depression. Still, they yielded a considerable sum. The local struggle against the *routiers*, court festivities, and preparations for the crusade absorbed most of it. With what was left the government was not even able, in three years, to make up the first million of the ransom.

Being in possession of the ceded territories, and having in his pocket nearly a third of the sum demanded, the King of England should have hastened the exchange of the renunciations, which would have set the seal of finality upon the cessions carried out. But the renunciations were not exchanged, either in November 1361 or later. It would be wrong to see in this a fresh proof of the cleverness of the Dauphin, who, now that his regency was over, had nothing to do with the kingdom's government, or of the heedlessness of John, who, on the contrary, was anxious to apply the treaty faithfully and fully in order to vindicate his honour. It was in fact the doing of Edward, fertile in fresh diplomatic schemes, always on the lookout for further advantages. He had stopped calling himself King of France, and he knew that John deemed himself to have no further right of sovereignty over Aquitaine. Surer material gains occupied his attention: he could leave until later a ceremony devoid of immediate meaning.

Meanwhile, since the ransom had not been paid on time, the hostages in London were kicking their heels in prolonged exile. It was an intolerable wait for the princes of the lilies: the king's brother, Philip of Orleans; his two younger sons, Louis of Anjou and John of Berry; his cousin, Pierre of Alençon, and the Dauphin's brother-in-law, Louis II of Bourbon. In order to hasten their freedom, they pledged the King of France's word and concluded the disastrous 'Treaty of the Hostages' with their jailer (November 1362). In it they were generous with other people's property. They promised the immediate payment of 200,000 *écus*, the definitive cession of the contested territories, and the handing-over as a pledge of the chief castles in Berry. In return for this, they were transferred to Calais, where, as prisoners on parole, they were to await the royal ratification, only after which would the exchange of ratifications again be considered. John would have asked nothing better than to agree to these fresh surrenders. It meant paying a little more for peace; but it would free his relations and hasten his departure for the crusade. But Edward had stipulated for the approval of the Three Estates. At their meeting, held belatedly at Amiens in October 1363, they proved stubborn. Once again, the Dauphin and his councillors defended the crown's real interests better than the king. They were the heart and soul of resistance to the treaty and secured its rejection.

It was the first hitch in the peace, the first cloud passing over the eternal friendship which the two sovereigns had sworn at Calais. Where a diplomat would have seen only political necessity, John deemed himself dishonoured, suspect of perfidy by an adversary who indeed was in no position to reproach him on this score. A personal incident strengthened this painful feeling of John's. His second son, Louis of Anjou, who was kicking his heels in Calais, had obtained permission to go and make his devotions at the sanctuary of Our Lady at Boulogne. There he met his young wife, Mary of Blois or Brittany, whom he had not seen for thirty months and with whom he was very much in love. The princely couple decamped and did not reappear in Calais. As a result, Edward III was in a position to say to Louis: 'You have much dimmed the honour of your lineage.' The laws of honour were exacting. In politics, only too often, they covered the worst surrenders.

Chivalrous to the last, John remained faithful to his code. Early in 1364, he returned to London to give himself up as a prisoner. His person would answer for the unpaid ransom and the escape of a distinguished hostage. He did not on this account abandon his plan for a crusade. As Edward had a liking for him, he undertook to negotiate a fresh 'final agreement' to replace the Treaty of the Hostages. It had just been concluded when John fell ill. He died, still young – he was only forty-five – on April 8th. His former jailer held a sumptuous funeral service for him in St. Paul's cathedral. Then, by way of Dover and Calais, his body was taken with great pomp to Paris and Saint-Denis.

Part IV
CHARLES V
1364-1380

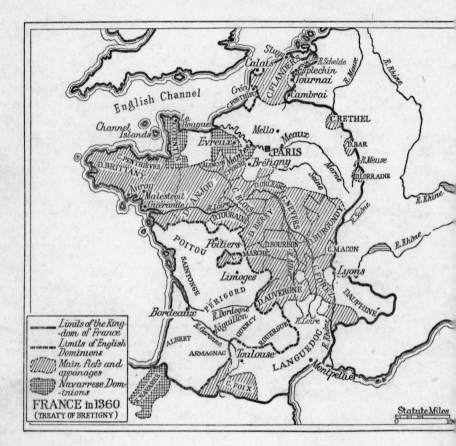

English Channel

Sluys
Calais
C.FLANDERS
Esplechin
Tournai
Cambrai
R.Schelde
C.RETHEL
R.Meuse
R.Rhine
Crécy
C.PONTHIEU
Channel Islands
La Hougue
C.PENTHIÈVRE
D.BRITTANY
COTENTIN
Evreux
ALENÇON
Mantes
D.PERCHE
Mello
Meaux
PARIS
Bréligny
D.BAR
D.LORRAINE
R.Meuse
Marne
Seine
R.Saône
R.Rhine
Auray
Malestroit
Guérande
ANJOU
R.Loire
D.TOURAINE
D.BLOIS
D.ORLEANS
D.BERRY
C.NEVERS
D.BURGUNDY?
R.Saône
R.Rhône
POITOU
SAINTONGE
Poitiers
MARCHE
D.BOURBON
C.MACON
Lyons
C.FOREZ
DAUPHINE
Limoges
PÉRIGORD
D.AUVERGNE
Bordeaux
R.Dordogne
Aiguillon
QUERCY
R.Loire
ALBRET
R.Garonne
ROUERGUE
R.Rhône
ARMAGNAC
Toulouse
LANGUEDOC
Montpellier
NAVARRE
C.FOIX

Limits of the King-
-dom of France
Limits of English
Dominions
Main fiefs and
appanages
Navarrese Dom-
-inions

FRANCE in 1360
(TREATY OF BRETIGNY)

Statute Miles
0   10

Part IV

CHARLES V
(1364–1380)

THE sixteen years which followed John the Good's death were a period of revival for France, unexpected and incomplete to be sure, but rapid. In England, however, it was not possible to stop a decline that gradually lowered her from the pedestal to which Edward III's genius had raised her. One personality dominated the two countries; the French King, Charles V.

1. THE KING AND HIS ENTOURAGE

CHARLES V has benefited from the popularity which, in times of misfortune, clings to the memory of a leader, who dies prematurely in what seems to be a vanished golden age. It was after his death, in the unhappy phase of anarchy into which his son's madness plunged the country, that this wise king was most appreciated. Then, among other incense-bearers, he was fortunate to find a kind Italian woman, the daughter of one of his physicians, Christine of Pisa or Pisan, whose laudatory pen helped not a little to surround the memory of his restoring reign with a halo of legend. Modern historians have had difficulty in freeing themselves fully from her touching anecdotes, her forced admiration, her dutiful praise, in order to disclose the real man behind the official compliments.

Physically, his excellent statue from the church of the Celestines, now an adornment of the Louvre, brings him fully to life again for us. He was of frail constitution, with a slender, sickly body, very different from those athletic giants, the first Valois, or those fine figures of men, the last Capetians. He had a long, narrow nose, an emaciated face, a heavy head slightly hunched over bony shoulders. A mysterious disease, contracted when he was still a youth, often kept him in bed and carried him away as soon as he reached his forties. These physical failings made him a man of the study rather than a man of action. A child at the time of Crécy, a youth at Poitiers, he retained from the profession of arms the memory of a long series of reverses. His tastes, even more than his health, kept him far from the battlefield. He was the first of the sovereigns of France – and the only one before Louis XVI – who dispensed with commanding his armies, even nominally. Professional leaders did so in his place. Not that he was a coward – no one dared to reproach him with his flight at Poitiers during the last hours of the battle – but the life of camps was not for him.

From his Valois predecessors, on the other hand, he had inherited a taste for luxury, fine dwellings, court festivities, the indispensable tokens of the royal majesty. While the country groaned beneath ruin and taxation, while he himself preached economy to his administration, he reconstructed the Louvre and Vincennes, and built a country house at Beauté-sur-Marne and a town house, the Hôtel Saint-Paul near the Bastille, in the Marais, which in his time became the meeting-place of fashion. Like his brother Berry, he loved collecting fine things, jewels, plate, works of art, tapestries. More than Berry, however, he had a taste for books, which he did not pile up in the tower of the Louvre solely out of regard for costly bindings and rare illuminations. He knew his library from actual perusal of the books and meditating over them. He had the political works of Aristotle and the Latin historians translated into French, and he commissioned Nicholas Oresme to explain the theory of stable currency in simple language.

For no king since Philip the Fair had such a sense of the royal majesty, nor was any king since Saint Louis so conscious of the duties of his office. Scrupulous sometimes to excess, he wanted to convince himself that he was in the right, that his taxes had no object other than the good of the kingdom, that his wars were just, and that justice presided over all he did. During his reign the jurists were supreme: Edward III once contemptuously referred to him as a lawyer. His honesty might appear casuistical, his cleverness cunning, his arguments specious. But in this he renewed the tradition, unfortunately interrupted, of a long line of Capetians always anxious to have right on their side, even at the cost of intellectual gymnastics which sometimes verged on virtuosity. The hard apprenticeship of a twofold regency, first from 1356 to 1360, and then during the early months of 1364, had taught him to distrust men, to circumvent difficulties, to bow to the storm, to dissolve the most dangerous coalitions by dint of patience and tenacity. Charles was indeed the right king for a France weakened and temporarily dismembered: a king who doubted his present, if not his future, and combined with a very high sense of the justice of his cause the employment of petty means, ruses, quibbling, bad faith, in order to escape disaster. Necessity knows no law, so the politicians say.

Historians still repeat that Charles, distrusting his brothers, systematically thrust them aside from power. Nothing could be further from the truth. A good husband (Joan of Bourbon's early death left him inconsolable), a good father (with what joy did he greet the birth of the future Charles VI!), he was equally a faithful, generous brother, sometimes weak to excess. Louis, Duke of Anjou and Maine, was an ambitious man, greedy for power and money, but by no means devoid of political sense. In 1364, when he became heir presumptive to the throne, he demanded that the king should give him Dauphiné in addition to his appanage. Charles promised him only Touraine, which would come into his possession on the birth of the Dauphin. The king also entrusted him with the lieutenancy of Languedoc, which he kept throughout Charles's reign. It was a choice post, which enabled Anjou not only to bleed the richest province in the kingdom, but also to conduct a personal policy which, as a rule, supported that of the king. Designs on the former kingdom of Majorca; intervention in the affairs of Castille; secret obstruction of the Black Prince's administration in Aquitaine – there was not one of the steps that paved the way for a renewal of the war in which Anjou did not play his part, sometimes outrunning his brother's wishes.

John, the second prince of the lilies, had no such high ambitions. Already Count of Poitiers and Mâcon, he was given, after Brétigny, Berry and Auvergne with the title of duke. From his long stay as a hostage he had maintained contacts in England, which the king turned to account in delicate negotiations. With Anjou, he was to take part in the reconquest of Poitou, which went to swell his appanage still more. Finally Philip, his father's favourite, was still in 1363 only Duke of Touraine. John the Good had entrusted him with the lieutenancy of Burgundy, recently reunited to the royal domain, with a secret promise to give it to him as an appanage. Charles could not have been in more of a hurry to fulfil his father's promise. He heaped privileges, gifts of land, grants of taxes on his younger brother. We shall see how much he soon increased his power by securing him the rich inheritance of Flanders. If Charles had distrusted his brothers, would he have shown them such favour?

But, if he conceded them provinces, employed them in his embassies, and entrusted lieutenancies to them, the essential of power escaped them. This was quite natural, and there was nothing very novel about it. It was not in the royal tradition to let the princes of the blood speak as masters in the councils of the crown. The case of Charles of Valois under the last direct Capetians had never had any imitators. Like his predecessors, Charles V trusted more to small fry, squires who owed him everything, devoted clerks and burgesses, sometimes adventurers or upstarts, but more likely than the great to submit to governmental routine and maintain administrative continuity. Some of them had been left to him by his father, and were perhaps not very disinterested souls: for instance, the dubious John de La Grange, Abbot of Fécamp and Treasurer of France before becoming Cardinal of Amiens and aspiring to the papal tiara. Most, although mindful of their own fortunes, were honest officials or conscientious parliamentarians, such as John and William of Dormans, who were successively chancellors, the presiding judge Peter of Orgemont, and the provost of Paris, Hugh Aubriot. I must deal separately with Bureau de La Rivière, a small squire from Nivernais, who was Charles's confidant during his later years, and especially with the military leaders, Duguesclin and John of Vienne.

Even during his lifetime Duguesclin, that impoverished Breton knight, enjoyed a popularity out of all proportion to his talents and his exploits. Ever since, in the memory of mankind, the name of Charles V remains inseparable from that of his Constable, the consecrated paladin of legend. This is not wholly the fault of Cuvelier's crude poem about him, a long rhapsody stuffed with artless anecdotes and incredible fictions: the French retort to the dithyrambs with which the Chandos herald puffed up the glory of the Black Prince and his Gascon captains. Froissart, a sound judge on this subject, and a faithful echo of the feelings of chivalrous society, was nevertheless astonished at the favour shown to Duguesclin, nor did he less complacently marvel at his deeds. In this mediocre captain, incapable of winning a battle or being successful in a siege of any scope, just good enough to put new life into the bands of pillaging *routiers* who recognized their master in him, swollen with self-importance and at the same time punctilious about chivalrous honour, the France of Charles V found a fitting leader for the commonplace tasks which alone remained within her power.

When he entered the king's service, on the eve of Charles's accession, after an impecunious youth rich only in buffets, Duguesclin was no more than a captain of *routiers*, fond of pillage and raids; but he surpassed his fellows by his iron authority and the strict discipline he imposed on his mercenaries. His tomb at Saint-Denis shows us his uncouth appearance, his big head, his square shoulder, his broad, flat nose, his mouth on which only the smile seems human. By force of circumstances, he was a man of petty means, limited effectives, short raids, surprises, skirmishes. He had not even the merit of frankly adopting a temporizing strategy, which in fact was imposed upon him by the king. Whenever he escaped from the royal tutelage and fought on his own account, he invited a pitched battle and got himself defeated, as he did at Auray and Nájera. He was grasping, and gloried in his newly acquired titles: Count of Longueville by the grace of Charles V, Duke of Molina by the favour of the King of Castille. Nevertheless, at the moment of danger, the wise king did not hesitate to silence those who envied him and entrusted him with the Constable's sword, in other words the command of the royal armies. Duguesclin adapted himself wonderfully to the needs of the hour. During the remaining ten years of his life, he became the man who, with slender resources, wiped out the shame of the Treaty of Calais. His glory eclipsed that of all other captains, all the king's other associates. Beside him, what did John of Vienne count, that landsman who, about the same time, was entrusted with the post of admiral and, though he never went to sea, created a royal fleet out of nothing?

2. THE REVIVAL OF FRANCE

AN ENGLISH spy, entrusted with picking up information for the Prince of Wales about Charles V's intentions in the spring of 1364, wrote to his government:

> The policy of the new king is to give fair replies in words to the English until such time as he has recovered the hostages who are in England, or at least the most important; and meanwhile he will make war on the king of Navarre and continue that of Brittany; and, under cover of the said wars, he will go on assembling men-at-arms; and, as soon as he has recovered the said hostages, he will make war in all parts on the English and on the principality [of Aquitaine] . . . and he will recover what he has lost from the English and finally will destroy them.

The Dauphin's past policy justified this vision of the future, which, perhaps not so much in intention as in fact, came true point by point. That the English should distrust Charles went without saying. The man who had resisted the hateful Treaty of London, stood up to the great raid of 1359, hastened his father's liberation and secured the rejection of the Treaty of the Hostages, could not indefinitely accept the surrenders at Calais. But to say that from his accession he prepared for a breach and assembled forces with a view to an early renewal of the war is to accuse him of a degree of duplicity, or flatter him with a degree of foresight, which he did not possess. Too many problems endangered the very life of the kingdom for him to think, in addition, of reopening the Anglo-French conflict. Moreover, to get out of his difficulties it did not suffice for him to lull his suspicious adversary with fair words. Charles had to convince Edward of his good faith, gain his confidence and, to this end, meet all the obligations of the treaty with the utmost possible zeal. Such, as we shall see, was his attitude towards England for nearly four years. Let us never forget the constant presence of Edward the conqueror, touchy, meddlesome, ready to intervene the moment he suspected any false play. This fact merely makes the results achieved by the wise King Charles seem all the more remarkable.

After keeping quiet since 1359, the King of Navarre rebelled again in March 1364. Once more he did not lack good reasons for taking up arms against the Valois. This time it was the succession in Burgundy which was in question. On the early death of the last duke, the sickly Philip of Rouvre (1361), the duchy had to devolve on the descendants of his great-aunts. There were two: Charles the Bad, grandson of the elder, Margaret, and John the Good, son of the younger, Joan. As in Brittany, was successional representation admissible in Burgundian custom? If so – and this seemed to be the case – the King of Navarre was the heir. But here again the King of France, as supreme lord, found himself both judge and party. After a pretence of inquiry, he proclaimed himself heir and annexed Burgundy to the royal domain. When he proceeded to promise it to his younger son Philip, Charles of Navarre could restrain himself no longer. After John had set off for England, he began war against the Dauphin. The grave danger of this rebellion was that, with a few bands of mercenaries, Charles the Bad might starve Paris. His Norman possessions made him master of Meulan and Mantes on the lower Seine. He could easily threaten Pontoise and Creil on the Oise. His aunt Joan, widow of the last Capetian for the past forty years, and his sister Blanche, widow of Philip VI, gave him access to Melun, which they held as their dower. All the rivers except the Marne were in his hands.

A stroke of luck enabled the danger to be averted. Duguesclin, entrusted with the defence by the Dauphin, presented him, by way of a gift to celebrate his accession, with the most brilliant victory of his career. On May 16th 1364, at Cocherel, near Mantes, the Gascon contingents of the Captal of Buch, John of Grailly, in the King of Navarre's service, got themselves cut to pieces. As the Plantagenet, duly circumvented by the new King of France, did not support Charles the Bad, Duguesclin was able to conquer Cotentin and seize Valognes, though he failed to take Évreux. The King of Navarre soon preferred to lay down his arms. The treaty which he concluded in March 1365 removed for ever the threat he had held over Paris. He was deprived of the fortresses on the lower Seine. Henceforth the charming chapel of Navarre in the collegiate church at Mantes alone served as a reminder of his fleeting domination. In exchange, he received the barony of Montpellier, in other words the co-lordship of a distant town, where the Duke of Anjou's officials reduced this illusory compensation to very little. After this the King of Navarre fell back to the rank of an obscure conspirator. The King of France had nothing more to fear from him.

The Breton affair did not turn so completely to the advantage of the Valois. It will be recalled that in the Treaty of Calais Edward and John, now reconciled, promised to consult about the pacification of the duchy. But each of them adhered to his own candidate: Edward to his ward John IV, brought up at the court of London, nurtured in hatred of the Valois, taught deceit and bad faith by his exile; John to Charles of Blois, who would willingly have abandoned the struggle if his imperious wife had not kept him uncompromising. Conferences under the aegis of the two kings, at Calais, at Saint-Omer and then in London, tried in vain to restore peace in Brittany. John IV of Montfort, emancipated by his guardian, returned to his duchy in the summer of 1362. At once the war flared up again, with its sad succession of destructive raids, attacks, surprises, and sieges. For long it remained undecided, until the day came when the two adversaries resolved upon a pitched battle. At Auray, on September 29th 1364, Charles of Blois suffered a crushing defeat. The saintly man – the Church was to raise him to the rank of blessed – died as a brave knight. Duguesclin, who had hastened to the defence of his 'natural lord', was among the prisoners. The cause of Joan of Penthièvre, and through her that of the Valois, was lost.

Nevertheless, relying on the apparently correct attitude of the new King of France, Edward, faithful to the terms of the Treaty of Calais, did not seek to derive profit from a favourable situation. This enabled Charles to save his face. The Treaty of Guérande, concluded in April 1365, gave Joan of Penthièvre, whose cause no champion could now defend, some compensation for her renunciation of the duchy: the county of Penthièvre in Brittany and a life-interest in the viscounty of Limoges. John IV remained sole Duke of Brittany, but Charles V received his homage. So the great duchy returned to the sphere of influence of the kingdom of France, from which the Montforts' treachery had removed it. Full of his success, the new duke thought little of his subordination to the hated Valois. In fact, he was not slow in betraying him too; but, for the time being, Brittany was freed from the English mercenaries who had occupied it for the past twenty years. This was the most that could be hoped for after the disaster of Auray.

With Navarre crushed and Brittany temporarily neutralized, all the 'gates' through which the Plantagenet could penetrate into the diminished kingdom of France were closed one by one. Edward III's neutrality had permitted these easy successes. In Flanders it was going to take all Charles V's cleverness to set himself victoriously against English diplomacy, without at the same time inclining it towards war. The settlement of the Flemish succession, with which future historians reproached the wise king, in which they saw nothing but blind imprudence, was in fact, if we place ourselves in the midst of events, the most striking diplomatic victory of his reign. At Calais, in the general peace which embraced the whole of the West, Edward had become reconciled with Louis of Nevers's son and abandoned Artevelde's last partisans to the count's revenge. This reconciliation soon turned into a friendship which was disturbing to the Valois. For, when Louis of Nevers died on the battlefield of Crécy and his son Louis of Male succeeded him, this meant a change in the policy of Flanders.

Louis of Nevers, like all his predecessors since the beginning of the century, had been a faithful vassal of the crown of France. To fulfil his feudal duties, he had estranged the richest of his subjects, the great industrial towns of maritime Flanders, and ruined himself in frightful civil wars. His son Louis of Male, who, during the darkest days of the rebellion, had been held as a hostage by the burgesses of Bruges, wanted no such humiliation again. He aimed at restoring the prestige of his power as count; but he knew that, without the financial support of the cloth-

They were men of war before all else, and the Treaty of Calais had deprived them of their living. In that treaty Edward III promised to make those of them whom he had hitherto paid evacuate the provinces which remained French. But he had no means of influencing them, once he had stopped their pay. His orders were inoperative and could not be enforced short of compulsion; and as the Black Prince, mindful of good order, resolutely closed the frontiers of English Aquitaine to the *routiers*, they flowed back over John the Good's kingdom, where nothing was ready to repel them.

They did not spread equally over all its territory, but had designs for choice on those provinces which, not having suffered too much as yet, would more readily lend themselves to pillage: Burgundy, the Central Plateau, Languedoc. For that matter, they had no concerted plan. Every company – a few hundred men at the most – operated on its own account. It sufficed for them to take two or three castles by surprise in order to terrorize a district, hold its inhabitants to ransom, requisition victuals, cut roads, and sell safe-conducts at extortionate prices, which were valid, as the case might be, for an individual or a whole village. Only at times did they gather together for some large-scale operation, as in the case of the 'Great Company', formed towards the end of 1361, which descended the valleys of the Saône and the Rhône, seized Pont-Saint-Esprit and held the Pope to ransom, or the '*Tard-Venus*' or 'Latecomers' – their picturesque name indicates that they were operating on ground already trampled upon by others – who, in the following years, threatened Lyons.

Neither John the Good nor Charles V could make the great financial effort necessary for the extermination of these elusive bands. The excommunications with which the Pope overwhelmed them, the ban laid on the faithful against having any dealing with them, were weapons even more inoperative. The weight of defence rested on the local populations. By bailiwicks and by great fiefs they were asked for grants. But the local Estates shrank from a long and hazardous war. It was less costly to pay the *routiers* to retreat, which merely meant shifting the problem elsewhere. Whenever it was decided to make a greater effort, the results were disastrous. This was what happened in 1363, when a strong army of knights, summoned by the Duke of Bourbon, was crushed by Seguin of Badefol at Brignais near Lyons.

The evil got worse and worse. The end of the Breton war and the Navarrese war, in the early months of Charles V's reign, set fresh bands flowing over the exhausted kingdom. The most dangerous lairs were in the central mountains: a line of fortresses stretching from the borders of Périgord to those of Dauphiné, across Auvergne, Velay, Forez, and Lyonnais, which cut off the southern seneschalships from the rest of the country. There was no getting rid of these brigands except by leading them to fight and pillage elsewhere. No one could succeed in this manœuvre better than Duguesclin, who shared their tastes and knew how to flatter their ambitions. Charles V encouraged him to try. His first attempt failed. This was a proposal to march these excommunicated miscreants right across Europe to the borders of Hungary, in order to stop the progress of the Ottoman Turks who had lately invaded Europe. The operation would be called a crusade, and the *routiers* would win Paradise from it. The offer struck them as risky, and the goal as too distant. It was then that a nearer theatre presented itself for their exploits: Spain.

Immersed as they were in internal strife, the Iberian kingdoms still remained outside the great Anglo-French conflict. For the past fifteen years King Pedro, rightly nicknamed the Cruel, had reigned in Castille. He was, indeed, intelligent, brave, and self-assertive, but so brutal that he estranged most of his subjects. Not content with taking a dislike for his wife, Blanche of Bourbon, Charles V's sister-in-law, shutting her up and then having her killed in prison, his suspicious jealousy made him persecute his father's bastard sons. One of them, Henry of Trastamare, had fled from Spain and taken refuge in Languedoc, where Louis of Anjou, more eager than his brother, had contemplated from the end of 1364 an early renewal of the war against the principality of Aquitaine. The exiled prince was given lands and money, employed in military tasks, and became a faithful instrument of the Valois.

About the middle of the year 1365 grandiose plans were built up and given shape. Pedro the Cruel had come into conflict with Pedro the Ceremonious, his neighbour in Aragon. It was an old quarrel about the possession of some frontier provinces, which envenomed the rivalry of these two equally treacherous kings. The King of Aragon sought allies and approached Louis of Anjou. Henry of Trastamare was brought into the plot, laid claim to the throne of Castille and promised the King of Aragon to cede him the contested provinces as the price of his military aid. Charles V, who had followed this manœuvre rather at a distance, saw in it only the long-sought opportunity to get rid of the free companies. At the invitation both of Pedro of Aragon and Henry of Trastamare, Duguesclin led the most dangerous of the *routiers* across the Pyrenees. Among the leaders of bands whom he took with him were some Gascons, but also formidable Englishmen, such as Hugh of Calverley and Matthew of Gournay. The campaign proved easy. Abandoned by everyone, Pedro the Cruel fled. Henry of Trastamare, at the head of his *routiers*, had himself crowned king. Thus Charles V gained a grateful ally across the Pyrenees, and at the same time rid his kingdom of most of the troopers who were pillaging it.

The English counterstroke was not long delayed. Henry of Trastamare had to struggle with the difficulties of every pretender who promises too much in his exile and cannot fulfil his undertakings once he is on the throne. The King of Aragon, the *routiers* and other hungry followers pressed him to keep his ill-considered promises. His rival had not lost hope. Since Henry was king by the grace of the Duke of Anjou, it was to the Prince of Aquitaine and Wales that Pedro the Cruel addressed himself in order to regain his throne. He knew that the Black Prince was eager for military glory. At Bayonne, where he had taken refuge, he promised the prince Biscay, a useful complement to Aquitaine, and assumed all the expenses of the war. Charles the Bad, from his capital in Navarre, intrigued between the two parties, according to his custom, and finally leant towards the side supported by the Plantagenet. The Anglo-Gascon, Navarrese, and Castilian coalition quickly raised a formidable army. At Nájera (called Navarette by the French chroniclers), to the south-west of Pampeluna, on April 3rd 1367, the victor of Poitiers won a fresh victory, as complete as the first. With Don Henry in flight and Duguesclin a prisoner, nothing was left of the scheme devised by Charles V, except perhaps the destruction of the *routiers*, many of whose bodies strewed the battlefield.

The Castilian comedy, however, was not finished. Its end is of less interest to us. It will suffice to recall that Pedro the Cruel, for the time being back on his throne, again heard rebellion growl around him; that Duguesclin, freed thanks to the King of France – he had boasted, in a shameless piece of bragging, that every peasant woman in the kingdom would contribute towards his ransom, which he himself had fixed at a very high figure in order to increase his own importance – returned to the service of Henry of Trastamare; and that finally, two years after Nájera, the two enemy brothers met face to face at Montiel and Henry treacherously killed Pedro with his own hands. At this moment, the war had broken out again in France, and Duguesclin, who now thought himself to be at the height of his power and comfortably settled in Castille, was recalled by Charles V to fight the English.

3. THE RENEWAL OF THE WAR

THE SETTLEMENT of the Navarrese, Breton, and Flemish affairs and the struggle against the *routiers*, together with the need to restore his ruined finances and reorganize the defence of his diminished kingdom, were so many good reasons why Charles V should remain on good terms with the victorious Plantagenet and show himself scrupulously devoted to peace, whatever sacrifices this might mean. Agreement over the disputed territories, payment of the arrears of the ransom, progressive freeing of the hostages: these were the questions to which the wise king tried to find satisfactory answers between 1364 and 1368. Legally his position remained unshakeable; he adhered solely to the terms of the Treaty of Calais. The Treaty of the Hostages, rejected by the Estates at Amiens, and the agreement which John the Good had substituted for it on the eve of his death – its clauses remain unknown to us – did not bind the new king. But in the execution of the peace of Calais he showed a zeal, real or feigned, which inspired confidence in Edward III, who was in less of a hurry than his adversary, it seemed, to settle the outstanding questions as soon as possible. Negotiations undertaken during the last months of 1364 did not come to a rapid conclusion. Charles, who was determined not to surrender a shred more than he was bound to do by the treaty, rendered the King of England small services which kept him patient.

At length, in February 1366, an agreement was reached by the Duke of Berry. Charles paid the balance of the first million at once, and promised to discharge the remainder of the ransom by instalments as close together as the sorry state of his finances allowed. In fact, he paid 400,000 *écus* in the course of the year, and in 1367 he made up and indeed surpassed half the total sum promised. In return, the hostages of the blood royal, John of Berry and Peter of Alençon, were definitely set free. Others, like Bourbon, were freed provisionally; but they never returned to captivity. There remained in London as hostages only the small fry of petty barons and burgesses. Individual measures of clemency set some free, and others married and settled permanently in England, for example Enguerrand of Coucy, who became Edward III's son-in-law. It was finally agreed that the frontiers of French and English territory should be delimited by mixed commissions of enquiry working on the spot. Did Montreuil belong to Ponthieu or Picardy? What were the exact dependencies of the lordship of Belleville, connected with Plantagenet Poitou? Charles was in a hurry to make an end of such questions. The delay of the English commissioners and the slowness and contradictions of the inquiry – nothing could have been more complicated than feudal geography – made the discussion inconclusive.

But these were unimportant details, unlikely to disturb the peace. In the early months of 1368 the execution of the treaty of Calais seemed to be a certainty. To be sure, the rivalry between Valois and Plantagenet had come to light elsewhere. But neither Charles V nor Edward III had officially intervened in the affairs of Spain. This fiction of non-intervention maintained friendly relations between them. Such was the situation when an unexpected incident called the very basis of the peace in question by raising once more the still unsettled problem of the renunciations. This was the appeal of the Gascon lords.

The Black Prince's administration in Aquitaine had not satisfied everyone. He had brought with him the harsh requirements which made up the strength of the Plantagenets: a meddlesome administration, a great need for money, a resolve to be obeyed without a murmur by all, whether villagers, vassals, or clergy. The recently annexed provinces, accustomed to the bureaucracy of the Valois, might put up with all this. But the Gascons thought otherwise. They were 'anti-French' only in so far as they disliked the interference of the king's officials and preferred the mild tutelage of a distant Plantagenet. Everything set them against the pretensions of the Prince of Wales: their long-standing habit of autonomy, of which they had never been broken by the weak 'lieutenants' sent out from England; their inveterate taste for anarchy. The independence granted to the Prince of Wales in his appanage had its reverse side: he had to meet the costs of an ambitious policy from his own resources. Already, in 1364, 1365, and 1366, he had had to raise a heavy hearth-tax from his subjects. On the morrow of Nájera the situation got worse. Pedro the Cruel had neither handed over Biscay nor paid a halfpenny of the costs of the campaign. The victorious *routiers* flowed back over Aquitaine. To prevent them from pillaging they had to be paid. Early in 1368 the victor of Nájera, undermined by fever, which was to make him an early invalid, presented himself as a supplicant before the Estates of Aquitaine, assembled at Angoulême. He wrested from them the grant of a hearth-tax of ten *sous* per hearth, valid for five years: a stiff price to pay for the Spanish adventure.

Once again, no one protested in the provinces recently annexed from the King of France. But in the old English Gascony it was quite another matter. Forgetful of the favours heaped upon them since the Treaty of Calais, and alleging that their subjects could not be taxed without their explicit consent, two of the greatest vassals in Guienne, John I of Armagnac and Arnaud Amanieu, Lord of Albret, refused to let the hearth-tax be levied in their domains. In vain did the Prince of Wales retort that, since it had been voted by the Estates of Aquitaine, the tax was payable by all the subjects of the principality, whoever they were. The two lords appealed to the King of England as the suzerain of the princely appanage. Then, without awaiting the inquiry ordered by Edward III, they went to Paris, where at this moment the Lord of Albret was to marry the youngest sister of the Queen of France.

One may imagine Charles V's embarrassment and hesitation in face of the proposal which the wily Gascons made to him. Since the Prince of Wales, by rejecting their protests, had denied them justice, they appealed to the King of France as suzerain of Aquitaine and asked his court to pronounce judgement in their favour. Could he accept this Gascon appeal? Had he even the right to do so? To be sure, through Edward III's fault, the renunciations provided for by the Treaty of Calais had never been exchanged. But no one was misled by that. Edward had ceased to call himself King of France and quarter the leopards with the lilies on his arms. On the other hand, neither John the Good nor Charles V had acted as suzerain in the principality of Aquitaine. There had been no writs served by French sergeants, no summons to the royal hosting, no appeals to the *Parlement*.

If the present appeal was legally receivable, its acceptance would in practice be tantamount to breaking the Treaty of Calais and rekindling the war. Was battered France in a position to do so? Charles wanted to be sure of his rights, and also sure of his strength. He surrounded himself with counsels, asked his lawyers to enlighten him, consulted his barons and persons of standing. From the self-interested advice which he received, he derived the assurance that his cause was just. Since the renunciations had not been exchanged, the 'sovereignty and resort' of Aquitaine reverted to him by right. To reject the appeal would be to do wrong to his duty as king and supreme judge, surrender his subjects to the discretion of a disloyal vassal, and deny his coronation oath. The peace was not at stake. The Plantagenet had only to submit to his suzerain's just sentence, and the rest of the treaty would remain in force. If it was broken, the blame would lie with the King of England.

After two months of hesitation and palaver, Charles crossed the Rubicon. On June 30th 1368, the Count of Armagnac laid his appeal before the *Parlement* in the form required by custom. The king promised the two appellants his help in case of any reprisals by the Prince of Aquitaine. Meanwhile he gave them pensions and presents. But for the moment these agreements remained secret. The Valois could not disclose his game and resume the war until all the trumps were in his hand.

First of all, it was essential to increase the number of appellants and confront the Prince of Aquitaine with a quasi-unanimous rebellion of his subjects. This was left to the Duke of Anjou, eager as ever to renew the struggle against Gascony, with which he wanted to round off his 'lieutenancy'. In June 1368 the Count of Armagnac stood alone. The Lord of Albret did not lay his appeal until September 8th. By next May there were between eight and nine hundred appellants. By dint of distributing money, grants of privileges, promises, and even threats, Anjou had 'worked' Poitou, Périgord, Quercy, Rouerge, and Agenais. He had obtained the adherence of prelates, monasteries, great vassals such as the Count of Périgord, towns such as Agen, Cahors, and Millau. It was an irresistible movement which foreshadowed an easy reconquest.

Meanwhile the remorseless machine of legal procedure was set on the move. As the secret, badly kept, was beginning to be noised abroad, on December 3rd 1368 Charles V issued a great proclamation explaining that, by law, he was entitled to receive the appeals; that, in conscience, he was bound to receive them; and finally that peace could not be endangered except through the Plantagenet's fault. Most of the great vassals approved and gave this statement the desired publicity. Only the Count of Flanders – this was the most delicate moment in the negotiations for his daughter's marriage – replied to the king insolently: 'I suppose you know full well what you have to do. As for me, I shall not publish this letter in my States, as my subjects are untaught and simple people, and its publication would do no good to anyone.'

On December 28th a great council endorsed the king's policy. About mid-January, the seneschal of Toulouse was sent to Bordeaux, bearing a summons to the Prince of Wales to appear before the *Parlement* and publishing letters of safe-conduct to the appellants. We know the prince's proud reply, reported by Froissart: 'We shall readily go to Paris on the day when we are summoned, since it is so ordered by the King of France, but it will be helmet on head, with sixty thousand men in our company.' The prince threw the seneschal of Toulouse into prison. On May 2nd 1369 the appellants appeared in Paris, and the *Parlement* declared the prince contumacious. Then a fresh 'assembly of notables' acclaimed the king. On June 8th Charles announced his intention to make war on the Prince of Wales and his adherents. But he waited until November 30th before pronouncing the confiscation of Aquitaine from the disloyal vassal, thus repeating, thirty-three years later, the action by which Philip VI had started the war.

Until the last moment, Edward III had intervened in order to save both the peace and his conquests. First, in September 1368, his ambassadors in Paris demanded the surrender of the contested territories, the payment of the ransom, and the replacement of hostages who had died in captivity, and begged Charles not to receive the Gascon appeals, about which there was already talk. Charles promised to negotiate; but in January 1369 his envoys in London made complaints and adopted a new tone. If the ransom had not been paid, it was because the King of England had let his mercenaries pillage France. Quite recently, once more, the victors at Nájera, driven from Aquitaine without pay, had flowed back over Auvergne and threatened Burgundy. To finish with the contested territories, Charles offered in exchange to abandon his illusory rights over Rodez and La Roche-sur-Yon. This arrogance made Edward III conciliatory, and he then proposed an agreement. He consented to fresh postponements of the ransom, accepted the territorial exchanges, and even promised that, if the appeal procedure was quashed, he would accept the arbitration of the King of France between the Prince of Aquitaine and his rebellious subjects. Finally, but somewhat late, he proposed the immediate exchange of the renunciations. But Charles, determined on war, did not reply to his rival's offers.

This was because the kingdom of France, despite the dismemberment of its south-western provinces, could contemplate a renewal of hostilities with confidence. Chance, cleverly invoked, had it that Charles possessed more stable resources than his predecessors. It will be recalled that, immediately after his liberation, John the Good had decreed the levy of a salt-tax and indirect taxes on merchandise and wine throughout the kingdom. These taxes were to last as long as the payment of the royal ransom. They looked like becoming permanent, to the great benefit of the monarchy. Moreover in 1363, on the ground of meeting the menace of the *routiers*, the Estates, assembled at Amiens, agreed to a hearth-tax payable quarterly for one year, adding that it should be valid 'in case of necessity (which we hope will not arise) for other years on the same terms'. Charles continued to levy it regularly, except that in 1367 he reduced its rate on the demand of the Estates of Languedoïl. But in 1369 the renewal of the war enabled him to maintain the indirect taxes, the salt-tax and a hearth-tax of six francs a hearth in the towns and two francs in the country. Their levy continued until the end of his reign. Admittedly, it was not assured everywhere. The government had to reduce it in the impoverished provinces, cancel unpaid arrears, agree to the payment by lump sums from the towns, and share the yield with the great vassals, when they could be induced to make the levy in their territory – neither Flanders, Burgundy, nor Brittany contributed.

The taxes remained, in theory, temporary and subject to the consent of the tax-payers. But, except in Languedoc, where the Estates voted and assessed the taxes and expended them locally, Charles V, in fact rather than by law, enjoyed permanent resources. The proof of this is that he completed and stabilized the administrative machinery intended to raise and control these 'extraordinary finances'. In Languedoïl – about two-thirds of the kingdom – he maintained the institution of *élus*, that expedient of the Estates of 1355. But the *élus* were henceforth royal officials, not representatives of the Estates. In every one of the thirty odd fiscal districts or *Elections* into which the royal domain was then divided, they assessed the hearth-tax by parishes, employed collectors to recover the total, presided over the farming out of the indirect taxes, and adjudicated on fiscal cases in the first instance. At the head of the organization, six to twelve 'councillors general in the matter of aids' supervised the basis of the taxes, heard appeals, and audited the accounts of the collector-general, entrusted with centralizing the receipts, and of the war treasurers, who made payments. The collection of the salt-tax became strict. Warehousemen, inspectors, and measurers supervised the bonding of salt in the royal storehouses, where the tax was paid. When smuggling threatened to impoverish the treasury, the purchase of a given quantity of salt by the tax-payers was made compulsory. This was the 'duty-salt', that affliciton of the *ancien régime*.

Imperfect and unpopular though it was, this fiscal machinery enabled the king to maintain an armed force which, while not large, was better disciplined than in the past. In the military sphere, Charles V's numerous ordinances, both before and after 1369, presented few novel features: they simply revived and codified earlier ordinances. Where discipline, ranking, pay, and verification of strength were concerned, there was no innovation. Measures and mechanism were the same as under Philip VI or John the Good. If they proved somewhat less defective in practice, this was because the return to stable currency enabled pay to be fixed at a permanent and more remunerative rate, and because the war treasurers, among them the energetic John le Mercier, made payments more regularly. For the financial year 1370–1 alone they disbursed 300,000 *livres*; and this was only for the pay of the cavalry, since the infantry were paid by the clerk to the master of the cross-bowmen. There was, in short, nothing comparable with the later military reforms of Charles VII.

Let us note, however, some novel experiments, whose utility and aptness were to appear in the course of the coming operations. Interest was taken in the role, hitherto despised, which the infantry could play in combat. In 1367 an inquiry was ordered into the number of archers which every town could provide. Regular training was ordered, and armament was specified. In 1369, to encourage the artisans to practise archery, public sports were forbidden. It was in the sphere of fortifications that Charles V's military achievement was most original. The struggle against the 'free companies' had shown the danger of badly garrisoned or badly maintained castles. In July 1367 an ordinance prescribed an inspection of seigniorial castles. The lords were bound to keep them in repair and provide them with troops and artillery, with the king's financial help. All the castles which were not defensible were to be destroyed and razed to the ground. The measure was imperfectly applied, but sufficiently to enable the English raids to be confronted.

Curiously it was the Plantagenet who had not learned the lesson of 1359, and maintained the tactics which had taken up all the first part of the war. At great expense he prepared an expedition of a few thousand horsemen in his island, transported them to the continent, and there launched them at random on a devastating raid. He was ready to take badly defended towns by surprise, but waged war above all for pillage, not accepting pitched battle unless he found favourable ground on which he could entrench. A decision could not be obtained unless the enemy let himself be brought to an encounter. Charles knew what this had cost his grandfather and his father. He still preferred the pillage of the countryside to military defeat. The tactics he had followed at a difficult moment as regent were those of his war now that he was king. He imposed them, not without difficulty, on his impatient cavalry, and got Duguesclin, at last convinced of their value, to agree to them. Meanwhile the Duke of Anjou's forces, recruited in Languedoc, applied themselves methodically to reducing Aquitaine.

As the victor at Poitiers had his hands full in his principality, it was to other captains that Edward III, now too old to fight – he was nearing sixty – entrusted the fate of his raids. The last months of 1369 witnessed the landing at Calais of the king's third son, John of Lancaster, heir through his wife to a great name and a large fortune. He crossed Artois and Picardy and advanced into Normandy. But he was not in strength, and supplies were scarce with the approach of winter. He fell back on Calais without achieving anything more. The next year there was a fresh invasion. It was led – a novel and almost unique fact – by a mere knight, but a captain of great renown, Robert Knowles. From Calais he marched straight on the Ile-de-France, setting fire to the Parisian countryside. It was then that Charles V, urged by his entourage to accept battle, appointed Duguesclin as Constable, with the duty of harassing the enemy raiders, surprising their isolated detachments and forcing them to retreat. When Knowles, getting uneasy, retired towards Brittany, where the English cause still had disloyal sympathizers, at the end of the autumn his rearguard was overtaken and annihilated at Pontvallain, near Le Mans. The English aristocracy blamed the unfortunate leader of low rank who had been imposed upon them.

After these two checks, the English needed a breathing-space. But in 1373 they mounted a still more imposing raid – more than ten thousand men, it appears – and its leader, the Duke of Lancaster, decided to strike more deeply into the kingdom of France. At first he followed the itinerary which Edward III had chosen: Calais, Artois, Champagne, Morvan. But, instead of deviating towards Paris, when the autumn came Lancaster decided to go and lend a hand to the Gascons in Aquitaine. This meant a march across the Central Plateau which was made arduous by the winter. It was with decimated and exhausted effectives that, at the beginning of January 1374, Lancaster arrived in Bordeaux, without having accomplished anything lasting.

To these fruitless raids were opposed the tactics of the Duke of Anjou, supported at times by Duguesclin. The French reconquest of the provinces lost since 1360 was effected more by diplomacy than force of arms. The forces which the king's lieutenants in the south-west had at their disposal were never crushing. They succeeded because the ground had been cleverly 'worked' ever since the move of the Gascon appeals. Anjou, aided by the Count of Armagnac, had not waited until the breach was complete before starting his campaign. As early as January 1369 his troops occupied Rouergue almost without striking a blow, because the

Count of Armagnac's brother held a large part of it. Then they subjected Quercy and part of Agenais and Périgord, while, in the north, Abbeville and Ponthieu were occupied without resistance. With Duguesclin's arrival and despite Lancaster's presence at Bordeaux beside his sick brother, the campaign of 1370 was still more brilliant. The whole of Agenais, including Agen and Moissac, and almost all Limousin made their submission. Beyond the Garonne, Bazas capitulated. The bloody reprisals undertaken by the Prince of Wales, notably the sack of the city of Limoges, carried out to punish the bishop for treating with the French, did not avert fresh defections.

The main French effort was made in 1372 and 1373, when Anjou and Berry were joined by Duguesclin's contingents, hitherto detained in Brittany. It was aimed at Bigorre, Poitou and Saintonge. La Rochelle, the principal point for English trade, was ready for defence. But when a Castilian fleet, luckily sent by Henry of Trastamare, completely annihilated the English reinforcements who were arriving by sea, La Rochelle surrendered, on September 8th 1372. Poitou, Angoumois, and Saintonge were then cleared of the last enemy garrisons. At the beginning of 1374, when the capitulation of La Réole opened the way to Bordeaux, nothing of his recent annexations was left to the Plantagenet. Even old Guienne was penetrated and reduced, between the Garonne and the Pyrenees, to the four dioceses of Bordeaux, Dax, Aire, and Bayonne, into which the domains of the house of Albret thrust a salient.

4. THE DISAPPOINTING END OF THE REIGN

FIVE YEARS of war had yielded unhoped-for results. The domination of the Plantagenets was not far from having disappeared from the soil of France. Only a moderate effort, it seemed, was needed to complete the task of reconquest. But this effort Charles V could not make. Fortunate as his lieutenants had been, they had exhausted the country. Let us not forget that impoverished France could aspire only to limited successes. England, for that matter, was not in much better case. Nothing could better illustrate how winded were the adversaries than their common eagerness to lay down their arms. In January 1374, without consulting the king, Duguesclin concluded a local truce at Périgueux with the Duke of Lancaster, who had just ended his futile raid. The truce halted the armies where they stood throughout the south-west of the kingdom. The Constable took advantage of his leisure to hasten to Normandy, give chase to the English *routiers*, and lend a hand to Admiral John of Vienne, who was closely blockading the citadel of Saint-Sauveur-le-Vicomte, a lair of English bands. Despite the importance of the siege, in which artillery already played a large part, these operations were mere diversions. The hour of great enterprises was over.

That of negotiations had struck. It was hastened by the action of the last Avignon Pope, Gregory XI, who had ascended the throne of Saint Peter at the end of 1370. Like all his French predecessors, Benedict XII and his uncle Clement VI, Innocent VI, and Urban V, Gregory, a native of Limousin, aspired to Franco-English reconciliation. He desired it all the more because it seemed to him the essential prelude to the great design of his pontificate, the return of the Papacy to Rome. He spared no effort to bring representatives of the two kings together. At the outset he encountered distrust on the part of Edward III, who, outwitted by the Valois' diplomacy, suspected Avignon of complicity in the renewal of the war, and reluctance on the part of Charles V, who was in no hurry to halt his troops on the road to reconquest. Nevertheless the papal legates covered the ground tirelessly, approaching Anjou in Toulouse, the Black Prince in Bordeaux, the sovereigns in London and Paris, and finally establishing themselves in Calais, the better to keep an eye on the two courts.

In March 1372 near Calais, and again in February 1373, at Bruges, they managed to assemble French and English plenipotentiaries for a few weeks, but they did not succeed in finding a basis of understanding. The English, posing as the injured party, demanded either the kingdom of

France as a whole or a return, pure and simple, to the Treaty of Calais. Charles V's envoys, arguing from the sentence of confiscation pronounced by the *Parlement*, refused to discuss a 'just peace' until after the last English possessions, Calais, Bordeaux, and Bayonne, had been handed over to their troops. In the year 1374 the slowness of military operations and the exhaustion of the adversaries made these uncompromising positions untenable. Since the two countries had no strength left to fight, it was better to seek an understanding, difficult as it might seem.

In March 1375 a regular peace conference opened in Bruges, under the presidency of the Archbishop of Ravenna and with Louis of Male, glad to be in a position to impress the French, as mediator. Philip the Bold led the French delegation, and Lancaster the English plenipotentiaries. On June 27th, without too much difficulty, agreement was reached on a general truce, valid for one year, but in fact extended until 1377. Peace properly speaking demanded longer debate. Once the theoretical claims of the two adversaries were set aside, everything, as in the past, turned on Aquitaine. Territorially they came very close to an understanding. Vanquished since 1369, the English knew that they could not hope to reconstitute the great principality for which the Treaty of Calais had set too wide limits. Charles V, in order to obtain a lasting peace, agreed to restore at least part of his recent conquests. So the idea of a partition was reached: either that half the great Aquitaine of 1360 should revert to the King of France and the other half to the King of England; or that it should be divided into three parts, with Charles V keeping half his conquests, giving the remainder as a fief to an English cadet, and leaving Edward the territory which he still controlled. Agreement was also reached about Calais, which the Valois, having conquered Ponthieu, would leave to his adversary; and about the balance of John's ransom, of which only part would be paid.

But once more the corner-stone was lacking: there was no agreeing on the question of sovereignty. Conciliatory over the extent of territorial concessions, the English demanded that, however small the part retained by their master might be, at least it should belong to him in full sovereignty. Not for anything in the world would they revert to vassaldom to the Valois, which had been the primary cause of the war. But Charles, having learned the lesson of the Treaty of Calais and that of the Gascon appeals, was determined to keep 'sovereignty and resort' in all the provinces of his kingdom in which the Plantagenets maintained themselves.

Between these irreducible arguments the papal legates sought a compromise in vain. Their idea of temporary sovereignty – Aquitaine would be left to the English during the lifetimes of the present king and his eldest son, after which it would again become a fief of the crown of France – struck everyone as a joke. Edward III was nearly sixty-five, an age unusual at that time, and the Black Prince was dying. One side must give way if peace was to be possible. In the autumn of 1376, when everything was on the verge of breakdown, the mediators made a last appeal to Charles V. They reminded him of the misery which the war inflicted on his kingdom, pointed out that his obstinacy threatened to provoke a breach, and begged him make some concession, however small, on the question of sovereignty. But the Valois was not to be moved. He could not go back on his word without accusing himself of beginning the war unjustly. His interest and his duty as king forbade him to dismember his kingdom. This was what his lawyers had kept on telling him. This was what he instructed his councillor, John le Fèvre, to say to the legates. This was what a clerk of his household, perhaps the Breton Évrard of Tremaugon, was soon to set forth elegantly, in the fashion of the time, in an allegorical dialogue entitled *Le Songe du Verger*.

Since agreement on the question of sovereignty was impossible, all hope of peace vanished. To be sure, English and French met again, 'in the accustomed places' between Calais and Boulogne, to talk about peace or a long truce. But it was without conviction. In 1377 the war started again, and palavers of ambassadors could not longer stay its course.

The French might look forward to a successful and early conclusion of the reconquest. England was in mourning, a ship without a pilot. She had already lost the Black Prince, the symbol of her past victories, who, sick with fever, had returned home only to die (June 8th 1376). Then it was the turn of the old sovereign who had guided the destiny of his island kingdom for more than fifty years – the longest reign in its history since Henry III's and before Victoria's – and launched it upon its continental conquests. When he died (June 21st 1377), the crown devolved upon a boy of ten, Richard of Bordeaux, the Prince of Wales's only son. The English kingdom's readiness to take the offensive, already much diminished during the past few years, could not fail to be still further affected by this change of sovereigns.

In addition, there was France's successful progress in the naval sphere. Ever since Sluys she had had no fleet or any means of building a new one. In 1373 the lesson of La Rochelle, taken the previous year thanks to the Castilian fleet, went home to Charles V. He did not want to go on being dependent on an ally, however faithful, whose naval forces might not always intervene at the right moment. It was then that he entrusted the position of admiral to John of Vienne, whose powers were defined and extended by royal ordinances. It was at this time, too, that a reorganization of the Clos des Galées at Rouen turned it into a regular naval dockyard, which launched ten ships in 1376 and thirty-five in 1377. In case of urgency the requisitioning of merchant ships was accelerated. From the renewal of the war in 1377 it might be said that the Norman fleet commanded the English Channel: a situation unknown since the disaster at Sluys. Before the end of Charles V's reign, it repeatedly threatened the English in their island and made pillaging raids on their ports of embarkation, among others Winchelsea.

But it was not strong enough to stop English reinforcements reaching Guienne, Brittany, and Calais. On land the French campaign of 1377, begun under excellent auspices, did not achieve the anticipated results. Despite the capture of Bergerac, the troops under Duguesclin and Anjou marked time on the frontiers of Gascony, where they met with unexpected resistance. The following year the government in London sent an energetic lieutenant to Bordeaux, John Neville of Raby, who had no difficulty in restoring the situation. He contained the invaders' inadequate forces, recovered several fortresses from them, organized punitive raids, and even repulsed a raid by the Castilians on Bayonne. The French reconquest was definitely halted, and it was not resumed. Duguesclin devoted himself to humbler tasks. He swept Auvergne, which the *routiers* were still devastating. On July 13th 1380 he died beneath the walls of Châteauneuf-de-Randon, in Gévaudan, where he was besieging a company of pillagers. His death was a great grief to the king whom he had served so well. Once he was dead, there was no one to put new heart into the troops.

To military failures were added diplomatic failures. At the beginning of 1378, to be sure, the situation still seemed excellent. After nine years of almost uninterrupted success, the prestige of the Valois monarchy stood high in Europe. It could count on the alliance of the greatest Powers on the continent, among others the Empire. Thirty years earlier, Ludwig of Bavaria's death had meant the transfer of the imperial crown to a friendly family, in the person of Charles of Luxemburg, King of Bohemia. His father, King John the Blind, had served Philip VI faithfully and been killed on the battlefield of Crécy. Charles himself had married a sister of Philip VI, and married his sister Bona of Luxemburg to John the Good. Charles V had already met his uncle at Metz towards the end of 1356, when he was seeking support as Dauphin against the Paris burgesses. Now it was a question of turning this family union into a political alliance. The ageing emperor and his son Wenceslas arrived in Paris in January 1378. Grandiose festivities, complacently reported by the official chroniclers, marked the meeting of the two sovereigns. But behind the customary compliments, the oaths of friendship, the diplomatic agreements lay no political reality. The house of Luxemburg, absorbed in its German ambitions, remained firmly decided not to intervene in the Anglo-French conflict. Charles V's grand finale petered out in formal feasts devoid of meaning.

This same year 1378 brought harsh set-backs, some of them very serious. First, in the spring, came the King of Navarre's last rebellion. Charles the Bad refused to accept his defeat in 1365. His duplicity in Spanish affairs had made his Pyrenean kingdom a battleground over which the partisans of Pedro the Cruel and Henry of Trastamare fought with no advantage to him. On the brink of ruin, he had to revert to the game of see-saw between Valois and Plantagenet which had now become a habit. When the war flared up again, he was ready to sell his support to the highest bidder. In September 1370 he went to see Edward III at Clarendon and offered him an alliance and a prospective partition of France. This move did not succeed, for the Prince of Wales rejected any agreement with an ally whose perfidy was only too familiar. Then, once more, Charles V managed to appease the eternal conspirator by promising, in the Treaty of Vernon (March 1371), to put him at length in possession of the barony of Montpellier and admit him to homage.

This was the position when, in the spring of 1378, the unexpected arrest of two Navarrese agents enabled a fresh plot to be nipped in the bud. It involved nothing less, so we are told, than poisoning the King of France and rekindling the Navarrese war with the help of the confusion which his death would cause. How much truth was there in these police reports, which were skilfully exploited? The King of Navarre had an established reputation as a poisoner, which did not seem to be ill-founded and made the accusation plausible. He was suspected of having disposed of the cardinal of Boulogne, and was known to have got rid of the *routier* Seguin of Badefol when he was in too much of a hurry to demand his pay. It was a good opportunity to eliminate the Navarrese menace once and for all. Duguesclin was ordered to occupy the county of Évreux and Cotentin and hand them over provisionally to the King of Navarre's eldest son, Charles the Noble, who was known to be devoted to the Valois's cause. But Duguesclin was not quick enough. In return for cash, which he needed for his Spanish adventures, Charles the Bad had time to cede the port of Cherbourg to an English garrison, which maintained itself there for fifteen years.

The Breton affair was to turn out still more badly for the King of France. Emboldened by the apparent success of his operations against Charles of Navarre, he believed that an equally treacherous vassal would be unable to resist his strength. Ever since his victory in 1365, John IV of Brittany had shown what he thought about his vassaldom to France. Without openly siding with the Plantagenet at first, he had helped him secretly since the renewal of the war. In 1370 Robert Knowles, hard pressed by Duguesclin, had found refuge in his duchy after his unhappy raid. In 1372 the duke threw off the mask, repudiated his vassaldom to France and fled to England. The next year, he accompanied Lancaster on his raid, and had since been fighting without glory on the frontiers of Gascony.

With the support of the population, Duguesclin was able to subject almost all the duchy to the king's authority. The English retained only four fortresses, among them Brest and Auray. When the truce of Bruges was broken, Charles V felt that the time had come to punish the traitor. Some Breton nobles, including the greatest, such as Rohan and Clisson, and Duguesclin himself, who had grievances against John IV's perfidy, assured the sovereign that the operation involved no danger, but would be simply judicial ratification of the *de facto* occupation. So the majesty of royal justice was directed against the Duke of Brittany. He was accused of treason, summoned before the *Parlement*, found contumacious, and sentenced to confiscation (December 18th 1378): the whole procedure which, ten years earlier, had been so successful against the Prince of Aquitaine.

But the king's advisers had deceived themselves. The whole population, burgesses, clergy, and villagers, supported the duke. Even the nobles, who had approved the temporary occupation, jibbed at the annexation of their country to the royal domain. Thanks to the hard wars which had succeeded one another for the past forty years, Breton particularism – I might almost say Breton nationalism – had come to birth. The Bretons were concerned about their independence, quick to take offence, and preferred appeal abroad to any interference by the Valois. It was to take the French monarchy more than a century to overcome them. Deposed by Charles V, John of Montfort returned to his first love and renewed the English alliance. The French managed to prevent the Duke of Lancaster, a mediocre soldier, from seizing Saint-Malo. But they could not stop John IV landing at Saint-Servan, reinforcing the English garrison of Brest and keeping control of all western Brittany. Their blow had failed.

At the same moment the French monarchy lost the support of the Papacy. For the past three-quarters of a century, during which French pontiffs had succeeded one another in Avignon, surrounded by a majority of French cardinals, people had got used to seeing them support the policy of the Valois. To be sure, the Avignon Popes had not always been the servile puppets of Paris, as the English and the Italians called them. Neither Benedict XII nor Innocent VI had fully met the wishes of Philip VI and John the Good. On the whole, however, the monarchy had derived from Avignon, together with considerable pecuniary help, an authority, a moral prestige which made it the recognized mainstay of the Holy See. But the necessity of administering the dearly reconquered papal States on the spot, and getting away from the banks of the Rhône infested by *routiers*, even more than the ardent appeals of Italian public opinion, had led Urban V and then Gregory XI to think about returning to Rome.

As early as 1369 Charles V's entreaties had failed to prevent Urban from going to Italy. The turbulence of the Romans had brought about the dying pontiff's return to Avignon. Gregory XI took the plan up again, but postponed it in order to keep better watch on the peace negotiations. When Franco-English reconciliation proved impossible, at the end of 1376, he refused to delay any longer. In vain did a French embassy, supported by the Duke of Anjou, beg him to remain, vaunting the advantages of a further stay on the French side of the Alps, recalling the friendship of the Valois and making the most of the services they had rendered. Nothing was of any avail. The cardinals, unenthusiastic though they were, had to follow the Pope's lead. Gregory went to Rome, where Italian affairs at once engrossed him. Charles V was almost forgotten.

It was still worse when, on Gregory XI's death, the Roman populace imposed the election of an Italian Pope, the Archbishop of Bari, Barto-lomeo Prignano, who took the name of Urban VI in April 1378. The new pontiff, an austere and imperious old man, announced his intention to reform the Sacred College, restrain its luxury and banish French influence from it. In alarm, the cardinals developed doubts about the legitimacy of the election, though they had taken part in it. They thus informed the King of France, who was only too ready to take their word. Backed by the Cardinal of Amiens, the ambitious John de La Grange, who had visions of the tiara, they fled from Rome, took refuge in the territory of the Queen of Naples, and launched anathema against the intruding Pope. Sure of the support of Charles V, readily convinced of the justice of their cause, on September 20th, at Fondi, they elected as Pope one of their number, Robert of Geneva, who took the name of Clement VII.

To prevent a schism from afflicting the Church, it would have been necessary for all the Christian sovereigns to pronounce unanimously in favour of one of the two rivals. With a clear conscience, Charles V had already made his choice. As early as November, without awaiting the arguments of the Italians, still less listening to them, he imposed recogni-tion of Clement upon his clergy, the University of Paris, the whole king-dom. But he had mistaken his influence upon the other courts of Europe. Only the kingdoms of Naples and Scotland followed his choice. Henry of Trastamare, faithful ally though he was, remained deaf to Charles's appeals. Together with the other Spanish kingdoms, he maintained a provisional neutrality as long as he lived. The Emperor Charles of Luxemburg, on his death-bed, insisted on recognizing Urban VI. His son Wenceslas followed his example. He gave the lead for Hungary, Poland, the Scandinavian kingdoms, most of the German princes, and Flanders. Finally, through the Parliament sitting at Gloucester, England lost no time in pronouncing in favour of the Roman Pope, for the sole reason that he was not French. The schism was consummated. Rightly or wrongly, it looked like France's doing, enforced or even inspired by Charles V, especially when Clement, driven out of Italy, came back to reside at Avignon.

The 'Great Schism of the West' was to rend Christendom for forty years. It had disastrous effects on the development of the Anglo-French war. Hitherto the papacy had always intervened eagerly to calm the conflict. Its efforts, as a self-interested but on the whole impartial medi-ator, had prevented hostilities from lasting too long and secured pauses and sometimes lengthy truces. But now each of the Popes encouraged war. This was because neither could crush his rival without the military aid of the kings who supported him. An Anglo-French peace would be the ruin of their opposed hopes. Not only were they absent from all the coming peace congresses, but they systematically thwarted the talks.

It was not long before this took place. The Archbishop of Ravenna, who for years had been working for peace at Bruges, was now one of Urban VI's cardinals and his legate in Central Europe. He toured Germany, invited Wenceslas to break the traditional alliance between Luxemburg and Valois, and planned to unite the Empire and England in a common crusade against schismatic France. In vain did Charles V, whom his military reverses in his recent campaigns had rendered less uncompromising, make tempting offers to the English: the cession of all Aquitaine south of the Dordogne (he would retain from his conquests only Poitou, Saintonge, Limousin, and Périgord); the marriage of his daughter Catherine to young Richard II, with the county of Angoulême as her dowry. In May 1380 the Cardinal of Ravenna managed to break off the talks and arranged a marriage between Richard II and Wenceslas's sister, Anne of Bohemia.

At the end of the summer, when Charles V felt that his death was near at hand, a fresh English raiding force landed on the continent and demonstrated by its pillaging that the war was renewed once more. It was the youngest of Edward III's sons, Thomas of Woodstock, Earl of Buckingham – later Duke of Gloucester – who led it from Calais to Brittany, by a route now customary, through Champagne, Gâtinais, Beauce, and Anjou. Before re-embarking he besieged Nantes, without success; but he left a trail of destruction behind him.

The conflict was becoming endless at a moment when France, whose forces Charles had stretched to the limit, was no longer in a condition to maintain it. Even though it was reduced to short raids, surprise attacks, local operations, the war cost dearly, and taxation weighed heavily on the decimated people. Alarming symptoms revealed the government's growing unpopularity and the nation's fatigue. The king, whose good administration was later to be looked back upon with regret, was not beloved, because his officials had too heavy a hand. For the time being, there was no open revolt except in Languedoc, against the exactions of the Duke of Anjou, the chief contriver of the war. Exasperated by his continual demands for money, the inhabitants of Montpellier rebelled in October 1379, after other risings had broken out in Le Puy and Nîmes, and the most hated officials and some tax-collectors were put to death. Happily for the royal administration, the insurrection did not spread. To assert the majesty of the power with which he was invested, Anjou passed stern sentences on the rebels, but quickly lightened them by grants of pardon, and order was soon restored.

But the king took fright and deemed it necessary to recall his brother. For Charles was not unaware of the misery of the people, and knew that discontent was rife in the countryside. On his death-bed qualms of conscience assailed him. Had he not squeezed his subjects unjustly? Had he the right to raise taxes to which they had not agreed, or to levy permanently taxes which they had granted only temporarily? The pious sovereign's last act, amid all the advice he gave his entourage, was to ordain the discontinuance of the hearth-tax (September 16th 1380). It was a measure which strikes us as absurd and impolitic to the last degree. No more than his subjects did the king understand the need for permanent taxation. If he eased his conscience, with a stroke of the pen he deprived his successor of the means of governing.

Part V

TOWARDS RECONCILIATION
1380–1400

Part V

TOWARDS RECONCILIATION
(1380–1400)

DURING his sixteen years' reign, at once healing and exhausting, Charles V had accomplished a great task: the destruction of the Treaty of Calais, which was the master-thought of this persistent and crafty man. But he had rekindled the war, and his slender resources did not enable him to end it. The dilemma in which he had placed the kingdom was not removed by his death. Unable to win the war, France was forced to continue it, without hope of a definite success. Worse still, the Breton treachery, the defection of the Pope, and the internal disorder threatened once more to make the struggle turn out disastrously for the Valois. If fresh calamities were spared France during Charles VI's minority, it was because England, on her side, was passing through a grave crisis, both political and social; the price to be paid for an unduly long war, which was beyond her means. By fits and starts the two countries had outrun their strength. Neither one nor the other could achieve a decision. A lull – it lasted thirty-five years – was brought about by the very exhaustion of the adversaries. To discover the reasons for this a backward glance is essential. We must examine the wounded combatants, count their visible and hidden injuries and expose their weaknesses.

1. THE EXHAUSTION OF ENGLAND

FROM THE morrow of the treaty of Calais to the death of Charles V, how far had England gone down the slippery slope of decline! At the end of 1360 Edward III had reached the peak of his fame: a military fame, above all. The whole of Europe, used to French successes, had been astounded by the victories of Crécy and Poitiers. It was to the court of London that the knights of the West now thronged. Great lords sought admission to the Order of the Garter. Humbler persons, with swords to sell and a taste for tourneys, were eager to meet the heroes of the war, the Black Prince, Chandos, Knowles, and others. The country was prodigiously enriched by the heavy ransoms imposed on the prisoners of the wars in France and Spain. There was a regular trade in ransoms, which were sold and resold like merchandise. The largest of all, that of John the Good, went to the royal treasury. Even though only half of it was paid, this sum of a million and a half gold *écus* still meant something enormous. Its intrinsic value has been closely estimated (£250,000 at the 1351 rate); but the scarcity of specie of the period gave it a purchasing power infinitely higher. At a time when gold still remained the sole apparent sign of wealth, the transfer from one country to the other of such a mass of coin and bullion should have made abundance reign in England. Wisely administered, this treasure would have sufficed for the normal needs of the monarchy for several years and rendered unnecessary any resort to parliamentary grants, always a delicate matter.

Like all fortunate princes, Edward lived surrounded by a large and handsome family. His five sons were the adornment of his middle age. The eldest, Edward of Woodstock, Prince of Wales, Duke of Cornwall, and Earl of Chester, added to his great English appanage the principality of Aquitaine, which he conquered at the point of his sword. He might have made a royal marriage abroad. But, being a romantic soul, he fell in love with one of his cousins, the beautiful Joan, Countess of Kent, already the mother of grown-up sons. The nobility approved this love-match, though later they murmured about its irregularity. It was in Bordeaux that the sole surviving son of this happy union, the future Richard II, was born. Edward's second son, Lionel of Antwerp, was a more retiring man. Richly endowed in Ireland, where he was made Duke of Clarence and Earl of Ulster, he held aloof from the quarrels on the continent. He did not appear there until later, in 1368, when, now a widower, he went to fetch a wealthy wife in the family of the Visconti of Milan; but he died prematurely some months later.

John of Gaunt, Edward's third son, born in Flanders at the time of his father's magnificent raids, had much higher ambitions. His first marriage to his cousin, Blanche of Lancaster, made him the richest landed proprietor in England: Duke of Lancaster, in which duchy he enjoyed palatine privileges; Earl of Leicester, and as such hereditary seneschal of England; Earl of Lincoln and Derby. His son married the heiress of the Earls of Hereford. John believed himself to be a good general and sought fame and profit on the continent. After Blanche's early death, in 1372 he married Constance of Castille, the eldest daughter of Pedro the Cruel, whose rights he claimed to inherit. Henceforth he called himself King of Castille. This, to be sure, was still an empty title; but as his father, at the same time, concluded an alliance with Portugal – its memory was not forgotten in the twentieth century – directed against Henry of Trastamare, it was a token of designs in Spain whose danger was soon to take shape.

It was still too soon to estimate the characters of Edward's two youngest sons, both greedy youths. The fourth, Edmund of Langley, was the hero of the abortive Flemish marriage. Created Earl of Cambridge in 1362, he consoled himself for his disappointment by marrying another daughter of Pedro the Cruel. But the future Duke of York always remained a retiring, mediocre, and timorous prince. The harum-scarum spirit of the youngest, Thomas of Woodstock, later Earl of Buckingham, did not display itself until long after his father's death, when it made him sadly celebrated under the name of Duke of Gloucester.

Eight years of peace served only to increase Edward's self-confidence, while they relieved his treasury, hitherto deep in debt. The reconciliation with Flanders restored the normal flow of wool exports by way of Calais, and indirectly re-established English influence in the Low Countries as a whole. Edward knew that he had the support of public opinion, represented by Parliaments. Now that he no longer called upon them to provide excessive taxation, they were obedient to his suggestions and embraced his enmities and his hatreds. Their now habitual distrust of the French was all the more readily expressed because it involved no risk; their forced diatribes against the 'encroachments' of the papacy enabled him, either in agreement with the Pope or in defiance of him, to place all his protégés in ecclesiastical benefices. In 1364, when Urban V went out of his way to demand from the kingdom, as vassal to the Holy See, arrears of the feudal tribute which had not been paid for more than thirty years, Edward retorted that the sovereignty of the Plantagenet state was incompatible with payment of this intolerable exaction. Henceforth, in law as well as in fact, the promise once exacted from John Lackland by Innocent III would be regarded as null and void. The incident was of no consequence. But it showed that Edward III in his pride was as zealous to affirm his independence towards the papacy as he had been to win it from the Valois in Aquitaine.

The renewal of the war in 1369 brought him back to earth. He realized that nothing was left of the millions paid for John the Good's ransom. They had been spent as they were received, without thought for the morrow. Since raids cost much and brought in little, it was necessary to appeal to Parliaments again and extract fresh grants from them in the form of property taxes, whose yield was often problematical and always below expectations.

Edward was growing old. Widowed before he was sixty, he sank into senile pleasures and became infatuated with a mistress of low birth, Alice Perrers. But administration was maintained after a fashion under the direction of two experienced clerks, Thomas Brantingham, Bishop of Exeter, and William Wykeham, Bishop of Winchester. It was they who were held responsible for the military defeats and the French reconquest. In 1371, Parliament demanded and obtained their dismissal and their replacement at the chancery and the treasury by laymen, despite the unsatisfactory precedent of 1341. Meanwhile the Duke of Lancaster, in the intervals between his raids, acquired a growing influence over the government, which his weakened father and his dying elder brother could not dispute. An almost unanimous opposition accused him of leading the country to ruin. It found vent in April 1376, on the eve of the Black Prince's death, in the long session of what the chroniclers called the 'Good Parliament'. This strong opposition apparently arose in the ranks of the commoners alone, and found an eloquent spokesman in the knight Peter de la Mare. For the first time the baronage, among whom Lancaster had some partisans, bowed to public demands which they had not originated and perhaps endorsed only with reluctance. In these demands we find an echo of Étienne Marcel's: upright administration, controlled taxation, a vigorous purge.

But the measures adopted fell far short of these fine ideas. Parliament contented itself with getting rid of Alice Perrers, replacing a few high officials and, despite Lancaster's furious opposition, impeaching two of his partisans, William Latimer, an official of the royal household, and Richard Lyons, a leading London vintner, both of them tax-farmers, embezzlers, and rogues. For the rest, no sooner was the storm past than John of Gaunt resumed power, permitted the return of his father's mistress, recalled the banished, had the acts of the Good Parliament annulled by a fresh assembly more malleable to his wishes, threw the over-bold speaker of the commoners into prison, and secured Bishop Wykeham's condemnation for his guilt in supporting the Good Parliament's claims. It was amid these wretched intrigues that a life once glorious ended. In January 1377 Edward celebrated the jubilee of a reign of fifty years. Five months later he died, almost forgotten by his subjects.

Richard II's minority made a bad start. Around the young king, just ten years old, a number of influences crossed and clashed. First, there were the Black Prince's councillors, who thronged the royal household and were quite naturally ready to assume power in his son's name. There was

the Princess of Wales, the king's legitimate guardian; but she was surrounded by her other sons, the greedy, grasping Hollands. There were
the bishops and clerks dismissed since 1371, and anxious to regain favour
at this beginning of a new reign. There were the burgesses of London,
divided into rival factions, but on the whole hostile to the Duke of Lancaster since the Latimer-Lyons affair. Finally, there was John of Gaunt
himself. As the eldest of the king's uncles he could rightly lay claim to the
regency; but his ambitions offended too many influential people. He was
in fact thrust aside from the government, and during the early years of
Richard II's reign played an ill-defined and apparently secondary role.
The better to bar his way, no regent was named. Something like a reconciliation of parties was effected by the Parliament's election of an executive council of a dozen members, twice reconstituted, consisting of prelates,
barons, bannerets, and knights, but excluding the burgesses. It had to
maintain order, pursue the war against the Valois energetically, and to
this end find plentiful resources.

In all these tasks the elected council failed, and in its discredit it
involved the Parliaments which had appointed its members and endorsed
its policy. Still without money and finding the property tax hitherto in
force unprofitable, as early as 1379 Parliament passed a poll-tax, which
yielded a poor return at the price of great unpopularity. Towards the end
of 1380 money had to be found to meet the heavy cost of Buckingham's
raid, make ready the expedition which Cambridge proposed to lead in
Portugal, and finally provide for the expenses of the king's marriage. Anne
of Bohemia arrived without a dowry, and meanwhile the German and
Czech knights in Wenceslas's entourage had to be laden with presents and
pensions. A fresh Parliament passed a fresh poll-tax, payable in theory by
all the king's subjects except paupers, in accordance with a rate that
varied with wealth and social position, but struck hard at the very poor
and the rural communities, which were held jointly responsible for the
yield. When the beginning of the collection led to extensive evasions,
commissioners were dispatched to the south-eastern counties and entrusted with a strict reassessment and a stern recovery of the tax.

This was the signal for a terrible peasant rising, at the end of May 1381.
Its almost simultaneous outbreak north, east, and south of London and
its swift spread to East-Anglia and the Home Counties led to belief in the
existence of some previous conspiracy, some secret society which issued
orders at a given moment; but there is no proof of this. French historians
wrongly speak about a 'rising of the workers', as though it included the
artisans of the towns from the start. It was in fact a peasant rebellion, at
least at the outset. It was directed in the first place against the revenue
commissioners entrusted with assessing the poll-tax and hastening its collection. Some of them were massacred, their documents were burned, and
the collectors were robbed. Then the wrath of the peasants turned against
the lords, particularly the rich abbeys, not because they had increased to

any extent the labour services since the Black Death, but because the now more prosperous villein wanted to free himself from his despised condition. The peasants pillaged monasteries, such as St. Albans and St. Edmundsbury, burned their archives, and by fear and by force obtained individual or collective charters of freedom, known as manumissions. Simultaneously, after concentrating their forces in Kent and Essex, the rebels swept on against the government, the burgesses, all the rich and all the powerful. They broke into the city of London by the badly defended Aldgate, and played havoc with the houses and shops of the foreign merchants, whom popular legend accused of enriching themselves at the expense of the people and draining all its wealth out of the kingdom. They also burned the fine manor of Savoy, the property of the Duke of Lancaster, who, directly threatened by the rising, had found safe shelter in Scotland. Finally they took the Tower of London by assault. The young sovereign escaped from it just in time, but they murdered Simon Sudbury, chancellor and Archbishop of Canterbury, and the treasurer Robert Hales.

Can we derive any idea of the feelings which inspired the rebels from these acts of vengeance and devastation? To their very real and definite grievances against the revenue officials, the lords and the merchants was added an implacable hatred of the powerful, a vague belief in levelling equalitarianism. The idea, which can be found in all periods, was particularly dear to some popular preachers, vagabond priests or monks, who thundered against the rich and against power in the name of the equality of condition of the first of mankind. An example was to be found in Kent in the person of John Ball, an excommunicated priest, who joined the rebels perhaps in the hope of becoming Archbishop of Canterbury. He and his rivals were fond of quoting the couplet:

> When Adam delved and Eve span,
> Where was then a gentleman?

Further, in the rear of these hot-heads should we blame the theories of the heresiarch Wyclif? Thrust out since 1378 from the king's council, into which Lancaster had introduced him, and soon driven from Oxford, where his theological teaching ended by provoking brawls, he retired to his country parish to compile the political pamphlets, the doctrinal treatises, the scriptural translations which flowed from his facile pen. His 'poor priests', to whom he entrusted the spreading of his gospel, preached against the ecclesiastical hierarchy, but in favour of the civil power, against the rich, but in favour of evangelical poverty. Whether this preaching, badly understood, encouraged the revolt there is no knowing. In any case, it had nothing to do with instigating it. It is easy and tempting to draw a parallel between Luther and Wyclif, between the Saxon and the English peasants, between the beginning of the sixteenth century and the end of the fourteenth; but such a parallel is deceptive.

In any case, this tidal wave was deeper and more dangerous than the *Jacquerie* whose passing peril the Dauphin had survived in 1358. Large bodies of insurgents concentrated in the south-east, badly equipped, but spurred on by leaders hitherto unknown, such as Wat Tyler of Kent, or Jack Straw of Essex. There is no knowing whether they were peasants, servants, or bastards or cadets of some knightly family. Under their command the rebels converged on London and held the king at their mercy. A courageous youth, Richard did not weaken. He was supported by the Mayor of London, William Walworth, whose boldness saved the situation. There were stormy meetings between the insurgents and the king at Mile End and Smithfield. Here Richard harangued the rebels and declared himself to be on their side. But Walworth killed Wat Tyler before their eyes. Thrown into confusion, the rebels retreated. Then came the hunt, joyfully led by the lords, at first cowed, but now bent on vengeance. The repression lasted several months and continued throughout the summer of 1381. When Queen Anne obtained an amnesty, on the morrow of her marriage, there was nothing left of the nightmare of the rich or the dream of the poor, harshly replaced in bondage to the lords.

If it was without a morrow like all *jacqueries*, the revolt of the English peasants nevertheless provides us with proof that Richard II's island, though it was not directly affected by invasion and the pillaging of *routiers*, had experienced profound effects of the war: depopulation, an agricultural crisis, a monetary and fiscal crisis, and, to round things off, a social crisis, not to speak of continual political crises.

Yet, despite everything, from force of habit the Plantagenet government maintained the fiction of a policy of intervention in continental affairs. The Black Prince's former councillors wanted to put Richard at the head of a fresh raid across France as a source of glory and profit. Some of the bishops, with the support and guidance of the merchants of London and Calais, demanded an expedition to help the people of Ghent, once more in revolt against Louis of Male. Finally, the Duke of Lancaster was waiting impatiently to set off for the conquest of Castille. As John I, Henry of Trastamare's son and successor, had ended by siding with the Avignon Pope, this expedition would become a crusade with Urban VI's blessing. Of all these projects not one was successful.

The Flemish expedition, limited to some four or five thousand men, did not sail until May 1383, six months after the defeat of the people of Ghent by the King of France: in other words, it was foredoomed to failure. The Bishop of Norwich, Henry Despenser, who led it, also called it a crusade, directed in theory against schismatic France. But he was content to take Dunkirk and then, after making contact with the people of Ghent, besieged Ypres, which withstood him. In August Philip of Burgundy's advance induced him to retreat, the French bought him off, and his crusaders re-embarked. The whole affair ended in London with his impeachment in Parliament, the punishment of this peculiar prelate, and a big budget deficit. For his part, the king did not attack France, which was regarded as too strong. But, as it was essential at all costs to enhance the prestige of this young sovereign of seventeen, in 1385 the idea was conceived of a military promenade in Scotland, which was costly and perfectly futile. An absurd deployment of strength served only to lead to quarrels among the leaders and between the king and his uncle Lancaster. Then, after encamping for a few weeks in the region of Edinburgh, the army retired.

In the spring of 1386, after many delays and countermandings, John of Gaunt finally assembled his personal army, at the expense of the royal treasury, and set sail for Spain. Once again, his imposing expedition proved unsuccessful. At the outset he captured a few towns and castles in Galicia. Then, in the spring of 1387, large Portuguese reinforcements enabled him to carry out a short raid in Leon. That was all. As in the case of so many wars at this period, a family agreement stopped his conquest. The Crown Prince of Castille, grandson of Henry of Trastamare, was betrothed to Lancaster's daughter, grand-daughter of Pedro the Cruel. It was a poor outcome. The English treasury had been depleted to no purpose, since, despite this marriage, Castille remained the ally of France and a supporter of the Avignon Pope.

But at least Lancaster's departure on his Spanish venture in May 1386 had the advantage in England of getting rid of a nuisance and leaving the rival factions leisure to develop and become distinct. The king had now become an elegant young man, with regular features and a pensive air: later he grew a small red beard. He was known to be self-willed and capricious; but, apart from wanting to make himself obeyed without a murmur, he did not as yet reveal any very definite political ideas. With his queen, Anne of Bohemia, whom he loved dearly though she remained childless, he gathered a few favourites around him, adhered to them, and loaded them with favours: his two half-brothers, the Earl of Kent and the Earl of Huntingdon; his advisers, old courtiers of his father, who thronged the services of his household, notably the knight Simon of Burley, his 'tutor'; some young aristocrats, companions in his sports and spongers on his treasury, especially Robert de Vere, Earl of Oxford, whom he created Marquis of Dublin and then Duke of Ireland; and lastly Nicholas Brember, ex-mayor of London, and Michael de la Pole, an upstart, the son of a rich merchant of Kingston-upon-Hull, whom he made Earl of Suffolk and chancellor. Heteroclite though it was, this group formed a clique: it heralded government at the king's own will.

As under Edward II, three-quarters of a century earlier, it aroused the opposition of the baronage, who wanted to maintain their position as the sovereign's natural councillors and were jealous of unworthy favourites. Here again there was a curious coalition of interests: prelates like William Courtenay, Archbishop of Canterbury, who reproached the king with not being zealous enough in persecuting those notorious heretics, Wyclif's disciples; the king's uncle Thomas of Gloucester, harum-scarum, hot-headed, and brainless, and his cousin Henry of Lancaster, then Earl of Derby, crafty and narrow-minded; some great barons, such as the Earl of Arundel, an energetic admiral, and the Earl of Warwick, a good soldier, who demanded strong military action against France and constituted themselves champions of war, always popular until the bill came to be paid. All these knew that their criticism of bad government and the favourites would find a ready echo in Parliament. So they played the 'constitutional' card against Richard's untimely revival of royal absolutism. Thus, about the same time as in France a struggle among the princes of the blood for control of a weak king was taking shape, in England a political revolution, already fiercer and more desperate, set in opposition a king and a baronage equally obstinate.

The first phase of the struggle, which alone need detain us for the moment, was marked by the victory of the united barons over the king, still inexperienced and poorly supported. Scapegoat and first victim of the opposition, the chancellor Michael de la Pole fell on the morrow of Lancaster's departure. Parliament demanded his dismissal and insisted that he should be tried by the formidable process of impeachment which the Tudor sovereigns were to use so often to dispose of their disgraced favourites. Accused of misappropriation, he finally succeeded in escaping to Brabant. But this Parliament of October 1386, usually known as 'marvellous' – the epithet *mirabilis* in the text of a chronicler favourable to the baronial party in fact applies to the assembly in the spring of 1388 – also insisted upon dismissing the king's most compromised councillors, and placing the king under the tutelage of a committee of barons, entrusted with preparing a purge and essential reforms. When Richard looked like resisting, Gloucester talked about deposing him. The king had to bow beneath the yoke.

But, early in 1387, he escaped from the barons' tutelage and left them to govern in London in his name, while he scoured the south-west and centre of the country in search of faithful followers. He summoned the judges of his courts to Nottingham (August 25th), where they gave him their legal opinion, declared the baronial committee unlawful, and assured the king – a lesson not lost on him – that only in its plenitude could the royal power be legitimately exercised. In the autumn the leaders of the baronage, the five 'Lords Appellant' (Gloucester, Derby, Arundel, Warwick, and Nottingham), accused the royal councillors of treason and took up arms to thwart their manœuvres. After a semblance of civil war, marked by a skirmish at Radcot Bridge, where the forces of the favourites collapsed, Richard, who had returned to London, was replaced under baronial control. A fresh Parliament, 'merciless' according to some chroniclers, 'marvellous' according to others – in any case, the longest ever known, since it sat from February to the beginning of June – set the seal on the baronial reforms: banishment of all the favourites, severe purging of the royal household, execution of the most guilty persons such as old Simon or Burley, Brember, and the chief-justice Robert Tresilian, dismissal or translation of bishops favourable to the court and their replacement by prelates favourable to the baronage, absolute control of the council and the great public services by Gloucester and the Lords Appellant.

Richard was powerless. He kept silent and bent his head to the storm. He was ready to let the barons break down in power, quarrel among themselves, demonstrate their incompetence. By the summer of 1388, despite the support of another Parliament assembled at Cambridge, their control was so precarious that they dare no longer advocate the bellicose policy by which they had won over public opinion. No sooner were they installed in power than they recognized that they could seek no meeting with France other than a meeting of plenipotentiaries. Gloucester was the last to agree to negotiation.

2. THE YOUTH OF CHARLES VI

THREE YEARS after England, France too experienced the trials of a royal minority. Such an event had not occurred in England since 1216, with Henry III's accession; in France, since 1226, with that of Saint Louis. Charles V, in poor health, had foreseen his early death. His ordinance of 1374 settled the government after his death, fixed the royal coming of age at thirteen, and gave the shortened regency to Louis of Anjou and the guardianship of the royal children to his other brothers. But it entrusted the substance of power to a great council of fifty members, made up of prelates, high officers of State, chief officials of the household, judges of the *Parlement*, knights, clerks, and burgesses of Paris. Twelve of them, experienced in the handling of affairs, would form an inner executive council. It took an occasion of such gravity to make the king dream of defining the composition and role of a permanent council. Let us recall that nothing could have been more vague, more badly defined than the royal council in this period: it was a picture of the latitude left to the sovereign to seek advisers and assistants where he would.

The ordinance, as almost always happened in such cases, was not applied. As soon as Charles V was dead, Anjou, in his capacity as eldest of the new king's uncles, demanded the effective regency and fraudulently took over part of the royal treasure. His brothers Berry and Burgundy and his cousin Bourbon, the late king's brother-in-law, claimed a share in power. After Charles VI's coronation an agreement was reached. Anjou kept pre-eminence in power, though he abandoned the title of regent. Two at least of the uncles would sit on the permanent council of twelve members, who would be appointed by them, thus ensuring continuity of policy by the 'princes of the lilies'. This arrangement itself was only partially carried out. The 'appointed council' functioned belatedly and only for a short time, from October 1381 to January 1383.

In practice, Berry was thrust aside from power. He was sent as lieutenant to plunder Languedoc in place of his elder brother. Then it was the turn of Anjou. Busy with preparations for an expedition to Italy, he established himself in Provence, negotiated with the Avignon Pope, and finally, in 1382, set off for the conquest of the kingdom of Naples. In fact, Burgundy and Bourbon conducted general policy, with the help of a council from which the late king's courtiers were only partially eliminated. True, there were some resounding dismissals at the outset of the new reign. The provost of Paris, Hugh Aubriot, was sentenced to imprisonment for life, on the ground of infringing the University's privileges.

Bureau de La Rivière, the Cardinal of Amiens, and John le Mercier were temporarily banished. Peter of Orgemont had to hand over the seals to Milon of Dormans, Bishop of Beauvais. The pious knight Philip of Mézières, the young king's tutor, was rudely thrust aside. But these individual dismissals did not prevent some of Charles V's councillors from retaining positions of trust and an influence which remained great. Many of them slipped back after a few months in exile.

What was novel was the leading role which was demanded, thanks to a minority officially very short – Charles VI was a boy of twelve on his father's death, and he should have assumed personal power by 1381 – by the princes of the blood and the near relations of the late king. They were conscious of working for the welfare of the monarchy, but they did not divorce its welfare from their personal interests, their private ambitions. As princes with appanages they were endowed with a power which was a source of weakness for the kingdom; but they did not possess the revenue essential for the satisfaction of their ravenous appetites. This applied especially to Anjou, claimant to the kingdom of Naples, and Burgundy, who had his eye on the succession in Flanders. They were to put the whole strength of the monarchy at the service of their personal policies, and by this very fact increase their power and their independence. The danger that the young king would be kept in permanent tutelage grew greater day by day.

True, at the outset the situation scarcely seemed to lend itself to such ideas. But the princes were not the kind of men to moderate their ambitions to the measure of the kingdom's resources. Anjou had been nominated by Clement VII as the champion of the Avignon cause in Italy, and been recognized as heir by the old Queen Joan of Naples. He promptly made sure of the possession of Provence, the sole tangible result of these visionary plans. He proceeded to harry the courts of Paris and Avignon with demands for money, until at length a majestic French army advanced into Italy, thus foreshadowing by a century Charles VIII's disastrous mistake. Anjou was defeated by Charles of Durazzo, Queen Joan's dispossessed nephew, and died in Italy in 1384. His wife Mary of Brittany, a daughter of Charles of Blois, continued the struggle in the name of the young Louis II of Anjou; but she was allowed no voice in the government of France.

Philip the Bold of Burgundy did not aim so high, for the time being. He was impatient to reign in Flanders, from which his suspicious father-in-law systematically kept him away. Then, despite his policy of understanding with England, Louis of Male once more heard the muttering of revolt in the cloth-making towns. From 1379 the discontent of Ghent, its rivalry with Ypres, another industrial centre, and its pent-up hatred of the bankers of Bruges, the count's protégés, threatened to take a nasty turn. When revolt broke out in Ghent, in the spring of 1380, the town chose as its leader the son of the dictator of 1340, Philip van Artevelde, who at once asked for military and economic help from England. Louis of Male found himself forced to appeal to his son-in-law. Burgundy in turn referred the matter to the royal council. It was for the kingdom of France as a whole to take its revenge on the people of Ghent, the allies of the English.

But could the Valois kingdom bear the cost? Ever since Charles V's death financial difficulties had increased. His abolition of the hearth-tax had led the people to believe that no 'extraordinary finance' would be levied in future. The collectors went on levying indirect taxes, which were unpopular because they were vexatious; but in November 1380, in face of the threat of risings, all taxation had to be suspended and even demands for arrears were abandoned. Without resources, the government of the uncles appealed to local assemblies, which imposed conditions. In March 1381 the Estates of Languedoïl, repeating the procedure adopted in the darkest days of John the Good's reign, granted a hearth-tax valid for one year only on condition that they controlled its levy and use, and that the government should issue a fresh reforming decree aimed at the royal notaries and judges and the special jurisdictions of the constable, the marshals and the chamberlains of the household. Once it was hard up, the monarchy became powerless to protect its officials against unpopularity. But these concessions did not suffice. Everywhere there were risings against the hated tax-collectors. In Rouen the '*Hérelle*' broke out in February 1382, as soon as the levy of an increased hearth-tax began. In Paris, on March 1st, the day on which the levy of a tax on merchandise, extracted from an assembly of frightened burgesses, was due to begin, the populace rose, pillaged the arsenal, seized lead mallets, and hunted down and massacred the tax-collectors. With great difficulty, a few influential burgesses, led by John des Marès, mediated between the court and the insurgents and, in return for the abolition of the tax, secured the restoration of order. The example of these 'Maillotins' of Paris was followed in almost all the towns of the royal domain, especially in the Ile-de-France. The infection spread to Languedoc, which Berry's exactions had scarcely pacified. Béziers rose, and so – a graver event – did the villages. Bands of *Tuchins* terrorized the countryside.

This was on the eve of the Flemish expedition. Inwardly raging, the uncles played for time and came to terms with the insurgents. By dint of flattery and promises, they obtained meagre grants: in Paris a few thousand francs, in Normandy a few hundred men-at-arms. Borrowing provided the balance. Equipped by such makeshifts, the royal army set out, under the effective leadership of Philip the Bold. On November 27th 1382, in the plain of Roosebeke in maritime Flanders, it routed the Ghent militia. Deprived of Philip van Artevelde, who was killed in the battle, the town of Ghent continued the struggle; but it was reduced to the defensive and held out only in hope of the arrival of English reinforcements, appealed for by its 'admiral', Frans Ackerman. It sufficed for Philip the

Bold that he had made this example. He was now sure of controlling the affairs of Flanders.

On the return of the victorious expedition, the uncles affected to regard the town risings as on the same footing as the Flemish revolt. The heavy fines to be paid by the allies of Ghent, now returned to their duty, were matched by exemplary punishment of the towns in the royal domain. In Paris John des Marès was executed for restoring order by appeasing the insurgents. The provostship of the merchants and all the municipal privileges were confiscated by the crown and henceforth exercised by the provost of Paris, a royal official. Enormous collective fines were imposed on Paris, Rouen, Laon, Orleans, and Rheims. Languedoc had to pay 800,000 francs to win its pardon. Moreover, the taxes on merchandise, salt, and wine were soon reimposed throughout the kingdom at their former rate. The hearth-tax was restored shortly afterwards. There was no longer any question of seeking the consent of the Estates. Still more than under Charles V, the taxes became not only permanent but also crushing. But the terrorized country did not dare to stir.

With regard to the Anglo-French conflict, which had trailed along since the failure of the Bruges conference, the policy of the uncles, like that of Richard II's councillors, and for similar reasons, was sometimes timidly pacific, sometimes mildly bellicose. The Duke of Brittany's submission, obtained by the second Treaty of Guérande in April 1381, was only a semi-success for France; for the English were masters of Brest and stayed there. Since then, from time to time, there had been peace talks and short truces were negotiated. The talks were entrusted only to underlings: on the French side the Bishop of Bayeux, Nicholas Dubosc. They took place for a few weeks at a time in the parish church of Leulinghen, on the borders of Calaisis and Boulonnais, and were then adjourned without result.

From time to time, too, military operations were speeded up, but only, it seems, in relation to Flemish affairs, dear to Philip the Bold's heart. In 1383 it was a French army that advanced to meet the Bishop of Norwich and the Ghent contingents, forced them to raise the siege of Ypres and purchased the re-embarkation of the English. The following year, it was French garrisons which, on the long-awaited death of Louis of Male, occupied western Flanders, seized the port of Damme and kept Ghent under close blockade until, by the peace of Tournai in December 1385, the great town made its submission to its new count, the Duke of Burgundy. Then, satisfied with having laid hands on the inheritance he had so long coveted, Philip seems to have let Charles VI's government pursue a more independent, more specifically French policy. He urged on the preparation of a great invasion of England, for which, during the summer of 1385, and then during the winter of 1386–7, heavy concentrations of ships, men, material, and supplies were effected in the Norman ports, to the great dismay of Richard II's subjects. Enormous expense was incurred.

It looked as though the war was about to change its aspect and be carried on to the very soil of the former invader.

For some obscure reason the expedition was called off. Was the adventure found to be too risky, the strength available too small? Or did Philip put on a costly act simply to frighten England, and was he satisfied when he obtained the reopening of the wool trade between England and Flanders? We do not know. In any case, after this episode French policy reverted to the Duke of Burgundy's service and the support of his aims in the Low Countries. Once master of Flanders, Philip the Bold developed designs on the duchy of Brabant, which, with its dependencies of Limburg and the 'lands beyond the Meuse', controlled almost the whole of the great commercial route between the mouth of the Scheldt and Cologne. The old duchess Joan had no children by her marriage to Duke Wenceslas of Luxemburg. It was a question of thrusting the Luxemburgs aside from the succession, rendering services to the duchess, and forcing the Brabançons, despite their prejudices against the Flemings, to place themselves under the tutelage of Burgundy. As early as 1385 a preliminary manœuvre enabled Philip to secure the support of the Wittelsbachs, who, as holders of the counties of Holland, Zeeland, and Hainault, might be the arbiters in the struggle in the Low Countries. A double marriage united Philip's children to those of Albrecht of Bavaria; and, in order to bind the French monarchy more closely to this policy, a niece of Albrecht, Isabella of Bavaria, was chosen as Charles VI's wife (July 1385). Philip reckoned that this comely, buxom German wench, ignorant of the refined ways of the Valois court, would dominate her weak husband by her almost animal sensuality and plenty of pregnancies, and would be an instrument in his hands. The woman better known to history as Queen 'Isabeau' had not yet revealed herself to the wily Duke of Burgundy.

A final manœuvre brought about the downfall of the government of the uncles, or rather of Philip. In her territory beyond the Meuse the Duchess of Brabant encountered opposition from the Duke of Gelderland, son of the Duke of Juliers, who was threatened with the nibbling away of his estates by the encroachments of the Brabançons. The duke, a young hot-head, had struck up a friendship with Richard II and, in return for money, had become a vassal of the King of England. He conceived the mad idea of issuing an insulting challenge to Charles VI. Philip at once forced the royal council to undertake an expedition of reprisals, of which he would be the sole beneficiary. The king was now twenty. He dreamed about battle and glory. But the expedition to Gelderland (1388), across the Ardennes and the region of the Meuse, was no more than a dull military promenade, darkened by the autumnal rain.

It was on the way back, at Rheims, that the *coup d'état* took place (November 3rd). The doyen of the councillors, Peter Aycelin of Montaigu, Cardinal of Laon, declared the king of age and invited him to assume the government. Charles thanked his uncles, who had the audacity to demand compensation for expenses incurred in the sovereign's service. They were dismissed and in practice expelled from the council. A well-laid plot had paved the way for this change. The queen, impatient of Burgundy's tutelage, probably had something to do with it. But the heart and soul of it was the king's brother, Louis, Duke of Touraine—later Duke of Orleans – a youth of eighteen, who demanded his place in the sun. If Charles had hitherto lacked determination, Louis had enough for two. The previous year, the Avignon Pope had negotiated his marriage to the daughter of the rich Lord of Milan, Valentine Visconti. Her dowry consisted of the county of Asti and firm expectation of the inheritance of Milan. The king's brother wanted the first place, before the uncles who had hitherto thrust him aside from power and wealth. Behind him stood the compact group of Charles V's former councillors, relegated since the beginning of Charles VI's reign to minor posts, and exasperated by the plundering of the revenue to the advantage of the uncles and their favourites. Not all of them were small fry, 'Marmosets' as they were contemptuously called. Among them were prelates such as Nicholas Dubosc, and soldiers grouped around the Constable Oliver of Clisson, Admiral John of Vienne and the Viscount of Melun. They also included squires like Bureau de La Rivière and finally lawyers, together with the financial experts John le Mercier and John of Montagu, who became 'superintendent of finances' of the royal household.

Once masters of the council and all the important administrative posts, the Marmosets formed a coherent and enthusiastic team, whom Charles VI, weak already, allowed to govern as they chose. They were no revolutionaries: their ideal was a return to Charles V's good administration. They made no far-reaching reforms. The great ordinances which they issued between February and May 1389 only repeated rules forgotten for the past eight years and defined the organization and perfected the working of all the public services. Above all, they wanted to avert a return to the autocratic despotism of the princes. The council was limited to twelve members, linked together by an oath of friendship and an undertaking to work together for the welfare of the kingdom. To bar the way to favouritism, the chief central officials and the bailiffs and seneschals were to be chosen by the council. The *Parlement* would co-opt its new members. The mechanism of the financial services, which had become so important during the past quarter of a century, became specialized. Thus the corps of 'general councillors', who controlled taxation as a whole, was split into two groups, one of administrators, the other of judges, who formed the *Cour des Aides*. Similarly, for the administration of the royal domain, within the membership of the treasurers a legal department, the Treasury Court, made its appearance. Finally, in accordance with Nicholas Oresme's advice, an effort was made to revert to the stable currency of the previous reign, which the uncles had slightly devalued.

The smooth running of the royal services was complemented by an administrative purge. The princes' creatures were dismissed from the *Parlement*, the *Chambre des comptes*, the revenue department, the mint, the treasury, and the forestry department. The chief victim was the chancellor, Peter of Giac, an old servant of Berry. Five reforming commissioners were appointed to travel through the provinces, redress wrongs, stop abuses, suspend dishonest officials and replace them by 'good persons', and finally inquire into fraudulent alienations of the royal domain. As their work proved slow and difficult – one can follow its traces until 1395 – it was deemed essential to make a striking example at once. At the end of 1389 the Marmosets took the king to Languedoc, which had been bled white by Anjou's and Berry's lieutenancies. Anyone could bring grievances before the royal council. The Duke of Berry was dismissed and replaced by Gaston Phœbus, Count of Foix. One of Berry's most hated commissioners, Bétizac, a native of Béziers, in charge of the finances of Languedoc, was arrested. As his accounts were in order, he was accused of Albigensianism and went to the stake as a heretic.

Finally the Marmosets were anxious for a reconciliation with the burgesses of Paris, deprived since 1383 of all their municipal liberties. Their magistrates and their rights of justice were not restored to them. But the powers of municipal administration were taken away from the provost of Paris and entrusted to a 'keeper of the provostship of the merchants'. In this new post John le Mercier placed a nephew of his, John Jouvenel, hitherto a minor official, but a good administrator.

Hated as the government of the uncles had been, that of the Marmosets was no more popular. Public opinion dreamed about far-reaching reforms and longed for a reduction of taxes, a decrease in the number of officials, an end to administrative absolutism. All it was given was a quest of abuses and a regulation of administration. Above all, the oppressive taxes were maintained intact. Stern rulers, sometimes mindful of their own fortunes – Clisson was a case in point – the Marmosets needed money for the king and his brother. Louis was greedy. He obtained gifts, pensions, estates. In June 1392 he exchanged his appanage of Touraine for the duchy of Orleans, which was more productive.

Above all, he led the king into a life of festivity and pleasure which swallowed up the kingdom's resources. The knighting of the young princes of Anjou in 1389 served as a pretext for splendid and costly entertainments. The royal progress in Languedoc was a succession of festivities. Intended to relieve the oppressed people of Languedoc, it only increased their burdens; for, once the treasury reserve was exhausted, the salt-tax had to be increased and the currency manipulated to meet the cost. Then the festivities continued, tourneys, feasts, drinking-bouts, dances, until the famous 'ball of the burning' which sent the court into mourning in January 1393. In this tragic incident a group of courtiers, dressed as wild animals and tied to one another, their bodies coated with pitch and covered with tow, came into contact with a torch, caught fire and flamed into a frightful pyre. The king escaped death only by a miracle.

The life of pleasure which he led at the Hôtel Saint-Paul was scarcely calculated to give the young Charles VI a sense of his duty and responsibilities. At the age of twenty-four, he was still no more than a big boy, care-free, erratic, and slack. What a contrast with his father's precocious maturity! He neither governed nor fought except when he was impelled by his entourage. The lessons of Philip of Mézières, who tried to make him a good administrator, a good knight, a good Christian, the leader-designate of the coming crusade, were wasted on this feeble soul, who has been rightly called a 'perpetual minor'. He was a handsome, fair young man, with an inexpressive face, accustomed to sport and soldiering; but his health, already bearing a heavy burden of heredity, could not long withstand the excesses of court life. A few fits of faintness and some nervous disorders had already served as so many warnings; but no notice was taken of them. Then suddenly, in the summer of 1392, the tragedy happened.

The all-powerful Constable, Oliver of Clisson, had recently escaped an attempt at assassination. His attacker, Peter of Craon, took refuge in Brittany. Duke John IV, long since at odds with the Clisson family, was accused of having inspired the attempt. Despite his uncles' advice, Charles VI took up the Constable's quarrel and decided to go and administer stern punishment to his Breton vassal. We need not recall in detail the dramatic incident so often related. On August 5th the army was riding slowly across the plain to the west of Le Mans under a burning sun. A lunatic emerged from the edge of a forest and was allowed to reach the king. The man seized the bridle of the king's horse, shouted something incoherent at him, and declared that he was betrayed. Charles was much upset. The heat, the blinding light shimmering on armour, the striking of a lance against a bassinet brought on a fit of raving madness. The king flung himself upon his suite, attacking them at random. He was mastered with great difficulty. Berry, Bourbon, and Burgundy hurried to the scene and stopped the expedition. Charles's outbreak was followed by a daze. He lay still, recognizing no one and stammering nonsense. He was taken back to the capital and sent to rest at Creil. The quiet and the mildness of the climate effected a rapid improvement. In September he seemed cured; but it was only a respite.

The next year he had another attack, lay prostrated for weeks, and then recovered again. But gradually his relapses became more frequent and longer, his intervals of lucidity shorter. Everything possible was done to cure him. Physicians and charlatans were summoned, every kind of drug was tried, sorcerers were indicted, the people prayed fervently – it was feared that he was bewitched or possessed – pilgrimages were organized. Nothing did any good. The great French monarchy now had at its head only a mad king, the plaything of every kind of intrigue, a poor puppet whose name served to satisfy the most insatiable appetites. Saddest of all, he was to survive for thirty years.

During his attack of madness in 1392, his uncles seized the opportunity to take their revenge and put an end to their four years of a disgrace which was gilded, indeed, but damaging alike to their purses and their self-esteem. The team in power had to give way. Bureau de La Rivière and John le Mercier, guilty of opposing Burgundy more than once, were imprisoned and convicted, but then pardoned. John of Montagu fled to Avignon and the knight Bègue of Villaines to Castille; but they returned once the storm was over. The Constable, Oliver of Clisson, scapegoat of the princes' wrath and public emotion, took refuge in his Breton castle of Josselin. Harsher treatment was meted out to him. He was brought to trial, lost his constableship, was banished 'as a false and wicked traitor' and had to pay a heavy fine. The other Marmosets remained in office and were able to maintain their beneficent influence in the various branches of the administration until the end of the century. But henceforth they had to satisfy the ambitions of the king's uncles, whereas until now they had to content his brother alone. The monarchy hastened towards ruin and disorder.

3. PEACE OR A LONG TRUCE?

THE COMING to power of the Marmosets in France, in November 1388, like the victory of the English barons over the king's favourites a few months earlier, had a profound effect on Anglo-French relations. It inclined them more and more towards peace. The English barons claimed to be in favour of war, but they needed peace to secure their hold on the government and lighten the financial burdens about which the Commons murmured. Until now they had thwarted negotiation and refused mediation. When the fugitive king of Armenia (that is to say, Cilicia), Leo V, arrived in London in November 1386, sought the conclusion of peace and talked about an Anglo-French crusade against the Ottoman Turks and the Mamelukes, he was politely turned away. Another attempt at mediation by Albrecht of Bavaria, Count of Holland, father-in-law of Philip the Bold's children and uncle of the Queen of France, suffered a similar fate in the spring of 1387. There was still resentment against the Valois for spreading panic in England by their great preparations for invasion, and self-interested offers of mediation were distrusted.

In 1388 the situation was no longer the same. Sure of their power, but unable to meet the cost of a warlike policy on the continent, the barons modified their doctrine and their plans. In August the baronial council broke down the last resistance, notably that of Gloucester, and voted in favour of negotiation. The talks were resumed in November at Leulinghen, the usual place, at the very moment when the Marmosets came to power. As Charles V's old councillors, they remembered the late king's desperate efforts, in the last months of his reign, to induce the English to make peace. Faithful to their former master's policy, they were eager to renew those efforts, by similar means and on similar conditions, but this time with the hope of success.

On June 18th 1389 a truce for three years was concluded as the prelude to a more lasting reconciliation. It was the first time for twenty years that so long a suspension of arms had been arranged. Three years were not too long for discussing the very involved conditions of a definitive peace. During the following years there were numerous negotiations, sometimes confined to obscure experts, sometimes conducted, as was the case at Amiens in the spring of 1392, by the princes of the two camps: Lancaster and York for England, Burgundy, Berry, and Bourbon for France. There were many preliminary difficulties, but they were gradually smoothed away by the adversaries' mutual good will. Evacuation of the Breton fortresses, except Brest, by the English garrisons was arranged by 1391. That of Cherbourg took longer. Richard II pleaded qualms of conscience and was reluctant to hand the town over to Charles the Noble, because this prince, son of Charles the Bad and his successor, had recognized the Avignon Pope and was a hardened schismatic. Nevertheless the King of England evacuated Cherbourg in 1393.

Meanwhile the peace terms themselves were being defined. Contrary to all expectation, the question of sovereignty was no longer, as it had been in the past, the main obstacle to understanding. Abandoning the uncompromising position which Edward III had maintained for half a century, ignoring the lessons of the Treaty of Calais and the Gascon appeals, Richard II's councillors agreed that their master should again become the king of France's vassal for Aquitaine. All they wanted was that the formula and obligations of homage should be defined, strictly limited and confined to simple homage, which committed a vassal to nothing. The French, on the other hand, would not hear of anything but liege homage, as in the case of the other vassals of the crown. This merely meant shifting the problem, not solving it. In the sphere of territorial concessions, the divergencies seemed still more serious. The English wanted to reconstitute Aquitaine as it had been in the days of the Black Prince. Of all Charles V's conquests they would abandon only Ponthieu, which indeed was little enough. Everything else must be restored to them, either at once or later: they agreed that the Duke of Berry should keep Poitou for his lifetime. Confronted with claims so excessive, if we recall the diminished Aquitaine over which Richard II's control was effective, Charles VI and especially his uncles went beyond permissible concessions. They promised Saintonge, Angoumois, Agenais, Quercy, and even Rouergue, and would keep only Poitou, Limousin, and Ponthieu out of the conquests made since the renewal of the war. At least they demanded the cession of Calais and the dismantling of its fortress. But, to facilitate agreement, they also proposed to pay, as a war indemnity, the balance of King John's ransom, amounting to 1,200,000 *écus*, which they later raised to 1,400,000 *écus*. The English negotiators, however, adhered to their position and refused the tempting offers which Burgundy and Berry made them.

Once more, on the eve of success, peace was endangered. There would have been a fresh breach if a man had not been found who was determined on agreement, whatever the cost. This man was no other than the King of England. The pomp of the Valois' court and the apparent absolutism of the French monarchy fascinated this imperious young man. Doubtful of his own strength, he did not feel capable of shaking off the tutelage of his barons except with Charles VI's help. As early as 1386, when Gloucester had talked about deposing him, he had threatened his uncle with the vengeance of the King of France. Since then the idea had been at the back of his mind and made him impatient to rule. In May 1389 he copied what Charles VI had done six months earlier when he dismissed his uncles. In a proclamation to his subjects, Richard II announced that, as he was now twenty-two and his minority had been too long, he would henceforth rule by himself. The barons were still united and powerful, and he was wise enough not to thrust them rudely aside. He let them keep their positions on the council; but he filled all the minor offices with followers devoted to the cause of absolute monarchy. He had cleverly imitated Charles VI. Now he wanted a reconciliation with him. A personal loss furthered his plans in the long run. In June 1394 Queen Anne died young. Though she had given him no child, Richard loved her dearly, and at first he was inconsolable. He razed to the ground the manor of Sheen – south-west of London, in the present suburb of Richmond – where they had spent the happy years of their married life. But, once his grief was over, it occurred to him that his widowerhood might favour his policy.

Whatever opinion of Richard II one may have, there is no denying him the obstinacy which took the place of continuity of purpose. He wanted peace. It looked impossible in face of the clash of territorial demands. He had long desired a meeting with Charles VI, and there had been talk about it as early as 1390; but it had been repeatedly postponed on account of the King of France's continued relapses. Richard had turned away the Popes of Rome, first Urban VI and then his successor Boniface IX, when they urged him to renew the alliance with Wenceslas of Bohemia and wage joint war against the schismatic Valois. Now, defying unpopularity among his own subjects, he proposed another solution. A reconciliation could be effected by means of his marriage to a French princess and the conclusion of a long truce.

In March 1395 an embassy, consisting of his favourite Robert Waldby, Archbishop of Dublin, and his cousin Edward of York, Earl of Rutland, went to Paris to request, on behalf of their king, the hand of Charles VI's daughter, Isabella. Their difference in age did not deter Richard: he was nearing thirty, and Isabella was only just six. To make a better impression on his future father-in-law, Richard betook himself to Ireland, where, at great expense but without striking a blow, he reduced to obedience the chiefs of the Irish clans, who were intimidated by the ostentatious strength of the forces employed. The marriage of Richard and Isabella took place by proxy in Paris on March 9th 1396. It was agreed that all the English barons should endorse the contract, that Rutland too should marry a French princess, and that the truce of Leulinghen, several times renewed already, should be extended for twenty-seven years. Though peace was not formally concluded, it seemed ensured for a generation, since a renewal of hostilities was not contemplated before 1432.

The meeting between Charles VI and Richard II finally took place between Calais and Ardres on October 26th 1396. The King of England, impatient to see his new wife, had gone there two months earlier. As was proper, the meeting was marked by splendid festivities. The uncles of two kings and the bedizened barons swore friendship to one another. Richard promised everything he was asked. He became an upholder of French policy in Europe. He undertook to force the Pope of Rome to resign, in order to hasten the end of the schism. He talked about helping his father-in-law in Italy in the expedition to Lombardy which the Valois court was planning. He restored Brest to the Duke of Brittany. But he found scarcely anyone in his own country to approve and support this policy. It was endorsed only by John of Lancaster, who was growing old. Having given up his Spanish claims in return for a substantial pension from the King of Castille, and being endowed since 1389 with the duchy of Aquitaine for his lifetime, Lancaster was anxious for peace. All he thought about now was obtaining the legitimization of his bastards by his mistress, Catherine Swynford, whom he had belatedly married, and settling these children, who had been given the name of the Angevin lordship of Beaufort. When he died, in February 1399, Richard once more found himself without support. The maintenance of his pro-French policy now depended wholly on his ability to keep his throne.

The reconciliation, for that matter, remained incomplete, since there was no peace treaty to delimit the frontiers or settle the reciprocal rights of the former adversaries. *Routiers* and mercenaries, who would not resign themselves to complete inaction, went on waging war as usual during the truce. The English chancery could not hide in ambiguous formulas its embarrassment in the presence of a false situation. The man who had long been called 'our adversary of France' became 'our cousin of France' and then 'our father of France'. But he was still denied the title of King of France, which his son-in-law continued to bear, meaningless though it was.

At all events, Richard was approaching the goal at which he had aimed so long, ever since his barons had humiliated him ten years ago. He had on his side zealous officials and most of the prelates, having consistently filled the bishoprics with his own creatures. He had recruited in Cheshire a guard of archers and men-at-arms, ready to act at a moment's notice. Isabella's dowry had filled his coffers. He had only to give the word. He gave it in July 1397. The barons' outstanding leaders were arrested and banished or put to death. Gloucester was escorted to Calais and murdered there on the king's orders. Archbishop Thomas Arundel retired to Rome. A servile Parliament was entrusted with the duty of preventing any return of the baronial opposition. First convened in Westminster, it ended its long session at Shrewsbury. To avoid summoning a fresh Parliament, Richard got it to surrender its powers to a commission of eighteen members, whom he would assemble if necessary. He devised the most formidable safeguards: the excommunication of potential traitors; the exaction of a solemn oath from all his subjects; the imposition of heavy fines on the seventeen counties in the south and east which had formerly supported the barons; the extortion from many of them of 'blank charters', in which they recognized their debt to the king by sums left blank, but to be filled up in the event of rebellion. At first the aristocracy seemed to be cowed, and then even won over by the grant of titles – dukedoms, marquisates, earl-doms – which Richard bestowed profusely among its members. To all the sovereigns of Europe he triumphantly announced the restoration of the royal authority, in other words absolutism. Lest there should be any mistake about it, he asked Boniface IX to canonize his great-grandfather Edward II, treacherously murdered by his rebellious barons, and secured the annulment of the sentences passed on the Despensers in 1327.

All this was not without its dangers. Richard made the mistake of striking a hard blow at his first cousin and nearest male heir, Henry of Lancaster, Earl of Derby, whom he had just created Duke of Hereford. When Lancaster fell foul of a royalist lord, the Duke of Norfolk, the king banished both the rivals, as a prelude to depriving Lancaster of his enor-mous inheritance and confiscating it to the profit of the crown. In 1398 Lancaster arrived in France, where his pretensions were not taken seriously. In fact, Louis of Orleans struck up a friendship with him. But he proceeded to plot with other victims of Richard and recalled Arch-bishop Arundel from Rome. Above all, he kept watch on events in Eng-land. The very excess of Richard's precautions, his tyrannical ways, his praetorian guard's brutality, his plan of extending the life of Parliament through a small commission summoned when he wanted it to issue ordin-ances stored up hatred of him. In the spring of 1399 the king thought he could consolidate his power by going to Ireland for the second time to punish the turbulent chiefs. While he was away, Lancaster landed in Eng-land on the beach at Ravenspur with a handful of exiles and mercenaries, proclaiming to all and sundry that he had come simply to recover his paternal inheritance. Everyone rallied to his cause, even his uncle York whom the king had made regent during his absence. Richard was lost.

4. THE FRENCH HEGEMONY IN EUROPE

In the long run, the political upheaval into which England was plunged at this time had deadly consequences for France. In the meantime, however, by contrast it served only to raise the prestige of the Valois. Seen from inside, the kingdom seemed weakened by the madness of its king, the persistent poverty of the countryside, the nascent quarrels of its princes. But from outside it appeared to be still powerful. What State in Europe could vie with it, at this turn of the century when everything was collapsing? Not the papacy, still rent by the schism, disputed between rival pontiffs; not the Empire, where the princes, tired of Wenceslas, who was lazy and drunken, declared him deposed and replaced him by Ruprecht of the Palatinate, a feeble claimant; and finally, not England, plunged once more into a dreadful dynastic revolution. The throne of the Valois was indeed the most secure in Christendom, even with its pitiable monarch.

In spite of the king's precarious state of health, festivities were resumed at the Hôtel Saint-Paul. Between her frequent pregnancies, the queen revelled in them. The Duke of Orleans encouraged her, so much so that they were soon accused of being lovers and betraying the poor crowned madman together. The greedy Wittelsbachs sponged on the court. All the princes vied with one another in luxury and prodigality. Every one of them insisted on having his own motto, his own badge, his own livery, even his own order of chivalry. All the court purveyors, drapers, tapestry makers, jewellers, brokers, feathered their nests. Paris enjoyed a prosperity which, though artificial, was striking. It was increased by the presence of Italian bankers, who were at once merchants, money-changers, money-lenders, pawnbrokers, and tax-farmers. The Florentines and Pisans of earlier generations were now replaced by Lucchese, such as the Rapondi, the Cenammi, the Spifami, and the Isbarri, who had branches in the chief centres of commerce, in Bruges and in Italy, enriched themselves in the service of the court and soon became quite French. The most active of them, Dino Rapondi, became Philip the Bold's all-powerful factotum.

A very brilliant civilization developed under the aegis of the princely mansions. Next to nothing has come down to us of private residences, public monuments or churches built in Charles VI's reign. Perhaps there were not many, for such building took time and money, and there was neither to spare. Patronage was practised elsewhere and created other forms of art, less lasting, but more valuable in proportion to their size: tapestry, jewellery, miniatures, paintings. The French painters, now free from Italian and Avignon influence and not yet submerged by Flemish production, constituted an original school, still very close to the technique of illumination. It was at this time that John of Limburg painted for the Duke of Berry, that refined and lavish patron, the detailed little pictures of his *Rich Hours* which may still be admired at Chantilly. It was to French or Rhenish painters that Richard II turned to paint him in majesty in the Westminster Abbey portrait, and to represent him, together with his suite and azure saints and seraphim, all clad in flowing cloaks profusely spangled with argent couchant stags, the royal badge, in the angelic diptych in the National Gallery. Further evidence of a refined civilization were the extravagant fashions fostered by the court of France, which became more and more bizarre at the beginning of the fifteenth century: the high forked hennins of the feminine head-dress, the tight-fitting jerkins and breeches, the gaudy embroidered silks, the long fur-lined surcoats with wide flared sleeves, the queer hats, the shoes with long pointed toes.

Literature, still languid in Charles V's reign, acquired a new note at this turn of the century. I am not referring to Froissart, wholly devoted to the past, who was then writing his copious chronicles in a diffuse and provincial style, richer in information about the feelings of chivalrous society than in historical exactitude. The novelty was to be found elsewhere. True, the France of Charles VI had nothing to show by comparison with the first great national poet whom the England of Richard II knew. But, while Geoffrey Chaucer, in his *Canterbury Tales*, succeeded wonderfully in adapting Petrarchism to the genius of the English language, it was through the medium of France that he was acquainted with Italian humanism. His style itself was quite French, which was not surprising, since all cultured English society still naturally spoke French. By comparison with him, the French Eustace Deschamps was no more than a court rhymester, who put current political, military, and religious affairs into ballads. But, above all, this period witnessed the birth of a real French humanism in Charles VI's entourage. Through Avignon and the Angevin court of Provence some of its members became familiar with Petrarch, intoxicated themselves with him on the Latin classics, cultivated a Ciceronian style, and wrote works which, for correctness and elegance, were worthy of the great Latinists of the sixteenth century. Very few of the writings of this little group of refined connoisseurs have come down to us. It was a sign of the times that they broke away from scholastic routine, and that side by side with clerks like Nicholas of Clamanges were to be found laymen like James of Nouvion and Gontier Col, who was secretary to the chancellery and a servant of Berry. All this vanished in the civil war after its brief hour of brilliance.

The fact remains that French hegemony about 1400 was not exerted only in the sphere of culture. The monarchy of the Valois lived on its reputation in past centuries and profited by its acquired momentum, which was far superior to the strength actually at its disposal. It inspired respect in Europe and still seemed to be the indispensable guide of Latin

Christendom. It was in France that the idea of a crusade was most fervently maintained. The knight Philip of Mézières, who, before becoming the king's tutor, had spent many years in the Near East as chancellor of the kingdom of Cyprus, constituted himself the champion of this idea. He hailed the Anglo-French reconciliation with delight, and, in his *Dream of the old Pilgrim*, written in the allegorical fashion of the time, set forth a plan of joint action which the now united West could carry out.

The French nobility did not await this visionary's appeals to embark upon adventure. Now that the truce and the suspended state of the war left them without occupation, they were once more attracted towards the East and thronged in large numbers into the expeditions which were organized. In 1391 it was the king's uncle, the 'good' Duke Louis II of Bourbon, who, at the request of the Doge of Genoa, led them on a futile expedition to Tunisia, which failed beneath the walls of Mahdyia, called 'Africa' by the French chroniclers. In 1396 there was an undertaking of more importance. The Ottoman Turks had just conquered the Balkans, destroyed the Serb empire and crushed the Bulgar principalities. They reached the Danube and threatened the Hungarian plain. In response to the appeal of Sigismund of Luxemburg, Wenceslas's brother, who had become King of Hungary through his marriage, the French nobility gathered round Philip the Bold's eldest son, John of Nevers. They crossed all Europe and, despite the prudent advice of the Transylvanian and Moldavian contingents which joined them, rashly attacked Bayezid's troops at Nikopol on the banks of the lower Danube. In the rout which followed John of Nevers was taken prisoner. He was freed two years later thanks only to the good offices of the banker Dino Rapondi, and gained from the adventure nothing but a reputation for gallantry and the nickname of John the Fearless.

This disaster did not exhaust the fighting spirit of the French nobility. When the Byzantine emperor, Manuel Paleologus, surrounded on all sides by the Ottoman invasion, issued desperate appeals to Western Christendom, and then went in person to seek help in all the capitals of Europe, it was again Frenchmen who, under the leadership of Marshal Boucicaut, undertook the sole operation of any scope which was attempted on the shores of the Bosphorus. Compared with these expeditions, what was the worth of the meagre help which Henry of Lancaster gave the Teutonic Knights in their struggle against the pagans in Lithuania? Even in this sphere of distant expeditions, French pre-eminence was not to be denied.

It was further affirmed, and in a more tangible and more fruitful way, nearer the frontiers of the kingdom. For the past two generations Dauphiné had been administered by officials of the Valois. Thanks to the occupation of 1381, Louis of Anjou had Frenchified Provence, if it needed doing, and established Angevin and Languedocian officials there. The former kingdom of Arles, though technically it did not belong to the crown of France, had become a natural dependency of it, especially since

Amé, Count of Savoy, nicknamed the Comte Vert, had become linked by marriage with Charles V's family. As late as 1368, the Emperor Charles IV had been able to go to Arles and don the old crown of the kings of Arles in the church of Saint Trophime, thus showing that his domination extended to the banks of the lower Rhône. Not one of his successors did the same or demanded homage for Dauphiné and Provence from the Valois princes.

Through these south-eastern provinces French policy acquired an interest in Italian affairs, into which it had ventured until now only reluctantly and with extreme prudence. Charles VI's reign marked the beginning of great adventures across the Alps, which were costly and disappointing, but still glamorous. It is, however, scarcely exact to speak of a French policy towards Italy. A number of interests jostled and clashed at the court of the Valois, and in fact produced the utmost incoherence. There was an Angevin policy, wholly directed towards Naples, where Louis II of Anjou fought hard for the crown with his rival Ladislas. There was an Orleanist policy, entirely devoted to alliance with Milan. There was a Bavarian policy – that of the queen – hostile to the Visconti, but favourable towards Florence. Finally, there was an Avignon policy, bent on the conquest of Rome and the expulsion of the Italian Pope. Every one of these policies triumphed in turn and played havoc with the patient intrigues of its predecessor. The fact remained – and this was what mattered – that the Italian seigniories, irreconcilably divided, now saw salvation only in appeals abroad. Once the Empire was dead, or at least on the point of death, it was towards France that all of them turned. Despite the incoherence of his interventions, Charles VI thus exercised a regular protectorate over Italy. To satisfy ourselves on this point, it is enough to recall the most tangible results of this policy.

The Angevin adventure was the least lucky of all. Put on short commons alone among the princes with appanages, Louis II of Anjou and his imperious mother, Mary of Brittany, indeed managed to establish themselves momentarily, in 1389 and then again in 1399, in Naples and its neighbourhood. But they had only a handful of followers in the peninsular kingdom, and each time they had to let go after a few months. The Duke of Orleans's ambitions in northern Italy seemed more substantial. Since his marriage to Valentine Visconti, the king's young brother had become Clement VII's hope. The pontiff contemplated making the Papal States of Romagna and the Marches a kingdom for him, with the title of King of Adria, provided he could conquer these territories. With the complicity of the Marmosets, Louis at least got the government to decide on the dispatch of a French expedition to Lombardy and the conclusion of an offensive alliance with his father-in-law, Gian Galeazzo Visconti (1391). But obscure English intrigues secured the postponement of this campaign. Louis nevertheless continued to operate on his own account. His lieutenants established themselves in Asti, whence they intervened in the affairs of Liguria and supported Savona when it rebelled against Genoa. Finally, in November 1394, Enguerrand of Coucy occupied Savona on Louis's behalf. At this point, however, Queen Isabeau of Bavaria's policy came into play, with the Duke of Burgundy's backing. They secured the abandonment of the alliance with Milan, which was of advantage only to Louis of Orleans, and brought about an alliance with Florence, hitherto faithful to the Pope of Rome and champion of the anti-French cause. They encouraged the Doge of Genoa, Antonio Adorno, who was directly threatened by Louis, to place himself under the protection of the King of France; and it was the banner with the lilies that the French ambassadors in 1396, and later Marshal Boucicaut in 1401, hoisted on the walls of the great Ligurian port. It remained there until 1409, a tangible token of the hegemony of the Valois.

Still more significant was the part played by the French monarchy in the settlement of the schism which had afflicted the Church of Rome since 1378. After seeming to encourage its development and perpetuate its harmful effects, all of a sudden the court of Paris took the initiative to stop it and tried to obtain the support of all the other States. It was extraordinary that the University of Paris, sadly fallen though it was from its former glory, ever since nominalistic criticism had ruined the fine scholastic achievements of the thirteenth century, assumed the leadership in this movement. Its graduates and masters became great personages and had their say in affairs of State. John Gerson primed the king. Peter of Ailly, John Petit, and John Courtecuisse dictated the government's policy. In this intervention, which in the long run hastened its decline, the University reached a degree of power which it had never known.

From 1391 onwards it urged the secular princes, in view of the default of the pontiffs, to take the affairs of the Church in hand and work for unity. This was a magic word, which was soon on everyone's lips. The policy of force or 'way of fact', in which the armies of Europe had clashed without result in order to make one of the two Popes prevail, was now succeeded by the 'way of cession': the sovereigns would force the rival pontiffs to resign so that unity might be restored. At first sceptical about this policy, Charles VI's councillors, his uncles and his brother were won over to it at the end of 1392. Henceforth it was France which took the lead, rekindled enthusiasm, broke down apathy. She thought she had reached her goal by 1394, when Clement VII died. But, instead of postponing the election of a successor, the Avignon cardinals hastened to provide themselves with a new Pope in the person of the Aragonese Pedro of Luna, though he had declared himself a convinced supporter of unity. Once he had become Benedict XIII, the pontiff would hear no more about it; he came from a country where they bred good mules, so his enemies said. Nevertheless, the court of France went on with its activity. It induced Castille to adopt its viewpoint and converted Richard II – but not the English – though it failed with Wenceslas. It was more or less alone in advocating a powerful weapon against the obdurate pontiffs and using this weapon. The 'withdrawal of obedience', imposed upon the French clergy in 1398 by the apostles of unity, deprived the Pope of all power over the Church of France and all revenue from it, and gratified nascent Gallicanism by organizing a national Church, in which, under the pretence of freeing it, the lay power gained the upper hand.

Emboldened by the struggle, the Paris masters evolved a doctrine to justify their rebellion against the Papacy. The main thing was to restore unity despite the obstinacy of the two Popes. Hitherto a faithful supporter of the absolutism of the Holy See, from which it had profited greatly, the University reached the point of denying the Pope effective jurisdiction over the national Churches and, like England at the time of Edward III, preaching the restoration of Gallican 'liberties'. It went further, and in the heat of the struggle forged the formidable conciliar theory. To secure unanimity of the faithful against those who disputed the tiara with each other, these faithful, assembled in General Council, must be invested with the right to depose Popes, and therefore the right to judge them and govern the Church in their place. Of this effervescence of ideas, for which so fruitful a future lay in store, Paris alone was the focus. None of the other great European centres of learning, neither Oxford, Prague, nor Bologna, as yet showed such boldness. By persistently following the lead of the Paris masters, the government of the Valois took the government of the Church in hand. True, it was still some time before these ideas actually prevailed. The interval witnessed some sad relapses: the restitution of obedience in 1403; then the pursuit of the 'way of conference' between rival pontiffs who played hide-and-seek to avoid meeting each other; then again a second withdrawal of obedience in 1408. When at length the cardinals of the two obediences, sick of so much dishonesty, assembled at Pisa, disowned their respective pontiffs, summoned a Council and elected a new Pope (1409), it was, alike for the University of Paris and the court of the Valois, the triumph of a policy preached tirelessly for the past fifteen years.

So, wherever we turn round about the year 1400, French hegemony was strikingly displayed. Half a century after the disasters of Crécy and Calais, battered France had resumed her place in Western Christendom. She enjoyed a prestige such as she had not known since Saint Louis. Only fresh defeats, as yet unforeseen, could deprive her of it.

Part VI

THE LANCASTRIAN CONQUEST

1400–1420

Part VI

THE LANCASTRIAN CONQUEST
(1400–1420)

WITH the truce of Leulinghen and the royal meeting at Calais the first part of the Hundred Years' War came to an end. Punctuated by long but badly kept truces and even, in the middle, a period of highly precarious peace, these sixty years of conflict, with all their train of misery, mourning, and devastation, had dragged on for the sole reason that Valois and Plantagenet could not agree over the question of Aquitaine. In its origin, its development, and its objectives, the war therefore remained essentially feudal. If Edward III, a prince French by birth, in education and in taste, had dreamed of donning the crown of France and uniting the two kingdoms under one head, never, even after his most brilliant victories, had his dream looked like coming true. Had he succeeded it is probable that at his death he would have divided his kingdoms between his sons and given France to a younger son. The two countries would then have resumed their own lives under two closely related dynasties, as had been the case under Saint Louis and Henry III, who were brothers-in-law, and under Philip the Fair and Edward II, who were father-in-law and son-in-law. In fact, Edward III did not aim so high. Starting with Aquitaine, where Gascon particularism remained traditionally hostile to the French monarchy, he laboured to restore the old Plantagenet empire and extend it to the Loire and sometimes even to the coast of Normandy. But, in order to avoid past mistakes and dispose once for all of the ever present threat of a confiscation which would deprive him of them, he demanded that his continental possessions should be handed over to him in full sovereignty, without any link of vassaldom.

In this sense one might say that there was a conquest and a partition of the kingdom of France. But it was a conquest by the Plantagenet prince, and by no means an English conquest. Except for the presence of a few high officials from England, who for that matter enjoyed little respect from the population, there was no change in the life of the provinces detached from Valois control, which remained French in language and administration and retained their own institutions. Only Calais was an exception. Here military and economic reasons enforced harsher methods. Occupied by a strong English garrison, the city, which had become the wool emporium, was also colonized by English burgesses. The 'mayoralty of the staple' was usually entrusted to a rich London merchant. Everywhere else the Plantagenets ruled as French princes with French officials, and conformed to local traditions without conflicting with them.

But this did not mean that the two countries remained indifferent to the ruthless struggle in which their rival dynasties indulged. Between their peoples, who had hitherto paid no attention to each other, the war sowed seeds of hatred which bore fruit in the future. It is curious to find |them even in England, though the war had never been waged there. The royal proclamations which, for the past fifty years, had continually denounced the perfidy of the French, thrown responsibility for all breaches upon them, and asserted the right of the Plantagenets to recover their continental 'inheritance' ended by creating an odd mentality in all classes of society.

The barons and knights, who in the thirteenth century had taken no interest whatever in the dynasty's continental domains, and in the long run were responsible through their abstention for John Lackland's and Henry III's disasters, had now acquired a taste for raids, which were rich in plunder and ransoms. They demanded war, because it was a profitable operation for them. So long as they remained French in language and education, the upper classes had not bothered about overseas expeditions. Now that they were becoming more and more anglicized, they supported their king's French policy with all their might. It was a strange contradiction, which scarcely suggested that the English sovereign's hold on his still doubtful conquests would be lasting. To the populace the war meant levies of man-power, requisitioning of ships, heavy taxation. For these unpopular measures they blamed the French, without knowing much about them. On this point the testimony of the monastic chroniclers is irrefutable. Among the clerks Francophobia had become exacerbated ever since the introduction of papal taxation, which was the doing of the French Popes of Avignon. Finally, the French enemy were involved in the same hatred which embraced all foreigners, Hanseatic merchants, Italian bankers, Flemish traders, and sometimes found expression in extreme violence, as it did during the peasant revolt of 1381.

France, even more than England, had learned to know and detest the opponents who had trampled her soil for two generations. Before 1340 the hostility of the French and English peoples did not go beyond quarrels between Norman and English or Gascon sailors. But now hatred persisted in all the provinces which had suffered the *routiers'* ravages in time of peace, truce, or war. This kind of nationalism asserted itself all the more strongly because it combined two feelings equally deep-rooted, but often opposed: loyalty to the monarchy and local particularism. Since all those, whatever their origin, who remained in the field and pillaged the country-side were called English, defence against the enemy locally united the whole population. At the most tragic times, when the nobility, defeated and decimated on the battlefield, were unable to take the lead, it devolved upon the burgesses of the towns and the peasants of the countryside to assume the necessary initiative. The heroism of the humble was sometimes displayed in a striking way and compelled the admiration of the chron-iclers, whose accounts usually dealt only with the exploits of the nobility. For example, out of many unknown deeds we have been handed down those of a sturdy peasant of the Beauvaisis, nicknamed *le Grand Ferré*, who, at the height of the Navarrese war in 1358–9, harried the English bands established in Creil and met with a glorious death.

Still, we cannot as yet speak of patriotism, in the modern sense of the word. The majority did not see beyond the bounds of their parishes. They wanted to be done with disorder, death, pillage. If they were afraid to engage in a fight with the *routiers*, they bought them off and sent them to plunder a neighbouring district. True, even in misfortune they re-mained faithful to the king and the dynasty. But national consciousness was still ephemeral. There was a kingdom of France, not a French nation. Flanders and Brittany had shown as much. Even in the most faithful pro-vinces, loyalty to the monarchy was only a slender link. In response to their suzerain's summons, the nobles of the centre had hastened to their deaths at Poitiers, as they were to do again at Agincourt. But, in the wills they made before they left, they announced their intention to go and serve the king in France, as though France was still only the old royal domain north of the Loire. The sorrows of the civil war were to make their vague feelings all the more wavering. When hostile pillaging bands ravaged the country in the king's name, many of his subjects prayed for the restoration of order, even at the cost of foreign invasion. The possessing classes, the princes with appanages, the merchant burgesses, the higher clergy set the example as usual. Let us not cast the first stone at Joan of Arc's contemporaries: we have seen worse since. To pull the country together the lesson, always salutary, of a long occupation was needed. Before 1400 that had not happened. The accession of the Lancastrians made it probable.

1. THE ACCESSION OF THE LANCASTRIANS

To CONTRAST the two rivals, Richard of Bordeaux and Henry Boling-broke, who disputed the throne of England towards the end of 1399, Shakespeare made the first a dreamer, absorbed in his plans of absolute government, peace with France, an easy, luxurious life; and the second a calculating, practical, shrewd, matter-of-fact prince, who revealed his ambitions only so far as he could fulfil them. It is a poetic transposition of character, but it is not without foundation. Henry of Lancaster was a man very different from his cousin, though they had been playmates in child-hood and youth. His long stays abroad, in Prussia and the Holy Land, and his exile in France had not given him that cosmopolitan air which marked all the Plantagenets, including Richard II. If he still spoke French, like almost all his country's aristocracy, he was before all else an English prince and an English landowner: to his parents' great appanage he had added the extensive estates in the west of England brought him by his wife, a Bohun, the last scion of a distinguished Anglo-Norman family.

This middle-aged man had long concealed his hand. Had he any con-victions, any plans, apart from his desire to win the throne and keep it? We may doubt it. With cold, calculating cynicism he became the cham-pion of all the causes which his rival had combated: among others, respect for parliamentary privileges and war with France. That did not make him a sovereign sincerely constitutional or resolutely warlike. His theatrical piety, which his son inherited, also suffered many a lapse from Christian feeling. Duplicity during his rise, but courage in adversity: these two traits depict him better than a long analysis. His actions tell us all the rest about him.

When he landed in England in May 1399 Henry openly demanded only the Lancastrian inheritance, of which he had been unjustly deprived. In this object he received the support of all the malcontents: barons ousted from power, exiled prelates, the harshly oppressed citizens of London. When Richard hastily returned from Ireland he had no followers left. He wasted time wandering about for a few weeks in Wales, and then, feeling that his cause was lost, sought negotiation. At Conway he agreed to pardon the rebels, entrust them with power and summon a fresh Parliament. At this price, he imagined, he had saved his throne and reverted to his humiliating position at the time of the Lords Appellant.

But this was only make-believe. Once in London he was thrown into the Tower and kept prisoner. In Parliament Henry recalled the king's bad government. He presented a document in which Richard, 'with a smiling face', and in the presence of witnesses, was alleged to have recognized his faults, admitted that he was unworthy to rule and finally abdicated. Then Henry demanded the crown for himself, and the assembly recognized his title to it (September–October). King by right of conquest and by the assent of Parliament, Henry IV was not the kind of man to be satisfied with a usurpation. He must justify it after the event. Rumours had circulated that the Black Prince's marriage was irregular. As this was not enough, Henry proclaimed that he held the throne as direct and legitimate descendant of Henry III Plantagenet, who died in 1272. He cynically countenanced a popular legend according to which Henry III's younger son, Edmund of Lancaster, was really the elder, but had been thrust aside from the throne because of his physical deformity as a hunchback. As great-grandson of Edmund of Lancaster on his mother's side, the usurper pretended to believe that the glorious line of the three Edwards, from whom he descended on his father's side, was unlawful throughout. This audacious move – but whom did it deceive? – at one stroke set aside from the throne of England all Edward III's descendants, Clarence's daughter, the Duke of York's sons and even John of Lancaster's legitimized bastards, and left only Henry IV and his issue in the field.

If this argument was specious in the case of the crown of England, what was it worth in its application to the title of King of France, which Henry also assumed? If he repudiated his descent from Edward III, of whom, for that matter, he was not the most direct heir – Clarence, the old king's second son, had left a daughter, the widow of Roger Mortimer, Earl of March – by what right did he claim the inheritance of the Capets, to whom he was linked only by a distant and dubious relationship? Such niceties did not worry him in the least. The title of King of France was one of England's stage properties. Henry adorned himself with it and went on parading it from force of habit. No one dreamed of justifying it: it was part of the succession. For the rest, Henry owed his popularity to the anti-French feelings which he had professed. He was known to be hostile to the policy of reconciliation pursued by his predecessor. From his accession he proclaimed the necessity of renewing the war as soon as possible and reconquering his continental 'inheritance'. This kind of proof was more conclusive than any genealogical tree.

In France Lancaster's usurpation created consternation. The policy of peace, pursued for the past ten years, depended on Richard personally. Now that he was gone, anything was to be feared. At first it was hoped that the change would be fleeting. After his rival's coronation Richard had been kept in the Tower, and then taken to Pontefract Castle in Yorkshire. His rescue, his escape, a rising of his followers were still possible. Meanwhile it was better to gain time. As Henry, insecurely seated on his still unsteady throne, asked nothing better than to postpone his warlike plans, France welcomed his offer to ratify, to his own advantage, that very truce of Leulinghen which he had sworn to break (May 1400). This was also a respite for the usurper while he consolidated his position. Then Charles VI, seeing no hope of his daughter Isabella's restoration to the throne, demanded that she should be sent back to him, as was provided for in her marriage settlement. Assured that he was not endangering peace, Henry was in a position to humiliate the Valois, powerful though he was, as he chose. The fallen queen served him as a means of blackmail. He imprisoned her, limited her French entourage, refused to let her father's envoys see her, and laid down exorbitant conditions for her freedom. When he finally agreed to let her go, in August 1400, he kept the unfortunate queen's dowry and her jewels. It was, so he said, an instalment of King John's unpaid ransom.

For the moment, neither side went further. Henry of Lancaster was struggling with all the usual troubles of a usurper raised to power by a coalition of interested parties. He had to satisfy only too many appetites or encounter only too many opponents. To achieve success he had taken the opposite course to Richard in everything. This ambitious, self-willed, and violent man had protested against the Plantagenet's absolutism. Was he going to let himself be put in tutelage by the baronage from whose ranks he had emerged, or by the Parliament which had hailed him as king? Deceived by appearances, the liberal historians of the past century sang the praises of Lancastrian 'constitutionalism', which harmoniously combined the need for a strong monarchy with the idea of a controlled government. In fact, there was no change in English institutions, even in spirit. The only difference was that Henry IV, still unsteady on his throne, was reluctantly forced to use tact. Grand councils of barons and meetings of Parliament became more frequent. The king took unusual care to seek grants from the Commons. He led them to believe that he was ruling with their help. The result was a weak government, always ill at ease and often without adequate resources in emergency.

Henry IV was more successful – though not entirely – with the clergy. Richard II had become a convert to the policy of unity advocated by the court of the Valois. The bishops and the Universities had not followed him. Henry reverted to enthusiastic, though ineffective support of the Pope of Rome. Boniface IX and his successors Innocent VII (1404) – who, under the name of Cosimo Megliorato, had for many years been collector of the apostolic chamber in England – and Gregory XII (1406) were assured of the English kingdom's fidelity. Henry held firmly aloof from all the attempts made by France to induce the two pontiffs to resign or reach agreement. When finally in 1409 the cardinals at Pisa elected a third Pope, Alexander V, the court of London, after making difficulties, decided to recognize him. But at the same time, as Richard II had concluded a concordat with Boniface IX which divided the nomination to benefices between the Pope and the king, Henry cried shame and, claiming to defend the 'liberties' of the Church of England, officially restored anti-papal legislation. If nothing was changed in practice, at least he gratified public opinion and rallied the lower and middle clergy to his cause.

In addition, Richard had been reproached with not harrying Wyclif's belated followers with sufficient energy. Since they could not tax the fallen king with heresy, the Lancastrian chroniclers contrived to accuse his entourage of it. The fable of the four knights of the royal household charged with Lollard manœuvres has found an echo even among modern historians. The fact remains that the episcopate, Archbishop Arundel at their head, eagerly demanded the support of the secular arm to exterminate the heretics. Into this country hitherto very tolerant in matters of faith, where the Inquisition had never functioned, Henry IV had the dismal distinction of introducing religious persecution. By virtue of the statute *De heretico comburendo*, promulgated in Parliament in 1401, the stakes flamed, to the great delight of the orthodox bishops.

All this did not allay the growing political discontent. Henry was really supported only by south-eastern England, the seventeen counties punished by his predecessor, which roughly correspond with what geographers call the basin of London or the sedimentary region. All the rest of the country, apart from the duchy of Lancaster, the usurper's patrimony, but including the north, the midlands, the Cheshire plains with their formidable people, and the granite south-west, still contained a number of followers of the fallen king. In January 1400 a plot was hatched, in which the Duke of York, the last survivor of the 'uncles', probably had a hand, to set Richard II free and replace him on the throne. York's eldest son, the Earl of Rutland, until 1399 Richard's favourite cousin; the ex-king's half-brother Huntingdon and his nephew Kent, and another royalist earl, Salisbury, planned to rescue Richard. Their plot was discovered and they fled to the west, but were defeated at Cirencester, between Gloucester and Oxford.

Soon afterwards it was learned that Richard had died of starvation in his prison. Lest there should be any mistake about it, his body was exposed in public, but was not taken to Westminster until Henry V's reign. This crime did not stop revolts, which followed one another with alarming speed. The object of all of them was to overthrow the Lancastrian dynasty and raise young Edmund Mortimer, Edward III's legitimate descendant, to the throne. The most dangerous was that of the Percies, a great northern family, who had won a glorious reputation in an endless struggle against the Scottish incursions over the badly defended frontier. Their head, the Earl of Northumberland, and his son Henry Percy, nicknamed Hotspur, had been laden with favours by Henry IV. They were not satisfied. They rebelled and, by a lightning march, swooped down upon Cheshire, intending to join hands with the Welsh. The Lancastrian forces intercepted them in time, and, on July 21st 1403, crushed them at Shrewsbury. Hotspur was killed and quartered, his father was taken prisoner, and order was restored in the north. Then there was another conspiracy in Essex, followed by an attempt to carry off young Mortimer. In 1405 the Percies took up arms again, and obtained the support of the Archbishop of York, Richard Scrope. In the course of the ensuing repression, the prelate was beheaded, to the great scandal of the clerical world. Northumberland remained indomitable. He perished in his turn in 1408 in a final crazy attempt to raise Yorkshire. Meanwhile an impostor, who claimed to be Richard II escaped from prison, was received with respect at the court of Scotland and revived the hopes of belated followers even in the heart of England.

A still graver symptom was the fact that Wales rebelled in 1400, and the downfall of the Percies enabled the Scots to renew the war with impunity. The people of the Welsh principality had not stirred since Edward I's heavy hand had mastered them once for all at the end of the thirteenth century. Great castles, Carnarvon, Carmarthen, and Beaumaris, secured the maintenance of order. The country had been harshly subjected to English administration, though it enjoyed comparative autonomy in relation to the crown, being traditionally given as an appanage to the king's eldest son. In addition, districts which did not belong directly to the principality had been entrusted to the barons of the Welsh marches, stout soldiers and powerful vassals, among whom the Mortimer family was dominant.

Why then did the revolt break out in 1400? Its pretext was trivial. A Celtic chieftain failed in a lawsuit in the king's court against a neighbouring English lord, rebelled, and was deprived of his estates. Gradually his rebellion spread to all his fellow-countrymen. From the first the Welsh joined with Richard II's followers, who were numerous in these parts, and made the struggle against the usurper and Mortimer's cause their own. But the most serious feature of the revolt was that it very soon assumed a national and racial character: the Welsh of Celtic culture against the English. Their leader, who brought the glorious deeds of Llewelyn, Edward I's formidable foe, to life again, was named Owen Glendower, in Celtic Glyndwr, and gathered all the strength of Wales around him. Until 1409 almost annual expeditions, which were a drain on the exhausted kingdom, had to be organized against these hardy mountaineers. In this fighting the young heir to the Lancastrian throne, Henry of Monmouth, Prince of Wales, served his military apprenticeship in appropriate circumstances. But for some time the struggle remained undecided, and at the outset it was critical. This was because the Welsh took advantage of all the Lancastrians' troubles and synchronized their attacks with those of the barons. As late as 1406, they planned a common campaign with the Mortimers, thrust aside from the succession to the throne, and the disinherited Percies, with a view to sharing the new dynasty's spoils in the event of victory.

Outside England they were supported by the Scottish forces. From the outset of the Hundred Years' War the little northern kingdom, though still allied with France, had not seriously disturbed the Plantagenets. Its king, David Bruce, had long been Edward III's prisoner. A new dynasty, the Stuarts, sprung from a younger branch which bore the hereditary title of Stewards of Scotland, renewed the war and gained some success against Richard II, though with no result except pillaging the northern counties. Scotland was then included in the truce of Leulinghen and laden with favours by Richard II. Her king Robert III resumed the struggle against the Lancastrians. Only her alliance with the Welsh enabled her to threaten them seriously. The little kingdom had slender resources and was incurably divided by internal feuds. In 1406, on his deathbed, Robert dispatched his young son, the future James I, to France, where he could serve his apprenticeship to his profession in peace. By a lucky chance, the English intercepted the ship and took young James prisoner. Doomed to a stormy regency, Scotland was once more neutralized. But it took three more years for the Lancastrians finally to master the Welsh rebellion.

Prematurely aged and in poor health, Henry IV had barely surmounted all these dangers. The man who had won the throne with a programme of war to the death against the French enemy had been for years reduced to a precarious defensive. Collusion between Wales and France had developed in 1404–5 and threatened to carry the conflict on to the soil of England herself, hitherto miraculously saved by the failure of all the plans for French landings. What a wonderful opportunity for a strong king, if only Charles VI had been one! Even as it was, from the outset Henry IV's difficulties had aroused great hopes at the court of France. There were two possible policies. One was to take advantage of the chance to consolidate peace, maintain the truce and inspire the grateful Lancastrians with the idea of a lasting reconciliation. This was the policy of Philip the Bold, always anxious not to endanger Anglo-Flemish trade. The other policy demanded more activity. Since Henry was detained at home by all his troubles, and if necessary could be kept there by skilful diversions in the Welsh sphere, the moment seemed to have come to complete Charles V's work and drive the Lancastrians from their last continental footholds: Gascony and Calais. This was the policy of Louis of Orleans; but, to succeed, it would have required a more capable and less changeable leader. The struggle against England was no longer the main concern of the court of Paris. Amid all the plans that shimmered on the horizon, the essential one was let slip; and the opportunity did not recur.

Still, something was tried, and it is worth telling. From the beginning of the century Charles VI's entourage, though they renewed the truce of Leulinghen for the time being, wondered whether it was not possible to foster a revolt of his Gascon vassals against the usurper. Envoys were sent to Guienne to test the ground and provoke rebellion. Their hopes did not meet with success. The Gascons, as a whole, had no quarrel with their new master, who was remote, weak, and did not worry them. There was only one important defection, in 1401: that of Archambaud of Grailly, Captal of Buch, a leading noble of the Landes. He handed over a few frontier fortresses to the French, but was unable to induce Gascony to rebel.

In 1404 the situation seemed to be more favourable. While Charles VI eagerly welcomed overtures from the Welsh and sent them money and even a few troops, Louis of Orleans got the royal council to accept a great plan for the conquest of Aquitaine. There was no need to break the truce officially. Both sides had acquired the habit of violating it with impunity. In the course of the campaign of 1405, capable leaders came within an ace of success. Advancing from Poitou, the Constable, Charles of Albret, liberated all the fortresses situated south of Saintonge and on the frontiers of Périgord. The French advance reached the Gironde and the lower Dordogne. Meanwhile, having recruited an army in Languedoc, the Count of Armagnac operated in middle Gascony, south of the Garonne, and seriously threatened Bordeaux. But once more the enterprise was beyond the means available. The campaign, intended to be a lightning-stroke, dragged on to no profit. During the winter of 1406–7 Louis of Orleans, a poor soldier, failed in the siege of Blaye, an essential prelude to the investment of Bordeaux. On his side the new Duke of Burgundy, John the Fearless, entrusted with reducing Calais, was indolent in his attack on his objective. His heart was not in it. The struggle between the two princes was becoming keener, and led to the abandonment of the plans of conquest.

Freed from danger in 1407 in Gascony and a little later in Wales, Henry IV could now breathe freely. The period of his trials was over, and that of his hopes was beginning. If his health had allowed, he would doubtless have been tempted to intervene earlier in the affairs of France, where civil war had just begun.

2. ANARCHY IN FRANCE

IT IS time to analyse the disease which afflicted the monarchy of Charles VI, apparently so strong, so glorious in its European reputation. It was this disease, much more than the renewed danger of an English attack, which led to its downfall. Indeed, can one still call it a monarchy, when the kingdom was dominated by a group of magnates, territorial princes already only too powerful, but insatiably ambitious and eager to acquire the utmost of the wealth, still great, in the hands of the royal government? A verbal laziness, so to speak, still lets history text-books describe the heads of these vast appanages as 'feudal lords'. They go on to talk about the 'feudal revolts' directed against Charles VII and Louis XI in their turn. Nothing could convey a more false idea of the situation which existed in the kingdom of France in the fifteenth century. True, all these princes were vassals of the crown for their appanages and their French domains. But the feudal link had ceased to be anything more than an empty word, and no longer represented the true structure of society, the real aspect of politics.

The struggle was not, as it had been in the twelfth and thirteenth centuries, between feudal lords jealous of their autonomy and a monarchy whose encroachments they endured impatiently, whose officials they hated and whose sovereign power they denied. The princes had no intention whatever to destroy the royal edifice, slowly built up in the course of centuries and at the expense of the feudal system. Monarchs themselves – or very nearly – in their own estates, they wanted to dominate the royal government and control the monarchy in order to advance their own fortunes. Would a coalition of these magnates make use of the mad king to share the spoils of the kingdom? Or would one of them, more powerful than the rest, impose his will both on the sovereign and the other princes? That was the whole question. At the same time, the coming struggle threatened to destroy the royal edifice whose possession was in dispute.

The constitution of great appanages in favour of royal cadets, which had been increased since the accession of the Valois, had had the unfortunate result of reducing considerably the crown domain where the exercise of the royal authority was direct and undivided. It still comprised a compact group of provinces in the north of the kingdom, Ile-de-France, Champagne, Picardy, and Normandy; and another in the south, Languedoc, though the southern seneschalships enjoyed a quasi-autonomy, being governed by a lieutenant of the king who was usually a prince holding an appanage, and the taxes voted by the Estates of Languedoc were spent locally, with no control by the capital. In between, a few isolated outposts, such as Mâconnais and Lyons, did not suffice to maintain contact. All the rest of the kingdom was more or less permanently in the hands of the princes.

Louis of Anjou's sons governed Maine, Anjou, and, at the gates of France, Provence. The king's brother held Orleanais, together with Angoumois, Périgord, and the counties of Blois and Dunois. Berry had made a compact State for himself out of the three neighbouring provinces of Poitou, Berry, and Auvergne, between the Loire, the Central Plateau, and the Atlantic. His domains bordered those of the house of Bourbon, which, by a patient territorial policy, had grouped around Bourbonnais first La Marche, then Forez, then more recently (1400) Beaujolais, and, outside the kingdom, Dombes. Philip the Bold controlled the duchy and the county of Burgundy, Flanders, Artois, and the counties of Rethel and Nevers, and later he added Charolais to them. Charles VI was to be no less liberal in favour of his sons, sickly youths who died young, but left accumulated appanages to their younger brothers. The first Dauphin, Charles, who died before being invested with Dauphiné, was succeeded by Louis, Duke of Guienne – that is, the part of Aquitaine not occupied by the English – and he in turn by John, Duke of Touraine, and he again by Charles, Count of Ponthieu, the future Charles VII.

These alienations of the crown domain would not have been so bad if the princes holding appanages, as docile vassals, had been content with their domainial resources in their own lands, given support to the monarchy everywhere else, and left its taxation system, its judicial powers and its administration intact. But, in the course of the past century, the great fiefs of the crown had undergone an evolution parallel with that of the monarchy itself. They had become regular States, with all their own administrative machinery, all their own corps of officials; and these, inevitably, vied with those of the king. Every prince had his own household, swarming with his own creatures, his own personal staff, a regular nursery of officials. Every one of them had his own paid council, consisting of prelates, high officers, vassals, and clerks; his own chancellery, which dealt with his correspondence and issued his ordinances; his own bailiffs and seneschals, who administered justice.

True, the royal sovereignty was safeguarded in theory by appeal to the *Parlement*. But sometimes, as in the case of Berry as early as 1370, the holder of an appanage was granted the regular holding of '*Grands Jours*', which allowed a delegation of judges to come and hear appeals locally, without any occasion for the parties to go to Paris. Similarly the Duke of Burgundy inaugurated '*Jours Généraux*' at Beaune, a regular miniature *Parlement*, with its president and its twenty judges of appeal, assisted by 'knights of honour' for feudal cases. In the financial sphere the essential machinery, here again modelled on that of the crown, was the Treasury, with its receiver-general and treasurer-general, and the *Chambre des comptes*. The one at Bourges was created in 1379. The Bourbons had three, at Moulins for Bourbonnais, at Montbrison for Forez, and at Villefranche for Beaujolais. In 1386 Philip the Bold asked for officials from Paris to organize a *Chambre des comptes* at Dijon, which had jurisdiction over the two Burgundies, i.e. the duchy and the county. At the same time a Council of Flanders was created at Lille for Flanders and Artois, which was both an appeal court and an audit-office.

No more than the monarchy could the appanage States live on their domainial resources alone. They simply had to find other resources, in the first place by applying to their subjects, whose representatives, meeting in local Estates, voted aids and hearth-taxes from time to time. But the yield of these subsidies, coming on top of the royal taxes, was inevitably limited, except in the rather rare cases when a pressing danger induced the taxpayers to make exceptional efforts. In normal times, it was simpler to lay hands on the local yield of the royal taxes, for which there was a ready-made administration with long experience. So the 'gift of aids' was the first goal which the appanaged princes had in view, since without this concession they could not balance their budgets. As early as the reign of Charles V they managed to receive for limited periods, which were soon extended by continual renewals, a third, a half or sometimes even the whole of the taxes levied in their domains on behalf of the crown. In this respect Philip the Bold was in a privileged position. By dint of guile and persistence, he got his brother to agree that royal taxation should not apply to Burgundy, or at least that his own officials should levy it and that he should appropriate the whole of it. Flanders too was exempt from all royal taxation. Only Artois, Nivernais and the county of Rethel paid it, if the duke did not claim the yield on one ground or another. For pro-longed periods Berry received all the taxes in his appanage. So did Bourbon and several others.

Accordingly, the 'extraordinary finances' which the monarchy enjoyed were now levied, more or less, only on a royal domain continually reduced by fresh alienations. Even this was too much for the princes' taste. While they were in power they proposed to turn their services to account and have their costly expenses paid 'to maintain their state'. First calculated daily in proportion to services rendered, these expenses were soon paid monthly in advance, and so came to be fixed pensions. That of Philip the Bold reached 100,000 francs a year in 1402. To this permanent source of revenue were added special grants, at first given on some valid ground, but soon for no reason whatever. In Burgundy's case they more than doubled his pension. Other princes secured the grant of a whole category of royal revenues. Louis of Orleans, for example, appropriated the yield of all forfeitures and confiscations in 1392, and in 1402 the revenues of the fair of Le Lendit. Beneath this beneficent rain of manna, the princely budgets swelled enormously. Burgundy's takings, which were only 100,000 francs in 1375, reached and exceeded 500,000 in 1400.

To stop the flow of pensions and gifts drying up, the princes had to exercise vigilant control over the government and secure the renewal and increase of favours. Their presence on the council was not enough. They had to fill the departments of state with their creatures and have contacts in all the government services. The career of a royal official under Charles VI normally began in one of the civil services of a prince. Once he passed into the royal administration, the prince remained his patron and he remained the prince's client. One example among many was that of the Auvergnat lord Peter of Giac, who was chancellor of the Duke of Berry from 1371 to 1383, and was then promoted to be chancellor of France. His successor at Bourges, Simon of Cramaud, Bishop of Poitiers, later appointed Patriarch of Alexandria, became before the end of the century the crown's most influential adviser on ecclesiastical affairs, the promoter and supporter of the withdrawal of obedience. If anyone wanted to retain his place in the king's service, he had to continue to serve faithfully the prince to whom he owed everything. One day in the year 1407, the chancellor could find not one of the five presidents in the *Parlement*. All of them were in Burgundy, Poitou, or Anjou in the service of their princes.

But let influence pass from one prince to another, and then there was a purge throughout the departments, a hunt for jobs, a regular spoils system from top to bottom of the ladder. The dismissals of 1380, 1389, and 1392 were only a foretaste of what happened in the first fifteen years of the fifteenth century. The career of Gontier Col, a burgess of Sens in the Duke of Berry's service, is typical from this point of view. Secretary to the king at the beginning of 1388, he lost his post on the accession of the Marmosets, but recovered it when the king went mad and was employed on diplomatic and financial missions. In 1411, with Berry, he took the Armagnac side and his property was confiscated by the Burgundians. A brief return to fortune was followed, at the time of Caboche's insurrection, by the pillaging of his house. Restored to office by the Armagnacs, he was assassinated by the Burgundians when they seized Paris in June 1418.

These alternating purges did not suffice to satisfy all appetites and find jobs for all the princes' protégés. The multiplication of offices, a natural process in any bureaucratic State, about which there had been complaints throughout the fourteenth century, assumed inordinate and alarming scope under Charles VI. In the *Parlement*, the *Chambre des comptes*, and the *Cour des aides* the normal quota of councillors and masters was swollen by 'extraordinary' officials whose number kept on growing. In vain did solemn ordinances periodically decree the elimination of sinecures and scrupulously settle the maximum staff of every department. Very soon royal letters decreed fresh appointments, 'notwithstanding any ordinances to the contrary'. In the supreme courts the principle of co-option, laid down by the Marmosets, had never been applied. If there was any resistance, the chancellor went in person and enforced the installation of any princely protégé, who was appointed as a supernumerary. The plethora of officials was still more marked in the king's household and in those of the queen, the Dauphin, and the royal children, where supervision by experienced officials did not apply. The sums required to run these household services kept on growing. In 1406 ordinary expenses for the royal household swallowed up 60,000 *livres*, the *Argenterie* 30,000, and there was an account for special expenses which almost doubled the total. Since cash was lacking, the right of requisition and seizure which the household officials enjoyed weighed heavily on the court purveyors.

All these officials gorged themselves with gold and silver. As they were doubtful about the morrow, they had to make their fortunes as fast as possible by systematic pillage of the State revenues. Misappropriation by officials, that endemic scourge of medieval administration, assumed alarming proportions. The princes set the example, and everyone else followed it, from the highest to the lowest. The chancellor Arnaud of Corbie, whose annual salary was 2,000 *livres*, a large sum for the period, was by no means satisfied with it. He procured a further 2,000 *livres* of special salary on the yield of taxation, 2,000 more on the emoluments of the seal, and received a percentage on the chancery dues, not to speak of 'sweetenings' and bribes. Among subordinates salaries were paid irregularly. Everyone helped himself by every kind of fraudulent procedure.

For in this administration, which had developed slowly by successive growth under pressure of necessity, the instruments of inspection proved inoperative. The *Chambre des comptes*, the control-lever of the royal machine, should have been able to check the movement and give a lead to officials zealous in their opposition to princely absolutism. But, though it was guardian of the royal domain, it could not resist imperative orders which bade it accept alienations or ratify ruinous gifts. From time to time all alienations effected since a date sometimes remote were revoked. But no sooner was an inquiry instituted which would enable order to be restored in the domain than the beneficiaries secured confirmation of former grants and obtained new ones. Corrupt accountants defied the control of the *Chambre*, which had no means of coercing them. Finally the system of assignments and warrants, according to which expenses were charged on particular receipts, was so general that many collectors had to pay out more than they received and any control of expenses thus became illusory. Many of these assignments were surreptitious and avoided the countersignature of the financial departments. Drafts were issued in blank, and the payees filled in the amount as they chose.

Plundered in all directions, the State was driven towards bankruptcy. Yet the taxes, permanently levied since their re-establishment in 1383, were periodically increased. The tax on merchandise rose from 12 to 18 *deniers* a *livre*, that is, from 5 to 7½ per cent. and the tax on wine from 12½ to 25 per cent. The salt-tax, originally fixed at 20 francs a *muid*, was subjected to increases which doubled the total. The hearth-tax, which brought in 1,200,000 *livres* in 1402, reached 1,800,000 in 1408. Despite all this, the gulf deepened. The savings-fund, organized by Charles V to hold surplus receipts, was supplied annually by a payment on account of taxes, but was empty on the morrow of the transfer. In 1411 the tax coffers of Languedoc contained only 2,500 *livres*. The government lived on expedients which, while they were not novel, multiplied dangerously: anticipation of receipts; tenths from the clergy (on pretext of covering the expenses of the policy of unity); withholding of salaries; forced loans from officials and burgesses; advances on jewellery; mortgaging of domainial revenues. When the threat of foreign war loomed over the kingdom once more, Charles VI's government was more hard up than improvident Philip VI or needy John the Good had ever been.

This administrative anarchy, of which I have tried to paint as exact a picture as possible, had established itself only slowly in the machinery of the State. None of the abuses was altogether new in 1380; but they had gradually spread. Until 1400 those of the Marmosets who had clung to power had managed partially to limit their effects. Then the evil rapidly worsened, being hastened by the princes' rivalry. Their political struggles, to which I shall now turn, favoured negligence, fraud, and misappropriation; but they did not create them. By a reflex action, these abuses were quickened by the thirst for pelf and pillage which drove the princes to civil war.

Thanks to the king's madness, Charles VI's uncles and cousins regained their places in the council by 1392 and demanded their share in the favours of which Louis of Orleans alone had been the beneficiary during the past four years. This meant too many appetites to be satisfied simultaneously in the country's state of exhaustion. It was inevitable that rivalry should spring up among all these claimants. Soon two of them, Orleans and Burgundy, were to emerge from the ruck and engage in a desperate struggle. The rest did not forgo all ambitions, but they were only seconds in the coming duel. The young princes of Anjou were wholly immersed in their Neapolitan dreams, which they pursued persistently. Louis of Bourbon, who was growing old – he was succeeded in 1410 by his son John I – did not aspire to the first place, and was kept busy rounding off his States by purchase and inheritance. Berry found his expensive tastes as a patron of the arts easily satisfied by the rich spoils he extracted from his appanage and from Languedoc, of which he had again become lieutenant in 1401.

But thirst for power tormented Philip of Burgundy and Louis of Orleans alike. They strove for influence over the afflicted king and exercised it in turn. No sharing between them was possible. Very soon they reached a point where they opposed each other in everything, even in spheres in which their personal interests did not seem to be at stake, for no reason except mutually thwarting their policies. In Italy

Louis counted unreservedly on his father-in-law's support to create a great principality round Asti in Lombardy. At once Philip supported the queen and the Wittelsbachs in their anti-Milan policy, favoured an alliance with Florence and, by the occupation of Genoa, brought Louis' plans to naught. When it was a question of achieving unity in the Church, Burgundy, less strongly supported by the other princes, constituted himself the champion of the strong hand, pressed for the withdrawal of obedience and secured the dispatch of a small force to the banks of the Rhône, which held the obstinate Benedict XIII securely shut up in the papal palace. Louis of Orleans took advantage of a turn of fortune to be given the guardianship of the pontiff and, from a spirit of contradiction, became the apostle of conciliation. From 1401 he fanned the discontent of all those, prelates, incumbents, University graduates, whose interests had been injured by the withdrawal of obedience. He got into touch with the Angevin officials, helped Benedict to escape and take refuge in Provence, and finally brought about the restitution of obedience.

There was the same opposition, as we have already seen, where policy towards England was concerned. Faced with Henry of Lancaster's usurpation, Louis of Orleans, though he had been Henry's friend, favoured a renewal of the war and the conquest of Aquitaine from the usurper. He talked about nothing less than sending a personal challenge to Henry IV and meeting the enemy on the frontier of Guienne with eight hundred seconds on each side. Being unable to convert the royal council to his views, he organized a splendid tourney at Saint-Inglevert near Calais, where the French nobility, by their successes in the lists, avenged Isabella of France's affronted honour (1402). Taking the opposite course to this policy, Philip of Burgundy declared his desire for understanding with the Lancastrians, renewed the Anglo-Flemish trade treaty, doubtless had something to do with the marriages which united the English royal family with the Wittelsbachs, and forced the royal council to maintain the truce of Leulinghen, despite all the insults which Henry IV had heaped on the court of the Valois. When Duke John IV of Brittany died and his widow, Joan of Navarre, soon afterwards married the King of England, Orleans favoured a military occupation of the duchy. Burgundy secured the guardianship of the young John V and so scored another point against his nephew (October 1402).

But it was in the Low Countries that their rivalry was most acute. After patient manœuvres, Philip had reached his goal in 1396. He secured the administration of Limburg and the territory beyond the Meuse and enforced the use of Flemish currency in Brabant. The old duchess Joan, who was in debt to him, finally decided to recognize Anthony, a cadet of Burgundy, as her heir and bring him up at her court. Louis of Orleans was determined at all costs to check the power of Burgundy in this very spot where it flaunted itself. He negotiated the purchase of the lordship of Coucy, whose dependencies extended to the border of the county of

Rethel. He allied himself with the Duke of Gelderland and the Duke of Lorraine. He got into contact with Wenceslas of Bohemia, who, since the death of Joan of Brabant's husband, had become the head of the house of Luxemburg. From this needy King of Bohemia, now deprived by the German princes of the title of King of the Romans, and his uncle Jošt of Moravia he bought for cash a mortgage on the duchy of Luxemburg. After entering Toul his troops occupied the great Ardennes principality, and rallied around them all those who, in the Low Countries and on the banks of the Moselle alike, were disturbed by Burgundy's ambitions (1402). Henceforth two rival lilied banners floated in the region of the Meuse, one bearing a label, that of Orleans, the other a bordure, that of Burgundy.

So long as Philip the Bold was alive, this rivalry, though continually more acute, did not degenerate into open conflict. The uncle overawed his nephew and had too much support in the king's entourage to fear complete supplanting. In 1403, moreover, in order to allay quarrels, the presidency of the council was entrusted to Queen Isabeau. But Philip died in April 1404, and was soon followed to the grave by Margaret of Flanders. Their enormous inheritance devolved upon their eldest son, John of Nevers, since Nikopol nicknamed John the Fearless. He was a newcomer to politics, for he had hitherto lived in complete retirement in his appanage of Nevers on a meagre allowance from his father, or as his lieutenant in Burgundy. He proved at once to possess a strong and unpleasant character. Small and ugly, with a long nose, a wry mouth, and an undershot jaw, even more ambitious than Philip and therefore a bad administrator – he drew bills on his expectations – he was harsh, cynical, crafty, imperious, gloomy, and a kill-joy. Any means served to attain his ends, the first of which was permanent control of public affairs.

Between the two cousins rivalry turned into hatred. Since Orleans had chosen as his badge a gnarled stick, in token of the blows he meant to deal his enemy, John spangled his livery with argent planes for smoothing down his adversary's cudgels. John promptly proposed to speak with authority and overawe the court of Paris. He turned the queen against him, and she drew closer to Orleans, to such an extent that public opinion accused them of being lovers. When John, in his insatiable ambition, marched on the capital and threatened to impose his will by armed force, they plotted between them to kidnap the Dauphin Louis. In August 1405 they carried off the young prince, but only as far as Juvisy, where the Burgundians overtook them and brought him back to Paris. Henceforth the royal council was the scene of endless altercations between Louis and John, which were prevented with great difficulty from developing into civil war, for both parties raised troops on the slightest provocation.

Still, the situation seemed likely to calm down; but Burgundy, to bring it to a head, resolved upon assassination. One dark night in November 1407 Louis of Orleans, who had spent the evening with the queen, was lured into an ambush in the rue Vieille-du-Temple, where ruffians hired by Burgundy butchered him and his small escort. Inquiry soon showed who was the guilty party. Two days later John the Fearless took Berry and Louis II of Anjou aside at the royal council, and confessed to them that he had ordered the murder 'through the intervention of the devil'. Next day he was forbidden access to the council. Then, fearing for his life, he fled at full speed. He did not stop until he reached Lille, where he was safe.

3. THE CIVIL WAR

AT FIRST the assassination of Louis of Orleans seemed to be a colossal political blunder. All the princes gathered around his mourning widow, Valentine Visconti, and demanded vengeance in the name of the dead puke's children. But only armed force could get the better of his murderer. From this, however, the princes still shrank. Their nominal leader, Berry, the sole survivor of Charles V's brothers, was a peace-loving old man, fond of his comforts and averse from adventure. The Anjous and even Bourbon dodged the issue. Valentine needed a more virile champion. But she did not find one during her lifetime. It was only after her death that one presented himself in the person of Bernard VII, Count of Armagnac, a grasping veteran. In 1410 his daughter married the young Charles of Orleans, and later again, in 1416, he was given the Constable's sword. In the civil war Bernard brought his son-in-law the support of his formidable Gascon bands, whose badge was a white shoulder-sash. As a result, the Orleanist party came to be known by the soon hated name of Armagnacs.

But for the time being Valentine was alone in her mourning. The support of the queen and the Dauphin Louis of Guienne, married to a cousin of Burgundy, was of no value to her. The king, to whom she appealed for revenge, was at first overwhelmed by his brother's tragic death; but, in his rare moments of lucidity, he aimed only at restoring peace in the royal family. John the Fearless, in his Flanders retreat, was aware of this. He invited his uncle Berry and his cousin Anjou to come and talk things over with him at Amiens. He informed them of the terms on which he would sue for pardon. As early as February 1408 he ventured to return to Paris. His arrival, he knew, was the prelude to his restoration to favour, under cover of a general reconciliation. Many a mishap still delayed it. But at length, on March 9th 1409, the king insisted on a ceremony at Chartres. All the princes passed the sponge over past injuries, swore friendship with one another, and promised to maintain peace. It was the first of those sham peaces which were to recur for the next ten years, without stopping the civil war promptly flaring up again.

Even before he became the sole beneficiary of the peace of Chartres, John the Fearless coldly pursued his advantage. It was not enough for him, now that he was back in the council, to play the modest part, to all intents and purposes, of a pardoned rebel. With insolent effrontery he insisted on justifying his actions and posing as a defender of the common weal. He commissioned John Petit, a well-known master of the University, famous for his activity in the schism, to prove the justice of Louis's

228

assassination in 1407. He drafted a *Justification* which John the Fearless boldly presented to the king and his council in March 1408. It complacently detailed all the peculations, the frauds, the exactions of which Louis of Orleans had been guilty at the expense of the Treasury and the State. It welcomed all the gossip about him. Louis's brazen debauchery and his inquisitive but disorderly and inconstant turn of mind had given rise to slanderous rumours. His adultery, his shameful morals, his practice of magic – everything was there, and to-day there is no telling the true from the false. But the conclusion was clearly defined: Louis had behaved as a 'regular tyrant'. Christian morality and the teaching of history and the learned allowed tyrannicide, and indeed made it an imperious duty, 'lawful and meritorious'. In John Petit's eyes the crime of 1407 thus became an outstanding act of justice and devotion to the crown. In vain did Valentine Visconti hire lawyers to refute the propositions of Burgundy's audacious henchman point by point. A long polemic ensued. But the blow had struck home. John the Fearless had appealed to public opinion and, on the whole, it supported him.

A more clever move won it over wholly to his side. Anarchy in the administration had been growing continually, and it alarmed all classes of society, who suffered more from its effects than from the struggle between the princes. Public opinion demanded a purge of the departments of state, strict economy and a return to sound working of the government. The masters of the University, given a taste for public affairs by the leading role they had just played in church politics, felt themselves called upon to reform the State in accordance with the principles of reason. They had no practical programme, but their purely platonic desire for reform was stiffened by their pride as intellectuals inured to syllogisms. The burgesses of Paris, carping by nature, and hostile since the time of Étienne Marcel to the truculence of the royal officials, had endured affronts at the beginning of Charles VI's reign which they still remembered twenty years later, and they formed an opposition stronger and more effective because it was more practical. Meanwhile the State proved impotent to reform itself. In January 1401, alleging that the king was restored to health, a handful of far-sighted or frightened officials had secured the issue of a great reforming ordinance, which eliminated a number of sinecures, subjected the system of assignments to stricter control, and extended the method of recruiting by election or co-option to all the great departments of State and to local officials in charge of justice and finance. But not one of these reforms was enforced. Offices were multiplied by arbitrary nomination, and waste worsened. Again, on the morrow of Louis of Orleans's murder, amid the anxiety into which the threat of civil war plunged the court, an ordinance issued in January 1408 went further than that of 1401, eliminated a number of sinecures by a stroke of the pen, and forbade any fresh alienation of the royal domain. The disturbances which ensued stopped these theoretical reforms being carried into effect.

Now John the Fearless resolutely set himself at the head of the reforming party. As early as 1405, on the morrow of the Dauphin's attempted escape, he had secured the royal council's support for a programme of reform of the household, the administration of the royal domain and the law courts, loudly declaring his desire to protect the people against the exactions of which they were the victims. This proclamation, abortive though it was, had made him popular. After the peace of Chartres he tried his hand again. An ordinance was issued which decreed reform of the royal domain, simplified the staff and reduced pay. A commission of inquiry was appointed to restore order in the financial sphere. The supreme courts and the treasury administration were purged by mass dismissals. John of Montagu, the last survivor of the Marmosets and comptroller of all the royal finances, was arrested and executed in October 1409. These measures made the Duke of Burgundy the idol of Paris.

Dominating the king by his frigid determination, having filled all the most important posts with his creatures, and being assured of the unswerving support of the capital, John the Fearless was in a position to defy the opposition of the princes, all allied against his dictatorship. Contemptuously he forced them into illegality and drove them into rebellion. The civil war was renewed in a masked fashion between Burgundian and Armagnac bands in the course of the year 1410, after Orleans, Berry, and the Anjous had reached an agreement at Gien. The princes still shrank from open rebellion, however, and they accepted a fresh reconciliation in the peace of Bicêtre.

But, ousted from the council and banished from Paris, they resigned themselves to a breach in July 1411, when Charles of Orleans sent a further defiance to the Duke of Burgundy. By dint of gifts and flattery, John won the support of the turbulent burgesses of Paris, dominated by the guild of the butchers, with Simon Caboche, skinner at the great slaughter-house, at their head. The masters of the University were on his side, especially the theologian Peter Cauchon, the future Bishop of Beauvais of infamous memory. The democratic spirit of the former and the desire for reform of the latter were alike means of pressure for keeping the king and his entourage under his exacting tutelage. In the autumn of 1411 a manifesto by Burgundy invoked the wrath of the people by name on all those in Paris who still sided with the party of Orleans or were 'hateful' to the domineering duke. They were actively persecuted. The grand master of the cross-bowmen, the Constable Charles of Albret and others were dismissed.

But John the Fearless was reluctant to leave anything to chance. The princes were powerful, enjoyed a prestige which was still great, and controlled a good half of the kingdom. They had gathered round Berry, the last veteran of a bygone age which recalled glorious memories. Beside him stood Charles of Orleans and his father-in-law Armagnac, John I of Bourbon and the Constable Albret. The queen and the royal children secretly sided with them. John might need outside support in order to get the better of them. In any case, this French prince, bent on exploiting the fame of the Valois monarchy to his own profit, lightly took the first step along the road of treason. He invited England to dispatch a raiding force and promised – or at least so the rumour ran among his enemies – to hand Dunkirk and other Flemish fortresses over to it and help it to conquer Normandy on behalf of the Lancastrians. Sincerely or not, he let it be understood that if need be he would contemplate the dismemberment of the kingdom of France. Henry IV, despite the advice of his Beaufort half-brothers and his eldest son, was still suspicious and hesitated to commit himself before the fruit was quite ripe for plucking. In October 1411 he sent to Calais only a small force of two thousand men, enough to raise the blockade of Paris, which the princes were besieging, and to storm Étampes, but not enough to undertake the conquest of a province on its own account. This weak English force – the first to trample French soil for twenty-eight years – soon re-embarked.

Driven back into the provinces south of the Loire, and fearing the strength of the royal army which Burgundy organized against them during the winter, Berry, Bourbon, Orleans, Armagnac, and Albret in their turn appealed to Henry IV. The King of England wondered which side to take, was reluctant to intervene in person and equivocated for some time. Finally, in May 1412, an agreement reached at Bourges, which soon became known to Burgundian spies, committed the princes to following Burgundy's treasonable example. In return for the dispatch of an expeditionary force of 4,000 men, which would be at their service only for three months, the rebels promised to surrender to the Lancastrians the provinces reconquered since 1369 and hand over the Gascon fortresses held by French garrisons. In his old age, Berry thus went back on Charles V's whole achievement, though he had taken part in it. Happily for France, when the English troops under Thomas of Clarence, Henry IV's second son, landed in Cotentin towards the end of the summer, crossed Anjou and reached Poitou, it was already too late. The Burgundian army had forestalled the rebels, occupied Berry, threatened Bourbonnais, and rapidly forced the old duke to capitulate. The other princes immediately surrendered by the Treaty of Auxerre (August 1412). A fresh solemn reconciliation of the whole royal family then took place in the presence of delegates of the great departments of State, the Paris burgesses and the University. The amnesty which followed produced demonstrations of joy. It was sincerely believed that the civil war was over. Only the people of Poitou had to subscribe heavily to purchase the departure of the English mercenaries, who fell back on Bordeaux.

In fact John the Fearless emerged from the struggle with increased strength. Now that he had brought about the threat from England, rather late in the day he became anxious about it and wanted to make ready for the war which had become probable, if not inevitable. To obtain the necessary taxes and complete the purge pursued since 1411, he induced the royal council to summon the Estates of Languedoïl, which had not been consulted for more than thirty years. He thought that the representatives of the three orders would approve his policy. The humbled princes did not dare to put in an appearance and awaited events far from Paris. In view of the insecurity of the roads, deputies from the provinces were not numerous. So Burgundy and his Parisian allies were able to speak as masters in the assembly. No one foresaw that he was enjoying the last few months of a dictatorship which he had maintained for nearly four years.

From the start of the session, which opened on January 30th 1413, it became apparent that the Estates would not hear of taxes until the long-awaited reforms had been carried into effect. The speakers' grievances, at first vague, were followed by definite plans and pertinent charges. The Carmelite Eustace of Pavilly quoted the names of some thirty officials guilty of misappropriation and demanded mass dismissals and confiscations, whose yield would suffice to maintain an army. After a month's debate, the royal government had to give way to the pressure of its critics. On February 24th it suspended all the financial officials and appointed a commission of inquiry of twelve members, one of whom was Peter Cauchon, to propose penalties and prepare reforms. While this commission slowly started its work, the princes' partisans, whose lives and property it threatened, banded together. There were still many of them in the entourage of the queen, whose brother Ludwig of Bavaria enjoyed shameless favour, and in the household of the Dauphin Louis of Guienne, to which the energetic Peter des Essarts, the former provost of Paris dismissed by Burgundy, was recalled. Envoys set off to negotiate with the princes of the party of Orleans, in voluntary exile in their appanages.

Against them John the Fearless fomented insurrection. Led by the formidable butcher Simon Caboche, the Paris burgesses rose on April 27th, besieged the Bastille, from which they carried off Peter des Essarts, broke into the Dauphin's mansion, imprisoned his favourites and massacred the hated Armagnacs throughout the city. For four weeks one riot followed another. Almost daily the crowd entered the Hôtel Saint-Paul, exacted fresh victims from the terrorized king and demanded the issue of reforms. The royal government lost no time in satisfying them. It took two whole days, the 26th and 27th of May, to read before the *Parlement* the text of the great ordinance, consisting of 259 clauses, to which French history gave the ignominious nickname of '*cabochienne*'.

Once again, though it was dictated by insurrection, there was nothing revolutionary in this text. It dealt simply with reforming administration, simplifying the civil service, preaching economy and balancing the budget. As a rule the reformers were content to revive, amplify, and codify earlier ordinances which had remained dead letters or lapsed since the fall of the Marmosets. But some novel features are worth noting, in order to measure the ever-growing ascendancy which the royal government exercised over the country. Now it was not against the royal officials as such that complaint lay, but against their misconduct. In 1315 the nobles had murmured against the royal institutions. The opposition led by Caboche wanted only to improve the working of these institutions, and did not demand any supervision except that of the officials themselves. There was no more talk about the Estates: they had surrendered every ambition into the hands of the officials. There was no question now, as there had been in 1356, of putting the needy monarchy into tutelage, still less, as has been wrongly repeated, of giving the kingdom a 'constitution'. This progress towards absolute monarchy was a legacy of the war with England, which had shown the need of strong and effective power.

In the ordinance promoted by Caboche one can distinguish very clearly anxiety to restore the *Chambre des comptes* as the centre of all supervision. Its staff, reduced to a reasonable size, would take part in the appointment of almost all officials, inaugurate more rapid methods of accountancy, and receive a statement from the Treasury every month, a balance-sheet from the bailiffs and seneschals every year, and a rendering of account from the receiver-general of taxes six times a year. Any fresh expenditure must have its approval before being undertaken. In the sphere of simplifying administrative machinery, the ordinance provided for a fusion which, if it had been carried out, would have changed mistaken methods that persisted until 1789. In the provinces it did not venture to merge under one control the receipts from the royal domain, which were collected by bailiwicks, and those from taxation, which were collected by fiscal districts called *élections*. But at the centre it eliminated the two bodies of treasurers for the domain and *généraux* for taxation, and replaced them by two 'stewards accredited for the management of all the finances of the kingdom', who were regular ministers of finance and supervised all receipts from whatever source.

The elimination of offices, the reduction of pay, the merger of certain services, the improvement of means of supervision had but one object: the reorganization of finances. As a beginning, a forced loan would be raised from the recipients of royal favours. All those who had received grants from taxation since 1409 must return half of them to the State in the form of a loan. In future half the yield of taxes would be deposited in Paris in a special treasury, strictly reserved for the war. This treasury would be further increased by the proceeds of fines and confiscations from dishonest officials. If everything was accomplished within the appointed time, there would be no need for fresh taxes. The country was still rich enough to meet the attacks of the English enemy without additional burdens.

This monument of administrative wisdom suffered the sad fate of reforms that come too late. Promulgated under pressure of insurrection, Caboche's ordinance looked like a partisan piece of work. General co-operation, essential for its enforcement, was lacking. The turbulence of the Paris butchers, dangerously aroused by the Duke of Burgundy, did not stop at the end of May. The rioters continued their practices, imprisoned suspects and carried out summary executions. The moderate burgesses took fright. Cleverly handled by John Jouvenel, formerly guardian of the provostship of the merchants and king's advocate, they approached the Dauphin and helped him to negotiate the peace of Pontoise with the princes, which was concluded at the end of July. On August 4th Louis of Guienne made a triumphal progress through the streets of the capital, which infuriated the butchers, who tried in vain to storm the Town Hall. On August 23rd, feeling that the game was lost, John the Fearless made a futile attempt to kidnap the king. Then he left Paris, to which he was not to return for five years. On September 1st Orleans and the other princes of his faction arrived in Paris. On the 5th, at a solemn 'bed of justice', they annulled the reforming ordinance, on the ground that it had been imposed upon the king without discussion by the council or consideration by the *Parlement*.

Henceforth the Armagnac faction was triumphant. Burgundy's friends and Caboche's protégés experienced in their turn the hardships of exile, imprisonment, confiscation, sometimes death. The princes' followers recovered their posts and their property. Charles of Albret regained the Constable's sword, and after his death on the field of Agincourt it was taken over by the formidable Count of Armagnac. Meanwhile Armagnac's Gascon bands kept watch on the capital and maintained order with an iron hand. A 'council of the faith', presided over by the Bishop of Paris, was moved by Gerson's flights of oratory to condemn John Petit's defence of tyrannicide as tainted with heresy, and this *auto-da-fé* purged the memory of the late Duke of Orleans. Everything was restored to order, or rather disorder. The monarchy was once more pillaged and despoiled by those who should have defended it. This was the moment chosen by the rulers of England to embark upon the conquest of the kingdom of France.

4. FROM AGINCOURT TO THE TREATY OF TROYES

AT THE moment when the Estates of Languedoïl were debating in Paris the possibility of a renewal of the war, the death of Henry IV, in March 1413, brought to the throne of England his eldest son, Henry V, a young man of twenty-five. With the new king's accession war became almost a certainty.

The military success of the second Lancastrian sovereign, and his premature death at the peak of an unprecedented fame, has raised him very high, perhaps too high, in the esteem of posterity. By a singular irony of fate, the first King of England who had some English blood in his veins, who started having certain deeds of his chancery written in English, was precisely the man who at length all but achieved the dream of his Plantagenet predecessors: the union on his head of the two most glorious crowns in Christendom. To succeed where Edward III had failed took outstanding qualities, and in these Henry V was certainly not lacking. He was later reproached with his debauched youth, very much out of keeping with the affectation of piety which marked him when he became king. In every respect his youth was alike stormy and revealing. He served a hard military apprenticeship in the Welsh campaigns. He had a thirst for power which shrank from nothing. From 1408 onwards, when Henry IV felt weakened by illness, the heir to the throne, copying the boundless ambition of Henry II Plantagenet's sons, thrust himself to the front, gathered followers and allied himself with his uncles the Beauforts against his father. He insisted on having his say in politics, pressed for the alliance with Burgundy and condemned the dispatch of reinforcements to the Armagnac princes. At one point, in the autumn of 1411, he demanded that his father should abdicate in his favour.

All this barely restrained impatience in itself bespoke a prince sure of himself, his strength and his rights. His exercise of power denoted further traits. A good soldier, he was also, like his ancestor Edward I and the great Plantagenets, a businesslike bureaucrat, a sound administrator, and a stern judge. He was, in short, a formidable adversary for a France full of faction and a Europe ruled by puppets. He was all the more formidable because his talents were coupled with a character with unpleasant features. His hypocritical devoutness, the duplicity of his conduct, his pretence of defending right and redressing wrongs when he sought solely to satisfy his ambition, the cruelty of his revenge – all this heralded a new era. Henry indeed belonged to his age, the age of the Italian tyrants and

Louis XI, a world far removed from the knightly kings whose inheritance he received and whose plans he took up again.

His policy at home need not detain us long. From his English subjects Henry expected above all the support required for the fulfilment of his continental ambitions. The maintenance of order and military preparations: these sum up England's internal history for years. Tired of disturbances, the country let itself be led by a strong king. This is the more remarkable since the Lancastrian dynasty was far from being universally accepted. Henry V's accession was the occasion for fresh troubles. Richard II's last supporters stirred up agitation in Yorkshire. A country knight, Sir John Oldcastle, indicted for his Lollard leanings, managed to escape and foment a rebellion of the western towns. As late as the summer of 1415, on the eve of the king's departure for France, a baronial plot for the overthrow of the dynasty was discovered just in time. Henry boldly chose to ignore those dangers.

Nothing could be more significant than the readiness with which the country accepted fresh sacrifices and let crushing military burdens be imposed upon it. Whereas Henry IV had had endless trouble in financing his Welsh campaigns, his successor had little difficulty in preparing for a new expedition on the continent. There was no need for legislative reform. The existing organization, backed solely by the authority of a popular sovereign, was enough. Henry was able to stir up public opinion against the perfidious French and associate it with his ambitions of conquest. In November 1414 Parliament made no bones about granting the heavy taxes he demanded from it. The hiring of mercenaries, the raising of the feudal army and of contingents of infantry by the commissions of array, the concentration of stores and supplies in the Channel ports and the requisitioning of ships proceeded fairly fast. When the breach came, in the summer of 1415, Henry had assembled a compact army, stronger than those of Edward III, amounting to nearly twelve thousand combatants, a considerable figure for the period.

He showed similar strength and skill in his diplomatic steps, which were aimed at driving his adversary either to surrender or war. Until his accession, Henry had been in favour of the Burgundians and hostile to the princes of the Armagnac faction. Once he was king, he negotiated simultaneously with both, though he expected more from the second than the first, now that John the Fearless was only an exile, an opponent reduced to champing the bit in his own domain, whereas the Armagnacs dominated the French monarchy with their mailed fist.

A refugee in Flanders since September 1413, John the Fearless dreamed of revenge on the hated Armagnacs. But the army which he hastily assembled failed to take Paris in February 1414, and the Armagnacs, bringing the king with them, proceeded to advance into Picardy, arrived beneath the walls of Arras, and talked about nothing less than disinheriting Burgundy by force. Like his father, however, John never forgot that before all else he was a Valois prince, a vassal of the crown of France. Extending the Burgundian State to the point of making himself independent at France's expense, and, by way of preliminary, surrendering France to the foreigner, was no part of his plans. Nor, whatever may have been said to the contrary, was it to be the policy of his son. But he wanted to resume the first place in Charles VI's counsels which belonged to him by right, rule the kingdom and dismiss the rival princes. Since his own strength was not enough, however, he must find on what terms the Lancastrians would provide the necessary aid. He sent messengers to London and received English agents at Lille and Bruges.

At a conference held at Leicester in May 1414 Burgundy's proposals were defined. At this time only modest operations were contemplated. John would raise one thousand men-at-arms and he asked for twice as many from the Lancastrians. Together they would make war not on Charles VI, but on the rebel princes, as in 1411. Together they would share the spoils of victory. Henry would confiscate to his own advantage the Gascon domains of Albret and Armagnac. He would annex Angoumois, which belonged to Orleans, and also have his share in the appanages of Bourbon, Alençon, and Eu. The talks were resumed at Ypres in August. Dissatisfied with these complex plans, the English wanted to know how far Burgundy's concessions would go. Would he give them the great Aquitaine contemplated at Brétigny? Would he, as they demanded, add Berry to it? Or would he go to the length of recognizing Henry's claim to the title of King of France? Scared by the scope of these demands, John dare not grant them and so spoil his personal plan of hegemony. At the last moment he dodged the issue and broke off the talks.

Henceforth the English negotiations with the Armagnacs took a more favourable turn. Like his predecessors, Henry V demanded the crown of France; but, again like his predecessors, he let it be understood that he would be content, at a pinch, with territorial concessions. So nothing seemed to be changed in the conflict which set the two sovereigns at odds. At first there was discussion about John the Good's ransom, of which the English demanded payment after a lapse of half a century, and about Aquitaine, which they wanted to restore as it had been defined by the Treaty of Calais. In addition, repeating what Richard II had done, the Lancastrian king asked for the hand of Charles VI's daughter Catherine. But, at every fresh meeting of the negotiators – in Paris in August 1413, at Leulinghen in September, in London in November, then in Paris again in January 1414 – the territorial demands of the English increased enormously. They talked about nothing less than the old Angevin empire: Anjou, Maine, Touraine, Normandy, the homage of Brittany. Then, claiming the maximum to get the minimum, they demanded sovereignty over Flanders and Artois, in order to thrust the Valois away from Calais and make the Duke of Burgundy a vassal of England. Even outside the kingdom of France, they demanded from the princes of Anjou the cession of Provence, by virtue of rights which Henry III's wife had held there a hundred and fifty years earlier.

Frightened by all these ambitions, Louis of Guienne and the Armagnacs went as far as possible along the path of concession. They agreed to go back to the unhappy time of John the Good, pay the balance of his ransom, fixed at 1,600,000 *écus*, give young Catherine a dowry of two million francs, and restore a great sovereign Aquitaine. But Henry V would not agree to renounce the throne of France except on condition of enslaving its occupant. Aquitaine did not interest him. He knew that, if they remained masters of the provinces north of the Loire, sooner or later the Valois would manage to shake off his tutelage. A shrewder politician than Edward III, he demanded that at least he should be given Normandy. Hemmed in between the great fief which had been wrested from the Plantagenets under Philip Augustus and the Burgundian domains, the French monarchy would be at the mercy of the government in London and definitely reduced to inferiority.

At the end of February 1415 the negotiations in Paris were broken off. In vain did Charles VI's envoys return to Winchester in July, complain about English perfidy, recall all the injuries France had already suffered, denounce the violations of the truce which had multiplied in the past few months – the Gascons, spurred on by the Duke of Clarence, had recovered all the fortresses lost since 1403, invaded Saintonge and threatened La Rochelle, while the English fleet had made a raid on Dieppe – and repeat their offer of concessions. Since they would not surrender Normandy to him, Henry dismissed them, declaring that he would soon follow them and throwing on France the responsibility for war.

It was too late in the year for him to think about a long campaign. But his army was ready, and he must make use of it. He must also take advantage of the favourable attitude of the Duke of Burgundy, still furious at his ostracism by the Armagnacs. In the autumn of 1414 the moderates, who had found a leader in the person of Louis of Guienne, the young Dauphin of seventeen, had indeed tried once more to reconcile the rival factions. But the peace of Arras, negotiated in September and ratified with difficulty in February 1415, though it annulled the sentence of banishment passed on John the Fearless, did not restore him to power, did not even make him the apology which his vanity demanded, and excepted from amnesty five hundred of his most faithful followers. So he shut himself up in an attitude of hostile neutrality, though he allowed his brothers Anthony of Brabant and Philip of Nevers to join the royal army, with which they met their deaths. For his own part he did not stir and sent no contingents to it.

After entrusting the regency of England to his brother John, Duke of Bedford, and issuing insolent proclamations in which he boasted that he was coming to restore peace and prosperity to battered France, Henry V sailed on August 10th. During the night of the 13th to the 14th he landed at Le Chef de Caux, at the mouth of the Seine, in Normandy, which he wanted to conquer first. It took him nearly a month to capture Harfleur, which was not relieved in time and surrendered on September 14th. He dreamed of turning it into a second Calais, expelled the inhabitants and sent for English colonists. Then, like Edward III in 1346, he retired northwards, not wishing to spend the winter on enemy soil. Meanwhile the Armagnac government had managed to concentrate an army of vassals around Rouen, though the absence of Burgundian and Breton contingents left unfortunate gaps in it from the outset. Still, it was stronger and more combative than that of the invader, who had to leave garrisons and casualties through illness behind him. It set off light-heartedly in pursuit of the retreating English, despite the prudent advice of the old Duke of Berry, who favoured Charles V's delaying tactics.

Seventy-nine years afterwards, the mistake at Crécy was repeated. Finding his retreat cut off by Marshal Boucicaut, who dogged his footsteps tirelessly, Henry awaited his pursuers at Agincourt on the plateau of Artois, not far from the Burgundian residence of Hesdin. The entrenchment of his infantry, the well-aimed fire of his archers, and the soaking of the ground by driving rain forced the French knights to fight on foot. They were cut to pieces, on October 25th. The victor hastened to set sail again from Calais (November 16th).

The campaign of Agincourt meant nothing decisive. It was only one raid more after so many like it. Beaten, but not overthrown, Charles VI's government tried to get its foreign friends to intervene. While Armagnac, appointed Constable, tried in vain to recapture Harfleur, the government accepted the Emperor Sigismund's mediation. A younger brother of Wenceslas of Bohemia, Sigismund of Luxemburg, whom an advantageous marriage had made King of Hungary, was a weak but vain prince, convinced that he was born for great things. For some years fortune had smiled on him. On the death of Ruprecht of the Palatinate in 1410, despite the fact that Wenceslas, sunken ever deeper in drunkenness, was still alive, the German princes had elected him King of the Romans. In Sigismund's eyes, the imperial dignity conferred upon him supreme dominion over all Christendom. He took resolutely in hand the union of the Church, which the Valois had abandoned since the Council of Pisa and the opening of the civil war.

Though most sovereigns had recognized Pope Alexander V and then John XXIII, who had sprung from the Council of Pisa, two other pontiffs, Benedict XIII and Gregory XII, in refuge at Perpignan and Rimini respectively, still retained some followers. To bring this tripartite schism to an end a General Council was clearly essential. Sigismund demanded that it should be held on German soil at Constance. At once he proclaimed himself its guide, supporter, and master. He backed the Fathers in their struggle against John XXIII and secured his deposition. He forced the Bavarian princes to abandon the cause of Gregory XII.

Towards the end of 1415 he went to the south of France, got into touch at Narbonne with the Spanish sovereigns and induced the Kings of Castille and Aragon to give up their support of Benedict XIII. At Constance quarrels between Burgundian members of the University and Armagnac delegates, and between English and French, threatened to postpone indefinitely the election of a sole Pope and the reform of the Church. To complete his work, Sigismund imposed his mediation between Lancastrian and Valois.

He went first, in March 1416, to Paris, where he had a niggardly reception at the impoverished court, overwhelmed by defeat and mourning. The Hôtel Saint-Paul was now the residence only of a mad and needy king: the echo of past festivities had died away within its melancholy walls. Then he went to England. Henry V flattered his vanity, staged splendid entertainments for his benefit, showed off his people's adulation, and made a great parade of pomp and strength. No more was needed to make up Sigismund's irresponsible mind. By the Treaty of Canterbury, on August 15th 1416, he allied himself with the Lancastrians, recognized their right to the crown of France and promised to go to war against the Valois usurper. In fact, he had neither the intention nor the means to put his promise into practice. But his defection was the death-blow to the prestige of the Valois. Feeling that the wind was veering, at the same time John the Fearless resumed his negotiations with the court of London. He met Henry V at Calais on October 6th. With his usual duplicity, he let the King of England understand that he would become his vassal and help him to overthrow Charles VI.

It was time for Henry V to exploit these diplomatic successes, which he followed up with alliances with the Rhenish princes, the Hanseatic towns and Aragon. A fresh effort was demanded from the English people and a new army was equipped. In August 1417, after an absence of two years, Henry V once more trod the soil of Normandy. But this time it was no question of a mere raid. As a result of the inactivity of the Armagnac government, which could not at one and the same time face the invader and the Burgundian army encamped in the region of Paris, the Lancastrian was able to begin a methodical conquest of the province he had so long coveted. The fortresses and towns of lower Normandy and Cotentin fell one after another. The castle of Caen, stubbornly defended, capitulated on September 20th. In October it was the turn of Argentan and Alençon. Before the end of the next spring the whole province from Cherbourg to Évreux was conquered. Only the monks of Mont Saint-Michel held out, shut up on their rock with a handful of faithful knights.

By this time the Armagnacs were in desperate straits. One by one the leaders of the princes' faction had disappeared. Charles of Orleans and John of Bourbon were in England, prisoners since Agincourt. Berry had died in June 1416. Dead, too, were the Dauphin Louis of Guienne (December 1415), his brother John of Touraine (April 1417), and their cousin Louis II of Anjou. Of all Charles VI's descendants there remained only a young hobbledehoy, Charles, created Dauphin and Duke of Touraine after his brothers, the sole hope of the party, who since June 1417 had borne the title of 'lieutenant-general of the king'. In fact, the domineering Constable ruled in his name. The two of them had made the fatal blunder of quarrelling with Queen Isabeau, whose profligacy had increased with her years. They had cut off her allowance and banished her to Blois and then to Tours. The Armagnac reign of terror had ceased to overawe the exasperated people. Already Picardy and Champagne, which had been promised exemption from taxes, had in large part gone over to Burgundian garrisons. In Paris, where a first attempt at rebellion as early as April 1416 had been sternly repressed, the populace only awaited a sign to rise and hoist the cross of Saint Andrew, the banner of the Burgundians. After five years of disfavour, the hour of John the Fearless had struck.

On November 8th 1417 Isabeau of Bavaria escaped from Tours. A Burgundian escort brought her to the duke, who awaited her at Chartres. The two of them then established themselves at Troyes, where the queen presided over a shadow government, a rival to that of her son, calling herself 'Queen of France, having on behalf of our Lord the King government and administration of the kingdom'. A chancery, financial services and a *Parlement* were hastily organized. Then, on May 29th 1418, came a rising in Paris, which opened its gates to John the Fearless and hailed him as a saviour. The bewildered king was 'delivered' from the Armagnacs, and a massacre of them was set on foot. The chancellor, the Constable, and others fell beneath the blows of assassins. The Dauphin managed to escape, and even returned a few days later with such scanty forces as he could muster and began a siege of the capital. His unruly veterans forced their way into the town on the east side; but they scattered through the streets in search of booty. Burgundians and burgesses drove them out. The Dauphin made no further effort and let the victors rage against his followers. The massacres claimed nearly two thousand victims. Charles retired south of the Loire to his appanage of Berry leaving his father, his mother, and the whole north of France to Burgundian domination.

These last civil upheavals had no effect on the fate of the war. John the Fearless was no more capable than the Armagnacs of checking the English advance. To maintain his reputation as friend of the people and promoter of reforms he had had to decree the removal of aids, hearth-taxes, and *maltôtes*. His government lived meagrely on the income of the royal domain in the few provinces it controlled effectively, the salt-tax, the sparse and infrequent subsidies it secured from the towns, confiscations and forced loans from Armagnac partisans, and above all heavy monetary devaluation.

When the people of Rouen, invested since July 1418 by Henry V's overwhelming siege equipment, asked him for help, John advised them to rely only on their own strength. On January 13th 1419, after six months of heroic and desperate resistance, the town surrendered and was sentenced by the victor to pay a heavy war indemnity. Henry went on to reduce the fortresses in the region of Caux. Then, leaving lieutenants to conquer Perche, he invaded Vexin, made a stay at Mantes, and in July reached Pontoise, which he took despite the Burgundian garrison's resistance. While he negotiated separately with Burgundy and the Dauphin, he contemplated a final attack on Paris and wrote to the Pope, the cardinals, his Rhenish allies, and the princes of Lorraine, proclaiming the justice of his cause, denouncing the faults of decadent France and inviting his friends to take part in the kill.

In the presence of this danger, the Burgundians and what was left of the Armagnacs drew together. For the past year the moderate elements had been seeking a ground of reconciliation in the form of a sharing of power between the two leaders of the parties. But the Treaty of Saint-Maur (September 1418), imposed by Burgundy on the Dauphin's councillors, had never even begun to be carried into effect. It left Charles his appanage of Dauphiné, Touraine, Berry, and Poitou, and allowed him to name one of the three officials who would have the handling of finance. It was, however, no part of John the Fearless's plans to play the game of the English, who were too powerful for him to hope to rule in their name. A real reconciliation with the Dauphin would enable him to get rid of the last Armagnacs and impose his will, under cover of a government of the Dauphin, on the whole kingdom. A first meeting between them, at Corbeil in July 1419, led to a preliminary agreement, but this was hard to enforce in the face of pent-up hatreds. They met again on the bridge at Montereau on September 10th. When the discussion between the princes became heated, Charles's suite, led by the Breton Tanguy du Châtel, formerly provost of Paris and a protégé of Orleans, fell upon John the Fearless and stabbed him to death. From the scuffle which followed Charles escaped unhurt; but the Burgundians were unable even to recover their master's body.

His murder at Montereau, this belated revenge for Louis of Orleans's assassination, completed the discredit of the Armagnacs throughout the north of France. Though the people of Paris had murmured against John the Fearless for his failure to relieve Pontoise, they now reverted with enthusiasm to the Burgundian cause. The upshot was that the Dauphin, save for a few exceptions, was confined to the centre and south of the kingdom. The new Duke of Burgundy was Philip, Count of Charolais – soon to be nicknamed the Good – son-in-law of Charles VI, whose daughter Michelle he had married. This young prince of twenty-five, indolent and luxury-loving, very unlike John the Fearless, had been brought up by his father in Flanders, and become familiar with its feelings and its interests. He found his advisers and his family divided, and was personally much perplexed. He was a faithful heir to the policy of the first two dukes, and it was repugnant to him to betray his lineage and surrender the kingdom to the victorious Lancastrian. Those modern historians who think that he was ready to abandon French affairs and devote himself wholly to his ambitions in the Low Countries are very much mistaken. It was always his goal to resume the first place in the government of France and keep it, if possible.

But he could not avenge his father and overthrow the guilty Dauphin except with Henry V's help, though he was fully determined to support the Lancastrian only in so far as English arms would allow him to crush his personal enemies. A family council held at Malines on October 7th urged Philip towards revenge, or, in other words, thrust him into the false position whose dangers I have just outlined. In December he made an agreement at Rouen with the invader which seemed to be entirely to his advantage. The Lancastrian and Burgundy would carry on the war against the Dauphin together. A marriage would unite their families. If, as was now probable, Henry V donned the crown of France, Philip would retain a privileged position beside him.

Burgundy's choice involved that of poor Charles VI. Queen Isabeau was filled with a fearful hatred of her last son ever since he had condemned her to exile, and she was Burgundy's closest supporter in the long negotiations which finally ended, on May 21st 1420, in the conclusion of the Treaty of Troyes.

Whereas the Treaty of Calais had allayed the feudal quarrel by the creation of an Aquitaine outside French control, the Treaty of Troyes settled the dynastic conflict by making Henry V heir to the throne of France. The Dauphin was rudely thrust aside, since this 'so-called Dauphin' was, by his own mother's confession – a somewhat belated one to be sure – nothing but a bastard, born in adultery: his father's name was not disclosed. Banished from the kingdom for his 'horrible and enormous crimes and offences', the future Charles VII was disinherited by his own parents. Charles VI now had only one unmarried daughter, Catherine. He gave her in marriage to the Lancastrian, together with the expectation of his kingdom.

'True son' and heir presumptive of the mad king, Henry V, pending the death of his father-in-law, who lived on in his unhappy state until the age of fifty-two, would exercise *de facto* regency of the kingdom, while he retained Normandy as an appanage and the homage of Brittany. For the keeping of order, the struggle against the Dauphin and the control of affairs of State, the regent would act in agreement with Philip. There would be no change in the kingdom's institutions as they had been maintained for the past two years by the Duke of Burgundy. In addition, Henry undertook to respect all rights, privileges, usages, and customs. Only the kingdom changed its head, in the person of the heir of those Plantagenets who for centuries had been the most powerful vassals of the crown. Thanks to a dynastic arrangement and a French marriage the Lancastrians were substituted for the Valois.

North of the Loire no voice was raised against the treaty. When he negotiated it, Philip of Burgundy probably anticipated that Henry would be overburdened by his two kingdoms, and would leave him the *de facto* administration of France, while helping him to conquer the rebel provinces: a calculation which, I may remark in passing, was partly upset. On June 2nd the Archbishop of Sens solemnized the royal marriage. The *Parlement* had endorsed the treaty and the University had approved it. In December the two sovereigns, father-in-law and son-in-law, accompanied by the young Duke of Burgundy, made their entrance into Paris, and were greeted with cheers by the burgesses, delighted to have the court back in their midst after two years of absence. Then the Estates of Languedoïl were summoned to ratify the treaty in their turn. The nightmare of the civil war, which had raged for thirteen years, and of the foreign war, which had been added to it for five years, seemed to be definitely banished.

Henry V had reached his goal: the formation of a 'dual monarchy' which, through personal union, governed both England and France. But in fact he controlled only Burgundian France. Far from unifying Western Europe under one powerful dynasty, the treaty of Troyes dug a deeper ditch than ever between the two parties which divided France. Which of them would prevail? To answer this question, we need only survey this France separated into two hostile halves.

Part VII
DIVIDED FRANCE
1418–1429

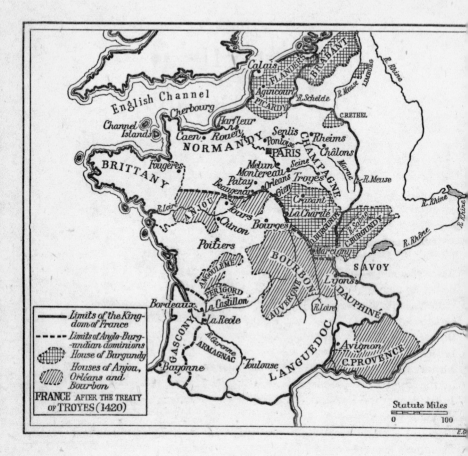

English Channel

Channel Islands

Calais
FLANDERS
BRABANT
Agincourt
PICARDY
R.Schelde
R.Meuse
LIMBURG
R.Rhine

Cherbourg
C.RETHEL

Harfleur
Caen · Rouen
Senlis
Rheims
NORMANDY
Pontoise
PARIS
CHAMPAGNE
Châlons

BRITTANY
Fougères

Melun
Montereau
Seine
Marne
R.Meuse

Patay
Orleans
Troyes

R.Loire
Beaugency
Gien

ANJOU
Tours
Cravant
La Charité
R.Rhine

Chinon
Bourges
C.BURGUNDY
R.Saône
C.BURGUND
R.Rhône

Poitiers
Marcigny

BOURBON
SAVOY

Lyons
ANGOULÊME
AUVERGNE
R.Loire
DAUPHINÉ

Bordeaux
PÉRIGORD
La Castillon

GASCONY
La Reole

R.Garonne
ARMAGNAC
LANGUEDOC
Avignon
C.PROVENCE

Bayonne
Toulouse

Statute Miles
0   100

─── Limits of the King-
      dom of France
- - - Limits of Anglo-Burg-
      -undian dominions
▨ House of Burgundy
▧ Houses of Anjou,
   Orléans and
   Bourbon

FRANCE AFTER THE TREATY
OF **TROYES** (1420)

E.G.

Part VII

DIVIDED FRANCE

(1418–1429)

UNTIL quite recent times the Treaty of Troyes was unanimously denounced as the most shameful surrender known in French history. But not all contemporaries, unfamiliar with modern patriotism and unaware of coming events, regarded it in that light. It is essential that we should place ourselves in their period in order to understand their different reactions.

Legally the Treaty of Troyes contained flaws both of form and substance which the Dauphin's advisers were in a position to denounce when the time came. Custom had made the crown of France a hereditary monarchy which had been handed down from father to son for more than three centuries. The succession of the last direct Capetians had excluded the king's daughters and their children from inheriting the throne. To go back on this decision, now nearly a century old, was a breach of custom, a supreme act of illegality in the eyes of the men of the Middle Ages. In 1316 and in 1328 the right of succession had been 'said' by the assembly of barons and peers, a solemn form of the king's court. It was not for the sovereign arbitrarily to revoke this decision and change the right of succession by disinheriting his son in favour of his son-in-law. Elevating themselves to an abstract concept of the common weal, the Dauphin's lawyers declared that the crown was an inalienable property, that the sovereign was only its trustee, and that he could not dispose of it in favour of anyone he chose.

The people at large paid little attention to these theories. They were more concerned about their immediate conditions of life and about what the agreement between the two sovereigns might mean to them now and in the future. Everything, indeed, suggested joyful endorsement of the peace which had at last been concluded. The treaty had been readily accepted by the king, for whose return to health his people had ardently longed for the past thirty years, and with whose efforts to restore unity in his family they were familiar. It was supported by the Duke of Burgundy, whose father had enjoyed unbounded popularity north of the Loire. It was approved by the highest religious and political authorities, the University, the *Parlement*, and the Estates. It provided for an heir to the throne who publicly proclaimed his desire to restore order, make justice respected, fill all posts with capable and honest officials, and banish the nightmare of civil war for ever. This combination, powerful alike in its strength and its prospects, was opposed only by the young Dauphin, lacking in initiative, hitherto a puppet of the hated Constable, doubtful about his own rights and aware of his extreme weakness.

The success of the Anglo-Burgundians seemed to be a foregone conclusion. But it was nothing of the kind. Despite all the trump cards it held, the 'dual monarchy' was doomed to failure. The complex and inconclusive events, political and military, which happened between the signing of the Treaty of Troyes and the appearance of Joan of Arc do not suffice by themselves to explain this failure. We must consider how the provinces behaved, how they were administered, what support they gave the rival governments. It is a difficult subject of study, for on many points research has not yet been carried far enough for definite conclusions. Still, one may attempt a sketch, lacking in detail but provisionally valid in outline.

1. LANCASTRIAN FRANCE

AFTER THE English invasion in 1417 and the entrance of the Burgundians into Paris in 1418 there were, in fact, not merely two Frances, but three: the provinces conquered and administered by the Lancastrian; those controlled by the Duke of Burgundy; and finally those in which the Dauphin maintained himself. We must survey them in turn.

Wherever force of arms had given him power, Henry V, even before the Treaty of Troyes, organized military occupation and set up an autonomous administration, which continued in its broad outline after 1420 and was barely changed in 1422, when Henry VI was proclaimed King of France. This administration concerned, above all, the duchy of Normandy, which Henry V governed not in his capacity as Charles VI's heir, but as the patrimony of the Anglo-Norman dynasty, recovered after more than two centuries of Capetian rule. To Normandy was added the 'conquered country' occupied before 1420, in other words Vexin, with the bailiwicks of Mantes and Gisors, as far as the neighbourhood of Pontoise, part of the region of Chartres, and the north of Maine. Rouen became the capital of this provincial State, which, though not large, was wealthy and compact. Here Henry V established a chancery, which drew up administrative documents and compiled the Norman Rolls, now preserved in London, and a great council, which was entrusted with executive decisions. He revived the office of seneschal of Normandy, who had supreme control over all administration, civil and military, and created the office of Admiral of Normandy. The *Échiquier*, which since the Capetian conquest had been only a temporary annual delegation of the Paris *Parlement* and of the *Chambre des comptes*, was reorganized. The *Échiquier* proper became a supreme court of justice sitting at Rouen. A *Chambre des comptes* dealing exclusively with Norman affairs was created at Caen and then, after a brief eclipse, transferred to Mantes. A treasurer and a receiver-general managed finance. By way of completing separation from the rest of the kingdom even in the intellectual sphere, later, in 1431, Bedford founded a Faculty of Law at Caen, despite the opposition of the Paris professors.

In all this there was nothing specifically English. Henry V was content to take over existing institutions and adapt them to a localized administration, or to restore those which the Capetian occupation had suppressed. The civil service was not affected, and the local officials, bailiffs, viscounts, provosts, *élus*, and collectors were maintained in their posts. So the people had to deal only with officials of their own nationality. Even in the central departments the French, or to be more exact the Norman, element was predominant. Only a few posts were given to Englishmen. John Kemp, Bishop of Rochester, became chancellor and the Earl of Suffolk admiral. Even in the great council the English element was neither the most numerous nor the most active. Lancastrian rule managed to secure the support of a few faithful Normans, who served its cause and were given its favour. Among them were the knight Raoul le Sage, lord of Saint-Pierre in Cotentin, who, when disaster came, withdrew across the Channel and became a naturalized Englishman; and Robert Jolivet, Abbot of Mont-Saint-Michel, who was unable to take possession of his abbey, where the monks remained persistently loyal to the Dauphin, but found fruitful compensation for his loss in the conqueror's service. The persons and property of the acquiescent people were left undisturbed. Henry V did not pursue his plan, at the outset of the conquest, of turning Harfleur into an English colony. Its inhabitants had been expelled, but were afterwards allowed to return home. Henry V and especially, after his death, his brother and heir to his ideas, Bedford, made a point of securing the good will of the Normans. They solemnly confirmed local privileges and particular or general franchises, notably the Charter to the Normans of 1315. Bedford, anxious to curry favour with the burgesses, remitted to Rouen part of the war indemnity imposed on the town.

But the military organization showed the occupation system in a very different light. Only garrisons from England could keep Normandy obedient and prevent any return to attack by the Dauphin's followers. The iron hand of foreign soldiery led the country to ignore the benefits of orderly administration and the fairness of officials chosen from its own nationals. A 'conquered country' in every sense of the word, it resented still more keenly the burdens which were thrust upon it. From the outset of the occupation all concern with defence and policing was reserved to Englishmen. A lieutenant general, the first of whom was the Earl of Salisbury, was given general control of military administration and exercised it harshly, despite the rival claims of the seneschal. Order was maintained by means of small English garrisons distributed among the castles. They numbered only 5,000 men-at-arms in 1421, and indeed were later reduced to 1,500 or 2,000. But they overawed the rural communities thanks to the system of *pâtis* or collective safe-conducts, which were issued for cash to the scared inhabitants and enabled heavy fines to be imposed in case of rebellion.

Henry V wanted to attach these garrisons to the soil and establish them in the Norman feudal system. Almost all the local nobility had remained faithful to the Dauphin and preferred exile to servitude. Their fiefs were confiscated *en bloc* and given to English captains in return for an obligation to garrison the castles and maintain a contingent of men-at-arms in proportion to the value of the fief. In this way the king set up in the country, above the native population, a feudal class of conquerors, paid for services rendered during the conquest without opening his purse-strings, and secured supervision and defence of the country without expense. To prevent any failure by these new colonists to perform their duty, Henry V forbade the English holders of fiefs to leave Normandy on pain of death. This measure was too severe and was rescinded by Bedford. A few defections followed, due to home-sickness. But those who left were replaced by new arrivals, and this harsh military occupation was maintained to the end. As any opposition was ruthlessly punished by stern measures of confiscation, the result was that a large part of Norman soil, consisting of castles and rural lordships, fell into the hands of foreign immigrants, eager to make their fortunes and hard on their new subjects.

How far did the people reconcile themselves to this state of affairs or display hostility? That depended on the period, the region or the social class concerned. Bent on consolidating his conquest quickly, Henry V behaved brutally and injured every interest without compunction. Expulsions, confiscations, and fines set up a reign of terror. After Henry's death Bedford, from self-interest and preference alike, showed more mildness and used a lighter hand, though he did not substantially change the situation. He avoided colliding head-on with his subjects' susceptibilities, and so fostered some rallying to the Lancastrian cause, some increase in co-operation. Nor were all parts of Normandy treated with the same severity. The ports, as landing-places of strategic importance, were subject to special rules. Such mass expulsion as we have noted at Harfleur was also initiated at Honfleur and perhaps at Cherbourg. On the other hand, once they had surrendered, the large inland towns, such as Rouen, Caen, and Lisieux, were treated more mildly. They kept their municipal liberties and co-operated satisfactorily with the occupying authorities.

There was a similar difference among social classes. The rally to the Lancastrian cause was effective and more or less complete only in two spheres, which were influential through their importance rather than their number. First there were the clergy, especially the higher beneficiaries, bishops, abbots, and prebendary canons, who, by virtue of the system of concordats with the papacy inaugurated after the council of Constance, were in practice appointed or controlled by the government. It was among them that Bedford found the most active co-operation, since it was he who placed Louis of Luxemburg, a follower and counsellor of Burgundy, on the archiepiscopal throne of Rouen. Next, the merchant burgesses of the towns, after heroically resisting the invader, made no bones about rallying to him once restoration of order meant prosperous trade. This applied particularly to Rouen, the seat of the government, the council, the chancery, and the *Échiquier*, which thereby had a fine time and did good business. The renewal of trade with England rounded off the rally of the burgesses.

In the countryside it was very different. With very few treasonable exceptions, the local nobility made common cause against the invader and went into voluntary exile, preferring to lose their lands rather than submit to his domination. Fundamentally the rural masses remained deliberately hostile. All they could see in the new order was a foreign lord, harsh in exacting dues and services, and a nearby garrison, as usual given to pillaging. The French and Norman chroniclers, to whatever party they belonged, stress the indomitable opposition of the peasants and their spirit of revolt. Some of these chroniclers present the English occupation as a barbarous iniquity, never accepted but merely endured. This fine show of resistance was not equally effective all the time. At the outset guerrilla warfare, led by outlawed squires with large numbers of local supporters, was waged actively. But it was sternly suppressed by the enemy, and gradually died down as liberation seemed more and more remote. After 1424, when the Dauphin lost the sole strong force he could still muster at Verneuil, on the threshold of Normandy, the people lost heart and became resigned to their fate. Henceforth there remained in the field only a few indomitable hotheads and daring guerrillas coming from the south, who sowed terror by their lightning raids. The peasants dreaded their approach as much as the English garrisons. To overcome these patriots the English branded them as 'brigands', which was a handy way of hanging them without trial whenever they managed to lay hands on them. But the endless struggle against these elusive irregulars preyed on the nerves of the occupying authorities by reminding them that they were in hostile country and never safe. Increased executions did not restore order, but only aggravated hatred. Plots persisted. At the time when Joan of Arc began her glorious career there was one even among the pacific burgesses of Rouen, which was discovered just in time.

All these troubles together speak volumes for the unpopularity and the precariousness of the English occupation. Still, according to Henry V himself, Normandy remained the province where his rule was most firmly based. On his death-bed he advised Bedford to maintain himself there at all costs, even if he had to abandon Paris. In fact, the loyal and energetic regent succeeded to the utmost in keeping this valuable conquest. But, if he did not lose it, he failed to win it over. His measures of clemency and his condemnation of the excesses of some particularly hated garrisons could not gain the loyalty of the people. Nevertheless, in this fundamentally hostile country the English maintained themselves for thirty years. It was a notable achievement in view of the difficulties of the task.

2. ANGLO-BURGUNDIAN FRANCE

By 'Anglo-Burgundian France' I mean those provinces which, after the Treaty of Troyes, were ruled jointly by English officials and Burgundian supporters. We must exclude from it the domains proper of Philip the Good and his cousins and cadets, which, by virtue of the same treaty, Henry V promised not to disturb, but to leave in the hands of the young duke. These domains, inside the frontiers of the kingdom of France, were Flanders, Artois, the counties of Rethel, Nevers, and Charolais, and the duchy of Burgundy. To them we may add the county of Boulogne, vassal to Artois, whose legitimate heir, George de La Trémoïlle, had been dispossessed by John the Fearless since 1416; Tournai, an outpost of the royal domain on the Scheldt, which came under the protection of Flemish officials from 1420; and Mâconnais, which was occupied from the outset of the war with the Dauphin by Burgundian troops.

If we look at a map, we cannot fail to be struck by the very small size of the territory actually controlled by the Lancastrians, even at the time of its greatest extent. Between Normandy, definitely English, and the Burgundian State on the one hand, and the large area which remained loyal to the Dauphin on the other, this Lancastrian territory was in fact limited to the royal domain at the time of Philip Augustus between the Somme and the middle Loire, in other words the old bailiwicks surrounding Paris: Amiens, Vermandois, Senlis, Meaux, Melun, and Chartres. It should have included Champagne. But in practice this province, occupied by the Burgundians since 1418, was outside the area of the condominium. After 1424 Bedford no longer exercised even nominal authority there.

Limited in area though it was, the region under Lancastrian rule derived an inestimable advantage from the possession of Paris and the central departments of the royal government. Here there was no need for the Lancastrians to make any change or even carry out any purge. They found a civil service entirely reorganized by John the Fearless, staffed by the powerful duke's nominees, and quite ready to co-operate with the new dynasty. The Treaty of Troyes could bear all the fruit on which the Lancastrians counted only if the master of northern France remained a faithful friend of Philip the Good. In the political sphere, despite plenty of storms with which I shall deal later, Bedford sought sincere agreement, and for ten years managed to maintain good terms, which were strengthened by his marriage to Anne of Burgundy.

On the administrative plane there were fewer difficulties, since the part of the kingdom of France under Bedford and Burgundy was still governed by Frenchmen, or rather Burgundians. Foreign rule remained in the background and was therefore more acceptable to the people. The royal council indeed included a few Englishmen of note, soldiers, diplomats, 'distinguished visitors', such as Cardinal Henry Beaufort. But all the other members, and the most influential because they were permanent members, were French and clients of Burgundy. Among them were the chancellors John le Clerc and his successor Louis of Luxemburg, belonging to the family of the counts of Saint-Pol, who was Bishop of Thérouanne before becoming Archbishop of Rouen and had won swift promotion as an official in the Burgundian civil service, being president of the *Chambre des comptes* and governor-general of finance; Peter Cauchon, who, after his exploits as a member of the University and a supporter of Caboche, became master of requests of the household and soon afterwards, in 1420, Bishop of Beauvais; Simon Morhier, a knight from the region of Chartres, who was made provost of Paris; and the master-butcher John of Saint-Yon, who became governor of finance.

To these officials with long service and secure in their posts Henry V and Bedford after him left the substance of power, reserving to themselves in general only appointment to military commands and the bestowal of gifts and pensions. The departments of State continued their routine work with the Burgundian staff in office since 1418. The *Parlement*, carefully purged by John the Fearless and with its presiding judge, Philip of Morvilliers, faithful to the Burgundian cause, on the whole supported the regent's views. It is true that, being traditionally Gallican, it made some difficulty in 1425 about endorsing the concordat which Bedford accepted from Pope Martin V; but its opposition was limited to one or two short-lived protests, which were stifled by the servile support of the higher clergy. In the *Chambre des comptes* and the *Cour des aides*, which Bedford re-established – John the Fearless had suppressed it in 1418, at the same time as the taxes – there was similar loyalty to the Lancastrian regent. The good relations and the administrative co-operation begun by the treaty of Troyes prevailed for more than ten years between the sharers of power.

If the prestige of a government is to be measured by its wealth of legislation, that of the Lancastrians could not be said to stand very high. Yet Henry V had arrived in France with the declared intention to restore order in a corrupt administration and put a stop to the exactions of its officials and the pillaging of the State revenues. The anxieties of the war, no less than his early death, prevented him from carrying out these ambitious plans of reform, though indeed it is hard to say whether he was really interested in them. But the Burgundian counsellors, who had also contemplated them, and some of whom, like Cauchon, had played a leading part in Caboche's movement, might at length have attempted, under the aegis of the Lancastrians, that complete recasting of administration which they had advocated. Whether it was from laziness, inertia, or impotence, they did nothing of the kind. The sole sphere in which they exerted themselves to repair past mistakes was the currency. But the very number of their monetary ordinances, one after another, shows how hard it was to restore and maintain a sound currency when the country was periodically flooded by the Dauphin's coinage, which was continually debased.

If the Anglo-Burgundian rule lacked the merit of introducing changes, one cannot deny it that of lasting some time. Its fundamental weakness must be sought elsewhere than in a routine administration unfavourable to initiative. It may be summed up under three heads: the troubles of the military occupation; the greed of the English captains and barons; and, finally, the poverty of financial resources.

Henry V had imposed on England a great financial and military effort, out of all proportion to the strength of the kingdom: the raid of 1415, the invasion of 1417, the dispatch of reinforcements to the continent during the following years. Once he was dead, the country could not continue to finance an endless war which swallowed up more and more men without any decisive result. The English people, through their regents and their parliaments, expressed the opinion that they had fulfilled their whole duty in giving their king the opportunity to don the crown of France. When that was done, if a number of rebel provinces remained to be conquered, the task devolved on his French subjects, not his English. Throughout his rule in Paris and Normandy, Bedford failed to obtain much money from England, whose coffers were but sparingly opened to him. Indeed in this respect the principle of the 'dual monarchy' was applied in all its strictness. English expenditure was England's business, and French expenditure was France's business. When Bedford managed to get reinforcements from England, never in adequate numbers, it was out of the French budget that he had to pay them.

The result was that he had not enough men to establish a strong enough system of permanent garrisons in the provinces which were entirely or partly subject to him. He could hold only the most important positions on the rivers and along the roads. His shortage of strength meant that all the men available had to be employed in active operations in Maine and Anjou and between the Seine and the Loire. Elsewhere the country remained badly guarded, in between punitive campaigns intended to chastise resistance. The apparent apathy of the people and the submission of the landed nobility, almost all devoted to the Burgundian cause, did not allow him, as in Normandy, to establish an English knighthood, paid without expense from the revenues of the fiefs granted to them. The Burgundian garrisons, of whose services he had to make use, played their own game and were not wholly reliable. This was to be observed in Champagne. Though the people offered less active resistance than in Normandy, the invaders controlled the country less closely and never exercised more than an unstable rule with a dubious future. Paris had surrendered with enthusiasm to the Duke of Burgundy through hatred of the Armagnacs. The English occupation made it forget the reign of terror from which it had escaped. It grumbled at the foreign garrison, though it did not go so far as rebellion. The countryside was much less secure. As a result, some strongholds managed to maintain their Armagnac captains for a long time, or, as the fortune of war allowed, were taken over by garrisons loyal to the Dauphin. They formed islets of resistance here and there, which made the roads unsafe and were bases for daring raids. It would be useful to mark them with red on a map and estimate their density and therefore their danger. But they varied greatly from time to time. At one period, the end of 1423, they were very numerous, not only round Paris and in Champagne, but also in Ponthieu and Picardy and on the borders of Rethelois and Barrois. At this time troops of the Dauphin roamed beneath the walls of Paris. A vigorous counter-offensive reduced them considerably. But some of them remained and others regrouped.

The epic of Joan of Arc presents us with two striking examples. On the eastern borders of Champagne and Barrois whole districts faithfully preserved the memory of Louis of Orleans, who had been powerful in this region, maintained their loyalty to the Dauphin and never embraced the Burgundian cause. Effective authority over the villages of the Argonne was exercised by Robert of Baudricourt, captain of Vaucouleurs in the name of the king at Bourges. In the heart of Ile-de-France, the campaign at the time of his coronation recovered Compiègne, within reach of Creil and the road to Flanders, where William of Flavy established a royal garrison. Relying on the Burgundians to maintain order, the Lancastrians were never really in possession of northern France. The ease with which first Troyes and then Rheims were able to open their gates to the royal forces on the eve of Charles VII's coronation proves to the hilt that Anglo-Burgundian rule there was nominal rather than actual.

The demands of the English barons and captains troubled Bedford's government no less. Everyone, great or small, who went to fight in France demanded his share in the spoils of conquest. Bedford had to pay for services rendered, keep the best captains on the continent by the grant of fine lordships, and dazzle the wavering by the prospect of favours to induce them to cross the Channel and keep up the flow of troops. The estates of the rebel vassals and the appanaged princes, Maine, Perche, Alençon, and Eu – some of them, to be sure, still had to be conquered – served to satisfy the largest appetites. Warwick, Salisbury, Suffolk, Talbot, and Fastolf got the lion's share. To others, and they were legion, lands had to be distributed and pensions assigned. It was for this reason that, in the government of the kingdom, Bedford had kept the control of favours in his own hands. He was soon overwhelmed by this endless task. As there were not enough confiscations to meet all demands, he was driven to alienate, bit by bit, the royal domain now pitiably impoverished by the civil war, and then to burden the treasury with all kinds of pensions, which continually widened the gap of the budget deficit. Burgundy's followers had helped themselves first. On pain of hastening their defection, Bedford could not oust them from their estates or cut off their allowances. Where was he to find the funds needed for all these greedy clients?

The Lancastrians inherited in northern France all the fiscal troubles of the Valois, aggravated by the calls of the war and the military occupation. In pursuit of his demagogic plans, John the Fearless had discontinued aids in the form of hearth-taxes and indirect taxes, and maintained only the salt-tax in the unpopular fiscal system. As early as 1420, at the time of the ratification of the Treaty of Troyes, Henry V induced the Estates of Languedoïl to restore taxation of commodities, though at a lower rate than before, fixed at one-twentieth on trading transactions and one-quarter on wine and beer. Soon the hearth-tax had to be revived as well. But the government, unsure about public opinion, could not impose it with a stroke of the pen. So it had to consult the Estates. On the other hand, it shrank from summoning the representatives of the whole of Anglo-Burgundian Languedoïl too often. It did so only once, on the morrow of its victory at Verneuil, when its newly enhanced prestige enabled it to obtain the grant of a heavy hearth-tax amounting to 240,000 *livres*. The provinces of the old royal domain, however, Ile-de-France, Picardy, Vermandois, and Champagne, had no long tradition of local Estates behind them. In his respect for all customs, Bedford appealed to them very rarely. There was a meeting for Champagne and Picardy in the spring of 1424, and that was all. Besides, these provinces, being the chief victims of the civil war, were exhausted and could not make any continuous or considerable fiscal effort. Though details of the Lancastrian administration in these districts are imperfectly known, it seems that Bedford had to be content, so far as direct taxation went, with meagre grants voted from time to time by delegates from a few towns and small assemblies of bailiwicks.

The main burden of taxation fell on the city of Paris, whose burgesses were squeezed by every government, and on Normandy. More firmly occupied, more sternly administered, and less ravaged by war than the other provinces, Normandy was indeed, in the full force of the term, the milch-cow of Lancastrian rule. Here the local Estates were traditionally more deeply rooted than in the old royal domain. Here, as elsewhere, Henry V and Bedford were careful to avoid changes. They summoned the representatives of the duchy frequently, in Rouen, Vernon, Caen, and Mantes, sometimes even in Paris. There were more than twenty sessions of the Norman Estates during a period of only thirteen years, between 1422 and 1435. At every meeting they were asked for money, which they voted obediently. The volume of the taxation thus granted varied from 100,000 to 300,000 *livres* a year; but it is impossible to say how far the collectors succeeded in levying these heavy sums from a single province of the kingdom. In any case, they fell below the government's needs, especially for the war. When we recall that at the beginning of the century the Valois monarchy exacted from the whole kingdom taxation exceeding a million *livres*, we can realize with what scanty revenue the invaders had to be content, at a time when the prosecution of the war and the conquest created continually increased needs.

Accordingly, all the resources available were strictly reserved for the war. The Lancastrians had regarded the occupation system as temporary; but it lasted as long as they did, and did not allow them to win over the people, since it never provided the peace which prevailed before the civil war. At least, however, the aggressive spirit of the Lancastrian troops, whether raiding separately in mobile columns or dispersed in garrisons in the castles, was carefully maintained by regular supplies of rations and stores and high pay at fixed dates: all things long unknown to the soldiers who fought in the Dauphin's name. It was this strict organization of an army with weak effectives which enabled the Anglo-Burgundian government to hold out, despite an incomplete military occupation and the precariousness of its fiscal resources. Seen from the inside, it seemed to be afflicted by an incurable weakness and to be moribund even when it came in being. The worth of the leaders who undertook this vain and hopeless task explains alike its partial success and its maintenance for more than fifteen years. Finally luck was on their side, above all in the fact that they did not find opposed to them men of their own measure, capable of flicking down the fragile house of cards of the 'dual monarchy'.

3. THE KINGDOM OF BOURGES

ALL CENTRAL and southern France, apart from English Guienne, remained faithful to the Dauphin Charles after his disinheritance. When they entered the capital in May 1418, the Burgundians flattered themselves that they were trailing the greater part of the kingdom in their wake. For a short time, indeed, the governors appointed by John the Fearless, notably John of Chalon, Prince of Orange, supported by Gaston of Grailly, Count of Foix, were accepted in Languedoc, where the exactions of the late Duke of Berry had stirred up public opinion against the Armagnacs. But a progress by the Dauphin in the southern provinces between March and May 1420, and the capture of Nîmes and Pont-Saint-Esprit, restored Languedoc to obedience to him. A little later, however (1425), after the Count of Foix had made his submission, these rich seneschalships were entrusted to him and, like all his predecessors, he plundered them systematically. He exercised in practice autonomous power and extended the scope of his lieutenancy over the neighbouring provinces of Agenais and Rouergue, for control of which he contended feebly with the English.

The frontiers of rival rule inevitably remained uncertain and varied in accordance with the vicissitudes of the war. While the struggle centred especially in the north for possession of the region between the Seine and the Loire, in other words from the marches of Brittany to Morvan, further east, on the contrary, after 1423 the Burgundian front became stabilized along a line which followed the Loire between Gien and Roanne – here there was a long contest for the two bridge-heads of La Charité and Marcigny, threatening Berry and Bourbonnais respectively – then ran eastward, between Mâconnais and Beaujolais, and ended in Bresse, a possession of the house of Savoy, whose neutrality on the whole favoured the Burgundian cause. In the south-west Saintonge, Limousin, Périgord, Rouergue, and Agenais were the theatre of an obscure warfare of siege and surprise.

Within these limits Charles was acknowledged in three groups of provinces. First there was the region of the Loire, protected on the north by the domains of the houses of Anjou and Orleans, and on the south by those of the Bourbons. This district comprised Poitou, Touraine, and Berry, and was the favourite region of the young prince, to whom his enemies soon gave the scornful nickname of 'king of Bourges'. Next there was a southern group, made up of Languedoc and its dependencies, whose fortunes I have outlined above. Finally, in the south-east Dauphiné was fortunately linked with the kingdom by the Dauphin's possession of Lyons, a strategic position of the first importance in relation to the Burgundian domains, which was loyal to him from the outset. Later, when he was victorious as Charles VII, the consuls of Lyons reminded him, with some pride, that their city had been 'the one that never wavered'. Almost entirely these provinces I have just mentioned had been appanages or lieutenancies of the princes of the Orleanist faction, and that quite recently. Touraine and Dauphiné had been possessions of Charles VI's sons and finally the Dauphin Charles himself. Berry, Poitou, and Languedoc had been ruled by the Duke of Berry.

It was, indeed, the loyalty of the princes which in 1418 constituted the sole strength of the youth of sixteen whom the Burgundians had driven out of Paris. Beside him stood the Anjous. He had been betrothed to Marie, sister of Louis III of Anjou and of René, who by a later marriage became Duke of Lorraine. When the Dauphin lost the support of the Constable of Armagnac, he found in his stead an imperious tutor in the person of his mother-in-law, Louis II of Anjou's widow Yolanda of Aragon, known in France as 'Queen of Sicily', who did her best to reconcile the interests of Anjou with those of her son-in-law. Beside the Dauphin also stood the house of Orleans. True, Duke Charles of Orleans had for several years been a prisoner of the English, beguiling his leisure in his long captivity by polishing the delicate rondeaux that made him the most charming French poet of the fifteenth century. But in his absence the Orleans appanage was administered by the Dauphin's officials. Moreover, the royal prisoner's half-brother, the bastard John, Count of Dunois, put his arms at the service of the Valois cause. Finally beside the Dauphin stood the Bourbons. In the absence of Duke John, who was also a prisoner and died in captivity, the Duchess Marie of Berry, who had added Auvergne to her husband's wide domains, served his cause faithfully. Her troops were useful in resisting Burgundian pressure on the borders of Charolais and Beaujolais. True, the kingdom of Bourges remained for several years a prey to anarchy, disorder, and decay. Nevertheless, thanks to the support of the appanaged princes, it formed a compact group of territories in which no serious dissidence appeared and there were no islets of resistance or guerrilla raids such as dangerously weakened Anglo-Burgundian France.

In the aimlessness of his roving and needy life on the banks of the Loire, therefore, the Dauphin was not so isolated, so friendless, as he has sometimes been depicted. To the support of the princes, moreover, was added the invaluable help of the royal officials, most of whom remained faithful to the service of the Valois. The Dauphin's government had had to abandon Paris to the enemy, and with it all the central departments of State. They had to be reconstituted in exile as best they could and housed in makeshift quarters south of the Loire. Just as Troyes had been for the queen and the Burgundians from 1418 to 1420, so Bourges became a capital of sorts, where the chief public services were established. It was here that the Dauphin's council sat as a rule, when it did not follow the prince in his travels. It was here that the headquarters of the chancery were organized, and here too, after a short stay at Tours, the *Chambre des comptes* joined it. Poitiers, another capital of Berry's appanage, became the home of the legal departments proper. Here, as early as September 21st 1418, the ordinance of Niort established the *Parlement*. In view of the fact that the purge carried out in Paris by the Duke of Burgundy had practically abolished the former *Parlement* and rendered the new one illegal, the Dauphin transferred the seat of the supreme court of the kingdom to the old palace of the counts of Poitiers. At the outset it was only a skeleton tribunal, comprising merely eighteen judges, councillors and masters of requests. They sufficed for the organization of no more than two chambers, the grand chamber and the criminal chamber. The chamber of requests and the chamber of inquests were restored much later, when the staff had become rather more numerous and cases came up for hearing in a more steady flow; for the insecurity which prevailed throughout the kingdom had reduced the jurisdiction and authority of this *Parlement* in exile to next to nothing. Between 1420 and 1428 the royal government was even forced to create a separate *Parlement* for Languedoc cases first at Toulouse and then at Béziers and allow it to continue, despite the definite dislike which the monarchy had always shown for decentralizing its supreme courts. Finally it was also at Poitiers that the *Cour des aides* was reorganized in 1425, again on a much reduced scale, since it had only seven members.

This duplication of institutions was facilitated as a whole by the loyalty of the royal officials to the Dauphin's cause. The mass dismissals carried out by John the Fearless in 1418 and rounded off by Henry V in 1420 in the *Parlement*, the royal household, the financial departments, and the supreme courts had affected a certain number of avowed partisans of the Armagnacs, but also many lukewarm and neutral officials, who desired above all, as at one point the Dauphin Louis of Guienne had done, a return to internal peace. Replaced by obscure Burgundians, inexperienced in the control of affairs and incapable of giving the Paris institutions the lustre which the representatives of the royal authority enjoyed, these dismissed officials were thrown back *en bloc* into the Dauphin's party and condemned to exile. They brought a self-interested devotion, sometimes dishonest but nevertheless loyal, to the kingdom of Bourges, in which they saw the sole legitimate continuation of the royal administration. Thus they formed the framework of a government which, but for them, might have foundered. There were more candidates than were needed for a civil service necessarily much reduced. The choice that was made among the swarm of applicants was not always happy. Only too many officials were corrupt and notorious for their dishonesty. Still, they possessed experience and capacity which later proved to be of value.

The presiding judge of the *Parlement* was John of Vailly, a trusted old councillor and long an enemy of the Caboche faction. His deputy was John Jouvenel, formerly keeper of the provostship of the merchants, then king's advocate, then chancellor of the Duke of Guienne, and finally president of the *Cour des aides*, who found posts beside him for his two sons, one of them the future Archbishop of Rheims and chronicler, best known by his Latinized name of Juvenal de Ursinis. A place in the *Parlement* was also found for Arnaud of Marle, son of the former chancellor massacred as an Armagnac in 1418. At the head of the finance department Queen Yolanda secured the appointment – though she later dismissed him – of John Louvet, the far from upright president of the *Chambre des comptes* of Provence. To the *Cour des aides*, in addition to two members of the old *cour* abolished by the Burgundians, were appointed two former members of the *Parlement* who had been protégés of Louis of Guienne and Louis of Orleans and three Poitevins, old servants of Berry. A similar mixture was to be found even in local administration. Here, side by side with self-seeking mediocrities, there were also energetic and faithful officials, such as Imbert of Grôlée, a nobleman of Bresse, who, from 1419 to his death in 1434, had a remarkable career as seneschal of Lyons, where he led a largely successful resistance to Burgundian attacks and Savoyard intrigues.

Superior to the Lancastrian government by virtue of the area under its control, its support by the appanaged princes and the ability of its civil service, the kingdom of Bourges also had at its disposal wider resources which, if they were not wasted by dishonest officials and greedy courtiers, would allow it to make a more intense military effort. Like his rival Bedford, Charles made use of existing taxes, continued to levy the salt-tax and the commodity taxes and asked the Estates for the grant of hearth-taxes which were continually renewed. The good old days when Charles V and his son decreed the rate of taxation on their own authority were not to return until the monarchy recovered its unity and its former prestige. But the sessions of the Estates, which were sometimes summoned several times a year, rarely opposed the government's demands; and, as the provinces loyal to it were as a whole richer and rather less impoverished than those ruled by Bedford, the King of Bourges obtained from them, at least on paper, considerable sums. For the year 1424 alone – obviously an exceptional one, since it witnessed, in the military sphere, the raising of a large army – he secured in March, from the Estates of Languedoïl meeting at Selles-sur-Cher, a hearth-tax of a million *livres*; in May, from the Estates of Languedoc summoned at Montpellier, 150,000 *livres*; and a similar sum in December from a session of the Estates General held at Clermont. Meanwhile local assemblies in Saintonge (June), Velay, Gévaudan, and Vivarais (September) granted supplementary aids, while Poitou by itself was taxed an addition of 50,000 *livres*. In all, this was five or six times as much as Bedford could hope to levy in his domains. In normal years, when the Lancastrian obtained 100,000 or 200,000 *livres*, the Valois was granted 500,000 at least, so that the difference still remained large enough.

It is, of course, another matter to what extent the country, whose resources were progressively exhausted, paid the enormous sums which were demanded of it. It is also another matter how far the money collected reached the coffers of the King of Bourges. One may suspect any amount of peculation and embezzlement, not to speak of the Dauphin's lavishness towards his unworthy favourites. During the early years of his exile, Charles lived in a state of absolute destitution, having scarcely enough to clothe himself suitably – and yet his taste for fine apparel was so strong that he was later to sacrifice to it all that his meagre budget produced – surrounded by a few faithful followers equally poor. His officials, badly housed in too small 'capitals', received their inadequate pay only irregularly. At Tours, Chinon, and Bourges his court was gradually reconstituted and wandered from one seat to another. But it still lacked money. The old makeshifts, notably monetary devaluation, were utilized to the full, so much so that the Estates of Chinon, summoned in 1428 on the eve of the siege of Orleans, opposed any fresh grant of taxation until the currency was revalued and stabilized.

Amid all this disorder, is it surprising that the Dauphin's military effort against the Anglo-Burgundians fell short not merely of his needs, but even of what economical Bedford managed to achieve with smaller resources? If the English army was small and inadequate for all the tasks that beset it, at least it was coherent, well equipped, and regularly paid, and its discipline was strict and effective. In his kingdom Charles could scarcely count on anyone except the Armagnac captains, survivors of the civil war, in which their habits of brutality, rapine, and indiscipline had become inveterate. Because they later took part in Joan of Arc's epic, some of them were to remain surrounded with haloes of glory. But La Hire, Xaintrailles, Ambroise of Loré, the Gascons Arnaud Guilhem of Barbazan and Amaury of Sévérac, and even 'noble Dunois' himself were still only brigand chiefs. To organize more effective campaigns Charles relied on foreign mercenaries, notably the formidable Scots sent him by the regent Albany. Their leaders, Archibald, Earl of Douglas, and John Stuart, Earl of Buchan, were received by the King of Bourges with open arms and endowed with estates and pensions; in 1421 Buchan girded on the Constable's sword. But they treated France as a conquered country, and the people hailed their extermination on the field of Verneuil as a deliverance.

The great weakness of the Dauphin's party, which in the last resort was responsible for its repeated defeats and its pitiable defence against the Anglo-Burgundians, was the personalities of its head and those who advised him or sponged on him. One could scarcely imagine a prince less fitted to evoke enthusiasm, defend a cause in peril and play the part of leader and later of king. Physically and mentally, Charles was a weakling, a graceless degenerate. He was stunted and puny, with a blank face in which scared, shifty, sleepy eyes, peering out on either side of a big, long nose, failed to animate his harsh, unpleasant features. The last born of too large a family – he was only sixteen in 1418 – the Dauphin was not expected to succeed to the throne. While still a child he was betrothed to Marie of Anjou, and from 1412 Queen Yolanda had taken charge of his upbringing. He was retrieved from this humiliating position belatedly, when he had to assume the leadership of the Armagnac party on John of Touraine's death; but it was only to fall into the stern grip of the formidable Constable. The sorrows of his childhood, surrounded by danger and enmity, had taught him to be deceitful and underhand. Though he denied it, the murder of Burgundy at Montereau appears in fact to have been premeditated. His excessive weakness made him diffident and indolent. He doubted himself, his followers, even his rights. Obsessed by the insult inflicted on him by the Treaty of Troyes, he wondered with mortification whether his mother had told the truth. Perhaps he was a bastard. If so, what was the good of fighting? Now and then he reacted against the insult and loudly proclaimed the justice of his cause. He did so in January 1421, when the Paris *Parlement* found him guilty of the murder of John the Fearless, declared him banished from the kingdom and incapable of succeeding to any lordship. He did so again in November 1422, when, on the announcement of his father's death, he proclaimed his accession to the throne of France and swore at the castle of Mehun-sur-Yèvre, in the presence of his handful of supporters, that he would never lay down his arms until he had recovered his kingdom.

But he soon relapsed into his timid apathy, of which his entourage took advantage to divide the spoils of his domains. Despite a few fits and starts, he had no faith in victory by force of arms – from 1422 he gave up personal command of his army – and often called off campaigns against the invaders before they were begun. Never, on the other hand, did he lose hope of obtaining by diplomatic means a reconciliation with the Burgundians, which alone, he felt, would enable the English to be ousted from France. But his counsellors barred the road to reconciliation and fostered anti-Burgundian feeling, which was their livelihood. Too weak to win the war, too indolent to negotiate peace, Charles consistently disappointed all those – and they were still legion – who regarded him as the legitimate heir of a glorious dynasty. Wandering gloomily from one residence to another, silent, sly, superstitious, this backward youth awaited the blows of fate before showing himself a man and becoming a king.

What can be said about those who held front rank in his entourage and gave orders to the submissive officials? The chancellor Robert le Maçon, the presiding judge Louvet and Tanguy du Châtel, who shared influence over him during the early years of the kingdom of Bourges, were the last survivors of the Armagnac faction, the instigators of the crime at Montereau, obscure hangers-on schooled during the civil war. They had learned to live by it and prosper from it, and could see no way of keeping power except the continuance of the faction fight. When they were threatened with the loss of their jobs, they resorted to the procedure of the civil war and rebelled in their master's name against those who supplanted them in his favour. Their successors, it must be admitted, were not much better. Quarrels, intrigues, plots, palace revolutions – everything happened all over again in the entourage of the too young sovereign just as it had under his mad father. As Charles took a long time to become a man, it was very belatedly that he got rid, by murder if need be, of this decomposing entourage. It was not until 1433 that the grasping George of la Tremoïlle, who for years had been the evil genius of the King of Bourges, was ousted after an attack by assassins.

4. THE COURSE OF THE WAR: THE SIEGE OF ORLEANS

THE MILITARY operations which took place during nearly nine years, from the signing of the Treaty of Troyes to Joan of Arc's appearance, on the Burgundian and the English fronts alike, do not lend themselves readily to a continuous narrative. Boldly conducted by an invader in strength, they might have led up to a deadly series of campaigns – such as that of Agincourt, which was in fact the last – and enabled a predestined victor to force a decision. But their failure to complete the conquest compelled the Lancastrians to disperse their forces, to lose valuable time in reducing islets of resistance and to be constantly on their guard against a counter-offensive by the Dauphin's followers. In the upshot, operations were confined to surprises, sudden attacks on fortresses, more or less deep raids into hostile territory, and a few more prolonged sieges. They make excellent material for the local historian, who may take a limited theatre in Anjou, Nivernais or southern Burgundy and follow the ups and downs of the war in detail in a particular area; or for the biographer, who may choose as his subject some outstanding captain, such as the Poitevin Perrinet Gressart on the Anglo-Burgundian side or the Castilian Rodrigo de Villandrandro on Charles VII's side, and let us accompany his hero wherever his deeds lead him.

The general historian, however, must forgo any idea of taking that sweeping, simplified view which military history demands in connexion with great armed conflicts, all the more so because, even during this unhappy period, repeated political difficulties in both camps and various attempts at diplomatic negotiation thwarted the plans made by the captains. To divorce the political and diplomatic events from the military events proper would give them an even greater incoherence than they actually possessed. At the risk of going too far in sorting out the tangle, we must try to distinguish some main phases, note the stages reached and take our bearings by a few particularly important dates. In doing so we can certainly see more clearly than contemporaries, who were concerned only with the passing show, and whose field of vision did not allow them to discern the outstanding changes in the sea of trivialities. To share in this myopia we need only read the very precious *Journal* of a Parisian burgess, an anonymous Burgundian supporter, busily engaged in noting the increase in the cost of living, talking about the difficulties of provisioning, and taking more interest in fleeting shifts of public opinion than in the gravest decisions of diplomats and captains; or even the engaging *Chronicle* in which Juvenal de Ursinis, some time later and with an obvious desire to show off, recalled the memories of a moderate among Charles VII's counsellors. While in both camps people felt more and more definitely how much was at stake, namely the fate of the glorious kingdom of France, they failed to see very clearly how events were shaping or towards what end, for all their passion, they were working.

The achievement of Henry V and the period following his death, until about the middle of the year 1423, make up the first phase of this confused story, whose main outlines we must retrace. Surrounded with a halo of unprecedented military fame, glorying in a diplomatic success which brought within his reach the crown he had so long coveted, the King of England nevertheless had not completed his task merely by his marriage to Catherine of France. The common purpose of his policy and that of his ally Burgundy was to overthrow the Dauphin, the sole obstacle to the unification of the kingdom under the Lancastrian dynasty. But the time had not come to attack him in his lair south of the Loire, though he seemed readily vulnerable there. The reason was that Henry, faithful to the systematic policy he had hitherto pursued, insisted on completing the subjection of the conquered provinces before pressing onward. Almost everywhere, in Ponthieu, Picardy, Champagne, and Ile-de-France, Armagnac garrisons threatened his communications. They were on the Oise, the Marne, and the upper Seine, and made the provisioning of Paris precarious. It would take months to reduce them one by one. For a start, Henry was content to make an example. His entrance into Paris with Charles VI for the ratification of the Treaty of Troyes was delayed to allow time for the lengthy siege and capture of Melun (September 17th 1420). Meanwhile a Burgundian force made a surprise attack on Montereau and brought back the body of John the Fearless to the Carthusian monastery at Champmol.

After this, a plan of attack against the Dauphin's forces might have been drawn up. But the Regent of France, without realizing the dangers involved, left matters to his lieutenants, and they were impatient to satisfy their personal ambitions. He had given Maine to his brother Clarence, and Perche to Salisbury. Each of them hastened to take possession of his new appanage and dispersed his inadequate forces in outlying regions. Finally Henry himself had to think about his island kingdom, to which he had not returned for over three years. In January 1421 he took Queen Catherine to be crowned at Westminster. There he summoned a fresh Parliament, made the most of the glorious results achieved since his last departure, foretold the early end of all organized resistance by the Dauphin's party, obtained the vote of a further subsidy for these final operations, and slowly started to raise reinforcements.

These mistakes and delays had grave consequences. They meant that final victory, which Henry reckoned quite close at hand, was postponed indefinitely. During his absence the conquerors of Maine let themselves be surprised by the French-Scottish army of the Earl of Buchan, who won the Constable's sword on the battlefield. Clarence, the best of Henry's lieutenants and his heir-presumptive, was killed in this battle at Baugé in Anjou (March 22nd 1421). No more was needed to revive the highest hopes in the Dauphin's camp. Throughout the country the garrisons loyal to him bestirred themselves and made life hard for the occupying English and Burgundians. At the same time, in a fit of unusual energy, the Dauphin in person led his army, by way of Maine and Beauce, to the walls of Paris. An immediate parry was essential. In July Henry landed at Calais with fresh troops, and the mere news of his advance sufficed to make the Dauphin retreat south of the Loire. But everything achieved during the past year had to be done all over again: the clearance of Picardy, upon which Philip the Good insisted; the reconquest of the districts of Dreux, Perche, and Beauce, which the king entrusted to his former prisoner Arthur of Brittany, Earl of Richmond (known as Richemont by the French), brother of Duke John V who had paid him homage; the relief of Paris by the capture of the river towns which surrounded it. All this took the remainder of the year 1421 and the first six months of the next year. Meaux surrendered in May 1422 and Compiègne in June.

Just as he was again in a position to undertake more extensive operations, the Lancastrian king was brought to a halt once more, this time by illness. He died on August 31st 1422, though not before he had time to appoint successors to carry on his task. Catherine of France had given him an heir, but he was only a child of eight months, who was at once proclaimed King of England as Henry VI and soon afterwards King of France. Now that Clarence was dead, Henry V had only two brothers left. To one of them, John, Duke of Bedford, a good soldier and a sound administrator, he left the control of French affairs, on condition that he should first offer the regency to Philip the Good, whose refusal he took for granted. Henry knew that in Bedford he had a faithful and intelligent successor, who would continue his policy. Before his death, he reminded Bedford of its essential points: to maintain agreement with Burgundy at all costs; to wage war energetically against the Dauphin; to rally the restive population to his side by just government; to try to hold Paris, but, if it so happened that he could not, to fall back on Normandy, the citadel of Lancastrian rule.

In England the position was not so clear. Logically the regency should go to the king's youngest brother, Humphrey, Duke of Gloucester. But Henry knew that, though he was thirty-one, he was a vain and brainless young man, whose muddleheaded restlessness might lead to serious trouble. While Gloucester could not be deprived of the title of protector of the kingdom, the essence of power would rest with the Beauforts, Henry's uncles or cousins and the surest supporters of his dynasty: Henry, Bishop of Winchester, soon to be cardinal: Thomas, Duke of Exeter; and John, Earl of Dorset. Though Henry V died in the castle of Vincennes, he was not fated to repose in French soil. His funeral service took place at Notre-

Dame in Paris, but after it his body was removed to Westminster, as though it was written that no Lancastrian should find his last resting-place beneath the paving-stones of Saint-Denis.

Another more melancholy death plunged France into mourning in this same autumn. Abandoned by everyone in the Hôtel Saint-Paul, which even Isabeau had deserted, surrounded only by a handful of faithful servants, Charles VI died on October 22nd 1422, two months after his English son-in-law, at the age of fifty-four, after thirty years of intermittent and incurable madness. Neither his son, nor his nephews, nor even the Duke of Burgundy attended his funeral. Alone behind the bier, Bedford represented the infant Henry VI, whom he immediately proclaimed King of France, despite his absence in England. Officially the dual monarchy, outlined by the Treaty of Troyes, was at last within sight of achievement. But it could become effective only with the downfall of the Dauphin, who now called himself Charles VII; and, to overthrow him, Bedford would need all the help he could get. Above all, he must tighten his bonds of friendship with Philip the Good. Hitherto, indeed, the Burgundian alliance had not yielded the results on which Henry V had reckoned. The masterful king and regent had taken little account of the traditional desire of the Duke of Burgundy to lord it in Paris. The English garrisons had roughly ousted the ducal livery with the cross of St. Andrew from all the important fortresses. The result was that since the Treaty of Troyes Philip had made only brief appearances in the capital. He had held aloof from the Lancastrian government and usually taken up his quarters in Lille or Ghent, his favourite residences. There had been regrettable quarrels between his captains and the English leaders, which revealed a disquieting state of mind. In January 1422, when Philip, taking advantage of a short trip through his duchy and faithful to his pledged word, insisted that the people of Dijon should pay homage to the heir named by Charles VI, the burgesses finally gave their forced consent to the Treaty of Troyes only at his express order.

These were grave symptoms, and it was essential to prevent them from coming to a head. Bedford, less imperious and less dissembling than his elder brother, laid the cards of honesty and trust on the table with Burgundy. Already, during Henry's illness, he had spontaneously sent reinforcements to Nivernais to ward off a threat by the Dauphin to his ally's patrimony. On the King of England's death, he offered Philip the regency of France. It was a tempting proposition, which would enable him to achieve peacefully the ambition of Philip the Bold and John the Fearless, the definite control of the kingdom's government. But Burgundy was on his guard. He weighed the risks. What would be his authority over a country maintained in allegiance only by foreign garrisons? Would not the regency bind him to service to the Lancastrians? Would he be any more than their servant? A man less shrewd, more eager for immediate advantage, however illusory, might have grasped the opportunity to reach his political goal, even though he got there on the foreigner's wagon train. History has shown that such a calculation, however profitable it might seem, never paid the fool or the weakling who let himself be lured by it. Philip refused the offer. The result was that Bedford besought his friendship and proposed to strengthen Anglo-Burgundian unity by marriage. At this point John V of Brittany, who hitherto had gone on hesitating between the adversaries, being sometimes Armagnac and sometimes Burgundian, sometimes offering his homage to the Lancastrians and sometimes becoming reconciled with the Dauphin, solely in the hope of sparing his duchy the horrors of war, joined Burgundy and Bedford and lined up against Charles VII. In April 1423 the triple alliance was concluded at Amiens. It was consolidated by a double marriage, between Bedford and Anne of Burgundy and Richmond and Margaret of Burgundy, the widow of Louis of Guienne.

The coalition of the three princes was in decay even before it was concluded. Despite all Bedford's shrewdness, the year 1423 ushered in a long phase of four years, a period of disappointments and rebuffs, during which Burgundy's friendship became transformed into underhand rivalry and his intrigues with the Valois king paralysed the military efforts of the Lancastrian armies.

An episode with some incidents of the burlesque was the starting-point of the coolness in Anglo-Burgundian relations. It linked Gloucester's scatter-brained restlessness and Jacqueline of Bavaria's romantic adventures in a perfectly constructed tragi-comedy. When John the Fearless's brother-in-law, William of Bavaria, Count of Hainault, Holland, and Zeeland, died in 1417, his inheritance was disputed between his brother John of Bavaria, hitherto Bishop of Liège, who hastened to abandon his mitre, return to lay life and take a wife, and his only daughter Jacqueline, widow of the colourless Dauphin John of Touraine, and after his death remarried to her no less colourless first cousin John of Brabant, son of the late Duke Anthony. Both were under obligations to the Duke of Burgundy. The ex-bishop had needed Burgundian troops to overcome the revolt of the Liège workers by the victory of Othée in January 1408. Jacqueline, by marrying the young Duke of Brabant, whose whole policy supported that of John the Fearless, entered the circle of his protégés. So it was to the powerful Duke of Burgundy that, after four years of strife, they appealed to settle the terms of an agreement. By this agreement, concluded in April 1420, the disputed domains were divided. John of Bavaria retained the administration of Holland and Zeeland for his lifetime, and Jacqueline was recognized as Countess of Hainault.

There the situation might have remained if Jacqueline, dissatisfied with the second husband who had been thrust upon her, had not suddenly left him in April 1421. Henceforth she found refuge in England, where Gloucester, hitherto unoccupied in his brother's continental campaigns, aspired to her hand and her inheritance. Philip the Good loudly protested first to Henry V and then to Bedford, accusing them of perfidy in giving asylum to the guilty runaway wife of his Brabançon cousin and protégé and countenancing her liaison with Gloucester. Conscious though they were of the embarrassment which Gloucester's foolish behaviour caused them, neither Henry V nor, still less, Bedford dared to take strong measures against him, for this scatter-brain had friends and had made himself popular by his prodigality. They merely advised him to be prudent, or, in other words, left him alone. Jacqueline, however, was not the kind of woman to wait on events. Since she could not hope that the legitimate Pope, Martin V, would agree to the annulment of her marriage to her cousin of Brabant, she hastened to seek it from the former pontiff Benedict XIII, that solitary but obstinate old man, who from the heights of Peñiscola, where he had found refuge, kept on launching anathemas against the rest of the world which had ceased to recognize him. Having obtained a bull from him, she married Gloucester in February 1423. Then, after making her husband heir to all her possessions, she urged him to go to the continent and conquer them.

Despite Bedford, Gloucester managed with some difficulty to recruit a few thousand men. He landed with them at Calais in October 1424, crossed Artois and proceeded to occupy Hainault in Jacqueline's name. Philip, feeling that he had been fooled, prepared for a stern revenge. At this point John of Bavaria conveniently died, leaving his custody of the counties of Holland and Zeeland to the Duke of Burgundy, and in March 1425 a Burgundian army, reinforced by Brabançon contingents and even – an unprecedented event – by a few companies of the Dauphin's forces, advanced into Hainault. Gloucester, on the point of being taken prisoner, fled to England, leaving his wife in the enemy's hands. But Philip had not yet heard the last of the fiery Jacqueline. She escaped from imprisonment in Ghent, rekindled the faction fight in Holland and forced the Duke of Burgundy to undertake several punitive campaigns before admitting defeat. At least, however, after his hasty flight, Gloucester had disappeared from the Netherlands stage. Repudiated by his imperious spouse, henceforth he devoted his restless activity to English affairs. He accused his uncle Henry Beaufort in so many words of usurping the regency and aspiring to the throne, and forced Bedford to return to England to settle the quarrel.

At every turn in this affair so rich in comic situations Anglo-Burgundian relations suffered a coolness which only the regent's skill prevented from developing into an open breach. In 1423, to ward off any unhappy results of Gloucester's marriage, Bedford asked for Anne of Burgundy's hand and allowed his Burgundian and Breton allies to contemplate seriously opening negotiations with the Dauphin. In 1424, to wipe out the bad impression created by Gloucester's landing, once more Bedford, anxious to stop his brother-in-law's resentment going too far, presented him with the counties of Mâcon and Auxerre, taking them from the royal domain of France. Finally in 1427 he averted a fresh *rapprochement* between Philip of Burgundy and Charles VII by solemnly undertaking to give no further help, direct or indirect, to Jacqueline of Bavaria. But agreement between Bedford and Burgundy, only just restored every time, remained unstable. Indeed, at the end of 1424 rumour had it that Bedford's English entourage planned to assassinate Philip the Good.

Thus the Duke of Burgundy gradually broke off his alliance with the Lancastrians. At the same time Charles VII, on his side, shaking off the tutelage of the surviving Armagnacs, sought a reconciliation with Burgundy. Or rather – for it would be paying the King of Bourges too high a compliment to credit him with a policy of his own at this period – Yolanda of Aragon managed to impose upon him an essentially Angevin plan for coming to terms with the Burgundian enemy. The ups and downs of the war explain alike the anxiety and the purpose of the Queen of Sicily. In 1423 Charles, with varying fortunes, directed the effort of his forces against the Burgundian domains. On July 30th, outside Cravant in Morvan, the Anglo-Burgundian allies halted an army of his which was seeking to advance into Champagne; but Charles's guerrillas, led by Imbert of Grôlée, took their revenge after a fashion in Mâconnais. At the end of the year the Duke of Burgundy managed with difficulty to stabilize his front along the line of the Loire and La Charité was taken by Perrinet Gressart.

Against the English the moves of the King of Bourges were on the whole even less successful. At the beginning of 1424, however, his government appealed to the people for a great effort to recruit and pay Scottish mercenaries commanded by Constable Buchan and others sent from Lombardy by Felippo Maria Visconti. At Verneuil, on August 17th, this considerable army met smaller forces under Salisbury. As at Poitiers and Agincourt, the numerically inferior enemy entrenched behind lines of stakes, brought their archers into play, and wrought havoc among the French knights, whose charges were broken before they reached their objective. Thus rid of the sole good army which Charles VII possessed, Bedford could now resume his plans of conquest, which were the same as ever: the clearance of Ile-de-France and Champagne, in which guerrilla bands had reappeared, and the seizure by Salisbury and Fastolf of Perche and Maine, with Angers, which the regent contemplated making an appanage for himself, as the final objective. By carrying the war into this outlying territory the Lancastrians invited the hostility of the Angevins, and above all that of Yolanda of Aragon.

The policy of this strong-minded princess aimed at saving Maine and Anjou. Though her object was simple, her plans had remarkable scope. She proposed to win Brittany over to the Valois cause, in order to buttress the seriously threatened Angevin domains to the west, and to arrange, if not a reconciliation, at least an armistice with the Burgundian State, so that the whole strength of the kingdom of Bourges might withstand the

English. The symbol and instrument of her policy was a man whom she proposed to place beside her son-in-law. He was Arthur of Richmond, brother of the Duke of Brittany and brother-in-law of Burgundy. After gallant conduct on the field of Agincourt, Richmond had served Henry V's cause; but Bedford, by relegating him to obscure tasks, had turned him into an enemy. He asked nothing better than to play the part of arbiter which the Queen of Sicily designed for him.

Her plan, launched on the ebb and flow of a stormy diplomatic sea, took years to achieve, and during them there was no stopping either the conquest of Maine or the enemy's establishment on the borders of Vendômois and Orleanais. But the two French sides did not wait long before seeking fruitful contact in negotiation. As early as January 1423, thirty months after the Treaty of Troyes, the Duke of Savoy, Amadeus VIII, succeeded in bringing together under his aegis counsellors of Philip the Good and courtiers of Charles VII. As yet the sole result was to set on record the arrogance of the Burgundians, through their spokesman Nicholas Rolin, who laid down exorbitant conditions for the 'pardon' which their master might grant to the King of France as the murderer at Montereau. But a start had been made. In May 1424, at Nantes, Brittany, Savoy, and Sicily agreed upon the terms of a possible reconciliation. In September, at Chambéry, the Duke of Savoy arranged a truce which, repeatedly prolonged, was to last no less than five years. For the first time, in the diplomatic instrument approving this truce, Philip the Good gave Charles VII the title of King of France. In November, at Mâcon, the Duke of Burgundy met, in addition to his brother-in-law Richmond, a royal delegation led by Charles of Bourbon, eldest son of Duke John I, who, after taking the Burgundian side, had gone over to the Dauphin after Montereau and was now on the point of marrying another sister of Philip.

All these contacts were bound to lead at least to a change of political personnel at the court of Bourges. In fact, Savoy and Brittany agreed to exercise a discreet tutelage over the young Charles VII, deprived by death or captivity of the presence of his nearest relatives. In March Richmond became Constable and took up his duties in Bourges, where he was welcomed by Queen Yolanda and the chancellor Martin Gouge, Bishop of Clermont. In a final attempt at rebellion, the uncompromising anti-Burgundians, the last Armagnac survivors since Montereau, carried off the young king to Poitiers and started a kind of civil war against the Breton Constable. Queen Yolanda joined her son-in-law. In July 1425 the obdurate Armagnacs, including Louvet and Tanguy du Châtel, were one by one deprived of power.

But the Franco-Burgundian understanding, thus so strongly foreshadowed in 1425, brought only disappointment to its promoters, just as Bedford had mostly experienced rebuffs from the Anglo-Burgundian alliance. This was because Philip the Good's policy urged him to play a game of see-saw. He never conceded anything definite to either adversary, but held his hand until he should finally find himself master and tutor of a monarchy once more united. For the time being the 'great duke of the West' was concerned only to subdue the rebel Hollanders by force of arms. To ally himself with Charles VII would mean forcing Bedford to support venturesome Gloucester; but he also wanted the regent to remain anxious about his borders with Maine – hence Philip's maintenance of his truce with the King of Bourges. It was a subtle diplomacy which did not suit those with whom he dealt. Through the downfall of the last Armagnacs Richmond had redeemed his devotion to the Burgundian cause; but he could not present Charles VII with the promised reward. The Constable's star waned rapidly. Bedford, back from England at the beginning of 1427, took advantage of the uncertain situation to win back by force of arms what he had lost through diplomacy. His troops threatened Anjou and the whole course of the middle Loire. At the same time John of Brittany, tired of staying too long in the same camp, reverted to alliance with the English, now that Salisbury's forces threatened the frontiers of his duchy.

Meanwhile at Bourges his brother was tottering. A fresh favourite, for whose rise he himself had paved the way, was making ready to dislodge him from power. This was George de La Tremoïlle, an unscrupulous schemer, who had been in turn a protégé of John the Fearless and Louis of Guienne, taken prisoner at Agincourt, freed through Burgundy, deprived by his protector of the county of Boulogne to which he could lay claim in his wife's name, and finally welcomed at the court of Bourges, where he sought to get rid of rivals by intrigue and murder. Entrusted with the office of grand chamberlain, he wielded absolute mastery over Charles VII, which was to last six years and to end only with his own dismissal by armed force.

At the end of 1427 Richmond was dismissed and had to flee to Brittany. An interlude of four years closed with this fresh palace revolution. In the year 1428 Charles VII was weaker than ever against the Lancastrians, who, having finally occupied the region between the Seine and the Loire, decided to strike a great blow. From the military point of view, they must hit Charles VII in the heart of his kingdom, Berry, which he was always reluctant to leave. So, in the first place, they must force a passage of the Loire. Amid all the points which presented themselves to him, Bedford chose the one whose fall would have the most resounding effect: Orleans, the strategic key to central France. Its importance was such that it quelled his qualms of conscience and made him break the rules of the code of chivalry. Orleans did not belong to the King of Bourges, but to his cousin Charles of Orleans. It was without precedent that a gallant knight should attack the territory of an enemy whose person he already held prisoner. But Bedford made no bones about it.

The summer of 1428 was spent in concentrating troops, material, and supplies and awaiting reinforcements from England. It was not until October 12th that the forces, under Salisbury's command, massed beneath the walls of the town. They were resolved to spend the winter there, despite the fact that Salisbury was killed by an arrow early in the siege. Around the town, especially to the west and north, but also to the south, opposite the sole bridge, they built a system of forts whose arc observed the ramparts, cut the roads and impeded supplies. The King of Bourges had managed to rush some troops into the town. Dunois, representing his absent brother, took charge of the defence. The town was strong and fairly well provisioned. But its fall was inevitable unless Charles VII could raise an army capable of breaking the vice of the besiegers. The somewhat modest effort of his troops failed pitifully. They set off to intercept a convoy of supplies for the besiegers coming from Paris, but received a bitter lesson from the escort, less numerous though it was, which protected the barrels of salt fish. This was known as the 'day of the herrings' (February 12th 1429).

Everywhere in the Valois camp dismay prevailed. It did so at the court of Charles VII, who, threatened for the first time in his beloved Berry, contemplated withdrawing to Dauphiné, or, if that was not safe, to Castille or even to Scotland. It prevailed in Orleans, where the burgesses, with surrender in prospect, begged Philip the Good to take their interests in hand. Burgundy was uneasy about the unaccustomed boldness displayed by Bedford; but all he could do was recall the contingents he had originally sent to take part in the siege. On all sides it was vaguely felt that the fall of Orleans, expected at any moment, would mark the end of France's tragedy and that victory would finally pass into the camp of the Lancastrians.

It was at this point that Joan of Arc appeared.

Part VIII

THE FRENCH RECOVERY

1429-1444

Part VIII

THE FRENCH RECOVERY
(1429–1444)

In the Anglo-French duel, during which one disaster after another had fallen on the frail shoulders of the weakened Valois since 1415, the year 1429 marked the awakening of national feeling in France, the reversal of fortune and the turning-point of the war. Henceforth there was no future for the Lancastrian dream, for that 'dual monarchy' which had nearly taken root in both England and France. Such, at least, is the verdict of posterity, in the light of perspective and the knowledge of subsequent events. But Joan of Arc's glorious adventure was far from giving all her contemporaries the impression that something definite and irrevocable had happened. The French recovery for which she served as the signal did not assume, after its first success, the surging, sweeping strength of a storm. The war still dragged on for more than twenty years, during which the Lancastrians and their supporters were entitled to cherish the illusion that they could easily retrieve a passing reverse. The exhaustion of a France bled white, the indolent slackness of her king, the blind selfishness of his favourites, all that human weakness which, in the course of history, makes the achievement of the finest plans uncertain and incomplete contributed towards prolonging the struggle. So the sacrifice of the Maid, though it heralded decisive victory, did so only remotely. Did she exercise that essential influence on the course of events which is always attributed to her? It is permissible to doubt it.

At the risk of seeming sacrilegious, the historian is bound to place her wonderful adventure back in its human context. He is bound to dispel certain illusions, which doubtless spring from the very way in which the heroine's deeds have been preserved in the memory of mankind. Few personalities of the period appear so well known to us. This is because we have the inestimable good fortune to possess the valuable testimony of her two trials: the one by which the inquisitorial judges, on Bedford's orders, led her to the stake, and the other, much later – too late, perhaps – which Charles VII had carried out in 1456 in order to rehabilitate Joan, to whom he owed the fact that he was King of France. The examinations of the first reveal to us Joan's very soul, her tranquil faith, her peasant common sense, her religious devotion to the legitimate monarchy, her absolute confidence in the justice of her cause. They convey to us a little of that fervour which she managed to instil into her comrades in arms, but which scarcely went beyond the limited circle of those who had the privilege of approaching her or living with her. The second trial is less conclusive, because it tried to prove too much. Its testimony relates memories already distant and, so to speak, hazy with legend. It comes from these same comrades of hers, legitimately and sincerely anxious to clear her memory of an infamous condemnation, and at the same time to rehabilitate a king now victorious. If these legal records were lost to us, how much should we know about Joan? The French accounts which have been preserved, notably the official chronicle by Jean Chartier, and the *Chronicle of the Maid*, which there is every reason to believe was the work of Archbishop Jouvenel, doubtless drew upon contemporary narratives of events, now lost, which were compiled without much regard for exactitude by some of her comrades in arms. They are of relatively late date and form, as it were, a prologue to the rehabilitation trial. They do not take us outside the circle of eye-witnesses, whom Joan's strong personality inspired with extreme devotion.

But beyond this group, beyond the region of the Loire where she was known and beloved, the echoes die away with surprising speed. In the part of France under Charles VII a silence scarcely disturbed by a few references brooded over her epic. Here, of course, the raising of the siege of Orleans and the king's coronation at Rheims were known and celebrated as was fitting. Letters from the king to the towns extolled the part played by the Maid, whose quasi-miraculous intervention gave added weight to these, so to speak, official bulletins. But the rest of her career, her failures, her captivity, her martyrdom, created, alike in the provinces long since loyal to the King of Bourges and those that rallied to the King of Rheims, a barely perceptible eddy, and any written traces of it that have been preserved for us are few. Everything happened as though Charles's subjects, following their sovereign's example, abandoned Joan of Arc on the morrow of his coronation. Among the enemy there was, on the whole, a similar apathy. True, the Burgundian chroniclers, by the venomous violence of their attacks, by the calumnies which they circulated to sully Joan's memory, proved that in government circles the Maid's early successes created such dismay that only the stake at Rouen could efface its memory. But public opinion in general was much less concerned. We may take as a witness the Paris burgess who, relating the unsuccessful assault on the city, recalled that the attackers were led by a woman, whom some people described as sent from heaven and others as a witch. 'What she was,' he added prudently, 'God alone knows,' Once the Maid was dead, tranquillity was restored.

What seems still more strange was the almost complete ignorance in which the Lancastrians' subjects were left about her adventure. They too, of course, learned, but very vaguely, about the events at Orleans and Rheims. But if Joan's feats of arms had created in the ranks of the English soldiers such dismay as legend would have been quick to exaggerate, fugitives and deserters would have communicated it to their fellow-countrymen. Moreover, if Bedford had staged the trial at Rouen in order to bolster up his tottering rule, he would not have failed to circulate its result widely in England. But nothing like this is to be found in the English chronicles, whose aridity, brevity, and inexactitude prove that there was little or no interest in England in the adventure which posterity turned into a wonderful epic.

Joan of Arc's example, therefore, did not stir the masses. It did not evoke a national outburst which, if it had spread to the whole people, would have enabled the guerrilla war, still active, to be transformed into a crusade of liberation. All that the heroine left behind her were actions. But they were actions whose imprint no condemnation could efface. There was the military fact that for the first time the Lancastrian arms were halted on the road to victory. There was the political fact that the King of Bourges was given the prestige of coronation. In this way Joan of Arc's intervention was decisive, and the page she wrote, contrary to all expectation, in the history of France deserves to be remembered as one of the finest. If her message went unheeded, she whom the French have become accustomed to call 'the saint of the Fatherland' nevertheless saved her king, in whom France was incarnate.

1. JOAN OF ARC

THE VILLAGE of Domremy, where Joan of Arc was born, belonged partly to Champagne and partly to Barrois. Her family was wholly of Champagne peasant descent. They were well-to-do farmers or village craftsmen, and one of her uncles was a priest. Like all peasants, and many others at this period, the child was illiterate. Though she was brought up in a very religious environment, all she knew about religion was a few prayers and lovely legends full of marvels. From her adolescence she had visions, heard voices, and talked to angels and saints. Though the English had never penetrated there, this remote frontier region had been hard hit by the kingdom's misfortunes. Its people recalled, like a bygone golden age, the happy days before the civil war, when Louis of Orleans held a protectorate over the nearby territories, in Toul, Luxemburg, and Barrois. The region had been Orleanist, then Armagnac, then under the Dauphin. It was administered by a forceful, heavy-handed captain, Robert of Baudricourt, who had been bailiff of Chaumont for the Dauphin, but retained only the castle of Vaucouleurs. Since 1419 war had raged between Charles's guerrillas and Burgundian *routiers*, both of whom sacked the countryside.

In 1428 Anthony of Vergy, the Burgundian governor of Champagne, led a punitive raid into the castellany of Vaucouleurs and drove the defenceless peasantry to flight. Joan's family found refuge for a time in Neufchâteau. Joan was now between sixteen and twenty years of age. More than ever her voices spoke to her about Charles VII, the kingdom which God intended for him, the English and Burgundian enemies who must be driven out of it. When news of the siege of Orleans became known, she took her decision. What must strike us as surprising was not the obstacles she had to overcome, but the ease with which those whom she approached let themselves be convinced by her. The war had exacerbated men's emotions. They relied only on some miracle to rid them of the nightmare. Prophets and seers swarmed, even in Charles's entourage. No one wondered at this country girl who declared that through her Orleans would be relieved and Charles crowned as king. Some people were shocked by the fact that she cut her hair like a boy and rode clad as a man. This struck them as scandalous and blasphemous; but it did not affect belief in the supra-human nature of her powers. In our sceptical days people would be inclined to regard Joan as mad, mentally deficient, visionary, or even bogus. Her contemporaries simply wondered whether she was sent by God or the devil. Very soon waverers let themselves incline towards the first alternative.

Two journeys by Joan to Vaucouleurs sufficed to move Robert of Baudricourt. He announced her impending arrival to Charles VII and gave her a small escort, horses and arms. She set off on February 23rd 1429 and crossed Champagne, Auxerre, Gien, the north of Berry, and Touraine with little difficulty, though all these regions were infested by brigands. She reached Chinon on March 6th and was received by Charles two days later. She managed to convey her faith to him and gave him a 'sign' of her divine mission. Was this 'sign', as has often been supposed, some satisfaction of his doubts about the legitimacy of his birth or some assurance of final victory? It is difficult to penetrate this 'secret', which a certain biographer's imagination has quite recently reduced to the level of a novelette. Though he was readily convinced, the king, with a prudence for which one cannot reproach him, insisted on seeking the advice of his clergy. Joan was taken to Poitiers, where bishops, theologians, and clerks of the *Parlement* were entrusted with the duty of attesting her orthodoxy. As she extolled their master's power and promised them early victory and consequently a return to prosperity, these Armagnac churchmen found no fault in her replies. After detaining her for a few weeks and asking her a number of not very difficult questions, they finally let her go when she had proved her virginity. Though they could not affirm that she was supernatural, they advised the king to let her have her way, since all she wanted was the welfare of the royalist cause.

Joan had made up her mind to go and relieve Orleans. Everything helped to favour her plan. After a siege of six months, the enemy's situation at the end of the winter had deteriorated. They numbered less than four thousand, and were unable to effect a close blockade or even to man adequately the forts they had built. Supply difficulties had led to sickness and desertion. It would have been easy to defeat them if panic inside the town had not created general suspicion of spying and treachery. For his part, Charles VII raised some troops and mustered a large convoy of supplies and stores for the besieged city. Joan had easily won over a young prince of the blood, the 'gentle' Duke of Alençon, lately set free by the English, and Charles let her accompany the expedition. On April 29th she entered Orleans. She knew nothing about the art of war, and thought that abstaining from oaths and brothels was enough to earn victory for the soldiers. But at that time the art of war did not amount to much. Courage, confidence, and boldness readily made up for it. For that matter, despite her ascendancy over the troops, Joan did not lead them. She left that duty to the captains, such as Dunois, Alençon, and Richmond. Though their decisions were often contrary to her wishes, she finally gave in to them. She was content to exhort the combatants, say what advice her voices gave, step into the breach at critical moments and rally the infantry. She was accompanied by a handful of priests and monks, to whom she dictated letters, several of which have come down to us. In them she summoned Bedford and the English captains to withdraw from the kingdom of France and restore it 'to the King of Heaven', invited the Duke of Burgundy to recognize Charles as his legitimate suzerain, and congratulated the people of Tournai, a royal enclave in Burgundian territory, on their loyalty to the sovereign of Bourges.

Combined action by the reinforcements and the communal militia in Orleans enabled successful sorties to be undertaken. The capture and burning, one after the other, of two English forts, to the east and south of the town, led the besiegers, numerically inferior and demoralized by these dashing tactics, to beat a retreat. On May 8th, ten days after Joan's arrival, the siege was raised. The moral effect was immense. It was now easy to overcome the small enemy garrisons which remained on the banks of the Loire, at Jargeau, where Suffolk was taken prisoner, Meung and Beaugency. On June 18th the rearguard of a reinforcing army was surprised and harried after a short pursuit. This led to a rout at Patay, where Talbot was taken prisoner and Fastolf was put to flight. Joan did not reach the scene until the engagement was over. As a chivalrous prince, Charles gave her all the credit for the victory. In fact, it belonged to Richmond; but the Constable, still out of favour at court, had to withdraw again to his Breton estates.

After this, the French might either have marched on Paris, where panic prevailed, or advanced into Normandy to join the guerrillas who were still active there. Bedford feared one attack or the other. Charles's advisers, rendered prudent and timid by years of uninterrupted reverses, did not feel strong enough. But above all Joan, probably with the support of the chancellor Regnault of Chartres, Archbishop of Rheims, insisted on a plan no less bold: the coronation of the king in the capital of Champagne. By dint of a supreme effort, twelve or thirteen thousand men were concentrated at Gien. The march to Rheims, though apparently hazardous, proved to be a mere military promenade. Feeling that the wind was veering and with no desire to fight, the people of the towns on the way, where Charles had created contacts, asked nothing better than to open their gates. Skilful negotiation obtained the neutrality of Auxerre on July 1st, and then surrender of Troyes on the 10th, Châlons on the 14th, and finally Rheims on the 16th.

Charles's coronation took place on the 18th. By force of circumstances it was a ceremony without pomp. None of the temporal peers was present and only three of the spiritual peers, and the crown, sceptre, and orb were at Saint-Denis. But the holy unction was the essential thing. Now Charles, whom Joan had hitherto persisted in calling only the Dauphin, was King of France, a new Melchisedec sanctified by the sacrament which bestowed upon him the power of a thaumaturge. Henceforth no believer could doubt who was the legitimate sovereign, since there was now a king crowned in circumstances so incredible that they seemed miraculous, opposed overseas by a boy of seven who called himself King of France, but whom his subjects had never seen. So the coronation annulled the deposition illegally pronounced by the Treaty of Troyes and restored to the Valois the legitimacy which had been questioned for the past nine years. It would be unfair to go on calling his supporters Armagnacs, when his coronation had raised them to the dignity of faithful subjects. How, moreover, could the Burgundians, contemptuously known at Bourges as the 'English-French', continue their obedience to Bedford without obvious treason? Such was the result, pregnant with consequences, of the coronation at Rheims.

Once the start had been made, it seemed as though nothing could now stop Charles's progress. The English had only weak garrisons to oppose the coronation campaign. Bedford and his council did not know which way to turn. They begged for aid from England and received just enough to strengthen the occupation of Normandy, which at least they must save from the wreck. Above all, they feared the defection of Paris. With the object of flattering the Parisians' Burgundian sympathies, on August 29th they entrusted the government of the capital to Philip the Good; but he had no desire to direct its defence in person, since at this very moment he had negotiated with Charles a truce for some months valid for all the territory north of the Seine. In these conditions Charles's moves, though hesitant and undecided, looked like a series of striking victories. On the morrow of this coronation he received the submission of Laon and entered Soissons. Then, by way of Château-Thierry, he advanced into Brie, where he obtained fresh capitulations everywhere, though he intended to withdraw soon to Berry. A small English force barred his way. He returned with his whole army to Valois, where Senlis surrendered, and captured Compiègne, whose defence he entrusted to William of Flavy. Then he marched on Paris and took up his quarters for some days at Saint-Denis. Siege material was lacking; but Joan, still confident in her star, believed that the capital, whose pro-Burgundian burgesses refused to surrender, could be entered by escalade. The assault was made on September 8th from the west, near the Porte Saint-Honoré. It failed. Joan, though wounded, wanted to try again; but the captains and the king thought otherwise. They led the army back south of the Loire. It had been in the field nearly three months, a long time for the period. The army was disbanded.

Despite the failure of the attack on Paris, the military results of the campaign were no less important than its political success. Champagne, Brie, Soissonnais, Valois, and even the neighbourhood of Paris had readily submitted to the hitherto hated Armagnacs. Picardy would have asked no better than to follow their example, if the royal army had entered its territory. But it had gone, leaving behind it weak garrisons and, as the king's lieutenant, Archbishop Regnault of Chartres, who made Soissons his headquarters. Nothing was done to provide against a counteroffensive in strength by the English, though this was unlikely for the time being, or against a Burgundian attack, which was certain when the truce expired. In the king's entourage there were wrangles over the Maid, whose reputation still stood high. Instead of letting her accompany Alençon, who carried on the war in Ile-de-France, La Trémoïlle, who was jealous of the 'gentle duke' and anti-Burgundian in order to maintain his post, sent her to take part in the attack on La Charité, still defended by Perrinet Gressart. But it was not now a matter of dealing with demoralized garrisons, as after Orleans, or with peace-loving and contemptible burgesses, as in Champagne. The siege of La Charité, led by Louis of Bourbon, Count of Vendôme, and Charles d'Albret, son of the former Constable, was undertaken in the depth of winter and came to nothing. Before Christmas it had to be abandoned.

Exhausted by the effort demanded for the coronation army, the royal treasury could not finance a fresh campaign in 1430. As so often in the past, Charles's government counted on loyal garrisons and a few bands of mercenaries, who were badly paid but lived on the country. It was to their captains that Joan was allowed to lend her help. From March onwards she took part in their surprise attacks at Melun, Lagny, and Senlis successively. Her presence was not enough to secure success. She was unable to stop Soissons surrendering to the enemy. Bedford, on his side, scarcely had any more troops at his disposal. His star was waning. In March a conspiracy with Charles, in which over five hundred people were involved, was disclosed in Paris. So, more than ever, the regent needed the Duke of Burgundy, who as usual greedily gathered the fruits of his duplicity. On March 8th Philip induced the Lancastrian to add Champagne and Brie to his appanage, though he had to reconquer them for himself.

So, when the truce expired in April, the main effort was made by the Burgundians. As the King of France had failed to hand over the fortress of Compiègne to his cousin of Burgundy, as the truce provided, Philip ordered his captain John of Luxemburg, brother of the Bishop of Thérouanne, to seize it by force. On May 13th Joan, with some reinforcements, was rushed into the town. The besiegers, who had not yet begun their blockade, had established their forces in several groups on the west bank of the Oise. Ten days later, a sortie, in which the Maid took part, was organized to surprise one of these groups. The French lingered to pillage, thus giving the enemy time to rally, and were then put to flight and hotly pursued. Lest the Anglo-Burgundians should enter the town on the heels of his own forces, William of Flavy had to reclose the gates before all his men were inside. Joan had not understood the reason for the retreat and had remained in the rear. She was captured by a Burgundian knight and handed over to John of Luxemburg.

The news very quickly reached Charles VII's court. In the region of the Loire it evoked amazement and consternation. As usual in such cases, the cry of treachery was raised against the king's counsellors. But, despite their petty quarrels, Joan was so useful to them that they would never have dreamed of betraying her. There were moving public and religious demonstrations on her behalf, but they were naturally fruitless. On the other hand, in Anglo-Burgundian circles, in Paris, where the University since Caboche had retained its influence, and in Rouen, whence as a measure of precaution Bedford and his council now controlled the government of the kingdom, there were outbursts of delight and calls for revenge. The masters of the University wrote to the Duke of Burgundy and demanded that Joan should be surrendered to the Inquisition, which was entitled to burn heretics. Pierre Cauchon, as Bishop of Beauvais, claimed her for his ecclesiastical court, since she had been captured within his diocese. This claim would probably have left her captor unmoved but for the fact that at the same time Cauchon, as counsellor to the King of England, proposed to buy her for ten thousand *livres*, charged on the subsidies voted by the Estates of Normandy. John of Luxemburg was not rich. He agreed to the bargain about the middle of November, just when royalist reinforcements had compelled him to raise the siege of Compiègne. Joan, who after stays in several castles had been placed for safety in Arras, was taken by way of Drugy, Le Crotoy, Saint-Valery and the region of Caux to the old castle in the Norman capital. The English regarded the ecclesiastical prison as insecure and preferred to keep her themselves.

Once the Maid's capture seemed to have stopped the series of disasters, Bedford's policy assumed a more definite purpose. First of all he must annul the moral effect of Charles's coronation. Henry VI was the legitimate King of France, but he was uncrowned. With all speed he must be made known to his continental subjects. At the beginning of June 1430 the boy king, accompanied by his English counsellors and tutors, took up residence in Rouen. Officially Bedford's regency came to an end, the king assumed the government and the ducal council was transformed into a royal council. Then it was decided to crown Henry. But Rheims remained out of reach and its archbishop sided with the Valois. So it was in Paris that the ceremony took place, on December 17th 1431, contrary to venerable custom, in the cathedral of a mere bishop, and not in the ecclesiastical metropolis of Champagne hallowed by the memory of Saint Rémy. This sufficed to render an unction which did not come from the holy ampulla invalid in the eyes of the pious masses. When Henry VI returned to England, after spending twenty months in France, he had not gained one more partisan or stirred enthusiasm among his own supporters.

Better results were expected from Joan's trial. If it could be proved that she was a woman of loose morals, a witch and an envoy of the devil, at the same time ridicule would be brought upon the overcredulous Charles, who had rashly entrusted his cause to her and made the most of her exploits at Orleans, Patay, and Rheims. His fleeting successes would be put down to an odious liaison between a criminal bastard and a shameless sorceress. That would deal Charles's cause a blow from which it might well be hoped it would never recover. To this end it was essential that the court, if its judgment was to be respected, should seem to be impartial. Fortunately matters of faith fell within the jurisdiction of the ecclesiastical court, in which the local bishop and the Dominican inquisitor sat side by side. Though he had been driven from his diocese by the advance of the Armagnacs, Cauchon was available to conduct the trial. As he deemed the case important and worthy of solemnity, he surrounded himself with a swarm of assessors, councillors, advocates, and investigators. He chose them among the canons of Rouen, the abbots of the great Norman monasteries and the most distinguished theologians and canonists of the University of Paris. All of them were devoted to Bedford and the Lancastrian cause.

Although the whole trial strikes us as a tissue of vile calumnies and odious nonsense, we should not suppose that all these judges had sold their consciences or cravenly let themselves be influenced by the holders of power. Most of them, reared in pro-English or Burgundian feeling, sincerely believed that Joan, since she had sided with their enemies, must necessarily hold her powers from the devil. There was no need for Bedford to exert pressure on the judges. They went more than halfway to meet him. Their whole past, especially that of Cauchon, who was rewarded on the morrow of the trial by his translation to the bishopric of Lisieux, answered for their servility and their blindness. These men felt only horror and hatred of the accused. Everything about her infuriated and scandalized them, even the dignified simplicity of her life, the vivacious readiness of her replies, the obvious modesty of her bearing.

The cruelty of the procedure shocks our consciences as modern men. But it was simply that of the Inquisition, which was daily applied, without offending anyone, to any number of poor wretches, whom public malignity, the stupid self-sufficiency of their accusers, and the suspicious fanaticism of their judges led to the stake in various places. This procedure involved absolute secrecy of investigation and testimony, about which the accused was left in ignorance; the absence of any advocate to defend him, his constantly repeated examination by fresh relays of interrogators; torture, threats, and false promises to obtain an admission of guilt or the signature of a confession. Nowadays any revival of such procedure is regarded as a relapse into barbarism, and any political police which covertly indulges in it is promptly branded by public opinion. But neither the judges nor the public of the period had any such scruples. They did not realize that by such methods one could get anyone to admit anything. In their arrogance as scholars accustomed to splitting the finest of hairs, the judges were obsessed by the idea that heresy hid itself everywhere behind the appearance of innocence. They would have consigned all the faithful to the flames, and no one could find favour in their eyes. There was no vice of form or substance in the trial itself; but, once it had begun, it could end only in a conviction. The means employed and the charges alleged mattered little.

At the court of the Valois Joan had admirers and supporters. They did nothing to save her, and they have been harshly blamed for their inaction. True, they could not contemplate either rescuing her by force or negotiating her ransom. But legal means were not lacking for stopping her trial at Rouen or suspending the enforcement of its sentence. Regnault of Chartres could have claimed jurisdiction, since his suffragan Cauchon had irregularly started the procedure in a neighbouring ecclesiastical province. An appeal to the Pope and the council would have been in order, and Cauchon, a respecter of formality, could not have challenged it. But nothing of the kind took place. Charles abandoned the Maid. She had been useful to him; but perhaps he thought he could replace her by any one of the seers with whom his court swarmed.

Her trial began on February 21st 1431 with four weeks of preliminary interrogation either before a bench of assessors or by an informal party of them in the prison. From the high-minded replies of the accused, who was in turn exalted, firm, vivacious, prudent, even wily, it was easy to derive every kind of heretical proposition. The judges and their assessors excelled at this subtle game. The trial proper opened on March 27th, and then dragged on in accordance with the rules. At the last moment, the court shrank from applying torture in order to obtain more complete and conclusive confessions. Twelve propositions were sent to the University of Paris, where the faculties of canon law and theology were unanimous in finding them tainted with heresy. But a church court could hand over to the secular arm only obdurate heretics. To spare Joan the supreme penalty, her judges therefore exerted themselves to obtain an abjuration of her errors. On May 21st, frightened by the prospect of the stake and weakened by long imprisonment, Joan flinched for a moment. Without quite realizing what she was doing, half crying, half laughing, she signed what was asked of her. As a result, she was let off with life imprisonment, by way not of punishment but penance.

Bedford's entourage were displeased, and informed the judges in so many words. The incident, for that matter, was of no consequence. Joan soon recovered herself. As a preliminary cause of scandal, she resumed male clothing. She felt that her abjuration had been a weakness, and proclaimed the fact. Interrogated again on May 28th, she was declared relapsed and liable to the death penalty. She was handed over to the English authorities, and on the 30th, in the old market-square, she was publicly burned.

2. THE FRANCO-BURGUNDIAN RECONCILIATION

WHILE Joan was slowly approaching her martyrdom, France went on living, and, above all, suffering from the successive blows of the war. Fighting continued on the Norman frontier, and the Ile-de-France, Champagne and Nivernais. Neither side put large forces into the field. Bedford received reinforcements from England only on the smallest scale. Philip the Good, with an eye to the future, did not intend to commit himself deeply. In these conditions, Charles VII might have lost no time in exploiting his successes in 1429–30. A few attacks should have sufficed to sweep away the enemy. He has been blamed for not making the attempt. His now inveterate apathy and his counsellors' intrigues are not an adequate explanation. We must remember, once again, the utter exhaustion of the provinces loyal to him. The Valois kingdom was not merely out of breath; it was at the end of its strength. Its government shrank from the apparently insuperable task of raising and maintaining an army of a few thousand men. All it aspired to do was to hold the conquests achieved by the coronation campaign.

On the whole, the royalist leaders managed to do so. In Champagne Troyes stood fast. Possession of Lagny assured control of the lower Marne and that of Compiègne control of the middle Oise: both supply routes for the capital. From these strongly held fortresses Barbazan, La Hire, Ambroise de Loré, Dunois, and the Castilian Rodrigo de Villandrando scoured the nearby countryside and thrust their raids as far as the walls of Paris. This meant a hard trial for the civilian population, the innocent victims of the devastation and pillaging of their greedy troops, whose unhappy exploits put the memory of the 'free companies' of the past century in the shade. Soon the people's macabre humour gave the nickname of 'Skinners' (*Écorcheurs*) to these men-at-arms, who pillaged districts already fleeced over and over again, and robbed the unlucky wretches of their last shirts and sometimes even of their skins. For that matter, from north to south brigandage was endemic, even far from the battlefields. Captains and adventurers, living in plenty in their lairs, maintained a host of clerks for their correspondence and spies for their expeditions, sacked the countryside and held abbeys and towns to ransom.

Yet, by carrying the war into the provinces still held under Anglo-Burgundian government, Charles VII's soldiers, far from damaging their master's cause, aroused hatred of the foreign occupation, which was held responsible for the whole trouble. Even those who had accepted the surrender at Troyes, because it promised to put an end to disorder, now

turned against its promoters, who had brought about only fresh ruination. After fifteen years of servitude Normandy was not tamed. In 1432
a plot, which the police discovered in time, nearly handed over Rouen
to Charles's supporters. In 1434 the peasants of the Caux region rose
against the English tax-collectors' demands. Other bands besieged Caen.
Each time order was ruthlessly and bloodily restored. In Paris public
opinion was more varied; but the mass of the people had become frankly
hostile to the English occupation. They suffered from the blockade, even
although it was not very strict, imposed by the royalist captains who roved
the countryside. The government had taken refuge in Rouen, and the
burgesses were impoverished by its withdrawal, while the cost of living
increased. In the Regent's council, the civil service and the University
there were still resolute supporters of the government which paid them,
men too deeply involved to gain any advantage from submission to
Charles VII. The visit which the young Henry VI had paid them at the
time of his coronation in 1431 had rekindled their loyalty; but the hopes
it had aroused proved fleeting. They felt that the game was lost. One last
resort remained: heavy reinforcements from across the Channel. They
addressed their laments to London, besought help from their king and
foretold disaster if it did not come in time.

If the capital had not yet surrendered to Charles VII, it was because
it remained deeply devoted to the Duke of Burgundy. There, after 1431,
was the whole problem. Since a military effort had become impossible
through the exhaustion of the treasury, nothing was left for Charles VII
except a reconciliation with Philip the Good. The war, which had been
brought about by the discord between the princes, could be ended only
by a settlement of their old feud. The thing was not simple: it would take
time. But everything influenced Charles VII to accomplish it. Indolent
and unwarlike, he preferred diplomacy to battle. Never since 1418 had he
broken altogether with his too powerful neighbour. Even after Montereau,
even after his coronation, there had been negotiations and short truces
had been concluded.

On Burgundy's side the obstacles to peace were greater. Though
fundamentally a realist, Philip was superficially chivalrous and upright,
and he was too deeply committed to the English alliance to be able to
break it overnight. But he did not propose to be trapped in it. Apart from
his doubtless sincere desire to avenge his father's death, he had signed the
Treaty of Troyes only with the object of playing the part of exacting tutor
to the Lancastrian sovereign, as his father had done to Charles VI. In this
he had failed. His prospect of success now seemed to him to be better if
he allowed the mad king's son to recover his capital. Charles was a weakling. It would be a long time before his resources approached those of the
Burgundian State. He might be made a docile and grateful ward. At the
same time, everything favoured a smooth breach in the friendship between
Philip and the Regent. In the past they had often had quarrels and

misunderstandings, but Anne of Burgundy, Bedford's wife and Philip's sister, had always managed to allay them. She died in November 1432, and there was no one left to reconcile the brothers-in-law as their interests diverged more and more. Philip felt that Paris would escape him if he continued an endless war. He knew, too, that Charles VII was testing the ground across the Channel, especially through Charles of Orleans, who was still a prisoner. If the peace party in England came to a direct agreement with the Valois, it would mean the collapse of the whole Burgundian policy.

But how could Philip disavow fifteen years of alliance with England? How could he free himself from his promises at Troyes? His lawyers managed to quiet his qualms of conscience just at the right moment. Nicholas Rolin, the chancellor of Burgundy, hitherto a strong supporter of Anglo-Burgundian unity, suddenly discovered that Henry VI had no valid claim to the crown of France. By the Treaty of Troyes the succession to Charles had been promised to Henry V, Catherine of France's husband. But, since the son-in-law had died before the father-in-law, he had been unable to inherit the crown, and consequently could not leave his future kingdom to his son. If Philip disavowed the Lancastrian cause, he would not be unfaithful to the spirit of the Treaty of Troyes or false to his undertakings. Nothing was said about the Dauphin's disinheritance, which would have shattered this feeble legal structure.

At the court of Bourges La Trémoïlle's influence hampered the cause of reconciliation. The brutal and grasping chamberlain's one thought was to overthrow Richmond and get rid of the Queen of Sicily, Queen Marie of Anjou and her brother Charles of Maine. In order to be free of them, he launched Villandrando's forces against Anjou and Touraine. But Franco-Burgundian peace could not be made without Richmond, Burgundy's brother-in-law, or without the Anjous, who as princes of the blood were natural mediators. A timely surprise disposed of the obnoxious favourite. La Trémoïlle was lured into an ambush, badly wounded and captured, and his life was spared only on condition that he left the royal court for ever. Yolanda of Sicily resumed all her lost ascendancy over her son-in-law, and the Constable Richmond returned to favour (June 1433).

We know that negotiations between the courts of Bourges and Dijon were opened as early as the end of 1432, and that they assumed a wider scope after La Trémoïlle's downfall; but their details remain obscure. It would be interesting to know the Burgundians' territorial claims at this time and their demands about the Montereau murderers, and the concessions urged upon the indolent Charles VII by the Angevin coterie. In any case, for the moment the negotiations led to nothing. Medieval diplomacy was never in a hurry. It was not until the beginning of 1435 that definite results were achieved. René of Anjou, Duke of Bar by inheritance from his great-uncle, the king's brother-in-law and Burgundy's former prisoner, acted as mediator. Under his auspices, Philip the Good had a series of conversations at Nevers with Regnault of Chartres, Archbishop of Rheims, and Constable Richmond. He was most attentive to his guests, and showed his good will by becoming reconciled to the Bourbons, those faithful supporters of Charles's cause, whose arms had often embarrassed him on the borders of Mâconnais. At the end of three weeks an agreement in principle was reached, and the parties undertook to put it into shape at a great international conference which was also to be held in Burgundian territory, at Arras.

For in no circumstances did Philip the Good want to convey the impression that he was betraying his former allies and playing his own hand. A restoration of peace in the West through his influence would give him more prestige than a mere family reconciliation. If, as he and his entourage calculated, the English were too unreasonable to let peace be made, that would leave him all the more free to abandon them. In this adroit calculation he had the support of the Papacy.

Since the Council of Constance had put an end to the schism by electing Otto Colonna (Martin V), the Holy See, once more Roman and Italian, had paid scant attention to the affairs of the West. A wary opportunist, Martin V had been a powerless spectator of the division of France, recognized the *fait accompli* without approving it, and negotiated simultaneously with Bedford and Charles about church affairs in their respective provinces. In Paris the Regent, despite the Gallican University and the *Parlement*, and in this respect running counter to the anti-Papist English tradition, had preferred to come to terms directly with the pontiff over a friendly division of nomination to clerical dignities and the yield of taxation of church estates. In Bourges, on the contrary, faithful to the Gallican ideas of the Marmosets and the Armagnacs, the Dauphin had been more exacting. Martin did not attempt to support the cause of the Dauphin, but he did not favour that of the Lancastrian either. His successor Eugenius IV, however, had to bow to the conciliar theories which were spreading in the clerical world. In 1431 Sigismund forced him to summon a new council, which Martin had managed to postpone. Again it was held in Empire territory at Basle. Conflict promptly broke out between the demands of the Council and the claims of the Pope. In 1436 it was entering upon its most acute phase. It was obvious that Eugenius would derive from the conclusion of an Anglo-French peace under his aegis an enhanced prestige which would subsequently enable him to bring the Council to heel. He dispatched the cardinal of Sainte-Croix to Artois with the title of legate. Not to be outdone, the Council at Basle sent a delegate of its own, the cardinal of Cyprus. As the leader of the English plenipotentiaries was Henry VI's uncle, the old cardinal Henry Beaufort, it was in a regular setting of the purple that the largest and most pompous diplomatic congress that Europe had ever known was opened. Grandees of the Church, princes of the blood, military leaders, and ministers, all attended by extensive suites, rubbed elbows with deputies from the French towns and a delegation from the University of Paris, which, since the schism and Caboche, felt that it should have a say in all affairs of State.

The real negotiators were for Charles VII, Regnault of Chartres and Richmond, and, for Philip the Good, that bountiful host, his faithful chancellor Nicholas Rolin. Throughout the month of August 1435, amid tourneys and banquets, peace between the English and the French was first discussed. These negotiations, the first for sixteen years, were resumed in an atmosphere remarkably different from that with which Henry V had been familiar in London, Winchester, Pontoise, and Troyes. Bedford was aware of the fact, and was prepared for what he believed to be substantial concessions. But it was impossible for him to abandon the cause to which he had devoted all his energy for the past thirteen years and give up the 'dual monarchy' outlined by the Treaty of Troyes. So he offered to let the Valois keep those provinces where he was unquestionably master; but Henry VI would remain King of France and master of Paris, and, for that half of the kingdom which he was allowed to retain, 'Charles of Valois' would pay homage to his Lancastrian suzerain.

Bedford, who lay dying in his palace in Rouen, could not understand the amazement which was evoked by this ridiculous offer. His proposal to treat the king anointed at Rheims as a mere rebel whom he would be good enough to pardon and endow, while denying him the crown and the capital, when he wore the one and threatened the other, meant that Bedford did not realize that his cause was lost. The Lancastrians might have reverted to Edward III's more realistic ideas, given up their dreams and retained a few provinces. But they did not understand this in time. Regnault of Chartres, supported by the eloquent Jean Jouvenel, first demanded complete evacuation of the kingdom, in return for financial compensation. Then he conveyed to the Lancastrians that they were required, before all else, to renounce the crown of France. No compromise between the two viewpoints was possible, and on September 1st Beaufort and his suite broke off the negotiations and left Arras.

With the papal legate's support, Philip the Good decided to come to terms without the English. A treaty was concluded on September 20th and ratified two days later. It seemed to be wholly to the Burgundians' advantage. Except for Champagne and Brie, Charles endorsed all the territorial concessions with which the Lancastrians had bought the alliance of the 'great duke of the West'. Philip retained Mâconnais, the county of Auxerre and Ponthieu, which had been granted to him by Henry V; the county of Boulogne, which he had occupied ever since Berry's death; and the 'towns of the Somme', Saint-Quentin, Amiens, Corbie, Saint-Riquier, and others constituting the line of fortresses protecting Artois and threatening Paris, which had been given to him as a pledge on his marriage to Michelle of France and which he had kept as compensation for her still unpaid dowry. The king could redeem them for the enormous sum of 400,000 écus.

Finally, a special clause exempted Philip, during Charles VII's life-time, from the homage due for his French fiefs, formerly or freshly acquired. By this clause the duke, whatever may have been said to the contrary, did not desire to make himself independent of the Valois monarchy. As a French prince, all his ambitions centred on Paris. If he broke the link of vassalage, he would doubtless have strengthened the cohesion of the Burgundian State; but he would have had to renounce control of the royal government as a prince of the lilies. If he freed himself from paying homage for a time, it was because he shrank from being the vassal of the man whom he regarded as responsible for his father's death.

The Treaty of Arras, in fact, gave Philip the supreme satisfaction which he had vainly sought in the Treaty of Troyes: revenge for the crime at Montereau. Charles humbled himself before his cousin, denied any personal part in the murder, and promised to punish the guilty parties, who were mentioned by name, to erect an expiatory monument, and to have masses said for the soul of the victim. One of his counsellors, in his name, would make due apology on his knees before the Duke of Burgundy. It was a hard blow to the vanity of the King of France. Before his over-powerful vassal he would cut the figure of a penitent and humble himself to ask pardon for an act for which he had loudly – perhaps too loudly – denied responsibility. It was a still harder blow for the belated partisans of the old Armagnac faction, for whom the knell tolled at Arras. But, by separating himself from those who had been his sole supporters in his youth, Charles VII completed the transformation begun by his coronation at Rheims. From a bitterly challenged party leader he turned into the king of all the French, and thereby the sole King of France. Harsh though it was, his humiliation had its reward.

Bedford died on September 14th, before he had time to realize the full extent of the Burgundian betrayal. A few weeks later, in complete isolation, Queen Isabeau died in the Hôtel Saint-Paul, to which she had finally returned. She disappeared at the same time as the Treaty of Troyes, which had been her achievement.

The fate of the dynasty, in the balance for fifteen years, was now settled. At once all the provinces formerly faithful to Burgundy and all the towns where there were not English garrisons reverted to their allegiance to the Valois. During the winter which followed the congress at Arras, Ile-de-France was virtually cleared of the enemy. The revolt spread to upper Normandy, where royalist forces were able to move about without opposition, and Dieppe surrendered. The capture of Paris, the natural climax of these operations, might have required a lengthy siege, for the garrison had orders to hold out. Richmond, who had opened his campaign in February 1436, completed his blockade of the capital by occupying all the river towns around it. The city faced starvation. Richmond proceeded to get into touch with Burgundian officials, who gave assurances about the feelings of the people. Timely incitement of an insurrection, on April 13th, enabled the royal troops to enter Paris without fighting. The English garrison, which had taken refuge in the Bastille, was allowed to withdraw; but it was amid the hoots of the burgesses who had once hailed it with delight.

The effect throughout the kingdom was enormous. With good reason Charles VII could dispatch ringing proclamations of victory in all directions. His recovery of the capital meant that the unity of the kingdom was restored and consolidated, to the greater glory of the Valois. It was the end of the Lancastrian dream. Henry V and Bedford had died in harness to it, and their work did not survive them. True, there were still in Rouen a regent representing Henry VI, an English seneschal, a royal council, a chancery, a *Chambre des comptes*, an *Échiquier*. These officials still controlled almost all Normandy, part of Maine and part of Guienne. But sooner or later they would have to give way to the restored kingdom of France, whose instruments of government rapidly adapted themselves to the new situation.

3. CHARLES VII'S REFORMS

THE TAKING of Paris and the submission of Anglo-Burgundian France virtually, if not completely, unified the kingdom which for a score of years had been disputed between two rival dynasties and before that torn by factional strife. Reorganization of the government in the reconquered capital could not await the total expulsion of the Lancastrians and the recovery of Normandy and Guienne. A delicate problem presented itself to the victorious king, as it did after all the great internal crises which shook the country in the course of its subsequent history, to Henri IV on the morrow of the wars of religion, or to the First Consul after the storm of the Revolution: the problem of uniting all his subjects now that they were reconciled and establishing a strong government which would efface the memory of past discords. True, the object of Charles VII's 'reforms' was not so much innovation as restoration. But the fact remains that the France which emerged from them was no longer, either politically or administratively, that of his grandfather Charles V.

The test of experience and the needs of the moment all contributed towards these changes, which in their turn exerted an influence sometimes decisive on the end of the war. The reforms were neither the work of a day nor the fruit of a preconceived plan. The administrative re-organization, begun on the morrow of Richmond's entrance into Paris, was pursued by fits and starts, without any controlling idea, over a period of years, and was encouraged especially between 1440 and 1450 first by the slowing-down of the war and then by the truce of Tours. It was this decade that witnessed the most numerous and the most decisive ordinances. We should lose sight of the importance of the work accomplished if we examined them in their chronological order. But, in the general sketch which I shall try to make, we must never forget the political circumstances that explain its outstanding features. For the sake of clarity, I shall now deal with them.

In the first place there was the question of unifying the central government, lately severed by the necessities of war into several sections. The king's advisers had frequently upheld the doctrine that the supreme courts and the essential departments of state were indivisible organisms, which exercised their authority over the whole kingdom. They were opposed to decentralization, which they could accept at the most as temporary. They could contemplate only one chancery, one *Parlement*, one *Chambre des comptes*. Since the time of Charles V ordinances had periodically forbidden the *élus généraux* in charge of taxation to split up the kingdom among themselves and had maintained them, sometimes against their will, as an indivisible central body. As early as 1428, when communications between Poitou and Languedoc had become easier, the *Parlement* at Toulouse was abolished and southern cases were heard before the *Parlement* at Poitiers. No sooner had the city of Paris surrendered in April 1436 than the chancery and the *Chambre des comptes* were transferred there from Bourges, and the *Parlement* and the *Cour des aides* from Poitiers. A small delegation of the *Parlement* stayed for a few months longer in Poitou to wind up current cases, but its activity ceased before the end of the year. Though the king continued to reside on the banks of the Loire, still keeping aloof from the city where only too many unhappy memories would beset him, Paris once more became unquestionably the administrative capital of the kingdom.

In these conditions a merger of staff became essential, since Burgundian France had had similar courts and similar government departments concurrently with the kingdom of Bourges. The difficulty did not exist in the case of the local and subordinate staff of bailiffs, collectors, *élus*, foresters, and provosts. In the north of France the Treaty of Arras simply meant that they changed masters. They served Charles VII as faithfully as they had obeyed Henry VI, and there was no need to dismiss them or purge their ranks drastically. In Paris the case was different. There is a lack of research into the administrative archives so that we cannot say precisely how the king managed to deal with this so skilfully. Somehow he preserved the illusion that he had no intention to dismiss his former enemies, while at the same time, smoothly and quietly, he eliminated tainted and suspect elements. The sole example more or less well known to us, that of the *Parlement*, gives us at least an idea of the procedure employed.

The Treaty of Arras had provided for the maintenance in office of at least fifteen members of the Burgundian *Parlement*. This gave an opportunity for a preliminary sifting. Only those Burgundians whose change of heart looked most promising were retained. Then the king let his supreme court evolve on its own account. He admitted the principle of recruitment by co-option, which had often been advocated since the days of the Marmosets, and in 1446 went so far as to decide that he would choose the new counsellors from a list of alternative candidates presented by the court. But by 1447, when he felt in a stronger position, he eliminated election for the time being, personally appointed the members of the *Parlement*, and expelled from it the last partisans of the English, overt or covert. We may assume that similar procedure led to similar results in the other corporate bodies. While there were no mass dismissals, the government at least managed to retain only the best elements in the two hitherto hostile administrations, without reference to their political past. It was doubtless to this skilful merger that Charles VII owed the fact that he was nicknamed, even during his lifetime, 'The Well Served'.

Some of his servants had travelled a long way, such as Thomas Basin,

Pierre Cauchon's successor at Lisieux, who was originally a client and counsellor of the Lancastrians in Normandy, but arranged at the right moment to negotiate the surrender of his episcopal city. He became a member of Charles VII's council and later, when Louis XI drove him into exile, his apologist and chronicler. Out of this body of good servants history has not handed down many names. Their master, more distrustful than ever, having suffered only too much from unworthy favourites, came to be less dependent on counsellors. Among the clerks, Basin, like Jouvenel, exaggerated his real influence in his writings. Posterity did the same for Jacques Cœur, who, in his capacity as *Argentier*, was never more than an exacting and enriched creditor of the court, and for the Bureau brothers, who were sound financial officials and also took an interest in the innovation of artillery.

What was important, for that matter, was not so much the individuals who made up the royal officials as the imposing number of them. Neither war nor reforming ordinances stopped their steady multiplication. For example, the taxation districts (*élections*) grew from about thirty under Charles V to seventy-five on the death of Charles VII, and in the northern half of the kingdom there were soon nearly a hundred and fifty salt warehouses, all with their own staffs of warehousemen and measurers. Such officials were henceforth numerous enough to form a highly particularized social class, midway between the burgesses from whom most of them sprang and the nobility to which they aspired. Their cohesion was strengthened at all levels by marriage. The capital witnessed the foundation of regular dynasties of lawyers, linked by marriage to the 'gentlemen of finance', and similar marriages were arranged locally in the lower grades. All these officials tended more or less to acquire a privilege comparable with that which the nobles had lately arrogated to themselves. Since they served the king with their persons and their time, they regarded themselves as exempt from royal taxation, and often successfully maintained their claim to such exemption in the courts. Thus, *de facto* rather than *de jure*, there came into being that 'gentry of the robe' which constituted first a strength and later a weakness for the monarchy.

The royal system of centralization, vigorously restored from 1436 onwards, soon proved unworkable, or at least cumbrous. The kingdom was so large that in most spheres, such as law, taxation, and accountancy, it was impossible to deal with everything simultaneously in Paris. There was no option but to create elsewhere other supreme courts and other departments which would bring the subjects closer to the royal administration. Hindered by the selfish opposition of the officials in power, this movement did not really take shape until, for obvious political reasons, the particularist feelings of Normandy and Guienne, after their recovery, had to be soothed by the grant of a special system of government; but its first symptoms appeared somewhat sooner. Even before 1435, the *élus généraux* had divided the fiscal administration between themselves into Languedoïl and

Languedoc respectively. A new area was formed from the territory 'beyond the Seine and the Yonne' as it was gradually reconquered from the English, and another again in Normandy. Every area was controlled by a *général*, who had at his side a receiver general for what was soon called the '*généralité*'. For closer supervision of the royal domain, which the war had reduced almost to nothing, the treasurers similarly divided the kingdom into four areas, with ordinary receivers, having their head-quarters in Tours, Montpellier, Paris, and Rouen. But the *Cour des aides*, the *Cour du Trésor* and the *Chambre des comptes*, reorganized by exact ordin-ances, still refused to follow this process of division. They remained indi-visible at the centre of financial administration, except the *Cour des aides*, which finally had to accept the creation of rival bodies, first one for Languedoc, which was established in Toulouse from 1439, and then a second for Normandy in Rouen (1450).

The Paris *Parlement*, for its part, did its best to resist this centrifugal tendency, whose first symptoms did not fail to alarm it. It believed that it was in a position to relieve the pressure of legal cases by the institution, as in the previous century, of *Grands Jours*, temporary and more or less periodical sessions of Paris judges in the provinces. These were held after 1450 in Poitou, Auvergne, Guienne, and even Orleans. But they had ceased to suffice. From 1443 the *Parlement* at Toulouse was re-established, with jurisdiction over all Languedoc and those parts of Guienne under the control of Charles VII's officials. A second supreme court was estab-lished at Bordeaux on the French entrance into this town (1451), but suppressed two years later to punish the Gascons for rebellion. About the same time, however, when the Dauphin Louis decided to set up a *Parle-ment* at Grenoble with jurisdiction over his appanage, the king raised no objection to its creation. All this proportionally reduced the jurisdiction of the Paris court in the more remote regions of the kingdom; but it was able to prevent the re-establishment of yet another *Parlement* at Poitiers, which would have robbed it at one stroke of all the central provinces. Thus were gradually sketched the features of modern France which the monarchy of the *ancien régime* inherited: financial '*généralités*', which later supplanted the historic 'provinces'; *Cours des aides* and provincial *Parle-ments* with jurisdiction over the outlying parts of the kingdom. To these must be added the administrative geography of the salt-tax and the dawning distinction between *élections* districts and Estates districts, with which I shall deal in a moment.

What differentiated Charles VII's government from that of the first Valois was the permanence of its resources and its armed forces. But to say that the king 'created' permanent taxation and a standing army would be a rough and ready expression of a truth much more complex. For some time back, and for long periods, 'extraordinary' taxes, chiefly the hearth-tax, which produced much more than all other forms of taxation, had been levied quasi-permanently. But the extreme weakness of the King of

Bourges had forced him, as we have seen, to request from the Estates the voting of subsidies, often crushing, which the prosecution of the war demanded. Until about 1435, it looked as though the French monarchy was evolving towards a government doubtless authoritarian, but tempered by the principle of consent to taxation. If this practice had continued, the Estates of Languedoïl, representing the whole kingdom except the Languedoc seneschalships, might have become a permanent institution and played the part taken by the English Parliament. The king's counsellors clearly perceived this danger, and they were encouraged to check it by the deputies themselves. The insecurity of the roads and the heavy expense of travelling meant that the townships shrank from answering a royal summons and that their delegates, once arrived, were in a hurry to get home again. Since the main business was the voting of a subsidy, everyone wanted it to be obtained without delay. The grievances of the Estates were received perfunctorily, and met with evasive or dilatory replies, with which they expressed themselves content. Only on two occasions, in 1431 over the currency and in 1439 over military discipline, were ordinances issued to satisfy the demands of the three orders. Immediately the financial vote was obtained, the assembly was dissolved, after a session which never lasted more than three days.

The monarchy, therefore, did not admit that its expenditure should be controlled or that a policy should be imposed upon it. But even the obligation to beg for taxes whose necessity was obvious was in itself excessive in the eyes of the royal officials. Already, even at the worst moments of the foreign war, they had sometimes decreed, without consulting the Estates, the continuance of a tax previously levied or imposed a new one. This was the case in 1425 after the disaster at Verneuil, in 1429 to prepare for the coronation campaign, and in 1430 to meet its very heavy cost. A further step was taken in 1435 and 1436, when the Estates agreed to the re-establishment throughout the kingdom of the indirect taxes which since 1418 had been levied only irregularly. These taxes on commodities, fixed at the rate of 20 *deniers* to the *livre*, or one-twelfth, henceforth continued to be levied without need to ask for their renewal from the deputies of the three orders. Then came the turn of the hearth-tax. The Estates of 1439 were the last from which the king demanded its concession. During the following years he continued to levy it. A yearly royal ordinance, issued in accordance with the estimate of the 'gentlemen of finances', determined its total, which kept on growing until the end of the reign. The financial administration, which had become more complex, also became more provident. Every year, for the royal council's guidance, it drew up a budget proposal which was called 'statement by estimation'. After the financial year, it presented its net accounts, or 'true statement'. From 1450 treasurers and *généraux*, merging the ordinary and extraordinary accounts into one, drew up a single proposal, the 'general statement of finances', which was used by the council to determine the rate of tax.

Henceforth, since the king himself decreed the scope of his needs and the total of his resources, it might be said that taxation had become permanent. This did not mean, however, that the government dispensed with the consent of the taxpayers always and everywhere. Languedoc, where fortuitous circumstances had forced the government to separate consultation, jealously retained its own Estates. As early as 1423, the king tried to tax the southern seneschalships in proportion to the sums voted by the deputies of Languedoïl. In response to their strong protests, in 1428 he had to recognize his obligation to consult the Languedoc deputies before taxing them. So the principle was maintained of frequent sessions, at least yearly, at which the deputies, while presenting grievances to which more or less account was paid, vented their feelings by nibbling away the demands of the royal lieutenants and then proceeded to divide up the subsidy among the dioceses of the province. But the Estates of Languedoc, confined to a comparatively small area, more and more assumed the appearance of a local assembly anxious to protect its individual interests and therefore not very dangerous to the royal authority.

There still remained, indeed, local Estates which, even within the crown domains, sometimes met for urgent and limited needs. In 1431 those of Champagne granted the money necessary for the maintenance of royal garrisons in the recently reconquered province. In 1436 those of Ile-de-France provided for the needs of the siege of Creil. Elsewhere they were asked to vote extraordinary subsidies for regions which were always restricted and for limited periods, usually in the form of increases of tax. They themselves assessed it or supervised its assessment by the *élus*. But these were exceptional cases and they became more and more rare after the extinction of the Estates of Languedoïl. All that survived, more strongly and more regularly, were the assemblies of the great fiefs, because the princes in control there needed them to request the grant of free gifts, aids or local taxes intended not for the royal treasury, but for the treasuries of the great feudatories. Since, as these provinces were reabsorbed into the royal domain, the monarchy made a point of not colliding head-on with local privileges, it scrupulously maintained the institution of Estates in them. The case of Languedoc was therefore paralleled in Dauphiné, in this respect comparable with a great fief, then in Burgundy, Artois, and Provence, and later again in Brittany. The old 'Languedoïl', which after the disappearance of its Estates became an '*élections* district', was girdled by a belt of '*Estates* districts' which preserved their provincial assemblies.

While it is difficult to speak of a system of financial 'reform' deliberately and logically conceived by Charles VII, the term may, on the other hand, very well be applied to the whole of the measures undertaken in the military sphere.

The situation was undeniably tragic and demanded prompt remedy. The Franco-Burgundian reconciliation, far from bringing peace to the buffeted country, had the result of disbanding a large number of mercenaries hitherto paid, though very poorly, by one side or the other and letting them loose hungrily on the whole kingdom. The State was too impoverished to hire them and launch them against the last strongholds of Lancastrian rule, and was not even in a position to drive them out of the provinces which they proceeded to pillage. Their excesses, in a country exhausted by twenty years of strife, seem to have surpassed in horror all that the kingdom had suffered under John the Good. The narratives of the chroniclers, with their gruesome details, are fully corroborated by the sorrowful laments of records in various archives. Pillage, burning, torture, rape, massacre: the whole story is to be found there. The *Écorcheurs* spared nothing, except the walls of the towns which they could not take by assault. They had no thought even for their own morrow, and multiplied senseless devastation for the sake of immediate but fleeting advantage. Beneath their repeated blows, the depopulation of the countryside increased and poverty bred poverty. All the provinces of the kingdom suffered from them in turn, not only those which had been the theatre of war, but also, and for choice, the others too, because they were less impoverished. The mercenaries were to be found in Languedoc, Albigeois, Auvergne, and Berry. They swept over Burgundy and even carried their ravages beyond the frontier into Lorraine and Alsace, where they were still called Armagnacs.

Their captains, now enriched by long campaigning, flouted the royal orders. For example, Perrinet Gressart, who had devoted all his energy to serving the Anglo-Burgundian cause, refused to surrender La Charité to the King of France. This obstacle was circumvented by appointing him captain in Charles VII's name. Others had higher ambitions. The Maid's former comrades in arms, such as La Hire and Xaintrailles, worked for their own advantage while accepting official posts. Xaintrailles was successively seneschal of Limousin and bailiff of Berry. The Aragonese François de Surienne, heavily paid in Normandy, continued to fight for the English. The bastard of Bourbon laid waste the central provinces before ending on the scaffold. The most formidable of all, the Castilian Rodrigo de Villandrando, long pursued his misdeeds with absolute impunity.

The government tried in the first place to restore discipline in the companies which claimed to act in the king's name. It was necessary to set about this several times over. Charles V's instructions were renewed in 1431 and again in 1438. In November 1439 a still more strict ordinance established in principle a royal monopoly in respect of recruiting, limited the maximum strength of companies to one hundred men, and endeavoured to settle them in garrisons. These orders were far from being effective at once. But stricter supervision of strength by the military authorities, the constable and the marshals, exemplary punishment of malefactors, and above all better and more regular pay did much to restore order and reduce extortion and pillage.

If the truce of Tours in 1444 had been followed by a general disband-ment of the army, as was customary in such cases, fresh bands of hungry *routiers* would have overflowed the kingdom. The great innovation made at this point was that the truce was not allowed to expire before the recruit-ment of fresh forces, but that, pending the renewal of the war, relatively large ones were maintained under arms. In the first place all dubious elements were purged. With the best of what remained large units were constituted which soon became known as 'companies of the king's ordin-ance'. They consisted of one hundred 'lances', comprising one man-at-arms with five more lightly armed attendants. If the strength of every 'lance' was not always reached, at least the number of companies hovered around a score. The next year (1446) this reform was extended to Langue-doc, which had to provide five fresh companies. Even before the renewal of the war the government was able to raise other contingents less well armed and less compact. These were the 'companies of petty ordinance'. For the first time in the history of the Western kingdoms, a sovereign had succeeded, in a period of peace, in raising, equipping and maintaining a body of cavalry with a strength of at least fifteen thousand men, dispersed in garrisons throughout the kingdom. Every town and district had to house a given number of 'lances', and the cost of their maintenance fell on the inhabitants. To this end they paid a tax 'for the upkeep of the men-at-arms'. Added though it was to already crushing taxation, this tax was paid without a murmur, for everyone appreciated the benefit of this armed policy aimed at once against *routiers*, pillagers, and all the king's enemies.

In April 1448 an attempt was made to institute, side by side with the permanent cavalry, a body of infantry equally permanent. To attract volunteers, they were exempted from all taxation: hence their name of 'free archers'; but every urban and rural community had to provide one *per* fifty hearths. The men armed themselves. They were a kind of civic guard, who pursued their normal occupations as artisans and farm-labourers, on the sole condition of practising archery once a week and joining their companies in case of war. This ordinance had only begun to come into force by the end of the Hundred Years' War. But it proved the fixed determination of the French monarchy to have at its disposal a military force always available, to which the swift and decisive strides in the use of artillery gave an offensive power hitherto unequalled.

4. THE TRUCE OF TOURS

THESE wise reforms, which have been briefly sketched, might easily convey the impression of a strong monarchy, sure of itself and marching resolutely towards a predetermined goal. In fact, they were simply a series of gropings, piecemeal measures spread over a period of more than fifteen years. The obvious proof that Charles VII did not pass overnight from the humiliated position of King of Bourges to the exalted state of a victorious sovereign is to be found in the mere fact of the slowness with which, after the capture of Paris, the reconquest of the provinces still occupied by the enemy was achieved.

Yet in the year 1436 Lancastrian England was very poorly equipped to restore her badly shaken position on the continent. She was paying the usual price of great epics, which devour men and money. She grievously lacked a leader, whom the troubled years of Henry VI's long minority had failed to provide. For, while Bedford had pursued the grandiose but hopeless task of the 'dual monarchy' in France, his fellow-countrymen at home were immersed in petty quarrels. Their details need not detain us long. Furious over being thrust aside from the regency, Humphrey of Gloucester had flung himself into intrigue. He was an accomplished prince, a sensitive humanist whose bounty enabled the University of Oxford to enrich its libraries enormously. But he was muddle-headed, violent, grasping, and crafty. As the faithful trustee of Henry V's last wishes, the royal council, dominated by his uncles the Beauforts, allowed him only a nominal authority. The dispossessed prince champed the bit for some months. But, when he returned in 1425 from his burlesque adventure in the Low Countries, both humiliated and out of pocket, he could stand it no longer. In open council he accused Henry Beaufort of having governed the kingdom badly in his absence.

The quarrel would have developed into civil war but for the mediation of Bedford, who hastily returned to England to smooth matters over and stayed more than a year to complete his task of reconciliation. It was arranged that Gloucester should keep his somewhat empty title of 'protector', and that Beaufort should leave the chancery, which he had directed since the beginning of the new reign. But, by way of compensation, the prelate received a cardinal's hat; and he remained, moreover, enormously rich and the largest creditor of the crown. Gloucester, jealous of him on all these grounds, resumed the struggle as soon as Bedford set off again for the continent. Against the luxury-loving prelate, who was the favourite of the aristocracy, he stirred up the middle classes, the London burgesses, and the Commons. He claimed the right to forbid him, as a churchman, from wearing the Order of the Garter, and, as cardinal, from administering the diocese of Winchester, which he had retained. Only the long stays which Beaufort made at this time on the continent, for the preparation of the crusade against the Hussites in Bohemia, prevented the rivalry from turning into a bloody struggle.

No one in England was of sufficient stature to master these intrigues. Bedford was too busy in Paris and Rouen to be able to repeat his visits home. Thanks to the princely quarrels favoured by the king's minority, Henry V's strict administration was relaxed. Above all, the budget deficit increased year by year. Henry V had promised an early victory, and for the sake of it his subjects had cheerfully agreed to heavy financial sacrifices. But existing taxation was insufficient to meet the ever heavier calls of the war. The equipment of the reinforcements which the Regent of France kept on demanding swallowed up its whole yield. Until the siege of Orleans, the English might believe that their reward would come soon. When the war became defensive, the burden seemed intolerable; but it was just at this moment that, faced with increased needs, the government had to seek new resources. Since the wool and property taxes and the customs and market dues proved insufficient, in 1431 Parliament agreed to the levy of a tax of five per cent. on all incomes over twenty pounds. Despite this, the treasury kept on borrowing recklessly and increasing its swarm of creditors.

Deprived by the Treaty of Arras of her sole continental ally, on Bedford's death England found herself without a leader. In London the rivalry of Beaufort and Gloucester around King Henry VI, a pious and weak youth, continued; but it now assumed a less personal and more political character. As a churchman anxious to recover the money he had lent the treasury, Beaufort became the champion of the party of peace and agreement with the Valois enemy. Part of the baronage, tired of so much vain sacrifice, grouped themselves behind him. Gloucester, like his namesake of the previous century, aroused the anti-French feeling of the London burgesses and the Commons, recalled Henry V's still recent glory, and advocated war to the bitter end. Neither of them was strong enough to control affairs in France. Bedford's succession was given first to the Earl of Warwick and then to Richard, Duke of York, who was feeling his way and leant towards either party in turn.

If the Valois government had not persisted in its now inveterate slackness, if the exhaustion of the kingdom of France had not continually paralysed it, the capture of Paris would have been the harbinger of a final assault on Rouen and Bordeaux, the last citadels of the Lancastrian empire. In fact, Richard of York, with the help of the energetic Talbot, was easily able to ward off the danger. By 1436 order was restored in threatened Normandy. The recapture of Pontoise even foreshadowed an English counter-offensive towards Ile-de-France. Not without difficulty, the Anjous and Richmond induced Charles VII to assume command of his troops, which he had abandoned after the epic of his coronation. But the campaign of 1437 miscarried. In October the French seized Montereau, the last enemy outpost on the upper Seine. Then the king made a ceremonial entrance into Paris, where his stay was marked by festivities and acclamations; but, three weeks later, he fell back on Touraine. Henceforth the military operations dragged on without other change than the recapture in successive years of one or two strongholds from the enemy, who were often successful in other directions. In 1438 there was an unfruitful campaign in Bordelais. In 1439 the English garrison of Meaux surrendered. In 1440 the French failed to take Avranches and lost Harfleur. It was a sorry achievement four years after Richmond's entrance into Paris.

Despite the French loyalty to the monarchy, Charles VII was not popular. He was blamed for his incapacity in face of the *routiers'* devastation. The ravages of the epidemics which spread through the exhausted provinces added to the people's distress. Finally, princely rivalry around the sovereign was resumed, to such a point that a relapse into civil war was feared. There was no question of feudal rising any more than under Charles VI. Ruined by the wars, the nobility, who had never been serious opponents of the Valois monarchy, could expect nothing from a revolt which they had no means to finance. The royal administration kept them in strict tutelage, gradually deprived them of their remaining privileges, abolished their courts of law, proclaimed the sovereign's sole right to ennoblement, legitimation, and the grant of fairs and markets, and even tried to limit by ordinance the occasions when the lords could demand extraordinary aids from their subjects. But, as under Charles VI, the princes kicked against the royal authority which exerted itself to thrust them from power and limit their revenues. Their need of money was more pressing, and so was their inducement to control the government and profit by the royal bounty. The former prisoners at Agincourt had had to pay crushing ransoms which nearly ruined them. When the Duchess of Burgundy decided to obtain the liberation of Charles of Orleans, the negotiations dragged on for years because the prince-poet could not find the sum demanded for his provisional liberty. If the king did not renew the favours they had enjoyed during the preceding reign, these needy princes would be reduced to poverty. They resented the fact that Richmond and Charles of Anjou, Count of Maine, alone influenced the king to their exclusive advantage. Charles I of Bourbon led the band of malcontents.

In 1437 they hatched a plot to overthrow the favourites. In addition to the Duke of Alençon, John V of Brittany – though he was Richmond's brother – and King René, brother of Charles of Maine, were involved. Rodrigo de Villandrando promised them the support of his mercenaries. A prompt march on Auvergne sufficed to scatter the conspirators. But in

1440 their threat became more definite and the plot was widened. John of Brittany and the Count of Armagnac supported it. Alençon got into touch with the English to obtain their military aid. Two recruits of note increased the danger: Dunois, who accused the king of doing nothing to free his half-brother Orleans, and above all the Dauphin Louis, a youth of sixteen already eager to reign. In February they opened hostilities. This revolt was known as the 'Praguerie', in memory of the recent upheaval in Bohemia. The royal army first occupied Poitou, and then subjugated Auvergne, where Bourbon and the Dauphin had taken refuge. Forced to submit, the plotters were pardoned in July. If they had failed pitiably, it was because their combined forces were so much inferior to those of the king. It was also because they lacked the support of Burgundy, without which no princely coalition could now succeed.

On the morrow of the 'Praguerie', Philip the Good felt that his hour had struck. If he sold his alliance to the princes and so resumed the leading place in the Valois kingdom which the Treaty of Arras had failed to gain for him, would this not be adapting to circumstances the traditional policy of his house? In December 1440 he formed a triple alliance with John of Brittany and Charles of Orleans, whose freedom he had finally secured. Alençon and then Bourbon joined them, travelled constantly from one court to another, and sent envoys to Rouen to sound the Duke of York's intentions. Finally, in February 1442, all the princes met at Nevers, set forth their grievances and demanded the summoning of the Estates General. Though apparently pacific, the coalition put the monarchy's independence in danger. Charles VII and his counsellors managed to thwart the princes' move. By means of timely largesse they bought Alençon's and Dunois's defection. Towards the other plotters they acted so firmly that they broke up without effecting anything.

But, in face of the continually renewed threat of these princely coalitions, could the king's government continue war to the bitter end against the Lancastrians until it recovered the last provinces? On the morrow of the Treaty of Arras, Charles VII, whose slackness had become a byword, had embarked upon serious negotiations, in which the Duke of Burgundy had played the role of mediator. In England all the hatred aroused by the disappointment at Arras had concentrated upon Philip the Good's 'betrayal'. Reprisals against him were ordered. Gloucester, fiery as ever, was given the county of Flanders as an appanage, landed at Calais and threatened to invade the Burgundian State. A blockade of the Low Countries was organized, and its inevitable result was a revolt of the Flemish towns, which it took Philip several months to master (1437–8). All the fruits of the Treaty of Arras seemed to be escaping the Burgundian. He might even fear a separate agreement between Lancastrian and Valois, which would be at his expense, while Charles of Orleans, impatient to regain his freedom after more than twenty years as a prisoner, would have an interest in negotiating it. It would pay Philip better to take charge of affairs, get into touch with Beaufort and negotiate directly for Orleans's provisional release, and finally arrange an Anglo-French conference through his own mediation and that of his third wife, the clever Isabella of Portugal, who was related to the Lancastrians.

So, in July 1439, a fresh peace conference opened at Gravelines, at which Beaufort led the English delegates and Regnault of Chartres was the spokesman of the French. At this conference there was no question of a 'final peace'. Each side put forward irreconcilable claims, which had changed little since Arras. The English still demanded possession of the kingdom of France, and would leave the 'Dauphin' – as they persisted in calling Charles – by way of an appanage, only the provinces lying south of the Loire. At a pinch, they would be satisfied with the old Plantagenet empire from Normandy to the Pyrenees, ceded to them in full sovereignty. On their side, the French first offered a diminished Guienne, and then added to it a few Norman bailiwicks; but they would not grant sovereignty. This was merely a resumption of the endless argument which had divided Valois and Plantagenet in the previous century. It was not realized that, since Henry V's time, the war had changed its aspect, and that no territorial or feudal arrangement could restore peace, now that the two nations stood behind their sovereigns. But at least, in order to relieve the exhausted peoples, the conclusion of a long truce was seriously contemplated. Above all, thanks to this conference, Philip the Good obtained an Anglo-Flemish commercial treaty, to the great delight of his subjects in the Low Countries.

The 'Praguerie' interrupted this diplomatic activity. With good reason, Charles VII took alarm about Burgundy's intentions. So far Philip had worked only for himself. Perhaps he was now going to work against the King of France. In July 1440, having obtained from Beaufort, at the cost of a ransom of 200,000 écus, Charles of Orleans's definite liberation, Philip welcomed the heir of the hated Armagnacs at his court, married him to one of his own cousins, Mary of Cleves, and made an alliance with him. This collusion of the Lancastrians, Burgundy and the princes was detrimental to Charles VII. The entourage of the King of France, now less apathetic and more provident, realized that, if he was to assert himself, he must hold more trumps. Diplomatic intrigue could be countered by military success. The war, which had been dragging along, suddenly flared up again.

With unaccustomed energy, the king assumed control of operations. In 1441 there was a brilliant campaign against the *routiers* in the plain of Champagne, that bastion of the royal domain thrust in a salient into the Burgundian State. It was here that the bastard of Bourbon expiated his crimes on the scaffold. Then the king turned towards the valley of the Oise, still held by the English and defended by Talbot. In succession Creil, then Conflans, and then, though not without difficulty, Pontoise were captured by the royal troops. Ile-de-France was definitely freed. Next year, on the morrow of the Nevers meeting, it was against Guienne that Charles VII directed his effort. In the south-west the princes' moves had resulted in strengthening the English position. The Count of Armagnac offered his daughter in marriage to Henry VI. After a long siege, the lord of Albret allowed his castle of Tartas to surrender. At the head of an imposing army, the King of France in person undertook its recovery. Not content with recapturing the fortress, he took Saint-Sever and Dax and, despite a temporary check at La Réole, seriously threatened Bordeaux (June–December 1442).

This vigorous show of strength bore fruit. The English warmongers had to lower their flag. Already Gloucester had had to throw in his hand, having been discredited when Henry VI's council secured the conviction for sorcery of his morganatic wife, Eleanor Cobham. The last supporters of the war insisted on replying to the French successes by a final campaign, which was launched from Normandy with the intention of reaching Bordeaux and reviving the spirits of their Gascon partisans. But the expedition, entrusted to the incompetent hands of Cardinal Beaufort's nephew Somerset, was a pitiable failure, and the English forces had to re-embark after roving for a few weeks on the borders of Brittany and Anjou.

Henceforth the peace party was triumphant. On both sides of the Channel the people, crushed by taxation and exhausted by all the ravages of war, clamoured for peace and demanded an end of the conflict. Philip the Good, still fearing negotiation without him, redoubled his attempts at reconciliation. For that matter, he had never lost touch with London. The new Duke of Brittany, Francis I, offered himself as mediator. Even the Pope, still involved in his struggle with the Council at Basle, and at the same time anxious about the advance of the Ottoman Turks, proposed his good offices. No more was needed to prevail upon the two enemies, equally anxious for agreement. Their general weariness completed the task. William de la Pole, Earl of Suffolk, was dispatched by Henry VI to 'his dear uncle of France'. On April 8th 1444 at Le Mans a local truce was arranged. Then negotiations were opened at Tours. They were conducted on the French side by Peter of Brézé, who, since Yolanda of Sicily's death and thanks to the favour of Charles VII's mistress Agnes Sorel, had become the king's chief counsellor. At once, as in the past, a 'general peace' proved impossible. Its place was taken, as in the past, by a marriage covenant and a truce.

On May 22nd, the plenipotentiaries agreed upon the betrothal of Henry VI, now a tall young man of twenty-three, to Charles VII's niece, Margaret of Anjou, daughter of King René. Six days later, a general truce was concluded between the adversaries and their respective allies. It was valid in the first place for ten months, but could be prolonged. To modern minds this result may seem meagre. But the marriage of a Lancastrian to a Princess of Anjou opened up a promising prospect. Above all, the truce, the first since the Treaty of Troyes, in other words for nearly a quarter of a century, set the seal on the recovery of the Valois and confirmed his conquests. A fresh phase of the conflict, the last phase, was soon to begin.

Part IX

THE END OF HOSTILITIES

Part IX

THE END OF HOSTILITIES

SINCE it was merely a suspension of arms, the truce of Tours left things as they were. The English still occupied the greater part of Normandy and Maine, large tracts of land around Bordeaux and Bayonne, and, in the north of the kingdom, the district of Calais. The armistice, as always in such cases, was precarious and suffered many breaches at the hands of the captains on either side. But so great was the need for peace that, in England and France alike, the truce was welcomed with an outburst of joy. Only a few peevish souls blamed Charles VII, on the one hand, for deserting his Norman and Gascon subjects, and Henry VI, on the other hand, for marrying his enemy's niece.

On closer examination, the respite granted to the combatants was not equally to the advantage of both camps. In England the political situation remained disturbed. Henry VI proved to be a weak prince, incapable of ruling by himself. The young wife who had been thrust upon him at once began to influence him, and her ascendancy kept on growing. In view of the self-effacement of Beaufort, who was growing old and losing interest in power, Margaret of Anjou entrusted her confidence to the negotiator of her marriage, the Earl – a little later the Marquis – of Suffolk. But, though the country was grateful to him for stopping the war, there was resentment of the humiliation which the truce implied. Gloucester continued to stir up discontent, until Suffolk finally managed to get rid of him in 1447 by a charge of treason. The king's uncle was arrested and died mysteriously in prison. In the eyes of indignant public opinion, this was one more reason for hating the all-powerful minister, who was regarded as simply the servant of the foreigner. In vain had Suffolk taken precautions and obtained from Parliament, in June 1445, approval of his peace policy. English nationalism was unanimously aroused against him, all the more violently because it was aware of its own impotence. The English did not want to abandon the dream of continental adventure, but they refused to make the material sacrifice necessary for its pursuit. To satisfy their vanity, they preferred to blame the incompetence and treachery of the minister upon whom fell the responsibility for military failure. As the architect of peace, Suffolk fell on May 2nd 1550, on the morrow of defeats which his policy of understanding unsupported by an uninformed public opinion, had been powerless to foresee or avert.

Very different was the position of Charles VII's counsellors. The four or five years of respite with which the truce presented them were turned to advantage to complete the reorganization of the kingdom, restore order in administration and begin the creation of a new army. Even the currency, which repeated devaluation had reduced almost to nothing, was brought to life again and stabilized at a rate which allowed trade to revive. Satisfied with a prosperity increased by the security of commerce, the burgesses became more than ever faithful supporters of the monarchy. Even at court the king slowly shook off his apathy. In this he was doubtless helped by Agnes Sorel, the 'Dame de Beauté', the first influential royal mistress known in French history, who until her death in February 1450 exercised a good influence over him. Against her and the minister Peter of Brézé the princes were powerless. Disunited since the failure of their meeting at Nevers, they did not venture to come together again. Only the Dauphin Louis persisted in his craftily underhand attitude. But from 1445 he had had to take refuge in his appanage of Dauphiné. The base intrigues of his agents in the king's entourage did not endanger the favourites' credit.

To them, moreover, belonged the merit of taking advantage of the truce to improve the Valois's diplomatic situation. In July 1445 a large French embassy, led by Jean Jouvenel, the new Archbishop of Rheims, and accompanied by Castilian, Breton, and Angevin plenipotentiaries, landed in England. Such an event had been unknown for thirty years, since the pitiable failure of the negotiations at Winchester. They were given a magnificent reception, but for the 'final peace', in which no one sincerely believed, they had nothing more to offer than territorial concessions smaller than ever: Guienne, Quercy, Périgord, Calais. In return for a renewal of the truce, however, they obtained from Suffolk and Henry VI two important promises: an early meeting of the two kings, from which much was expected, and the cession to René of Anjou of the county of Maine, in which English garrisons still maintained themselves. Doubtless fearing unanimous opposition from ultra-patriotic opinion, the London government dare not carry out its promises at once. Embassies and conferences succeeded one another for more than two years. The projected meeting between the kings was constantly postponed, and difficulties were piled up over the surrender of Maine. Conscious of the justice of his cause, Charles VII decided, despite the truce, to resort to arms. While negotiations were still in progress, French troops besieged Le Mans. Threatened by a large deployment of strength, the English garrisons in Maine decided to evacuate the province and retreat on Normandy (June 1448).

1. THE RECONQUEST OF NORMANDY AND GUIENNE

THE TRUCE was not due to expire until the spring of 1450. But the attack on Maine showed that the King of France meant to resume the struggle until he had recovered the whole of his kingdom. Everything drove him to this warlike policy: the influence of his lawyers, doubtless supported by the weight of public opinion, who regarded the truce as a mere halt before the final assault; the impatience of his troops enrolled in the new companies; the ill will and bad faith of the English officials in France, who split hairs endlessly and kept on going back on Suffolk's and Henry VI's most solemn promises.

At this moment a new lieutenant of the King of England had arrived in Rouen, his cousin Edmund Beaufort, Duke of Somerset. Despite the exhaustion of Lancastrian Normandy, he saw fit, doubtless in order to satisfy public opinion across the Channel, to embark upon a rash policy of provocation. Instead of withdrawing them to Caen or Rouen, he dispatched the garrisons ousted from Maine to the western frontier of the duchy to occupy the two fortresses of Mortain and Saint-James-de-Beuvron, hitherto neutral territory. This was a direct threat to Duke Francis of Brittany, whom his uncle Richmond had definitely won over to French allegiance. When Charles VII supported the duke's complaint, he was sharply snubbed by presumptuous Somerset and told that it was none of his business, since Brittany was a fief of the English crown. Moreover, needing a more striking success to enhance their prestige, Somerset and Suffolk carefully prepared a blow by way of revenge for the attack on Maine. They entrusted an infamous leader of *routiers*, François de Surienne, known as the Aragonese, who was champing the bit in Normandy, with the organization of a punitive expedition of which the Duke of Brittany, and in consequence his Valois protector, would be the victims. On March 24th 1449 a daring raid by the Aragonese made him master of Fougères, in the heart of Brittany. The town was sacked and occupied by an English garrison.

Charles VII might have made this flagrant breach of the truce a pretext for renewing the war at once. He chose to continue futile negotiations for a few months longer. But he let his captains continue 'the quarrel of Brittany' in the Duke's name. They captured Pont-de-l'Arche and Conches in Normandy and other fortresses in Beauvaisis and the Bordeaux region. The enemy were demoralized and unable to react. Meanwhile the French army concentrated on the frontiers of Normandy. Finally, on July 17th, a council specially summoned near Chinon decided upon the opening of hostilities, entrusted command to the veteran Dunois and broke off all relations with Somerset.

Though it was still stuffed with English garrisons, Normandy nevertheless succumbed in the course of an astonishing campaign which continued without stopping for a twelvemonth. Everywhere, especially in the countryside, the people welcomed the French as liberators. Very often they rose without awaiting the victorious troops. Thanks to all this support, the campaign amounted simply to a series of sieges, such as Louis XI later favoured, which saved casualties for the attackers and were quicker than in the past now that the progress of artillery allowed devastating and demoralizing concentrations of fire. A concentric attack was carried out by three main bodies. Setting out from Beauvais with the support of the Picardy nobles, the counts of Eu and Saint-Pol crossed the Seine upstream from Rouen, took Pont-Audemer, Pont-l'Évêque, and Lisieux, which was surrendered by its bishop, Thomas Basin (August 16th), and then proceeded with a systematic clearance of the district of Bray. In the centre, Dunois, supported on his left flank by the Duke of Alençon, first entered Verneuil without opposition, was joined by the king at Louviers, took Mantes and Vernon and then, breaking into lower Normandy, advanced to Argentan (October 4th). In the west, in a brilliant autumn campaign, Francis of Brittany and his uncle Richmond carried Coutances, Carentan, Saint-Lô, and Valognes and almost all the fortresses in Cotentin, and ended by recapturing Fougères (November 5th).

Meanwhile the king, after regrouping his army, appeared beneath the walls of Rouen on October 9th. The burgesses, already more than half won over to the royal cause, opened their gates to him. Hard pressed in the castle, Somerset and his garrison decided to retreat to Caen. Charles made a triumphal entrance into the Norman capital on November 20th. Finally other fortresses fell in the depth of winter, including Harfleur.

So far the English resistance had been feeble enough. At the outset Talbot tried to hamper the enemy's movements; but, with only a few hundred men, he could not succeed. During the winter, with great difficulty, Suffolk, already on the eve of his fall, made a last effort. On March 15th 1450 a small reinforcing army, barely five thousand strong, under the command of Sir Thomas Kyriel, landed at Cherbourg. It recovered several fortresses in Cotentin, joined up with the two thousand men still at Somerset's disposal, crossed the Vire and advanced into Bessin. On April 15th, at Formigny, it suffered a crushing defeat.

Military history has paid little attention to these last battles of the Hundred Years' War. If it had done so, it would have recognized their close resemblance to those of Crécy, Poitiers, Agincourt, and Verneuil. But now the roles were reversed. Instead of the squadrons of cavalry which the first Valois put into line, Charles VII had at his disposal only small armies, equipped with artillery and infantry, but numerically inferior to the enemy's forces, weak though these were. At Formigny the

Count of Clermont's strength was so small that he could not dream of attacking. But the accurate fire of his field artillery forced the English, who had entrenched as usual, to take to the open country. Their forces were engaged in detail. Richmond's arrival with a body of reinforcements clinched the victory. While the French suffered small losses, the enemy left nearly five thousand men on the field, killed or prisoners. Kyriel was among the captured.

Formigny decided the fate of Normandy. While the Bretons cleared Cotentin, the bulk of the royal army advanced on Caen. Somerset capitulated on July 1st and sailed for Calais and Dover with what was left of the English administration. A few fortresses still held out; but Falaise fell on July 21st, Domfront on August 2nd, and finally Cherbourg on the 12th, a year to the day after the opening of the campaign.

By now England was feeling the effect of these irreparable disasters and seemed powerless in face of the prelude to a cruel civil war. First came the fall of Suffolk, whose policy of peace with France and alliance with the Angevins had gone bankrupt. He was hated by the barons and the Commons, who sought only an opportunity to overthrow him. He was accused of the murder of Bishop Adam Moleyns, assassinated in Portsmouth in January 1450. When he defended himself, Parliament put him on trial for high treason. The king attempted to save his life by banishing him; but he was killed on May 2nd 1450 by a sailor on board the ship which was taking him to Flanders. There was no capable man to replace him at the head of affairs. Somerset, appointed as his successor, bore all the weight of his defeats in Normandy. The affront to the nation's honour, the burden of crushing though still inadequate taxation, the tide of beaten and pillaging soldiers flowing back from France and the general poverty led to a fresh peasant rising in the south-east counties, perhaps more dangerous than that of 1381, because it was supported by the gentry and some of the clergy.

It was led by an adventurer from the county of Kent, Jack Cade, who gave the signal for the rising on May 31st, demanded the dismissal of the king's bad counsellors, seized London, put the royal treasurer to death and resorted to plunder. It took Henry VI a month to assemble an army which finally crushed the rebels on July 5th. The rising had no sequel, at least in the social sphere. But it raised a grave political problem. At the height of the revolt Richard, Duke of York hastened from Ireland, where he was governor. He was the king's nearest relation and his presumptive heir, if the legitimatized Beauforts did not aspire to the throne. Succeeding Gloucester at the head of the war party, he promptly presented himself as an enemy of Margaret of Anjou and a rival to Somerset. Around the two adversaries the nobility soon began to group themselves in accordance with their preferences or their family alliances. The prospect of civil war paralysed England at the moment when her last continental possessions faced the assault of the French power.

Without waiting for the reorganization of reconquered Normandy, which he entrusted to Constable Richmond, Charles VII decided to turn all his available forces against Guienne. Preliminary operations, begun during the summer of 1449, had not yet yielded much result. Everything encouraged the Gascons to resist these attacks: their self-interested loyalty towards the ducal dynasty, their long-standing habit of political autonomy, the trade links with England which ensured their prosperity. Without the support of the people, the conquest proved much harder than that of Normandy. While the Count of Foix operated in the valley of the Adour, a small army under the Count of Penthièvre, strongly equipped with artillery, captured Bergerac on October 10th 1450, took possession of Bazas, and approached the capital of Guienne, putting the communal militia to flight. The winter halted operations. But in April 1451 a powerful army, under Dunois's command, embarked upon the decisive campaign. It advanced into the Bordeaux region, captured the fortresses of Blaye, Fronsac, and Saint-Émilion one after the other, and began the siege of Bordeaux, which could not long resist in the absence of English support. Gaston of Foix, Captal of Buch, who had remained loyal to the Lancastrians, was entrusted with negotiating its surrender. It was agreed that the town should capitulate on June 24th, if reinforcements from England had not meanwhile relieved it. Dunois took possession of it on the 30th. At once all the fortresses which still held out surrendered without fighting, except Bayonne, which had to be regularly besieged. In its turn the town surrendered on August 20th. The reconquest of Guienne, like that of Normandy, had taken exactly a year.

But it was soon called in question through the victors' fault. It is true that Charles VII almost everywhere granted liberal terms to the Gascons when they submitted. Only Bayonne was punished for its resistance by the imposition of a war indemnity and the suppression of its communal liberties. Everywhere else the conqueror confirmed privileges and maintained institutions. But he made the mistake of entrusting the government of Guienne to Frenchmen of the north, who were not inclined to be mild and were soon hated by the people: the Breton Oliver de Coëtivy as seneschal of Guienne and the financier Jean Bureau as Mayor of Bordeaux. Their unnecessary pin-pricks, the ravages of the soldiers, and the complete stoppage of maritime trade antagonized the burgesses, the nobles, and the officials ousted from all their posts. They were ready to revolt at the first opportunity, and they conveyed the fact to London.

Somerset, who had assumed power there, needed a military success to offset his growing unpopularity. Though beaten at Caen, he had been made Constable of England, to the great scandal of the warlike nobility. York, who had set himself up as his rival, denounced him before the council, assembled troops and threatened to start a civil war. Somerset managed to ward off this danger for the time being. The overtures which the Gascon conspirators had made to him, in August 1452, gave him a means of restoring his shaken prestige. Reinforcements originally assembled for the defence of Calais were available at the Channel ports. Somerset entrusted these four or five thousand men to old Talbot, Earl of Shrewsbury, the only leader who might be successful in supporting the Lancastrian cause. Though he was over eighty, Bedford's former lieutenant displayed remarkable energy. He landed in Médoc on October 17th and four days later entered Bordeaux, after a general revolt of the population. All the fortresses from the frontier of the Landes to that of Angoumois opened their gates to him after driving out the French garrisons.

Charles VII had let events outrun him. He was aware of Talbot's preparations, but thought that they were directed against Normandy, whose defence he had reinforced. Now that Guienne was lost again, it took him all the winter to organize his counter-offensive, and this gave Bordeaux time to receive fresh reinforcements from England. When the French army advanced into Guienne, in the spring of 1453, it was so superior in numbers that Talbot dare not attack it. He waited until it was split up into various bodies, let the Count of Clermont push forward towards Médoc, and then marched against the smaller force which had laid siege to Castillon, near Libourne. Talbot reckoned that his seven thousand men should win an easy victory. But he found the French, who had learned the lesson of Crécy and Agincourt, strongly entrenched behind stockades. Without pausing for reflection, he attacked them with his usual impetuosity. Jean Bureau's artillery decimated the Anglo-Gascon cavalry. Then battle was joined in bad conditions for the English. A flank attack by a force of Breton 'lances' carried the day. Talbot fell on the field, and with him died the last English hopes in Guienne (July 17th). A siege of Bordeaux, promptly undertaken and coupled with a naval blockade of the Gironde, marked the climax of the campaign. It looked like a hard task, for the burgesses and the Gascon nobility were ready for a fierce resistance. But, cut off from reinforcements and unsupported even by the last English survivors from the battle of Castillon, whose sole wish was to get back home, the people of Bordeaux opened negotiations at the end of September. On October 19th Gascons and English surrendered unconditionally.

The citizens could scarcely congratulate themselves on their revolt. This time they were shown no mercy. A collective fine was imposed on Bordeaux, and the burgesses most deeply involved were banished. The *Parlement* granted to Guienne in 1451 was abolished, and appeal cases were heard as before in Paris or Toulouse. French rule, harsh and vexatious, was as unpopular as ever; but at least it had the merit of lasting. This was the end of the link, three centuries old, between the Gascons and the kings of England. This was the end of the great fief of Aquitaine which had led to the Hundred Years' War.

In Joan of Arc's famous words, the enemy had been 'driven out of France'. True, Calais and the county of Guines were left to them. As early as 1451 Charles VII had contemplated attacking this last bulwark of Lancastrian rule on the continent. But the hostility of the Duke of Burgundy, without whose help the operation could not succeed, made him postpone the plan. It was taken up again later, with no more success. So the capture of Bordeaux put a full stop, not indeed to the war, for it was concluded by no treaty of peace, but at least to the hostilities which had extended, with more or less vigour, over one hundred and sixteen years. Let us take it, in accordance with conventional history, that the Hundred Years' War, begun in May 1337, came to an end in October 1453. It remains for us to measure its effects and its sequel for both belligerents.

2. FRANCE AFTER THE WAR

THE GLORY and prestige of the victor should not mislead us. Legal measures, royal proclamations, narratives by paid flatterers, even mottoes on commemorative medals were devoted to magnifying the French success, extolling the wonderful rise of the sovereign who had started from nothing and reached the peak of power, and singing the praises of the kingdom of France which had once more become the foremost in Christendom. Charles VII himself took care to efface all the memories of his past defeats, the mistakes of his youth, the failings which had darkened the beginning of his reign. The rehabilitation of Joan of Arc was the main work of this campaign. On the morrow of the capture of Rouen, the king ordered a preliminary inquiry, though it was impeded by the bad grace of the court of Rome. In 1452 a papal legate, Cardinal d'Estouteville, agreed to hear witnesses and receive memoranda and reports. But Pope Nicholas V was afraid of falling out with England if he reopened, for political purposes, a trial which was canonically closed. His successor, Calixtus III, finally agreed (June 1455) to the holding of a trial, which he entrusted to the Archbishop of Rheims, Jean Jouvenel, one of the judges of Poitiers. Henceforth the trial proceeded, with customary ceremony and slowness, to the verdict of rehabilitation, which was pronounced in Rouen on July 7th 1456. This had the effect of resolving the last doubts which might remain about the legitimacy of Charles's coronation. Joan was proclaimed a good Catholic, unjustly accused of heresy. Nothing stood in the way of belief in the supernatural character of her mission. Thus God had protected the Valois at the darkest moment of their decline, as he had continued to do in the course of the recent victories; for it was spread abroad that miracles and marvels had attended the campaigns in Normandy and Guienne.

But prestige was not everything. The price of victory often withers its fruits in advance. For France as a whole the Hundred Years' War had been an immense trial, from which she emerged weakened and worn and incapable for centuries of resuming her former position. Gone was the peaceful hegemony which the last Capetians, though with limited resources, had exercised over a Europe even less well equipped. The world had not stopped evolving while Valois and Lancastrian clashed; it reappeared different and more resistant to French influence.

The material impoverishment of France was patent. All the fighting, all the plundering, all the epidemics had greatly reduced both the population and its capacity for production. This calamity was not everywhere equally irremediable. There were regions comparatively untouched, such as Languedoc in the south, the Central Plateau and, outside the royal domain, Brittany and Burgundy, which, while it had not managed to recover from its severe blood-letting in 1348, had not on the whole suffered any further loss of population. Here recovery could take place in fairly favourable conditions. Before the end of the century travellers extolled the prosperity of these regions, which were public granaries by comparison with the more devastated provinces. But the district of the middle Loire, Normandy, Ile-de-France, and Champagne, in other words the heart of the kingdom and the cradle of the monarchy, remained in a state of prostration very much longer. In 1461, when Louis XI, on the announcement of his father's death, left the rich plain of Flanders to be crowned at Rheims and enter his capital, all he saw around him was ruin and desolation. Ten years of peace had not sufficed to heal the scars of a ravaged countryside.

For it was the rural economy which, as always in such cases, had suffered the most. The sanctimonious tone of letters of remission and the startling statements of the chroniclers, usually to be taken with so much reserve, are fully corroborated by the irrefutable testimony of contemporary records. Some districts were practically deserted; their inhabitants were either dead or had fled from epidemics or on the approach of *routiers*. Once the danger had passed, the more courageous returned, but in such small numbers that villages once prosperous now counted only a few families. Farming was so diminished that it threatened to be insufficient for feeding the towns, in which scarcity of food and the high cost of living endangered the wretched workpeople. Such a situation impoverished all those who lived on the land, and especially the lords, who found their rents reduced to nothing by the encroachments of heath and waste land.

In every province, once the war was over, vigorous measures of recovery were put in hand to restore ruined estates, encourage the revival of farming and review rents. Charles VII's detailed ordinances about the administration of the royal domain played a part in this task of reconstruction. Similar steps were taken by all the great landed proprietors, lay and ecclesiastical. The efforts of John of Bourbon, Abbot of Cluny, which a lucky preservation of archives has enabled us to study, doubtless did not stand alone. Everywhere an attempt was made to attract the peasants by the regrouping of tenures, the reduction of rents, the commutation of the most burdensome labour services into payments in cash, sometimes even the grant of settlement gratuities, which the lord hoped to recover from future rent. There is no denying that this policy led to definite results. They might indeed have been more rapid, but this revival of farming did not promise returns on a scale sufficiently attractive to encourage a great increase of population. The burden of taxation, especially heavy for the 'poor ploughman', increased continually until the death of Louis XI, and this inevitably put a brake upon the recovery of the countryside. Perhaps we should also take account of the fact that the middle class, which progressively acquired the seigneurial estates, were less liberal than the former landowning class towards their tenants. With all the arrogance of upstarts, they demanded strict payment of rents and dues, took defaulting peasants to court, and in short worked against their own interests, if they had properly understood them.

Yet there still remain in the French countryside indelible signs of the contemporary revival in the form of religious and civil buildings, churches, manors, and dwelling houses which bear witness to the fever for construction which seized upon the country once it was freed from the century-long scourge. True, building had never stopped, not even during the darkest periods, especially in the towns where the economic crisis was less severely felt. It was indeed during the first third of the fifteenth century, amid the disasters of the foreign and civil wars, that the characteristic style of the late fourteenth century, the last phase of the pure Gothic with its graceful and slender piers and vaulting, its large light stained-glass windows with their delicate tracery and its rather formal decorative sculpture developed into the freer and more robust style which flowered until the triumph of the Italian Renaissance. We are not very well informed about the influences which enabled French Gothic to acquire fresh life for more than a century; it might have been the example of English architecture, already evolving into a less rigid style, which impressed some architect in Anglo-Burgundian France whence the fashion spread to other parts of the kingdom. But, whatever the cause, side by side with the increasing complexity of the vaulting with its sharp groins and prismatic profiles, which had given a dominantly linear character to all architectural ornament, including the angular folds of the figure draperies and the conventional character of the floral patterns, there developed a more exuberant style with naturalistic ornament, curving profiles, less rigid foliage and drapery, while the tracery assumed those swelling and flame-like forms which have given this type of Gothic its name of 'flamboyant'. The first signs of this renewed vitality in architecture and decoration can be found in the towns long before 1450. Rouen, Troyes, and Bourges, to mention only three places, have preserved charming examples of it. Once peace was restored, it triumphed everywhere, even in the smallest villages, where a regular fever of reconstruction made haste to restore ruins, to reconstruct dilapidated buildings in accordance with the taste of the time, and give the wealthy more comfortable and spacious dwellings than the fortresses in which they had sheltered during the storm. More sober and less exuberant in country churches than in the towns, it adapted itself locally to provincial taste and sometimes gave birth to regular schools of architecture which, as in Brittany, enjoyed long and prosperous lives.

The towns on the whole had suffered less than the countryside. Their populations, sometimes much reduced, lived with plenty of elbow-room within walls too big for them, where the area without buildings left room for gardens, orchards, and fields. In some cases the fall in population was partly offset by an influx of people who had fled from the countryside and become used to town life. Despite sieges, fines, and plundering, the insatiable demands of the tax-collectors and the insecurity of the roads, trade had never ceased to enrich the burgesses and in spite of vexatious and restricting regulations, the craftsmen were still prosperous. Thanks to the restoration of peace, the towns of Champagne, Picardy, and Normandy, the capital itself, and, to a lesser extent, Bordeaux very soon regained the rate of their past production and commerce. A new era of prosperity opened for the towns of the Loire, especially Tours, which were enriched by the prolonged stays of the court. During the past century and a half the cloth-making industry had been largely decentralized and was no longer the exclusive possession of the Low Countries. Finally trade between different towns became active as the security of exchanges increased, enriching money-changers, bankers, and the shadiest of financiers.

But this revival of activity should not mislead us. In the commercial competition in which all the countries of Europe now took part, France's share was very much smaller than it had been before the long trial she had just experienced. Flanders, Artois, and Burgundy were no longer integral parts of the kingdom, and their wealth, greatly increased since 1450, did not profit the king or his subjects. The routes of international trade, which had formerly crossed the Capetian provinces, had definitely deserted them. From Florence and Venice they crossed the central Alps, brought prosperity to the fairs at Geneva, which Lyons never managed to rival seriously, then crossed southern Germany, a regular paradise for international banking, and, by way of the Rhineland, ended at Antwerp, whose rise now eclipsed the fading fame of Bruges. The French fairs, which multiplied through a kind of artificial emulation, took part only remotely and indirectly in this European development, from which the king's subjects were too often excluded.

Nothing better illustrates this illusory and, in short, inferior standing of the Valois kingdom than the meteoric career of Jacques Cœur, who has too often been regarded as the forerunner of an imaginary prosperity, whereas his powerlessness to create anything new and lasting is apparent. It is true that this son of a Bourges furrier, illiterate by enterprising, was the first in date of those merchant adventurers who made their way even into the king's councils. After him, Louis XI's court was full of them. Master of the mint to the king at Bourges, and then Argentier, in other words keeper of the royal jewels and furniture, and entrusted with fiscal and diplomatic missions, he made use of the favour of those in power mainly to promote his own fortunes. In two spheres he seems to have been an innovator. He was given a concession to work the silver-bearing lead mines of Lyonnais, which he believed to be full of rich veins. He flung him-

self enthusiastically into maritime trade, with the object of linking Montpellier directly with the fabulous wealth of the Levant. When he pros-
pected the mines, he realized that a fortune awaited the man who could
throw a fresh supply of bullion upon a world thirsting for gold and silver
and suffering from progressive monetary anaemia. Unfortunately the
veins in Lyonnais were poor and unremunerative – they were abandoned
after his fall – while at the same time through systematic working of the
silver mines of Styria the house of Habsburg was building up a fortune
which alone explains its astonishing rise.

In the sphere of Mediterranean trade Cœur's error of judgement was
no less great. Seeking to wrest the monopoly of Levantine trade from
Venice and Genoa, he fitted out and chartered a little flotilla – half a
dozen vessels – which with considerable exaggeration has been called
'France's first great mercantile fleet'. Let us ignore the modesty of its
beginning: one must start somewhere. But was Jacques Cœur right in
launching his ships in the Mediterranean? Faithful to a tradition five
centuries old, he believed that Alexandria and Cyprus would always
remain the wide-open doors of the Oriental warehouses, those inexhaust-
ible markets for silk and spices. He did not realize that, with the menacing
advance of the Ottoman Turks this spring was on the point of drying up.
He had the excuse that he was not alone in making this mistake, which
was repeated by his successors, Louis XI's counsellors. But whereas, at the
start of the fifteenth century bold Norman sailors explored the Canaries
and founded a fleeting colonial kingdom there, the lure of the Mediterranean subsequently led to the abandonment of Atlantic adventures.
When the sailors of Dieppe resumed them, in the very last years of the
century, they had been outstripped by others bolder than themselves. With
America in the hands of the Spaniards and the rounding of Africa achieved
by the Portuguese, all that was left to France was the crumbs from the
table and, here again, a humiliating situation. All this was foreshadowed
in Jacques Cœur's enterprises. For the rest, his resounding fall in 1451, his
imprisonment, his escape and finally his early death in Chios in 1456
swallowed up his fortune and frustrated his efforts.

But even though materially impoverished, did the French monarchy
emerge from the crisis stronger in the political sphere? In this respect its
definite gains seemed more obvious, though they were offset by some
weaknesses. Unquestionably the war enabled the kingdom to perfect its
administrative structure and to change, more quickly than if it had not
been impelled by military and fiscal exigencies, from a feudal monarchy to
that State, at once paternal, authoritarian and tyrannical, which was the
France of Louis XI. Despite crises, defeats, peasant risings, revolts of the
towns and the princes, the Valois had reached their goal. They had evaded
any tutelage, such as that of the Estates under John the Good or that of the
princes more recently. They had repelled any reform imposed from outside; but, at the right moment, the monarchy had managed to reform itself

on its own account, supervise its officials through themselves, and definitely increase the efficiency of the machinery of administration, without surrendering any of its power or giving its subjects the impression that they were more oppressed than before. Events had finally hastened the process of evolution whose main stages I have noted and which I need not recapitulate.

But the strength of its institutions does not by itself explain the popularity of a government. It forms its framework, but does not give it a soul. Thanks to his prestige, Saint Louis had been able to do without government departments, graded staffs, and supreme courts. Because they had swarms of officials at their command Charles VII and Louis XI were not necessarily better obeyed than the saintly king. The invaluable support which they received as a legacy of the Hundred Years' War was that of national feeling, which now and for centuries afterwards crystallized around the sovereign in a loyalty to the monarchy stronger than the fidelity of vassalage had ever been.

This feeling, as I have pointed out, still remained very vague at the dawn of the fifteenth century and even seemed to vanish completely at the time of the Treaty of Troyes. But experience soon brought it to maturity. The constant campaigns, the ceaseless raids of the *routiers* and, above all, the prolonged occupation of some provinces sufficed to effect this mental transformation, of which the last phase of the war provides any number of striking examples. The people – or would it still be too soon to speak of the nation? – learned to know and to hate the foreigner, because they could see the foreigner established in their midst. There is no example in the whole history of the world of a military occupation encouraging understanding between victor and vanquished. Hence arose those new expressions, with a strangely modern ring, which were employed in the entourage of the King of Bourges. The subjects who remained loyal to Charles were 'true Frenchmen', good Frenchmen. The others were 'renegade Frenchmen', 'English Frenchmen'. A deep-seated intuition branded them as traitors, despite all the legal arguments that could be advanced in their favour. What did the fiction of a regular dynastic succession count, what did an administration which remained French count, beside these foreign soldiers who spoke a different language, had different ways and, despite all precautions, behaved as conquerors?

So this national feeling, brought to birth in a negative fashion by common hatred of the English invader, carried with it a positive corollary, which was the devotion of the subjects to their legitimate sovereign. Loyalty to the monarchy, already so strong in the last Capetian century, was only reinforced by misfortune and ruination. It was supported by the proceedings of the lawyers, concerned to glorify the sovereign in the course of preserving his kingdom. To the disinheritance of which Charles was made the victim by the argument of the Treaty of Troyes they replied with a new theory of the crown, which foreshadowed that of the modern

State. The crown, or in other words the sum total of domainial estates, feudal rights, and royal prerogatives which the sovereign enjoyed, became in their eyes an inalienable inheritance of which the monarch was only the trustee, as he was already the guardian of the law and the dispenser of justice. Public law became separate and distinct from private law. As the servant of the people the king thus acquired an unquestioned authority which strengthened the old monarchical cult already so widespread under the last Capetians. In this respect as in so many others, legal theories were the reflection of changes in public feeling.

As the personification and symbol of the nation, the monarchy was all the stronger because no organized opposition could now be based on the propertied classes. We have already noted the extreme impoverishment of the nobility and the progressive disappearance of their most cherished privileges under the combined pressure of economic necessity and royal bureaucracy. To maintain their position they had only one course left: to enter the service of the king or the princes. It was they who formed the nucleus of the permanent army and applied for administrative posts, perhaps in the hope of obtaining positions at court or in the king's council. Thus the taming process began. When they followed a prince in a revolt in any given region, it was less with the desire to fight the sovereign than to sell their services to a protector. A bounty wisely distributed was usually enough to disband the rebels and attract them into the king's service.

Even more than the nobility, the clergy now found themselves placed in strict dependence on the royal power. They had counted on taking advantage first of the schism and then of the conciliar quarrels to shake off the tutelage of the Roman See, restore the 'liberties' of the Gallican Church and free themselves from the burden of papal taxation. On the whole Charles VII supported their claims and in frequent assemblies consulted them about the attitude to be taken towards the Council. The assembly at Bourges in 1438 ratified certain decrees of Basle, abolished annates and restored freedom of election to benefices, but did not deny the Pope all authority over the clergy. Its decisions were promulgated in the Pragmatic Sanction, the constitutive charter of the Gallican theory. But the king had no intention of breaking with Rome. When the Council of Basle, persisting in their revolt, instigated a fresh schism, he refused to recognize the anti-Pope Felix V – formerly Amadeus VIII, Duke of Savoy – and even worked actively from 1446 to 1449 to obtain the intruder's resignation and induce the Council to submit to the Roman authority.

He wanted still less to let the Church govern itself autonomously. As during the two previous withdrawals of obedience in 1398 and 1407, all the power denied to the Pope reverted to the king. The Sanction allowed the canons to elect their dignitaries; but it enjoined them to take account of the 'benign requests' of the lay power. It relieved the clergy of a large part of Roman taxation, but only to subject them all the more to that of the king. In practice the ordinance was imperfectly enforced. Charles did not refrain from asking Rome, or allowing the Curia, to fill benefices to the advantage of his protégés. He opposed papal decisions only when they were injurious to the royal interests. Whether there was agreement or conflict, it was almost always the monarchy that had the last word. More than ever the bishops and the higher dignitaries were recruited among the king's counsellors, his relations and his friends. He was assured of their subservience, which was even more strict than in the past.

But there remained some obstacles to the king's authority, and their danger was likely to increase with the progress of time. The civil and foreign wars had quickened provincial nationalisms, and here and there set back the advance of loyalty to the monarchy. Some provinces were grudging in their acceptance of the rule of Charles the Victorious. Normandy, fiercely anti-English though it was, clung to its provincial privileges and its judicial autonomy, murmured against the levying of royal taxation from outside and demanded confirmation of the Charter to the Normans. It would have been glad to be governed by an appanaged prince, who could stand up against royal centralization. Louis XI was to learn this to his cost when the conspirators of the 'Common Weal' demanded that he should hand it over to the nonentity Charles of France and its people welcomed Breton forces in opposition to the king. Guienne was still more recalcitrant. All the Gascon nobility, who had served enthusiastically in the English war, held aloof from the sovereign who had conquered it. It was not until the next century that its captains and adventurers entered the king's service.

Outside the royal domain opposition was more emphatic. In Anjou and Bourbonnais the people still set loyalty to their princes before obedience to the king. Brittany proudly maintained its habit of autonomy. Though temporarily loyal vassals, its dukes had their own church policy, their own diplomacy, which they insisted on keeping independent of those of the sovereign. When Constable Richmond succeeded his nephews in 1448 and became Duke Arthur II, it was upright and with sword at side that he paid homage to Charles VI, refusing to make the genuflexion which would imply liege homage. Two generations of Burgundian rule had sufficed to make some provinces, such as Artois, enthusiastically devoted to their duke. They opposed any royal intervention and blindly obeyed their foreign masters, Austrian or Spanish, and it was not until Louis XIV's conquests that they recovered the feeling that they were French.

So the provincial nationalisms dangerously supported the activity of the princes, a danger against which the State was not yet able to safeguard itself. The goal remained unchanged. It was still a question whether the monarchy would remain independent and strong, or be controlled by a 'polyarchy' of great lords eager for power and wealth. By now their selfish ambition was masked beneath altruistic proclamations. To relieve the people by reducing taxation, abolish the arbitrary power of the royal officials, demand the summoning of the Estates: such was the programme they outlined to stir up public opinion in their favour. The demands of the conspirators at Nevers in 1442 foreshadowed the 'Common Weal' of 1465. But as long as Charles VII lived they did not dare to regroup. The stern punishment inflicted in 1455 on John V, Count of Armagnac, whose territory was occupied by royal troops, and the example of the trial of the Duke of Alençon, who had resumed his treasonable intrigues with the English, was sentenced to death and then reprieved and imprisoned in the castle of Loches, sufficed to damp their ardour. Above all, before rebelling they awaited a breach between the king and his cousin of Burgundy, which was regarded as imminent.

For Philip the Good struck all of them as the inevitable head of any princely coalition. During his reign the Burgundian State had reached the peak of its power. Dynastic strokes of luck, cleverly contrived or exploited, had made him master of the rich Dutch inheritance of the Wittelsbachs and the important duchy of Brabant. In Luxemburg he had ousted, though not without difficulty, the last representatives of the house of Bohemia. The princes of the Rhineland were his clients. His bastard son and his cousin held the ecclesiastical principalities of Utrecht and Liège. This collector of territory controlled a great and rich domain, which extended from the Somme to Friesland and from the English Channel to the Moselle. His mosaic of principalities still lacked the cohesion which could be given it only by strong central institutions. But they were now taking shape, especially in the financial sphere, and after 1450 Brussels already had the air of the capital of the Low Countries.

Almost all these territorial annexations had been made at the expense of the Empire. It did not follow, however, that Philip had become a German prince. Towards the Imperial power he preserved an attitude of haughty independence and refused to allow the link of vassalage which bound him to the colourless Frederick III of Habsburg to find expression in practice. In 1447, when the Emperor, in order to obtain his help against the Swiss, proposed to elevate into a kingdom some of the territories which Philip possessed beyond the Scheldt, such as Friesland and Brabant, the duke laid down exorbitant conditions for his acceptance of this offer. The kingdom must comprise all his imperial domains and carry with it suzerainty over all the Rhineland and Lotharingian principalities which he did not possess directly. If he did not wish to commit himself too closely with the Empire, it was because his eyes were still fixed on Paris, where his predecessors had lorded it. His imperial possessions, of which he meant to remain the absolute master, were to serve him only as a fresh source of strength for the achievement of his French ambitions.

But, far from satisfying these underlying ambitions, the King of France kept his cousin of Burgundy remote from all French affairs. Some clauses of the Treaty of Arras, the very ones which Philip had most at heart, had never been fulfilled. The murderers at Montereau remained unpunished; the soul of John the Fearless got no help from the pious foundations which Charles had promised to institute; the royal officials continued to treat Burgundy and Artois as fiefs of the crown; they took proceedings there freely and notified appeals to the Paris *Parlement*. In 1451 the king took advantage of a revolt by the workers of Ghent, though without success, to demand from Philip restitution of the towns on the Somme, for which he did not now propose even to pay the stipulated indemnity. Busy with the preparation of a great crusade against the Ottoman Turks to which, as a faithful heir of the visionary Valois, he had devoted himself since 1454, the Duke of Burgundy saw France slipping from his grasp. Still worse, he was afraid lest the king's ever-increasing hostility should transform itself into open war. He was not even sure that, in such a duel with the monarchy, he would necessarily get the upper hand.

In 1456 an opportunity presented itself to him to pave the way for a better future and take his revenge for his present humiliations. Driven from Dauphiné by his father Charles, who was exasperated by his treasonable intrigues, the Dauphin Louis sought shelter in Burgundian territory. Philip hesitated to welcome him, lest he should precipitate an unequal contest. When he finally installed Louis at Genappe in Brabant, it was with the object of turning him into a protégé who, more than anyone else, would later restore him to the position in Paris once held by John the Fearless. Henceforth the exile and his host eagerly awaited the king's death, which would bring both of them power and wealth. Of all the dangers which beset Charles's recovered and reunited kingdom, the Burgundian problem was the one that loomed most darkly over its immediate future.

3. ENGLAND AND THE TWO ROSES

THE DANGER would have been still more urgent if England had been in a position to resume the struggle, ally herself with disgruntled Burgundy and once more call in question all the achievements of the Valois. It was not unreasonable, after 1453, to contemplate this development as quite close at hand, though it did not in fact occur until the reign of Louis XI. For it is a simplified view of traditional history to regard England under Henry VI as exhausted by her continental reverses, and the civil war in which she was engaged for a generation as an inevitable result of her military defeat. Quite on the contrary, the Lancastrian kingdom remained potentially formidable. Morally it had emerged from the struggle enhanced in the eyes of Christian Europe and, what was more important, in its own. The memory of past victory remained more green than that of recent defeat. Public opinion, as parliamentary petitions and the chroniclers' commentaries alike bear witness, still remembered Henry V's epic, rallied infallibly to anyone who promised to renew the war, and in short nurtured a dangerous spirit of revenge. In the course of the struggle the English had become conscious of their strength, of which they had been unaware in the previous century.

Moreover, their national cohesion was reinforced by linguistic unity, which was now strongly established. Despite the sovereigns' marriages, the nobility, the civil service, and even the court had gradually forgotten French. Catherine of France and then Margaret of Anjou appeared as foreigners, speaking a different language and incapable of understanding English mentality. Since Edward III's long reign the courts had already almost ceased to hear cases in the Anglo-Norman jargon. Under Henry IV the staffs of the privy seal and the signet had started to draft documents in the national language. French had progressively disappeared, to such an extent that the clerks had forgotten its use. After 1450, for the few documents still issued in the enemy's language the services of special officials had to be employed, survivors of the Norman administration, who were called 'secretaries of the French tongue'.

Materially the country's exhaustion was much less deep-seated than that of France. The people had been subjected to crushing burdens which in the end they had refused to bear, thus hastening the final disaster on the continent. But, apart from epidemics, their vital strength remained unaffected. The end of the war, by relieving the working classes of their fiscal and military burdens, should have enabled economic progress, which had slowed down for the past two generations, to quicken its pace. This

favourable development affected even the rural sphere, traditionally slug-
gish and unresponsive to change. Here the losses due to periodical recur-
rence of the plague had been made good fairly fast. Only some regions
remained partly devastated as a result of war, which earned them repeated
remission of taxes, especially in the counties on the Scottish border. Elsewhere the position of tenants improved rapidly. Manorial cultivation, so
out-of-date at the dawn of modern times, ended by disappearing through
division or transformation of the seigniorial demesne. Individual and
collective manumissions and redemptions skilfully obtained had abolished
performance of labour and made servile villeinage a rare and anachronistic survival. This increased the prosperity of the free tenants, who were
protected by long-term leases. The lords, deriving their incomes from the
soil, did not lose by these changes. They were eager to improve the yield
of their lands. Almost everywhere they tried to eliminate collective grazing
or common rights, which produced roving livestock of poor quality, to get
common lands into their own hands, to increase and enclose pasture land
and to drain marshland. Such was the process of 'enclosure', which reached
its peak under the last Tudor sovereigns and gave the English landscape
that wooded appearance which it still retains. All this was not achieved
smoothly. Political disturbances, growing disorder and bad harvests
created many anxieties for the landed proprietors. The letters of the Paston
family, small squires with estates in Norfolk, teem with vivid and picturesque testimony to this effect. But they also demonstrate the importance
and vitality of the rural economy on which the nation's prosperity still
largely depended.

To this was added the recent strides of industry in the towns. In the
course of the past century the ups-and-downs of the war and the sudden
changes in policy and diplomacy had disturbed trade relations with the
Low Countries and made the export of wool to the continental looms very
uncertain. Under pressure of economic necessity the wish earlier expressed
in theory by Edward III's Parliaments had come true. A cloth-making
industry had sprung to life in some towns, as well as in rural districts in
Essex, Wiltshire, or Yorkshire, encouraged by the exceptional quality of
English woollens and worsteds and by the technical skill of Dutch craftsmen, who were attracted by the grant of privileges. Even before 1450 the
export of wool was progressively diminishing in favour of finished cloth,
whose fineness was such that continental merchants bought it eagerly. In
response to the complaints of the Flemish and Brabançon weavers, and
despite the opposing interests of the Antwerp merchants, Philip the Good
repeatedly had to forbid the importation into his territory of English
cloth, which was manufactured in Bristol and many other towns. It was a
waste of effort. The supremacy of English cloth became so well established that the looms of the Low Countries, overwhelmed by its competition, gradually stopped working. To avoid dying altogether, they took
to production of lower quality, made use of short Spanish wool, and threw

serge on the market in a quantity which made up for its poorness of quality.

The result for England was a remarkable development of foreign trade. For a long time foreigners had enjoyed a monopoly in this sphere, which was favoured by the monarchy, anxious not to offend these indulgent moneylenders. Accordingly Edward III had granted foreign merchants the right to be treated by his courts like his own subjects, and the process of naturalization whereby they were regarded as nationals enabled them to recover their debts all the more easily. An exorbitant privilege had allowed the Hanseatic merchants, though not without violent opposition, to maintain their consular jurisdiction in London. The hatred of the people, so roughly displayed in the peasant risings of 1381 and 1450, piled up against these foreigners who flaunted their wealth so insolently. Above all, the profits of native industry and the prosperity of internal trade, handled by the craft guilds, had created a wealthy class of English capitalists, who were eager to enrich themselves still more in international dealings. The last-born of the London corporations, the Mercers Guild, from which the Guild of Merchant Adventurers later sprang, gradually eliminated the foreign traders and gave the country its maritime vocation.

The economic development of England was only temporarily halted by the political crisis under the Yorkists: but on the other hand this crisis threatened to destroy the strong royal administration on which the island kingdom had hitherto prided itself. The crisis came in 1450, on the morrow of Cade's rising, and at once crystallized around a dynastic and personal problem. It was a remote sequel to the Lancastrian usurpation by which in 1399 Henry IV had climbed the steps of the throne without taking account of the claim of Mortimer which had now devolved by marriage upon the powerful house of York. So long as the dynasty prospered its legitimacy was not called in question. Its continental defeats barely shook it. But personal quarrels and struggles for influence revived the ambitions and hopes of its enemies. Henry IV's descendants were almost entirely extinct. Clarence, Bedford, and Gloucester had died without leaving children. The last hope of the line, Henry VI, though married since 1444, had as yet no heir. Henry was a backward young man, extremely pious, of poor health, lacking in will power and probably in intelligence. A heavy burden of heredity weighed upon him. In August 1453 his mind gave way, as that of his grandfather Charles VI had done. It was not a violent madness in the case of this pitiful sovereign, but a vacant condition, a state of quiet stupor, which lasted for months before his return, always very briefly, to a semblance of lucidity.

Even before his madness the king was under the absolute domination of his wife. Margaret of Anjou was a foreigner, ambitious, active, and intense, and she knew nothing about English affairs. Brought up in the kingdom of France, where no one opposed the royal authority, she wanted to rule without the counsel of the barons and the advice of Parliament. In her eyes, the Estates of the realm (as Parliament was sometimes called, by analogy with the continental institution) were only a restraint on the royal power, whereas, skilfully utilized, they could increase its strength tenfold. French at heart, she stood for peace and did nothing to wrest from the Valois the provinces recently lost by England. She felt that Formigny and Castillon had definitely closed the Anglo-French quarrel. This was another source of her unpopularity, since public opinion unanimously demanded revenge for these defeats, though it was unready to bear the cost of a fresh war. The more isolated she felt, the more enthusiastically Margaret committed herself to the party which had put her on the throne. This was the clan of the Beauforts, the peace party, led by Somerset, vanquished at Caen but now Constable and all-powerful counsellor. Did the Beauforts aspire still higher? Could not this bastard but legitimatized branch of the Lancastrians hope to repeal the law which banned them from the throne? In this case, if Margaret remained childless, Somerset might aim at the succession to the king. Now that Henry was stricken with madness, he could at least demand the government of the kingdom.

But he found a rival in Richard of York. Grandson through his father of Edmund of Langley, he represented, against the Beauforts, Edward III's legitimate descendants. Through his mother, Anne Mortimer, he inherited the claims which the female line of Lionel of Clarence could have put forward against the Lancastrian usurper. This small, ugly man, wily but irresolute, had long been feeling his way. Since Gloucester's death he had become the leader of the war party. He had been sent in semi-disfavour to govern turbulent Ireland. But in 1450 he asserted himself and used the peasant rising as a pretext for returning to England without seeking permission. He still awaited events and imprudently let Somerset establish himself in power. Then, fearing that his enemy, in order to get rid of him, might indict him of treason, he issued a resounding manifesto against the favourite. But the hostile parties shrank from civil war. By an 'act of grace' which he readily obtained, York received, together with his pardon, a place on the council, which he turned to advantage to prepare for the last campaign in Aquitaine. The king's madness seemed to bring him nearer the throne. But two months later Margaret gave birth to a son, on October 13th 1453, the feast of Saint Edward, after whom the child was named. For the followers of the queen and the Beauforts he was, so to speak, a 'child of miracle'. In the Yorkist camp there were murmurs that this unexpected birth looked illegitimate.

York was no longer heir to the throne: but, as the doyen of the princes of the blood, he could demand the regency. In March 1454 a Parliament belatedly summoned and wholly on his side appointed him Protector of the kingdom. He changed all the ministers and imprisoned Somerset in the Tower. To pacify Margaret her son was created Prince of Wales, which wiped out calumnious charges that he was a bastard. But no compromise between the two parties was now possible. Henceforth in Henry VI's England, as half a century earlier in France, there was the scourge of civil war, the alternation of the parties in power, the raising of armed partisans, pitched battles, legal murders and, from time to time, false reconciliations.

The War of the Roses – the red rose of Lancaster against the white rose of York – is one of the most barren of all the domestic upheavals in England's history. If we considered only the monotonous story of its political and military vicissitudes, we should lose sight of the forces that made it possible, and disregard the circles which it affected and, more important for our purpose, those which it left untouched. It was, in fact, brought about by an aristocracy whose power had gone on growing for a century and who engaged enthusiastically in faction fighting in pursuit of the royal bounty, land, money, and power.

The evil was not of recent date. Throughout the fourteenth century the higher baronage, still numerous on the eve of the Hundred Years' War, had been thinned out by the progressive disappearance of its families. Marriage, inheritance, and royal grants had concentrated all its wealth in a few hands. To Edward II's Parliaments more than a hundred barons had normally been summoned. Under Edward III they scarcely exceeded forty. The richest of them, those who held one or more earldoms, were only a dozen in 1360. Their number did not increase much afterwards. Apart from the batch of 'petty dukes' with which Richard II sought to buy the consent of the baronage to his autocratic *coup d'état* and which created a scandal, the crown was parsimonious with new earldoms and these creations barely offset the disappearance of titles through extinction of the male line.

Conscious of the strength they derived from their small number, this upper aristocracy tended to close their ranks more and more. They relegated to oblivion the poorer nobility: needy tenants-in-chief and under-vassals. They alone had the right to be summoned to Parliament by virtue of their wealthy holdings. There they made up the assembly of 'peers of the realm', an aristocratic and oligarchic transformation of the old feudal council. Thus the 'council in Parliament', once consisting of the chief counsellors, the prelates and the still numerous body of barons, became the 'House of Lords', in which the lords temporal, numbering only about fifty in the period which we have now reached, claimed to dictate their policy to the sovereign, decide in the last resort on all the problems of the day, and turn themselves into a high court which, by the procedure of impeachment and attainder, tried fallen ministers, charged them with treason and imposed sentences that were always severe. Any fresh summons to Parliament was regarded as tantamount to the creation of a peerage, of which the beneficiary and his heirs male could not afterwards be deprived. Gradually the term 'baron', originally applied to all wealthy vassals, was limited solely to peers. It tended to become a title, borne by lords not holding earldoms or duchies.

This concentration of political power was accompanied by a comparable increase in landed wealth. The whole fortune of the Lancastrians derived from the fact that John of Gaunt and his son, through lucky inheritance, had united in their hands the property of several great families: the honours and dignities of the Montforts, the Lancastrian appanage, the estates of the Bohuns, in all five earldoms. In the first half of the fifteenth century, the Yorks had added to Edmund of Langley's scanty appanage the great estates of Clarence in Ireland and of Mortimer on the Welsh marches. There was only a difference of degree between these appanaged princes and the other baronial houses, linked together by manifold marriages. Possession of land was the basis of their power. All of them devoted themselves to extending and strengthening it. In the first place they concentrated their estates, hitherto widely dispersed, into great lordships all in one block. Exchange, purchase, grants from the crown: all these means were employed. Next they improved the administration of their fiefs. All these grandees now had their own households, modelled on that of the sovereign, with their own financial and administrative departments, which enabled them to live luxuriously and uphold their policies. Finally they created their own train of dependents.

Here again the monarchy's imprudent measures were the origin of this 'new feudalism' which threatened to put it in tutelage and destroy its power. To facilitate the recruitment of his army, Edward III had let his great vassals lead larger and larger contingents to it. This saved trouble for the sheriffs, who should have recruited the royal army by counties, but lacked the necessary power of compulsion. So the barons took into their service an ever-growing number of men-at-arms: the retainers who formed the baronial 'retinue'. Henry V's armies had reached the point of being almost exclusively composed of these feudal contingents at the expense of the royal retinue. Needy and greedy, the gentry, hitherto devoted to the monarchy, swarmed into the service of the aristocracy, all the more eagerly because the end of the continental war had deprived them of a lucrative pastime. They were paid by grants of land in return for homage – without realizing that he was chiefly responsible for them, Edward III had tried in vain to limit these subinfeudations – and above all by pensions. Almost all the knightly class had thus become clients of the grandees. They wore their 'livery' and were 'maintained' by them. Too late, at the outset of the civil war, Henry VI's government issued edicts forbidding 'livery and maintenance'. At the least pretext a handful of barons could assemble troops, go to Parliament in arms and impose their will on it.

Few though they were, the group of higher barons could not remain united. They flung themselves into the fight of factions, hoping that victory would enrich them still more at the enemy's expense. The civil war had no deep roots in the country, did not involve political principles or the social structure and did not set one region against another. Its leaders grouped themselves in accordance with their family alliances. Richard of York's wife was Cecily Neville, and around him rallied his Neville brothers-in-law and nephews, the heirs to the earldoms of Salisbury, Warwick, and Kent. Another nephew, the Duke of Norfolk, and another brother-in-law, the Earl of Essex, completed the Yorkist general staff. Somerset, the last male representative of the Beauforts, led the other side. Family ties bound him to the Welshman Owen Tudor, the heir of the Pembrokes. He derived increased strength from the support of the Percies, the earls of Northumberland, once fierce enemies of the dynasty, but now loyal Lancastrians, who brought the northern nobility over to the same side.

Before they disappeared completely in the storm, killing one another off with ever-increasing ruthlessness, this princely aristocracy imperilled the machinery of government and in consequence the royal authority. Under the last Plantagenets and the first Lancastrians the old Anglo-Norman institutions had continued to develop towards growing specialization of the central departments and stricter supervision of local agents. At the centre there were now three well-established departments, whose heads jointly controlled political affairs in the council: the Chancery, in addition to its administrative duties, had become a court of ever greater resort, since it judged in accordance with equity and did not concern itself with the narrow formalism of the other courts of justice. The Exchequer, on the other hand, had gradually lost its judicial powers and become purely a treasury and audit office. Finally the Privy Seal served as a link between the great government departments and the council. Since the middle of Edward III's reign the royal household, far from competing with the great departments of state, supported them in their tasks and complemented their activities. Specializing in the organization of military campaigns, the Wardrobe had created a 'great wardrobe', an equipment store in the city of London, and a 'privy wardrobe', a reserve of arms and ammunition in the Tower. A new secretariat had come into being in the household since the Privy Seal had been removed from it. This was the office of the Signet, whose head, known as 'secretary' since Richard II's reign, was the king's closest counsellor, so much so that in the following century the Tudors raised him to the rank of 'Principal Secretary of State', the ancestor of the modern ministers of the crown. In the person of Thomas Bekington, Bishop of Bath, Henry VI had a particularly competent secretary, a good administrator, and a shrewd politician and diplomat. In the provinces the monarchy, as in France, had multiplied commissions of officials, entrusted with temporary duties, directly responsible to the king and more malleable than the old local organisms, the county courts and the sheriffs. These were the tax inspectors and collectors, investigators or magistrates entrusted to '*oyer et terminer*' specific cases, and justices of the peace and of 'labourers' who enforced the old legislation about the maintenance of peace and the labour market.

But, once the political struggles around the weak Henry VI became acute, one has the impression that all this machinery worked in a vacuum. Were there, as formerly in France under the princes, a multiplication of offices, too frequent purges, a plundering of the State revenues? We cannot say so definitely. The very mass of the administrative archives preserved by the English departments of State has hitherto slowed down their systematic examination. Discouraged by the scope of their task, students have not yet been able to inform us adequately about the working of Lancastrian and Yorkist administration. But some indications lead us to suppose that all these offices, all these officials, all these judges, all this red tape did not result in making the royal will respected, keeping the country submissive or securing sufficient revenue. The Exchequer, hampered by routine and out-of-date methods, had no power to discipline dishonest accountants. The yield of taxation was low, expenditure was not controlled either closely or quickly enough, a budget could not be forecast or a balance-sheet drawn up. In the courts a ponderous procedure prolonged cases indefinitely and delayed verdicts, which could not be enforced if the defendant defaulted. The 'king's peace' was only too often an empty phrase. Force and violence and private war multiplied, and picturesque or grim echoes of them have come down to us alike in official letters of pardon or outlawry and in the Paston letters.

But we are not to suppose that the country reverted to anarchy in the wild escapade into which a belligerent aristocracy had dragged it. Apart from those to whom war was a profession, the great lords, the needy squires, the mercenaries of all ranks, no one was interested in the dynastic struggle. The urban communities asked only to preserve their wealth and carry on their trade in peace maintained by a competent government. In the countryside too the people lamented their lost tranquillity. Even in the royal council the lawyers weighed the rules of good government, extolled the monarchy, and praised the merits of the existing institutions, whose good working, temporarily interrupted, could be resumed if a stronger and more capable king ascended the throne. Sir John Fortescue, first chief justice of the court of King's Bench and then chancellor to the house of Lancaster, whom he followed into exile before joining the triumphant Yorkists, in his Latin and English treatises managed to reconcile the teaching of Roman law and the lessons of history with traditional custom and sing the praises of a well-ordered monarchy limited by the institution of Parliament as the expression of the will of the people. In his *De laudibus legum Angliae* and *The Governance of England* he did not desire to change the customary constitution or modify the existing laws. But the spectacle of the prevailing disorder led him to want better methods of government and in the first place a strengthening of the royal authority. It was essential to restore the king's choice of his own officers, prevent the

baronial dynasties from increasing their wealth by marriage among themselves, stop alienations of the royal domain and replace all influence in
the council in the hands of professional officials.

This generally felt desire for internal peace, which would be secured
by a strong government, worked in the long run in favour of the royalist
cause. It was because Richard of York and after him his son Edward of
March seemed capable of achieving this programme that their party
gained numerous adherents, despite the weakness of their dynastic claims.
In the course of his reign of twenty-two years, though it was disturbed
by many a revolt and even interrupted in the middle by a short exile,
Edward IV, who ascended the throne in 1461, laid the foundations of
that authoritarian monarchy from which, soon afterwards, emerged the
absolutism of the Tudors. First came the decline of Parliament as a
political organism. The lords temporal, less and less numerous – barely
thirty by 1485 – remained without any constructive programme. Under
their influence and thanks to their patronage knights of the shires and
even members for the towns were now nominated: hence the appearance
as candidates of squires and lawyers anxious to further their interests at
Westminster. The government of the day succeeded in suppressing any
opposition in the Commons by insisting upon the election of a Speaker
of its own choice. It was the king who now submitted his own legislative
plans for the assembly's approval, instead of turning into statutes the texts
of petitions presented by the lower chamber. On the whole, Parliament was
left with no function other than ratifying the last results of the civil war by
sentencing the vanquished to death, banishment, or confiscation and
granting subsidies to the victors. It was summoned more and more rarely:
in all only six times throughout Edward IV's reign, not counting the
Lancastrian Parliament which proclaimed Henry VI 're-adepted' in
1470–1.

To increase the power of the executive, hasten the processes of justice
and secure the monarchy's financial independence: such were the objectives of the dynasty of York. It did not last long enough to see them fully
reached; but it went some way towards their achievement. It was during
this period that the council developed its authority as an instrument of
government, and ceased to be a consultative committee of barons and
officials. One section of it sat permanently at Westminster. Another accompanied the king wherever he went. Others again were sent on occasion
to disturbed provinces. This was the origin of the Council of the North
and the Council of Wales, whose services the Tudors utilized to the full.
In the sphere of law, equity took precedence of the common law. It was
in 1474 that the chancellor delivered the first judgement in equity inde-
pendently of any intervention by the council. Litigants thronged his court
especially in the sphere of commercial law, in which the slowness of
procedure by writ could not be tolerated. On its side, the council supplanted Parliament in the punishment of political crimes. Its professional

jurists, sitting in the Star Chamber, now began to pronounce harsh sentences which could be justified only by 'reason of State'. For the examination of petitions addressed directly to the sovereigns there appeared the embryo of a court of petitions similar to that which functioned in the household of the kings of France.

Finally, the Yorkist dynasty tried to increase and stabilize its resources. It was because he found advantage in the pension – bashfully called 'tribute' in English documents – offered by Louis XI at Picquigny that Edward IV hastily abandoned his alliance with Burgundy. Both before and after this shameful transaction he employed and abused free gifts and forced loans known as 'benevolences'. Arbitrary though it was, this financial system aroused only moderate protests, because it corrected the injustice of the traditional taxes by weighing most heavily on the merchant class, which was the richest but hitherto the most lightly taxed.

4. THE IMPOSSIBILITY OF PEACE

So WE need not await the accession of the Tudors in 1485, but rather go back to that of the Yorks in 1461, to discern the first features of a new England, conscious of her wealth and her strength, endowed with renovated institutions, and on the way towards a system of government scarcely less authoritarian than that of the Valois. Henceforth, despite grave but fleeting disturbances, she might have resumed the continental policy of the Plantagenets and the Lancastrians and, by a fresh invasion, have reopened the Anglo-French conflict.

This would have been all the easier for her because no peace treaty, or even any truce, had ratified the reconquest by Charles VII of the last fragments of the Lancastrian empire. Exposed to Yorkist attacks, the Beaufort party, by the mere fact of its devotion to peace, dare not take the initiative in opening negotiations which would at once discredit it in the eyes of patriotic opinion. So one of the two factions which alternated in power between 1453 and 1461 could not, and the other would not, make peace with France. With Burgundy it was permissible for them to make agreements and consent to such suspensions of arms as would favour maritime trade. But towards Charles VII they must be all the more uncompromising because they lacked the means to pursue the war.

To break this deadlock the King of France found himself forced to take the offensive. He could attack Calais, stronghold of the Yorkists; or he could attempt a landing on the coast of England; or again he could sell his alliance to one or other of the English factions in return for acceptance of his peace terms. He tried these three courses one after the other; but not one of them yielded the anticipated results. In face of the veto of the Duke of Burgundy and the intrigues of the Dauphin who had taken refuge at his court, it was impossible for Charles to attack Calais with the large army he had concentrated in Normandy in the summer of 1456. As for a descent on England, a daring raid by Peter of Brézé on Sandwich in the following year led only to a strong counter-attack by the enemy upon Harfleur and the island of Ré and an unsuccessful naval engagement off Calais.

Nevertheless, on the eve of their decisive struggle, both the English factions sought the support and alliance of the King of France, just as Armagnacs and Burgundians had once done with Henry IV. Charles's sympathies naturally lay with his niece Margaret of Anjou and the peace party. But, if he committed himself definitely to their side, he ran the risk of a conflict with Philip the Good, an avowed supporter of

Warwick. He knew that the Dauphin, in his impatience to reign, was urging the duke to break with his father, and even inciting the English to take the offensive against the Valois kingdom and sending troops to support the Yorkist cause on the English battlefields. To commit himself definitely might mean renewing the Anglo-Burgundian alliance against him. So Charles shrank from allying himself with the Lancastrians and the Scots, just at the moment when such a coalition might have averted the civil war; and at the same time he rejected Warwick's overtures. All he did was send agents to advise Margaret, and, when the Lancastrian cause seemed to be triumphant and Richard of York perished at Wakefield (December 30th 1460), he granted free passage into his kingdom to his niece's followers. The final victory of Edward of York, in March 1461, marked the ruin of his hopes. On both sides of the Channel there were now preparations for war. At the very moment when each side feared a breach between Valois and Burgundy, a renewal of the Anglo-French conflict seemed to be imminent.

This was an urgent danger which must at least be postponed. When he became king on his father's death (July 22nd 1461), Louis XI did not rest until he had averted this formidable Anglo-Burgundian coalition, from which the Hundred Years' War might spring to life again, with all its fearful train of invasion, devastation, defeat, and territorial losses. To ward off the danger he applied all the resources of his subtle mind, his crafty calculation, his shameless effrontery. Here as elsewhere, in trying to be over-subtle, he sometimes lost his way in impenetrable coverts, from which only sheer good luck extricated him. The story of his intrigues and his mistakes may seem to lie largely outside our subject, since it involved all the political and diplomatic problems of this disturbed period: the princely coalitions, the death-struggle against the house of Burgundy, ambitions in Spain, intrigues in Italy. Yet all of it forms part of the Hundred Years' War, constituting its essential epilogue and foreshadowing its more remote results.

The first act of the new sovereign, hitherto an avowed supporter of the White Rose, was to become reconciled with the fallen Lancastrians. Henry VI was a prisoner in the Tower of London. But his wife carried on the struggle bitterly. She found refuge first in Scotland and then in France. Here, in June 1462, the king induced her to conclude a truce for a hundred years. On pain of losing all prestige with her English subjects, she had been unable to recognize either the French conquests or even the Valois's title as king; but this was a real peace except in name. As a more substantial concession, she surrendered Calais, in pledge for a loan of 20,000 *livres*, but with the onus on the French of recapturing it from its Yorkist captains. Once again the opposition of the Duke of Burgundy, whose territory it was necessary to cross, prevented any attack on the fortress. Moreover, the real masters of England, especially Warwick, followed by his protégé Edward IV, punished Louis XI's defection by a renewal of hostilities. The English fleet ravaged the coasts of Saintonge. Meanwhile French forces, led by Peter of Brézé, were dispatched to give help, without much effect, to the Lancastrian partisans on the Scottish border.

Louis XI saw that it would pay him better to come to terms with the Yorkists. Under Philip the Good's auspices, plenipotentiaries of the two kingdoms met at Saint-Omer in September 1463. This conference led to the conclusion of a short truce, at first limited to operations on land, but soon extended to the war at sea, and which could be renewed from year to year. It was a modest success; but Louis XI, always impatient, insisted on exploiting it without delay. He called the Duke of Brittany, Francis II, sharply to order when his subjects failed to respect the truce. Then, great match-maker that he was, he fancied that he could attach the sensual Edward IV to himself by marrying him to his sister-in-law Bona of Savoy. An impulsive act by the English sovereign made this plan miscarry. When his counsellors, headed by Warwick, now won over by the Valois's favours to the cause of reconciliation, pressed him to conclude this marriage, Edward IV had to confess that he was no longer free. He had secretly married a beautiful English widow, Elizabeth Woodville. All her relations had only awaited this declaration to scramble for posts and honours. But at least their intrigues allowed Louis to avert for the time being a coalition of his enemies. Embarrassed by his domestic troubles, by the incipient quarrel between Warwick and the Woodvilles and by the restlessness of Henry VI's persistent partisans, the King of England faithfully observed the truce while Louis XI was struggling in the hornets' nest of the Common Weal conspiracy, and to this Louis owed it that he was not completely crushed.

But what was to follow? The worst was to be feared from the Burgundian intrigues. Every attempt at Anglo-French agreement was at once thwarted by Charles the Bold, then Count of Charolais and soon to be Duke of Burgundy, and the King of France's sworn enemy since the Common Weal conspiracy. He had already forced Louis to give Normandy as an appanage to his brother Charles, who might become a pole of attraction for all the enemies, Breton, English, and Burgundian, of the Valois monarchy. But Louis, on the ground of his brother's intrigues with London, soon reoccupied Normandy. Then Charles the Bold, hitherto a friend of the Lancastrians, of whom his mother Isabella of Portugal was a descendant, suppressed his family preference in order to attract Edward IV to himself. In May 1466 Louis obtained a renewal of the truce and proposed its prolongation together with a pension and a fresh matrimonial alliance. In June 1467 he invited Warwick to Rouen, where a plan was outlined for a trade agreement among the English, the Normans, and the Gascons. But at this point Edward IV, urged on by the Woodvilles, allied himself with Brittany and Castille, came to a secret understanding with the court of Burgundy, and finally gave his sister Margaret of York in marriage to Charles the Bold (June 1468). He informed his Parliament that this was the prelude to an early landing on the coast of France, where he would recover the inheritance of his ancestors.

For a second time the formidable Anglo-Burgundian alliance was renewed. For a second time Louis XI managed to dissolve it. It was not enough for him to neutralize Brittany. An unhappy venture at Péronne, where he rashly put himself within Charles the Bold's grasp, at least had the advantage of making the triumphant duke forget that he could now count on English arms. Then, resolved to finish with Burgundy, Louis achieved the finest diplomatic success in his eventful career: a reconciliation between Margaret of Anjou and Warwick, followed by the restoration of the Lancastrians. Gradually ousted from power by the Woodvilles, Warwick did not resign himself to rebel until June 1469. Since he did not command enough strength to carry on civil war by himself, he took refuge in Calais and then in Normandy. Louis arranged a meeting at Angers between Queen Margaret and her worst enemy, the proud 'King-maker'. They agreed that a marriage should unite the young Prince of Wales and Warwick's daughter, whose dowry would be paid by the King of France. Margaret granted a truce for thirty years (July 1470). With 30,000 écus advanced by Louis, the Lancastrian party raised mercenaries. A landing at Dartmouth from the fleet of the allies was the prelude to a triumphal march on London. Released from prison and 're-adepted' on October 6th, the wretched Henry VI could refuse nothing to the King of France. Now that England was his client, Louis proposed to make use of her to destroy the Burgundian State. By way of Normandy, Picardy, and Calais, their joint forces would attack Charles the Bold and proceed to share the spoils. Defining the terms of this agreement with Louis XI, the young Prince of Wales went so far as to recognize the Valois's title as King of France, which was tantamount to renouncing the poor but persistent English claim. It is true that his father, treating his subjects' nationalism more tactfully, did not go to this length, or prolong the truce for more than ten years. But it was agreed that a very early peace conference should settle the dynastic conflict.

Within less than six months, however, all this structure had collapsed. Abandoned by everyone, Edward IV took refuge at Middelburg in Zeeland. His brother-in-law of Burgundy gave him the necessary support to prepare for his revenge. Catching his enemies off their guard, he made a daring return to England, seized London, defeated and killed Warwick at Barnet on August 14th 1471, and, a fortnight later, crushed the Lancastrians at Tewkesbury in the west. The Prince of Wales was killed, his mother was taken prisoner, and his unfortunate father was murdered in the Tower. Louis XI found himself back again in a situation worse than in 1468, since the Anglo-Burgundian alliance, nurtured in misfortune and hatred, now seemed indissoluble. The best he could do was to postpone the inevitable result for a few months or a year or two. A short truce was

concluded in September 1471, and a fresh suspension of arms was negotiated in Brussels in March 1473. But Edward obtained from Parliament
the necessary subsidies for an invasion of France, which was first contemplated for 1474. Delays and intrigues postponed it again. In July 1474,
however, a treaty was concluded between Edward IV and Charles the
Bold. Together, as Henry V and John the Fearless had done, they divided
up the Valois kingdom in advance. If he helped Edward to conquer his
continental kingdom, the Burgundian would receive the county of Guines,
Picardy, Tournai, and above all Barrois and Champagne, which would
weld the scattered parts of his States into a single whole.

Charles the Bold's folly saved Louis XI from this mortal peril, for the
third time in less than ten years. All his forces, which those of the French
princes, quivering with impatience, would have been only too ready to
join, should have gone to link up with the English invaders. At this very
moment Charles flung himself into a venture in the Rhineland and went
off to besiege Neuss, whose inhabitants were in revolt against the Archbishop of Cologne. Louis XI was therefore faced only by the twenty
thousand men with whom Edward IV landed at Calais at the beginning
of July 1475. Too late, Charles the Bold joined his brother-in-law, but
only with a small escort. As the French princes had not stirred, the King
of England deemed it better to negotiate. The two armies were drawn up
facing each other on either side of the Somme. On August 29th, on the
bridge at Picquigny, Louis and Edward came to an agreement which
ended the English invasion. By its terms a truce suspended hostilities for
seven years. Edward re-embarked with his whole army on receipt of an
indemnity of 75,000 écus. All differences between the two nations were
henceforth to be settled by arbitration. A life annuity of 60,000 écus would
be paid to the King of England, whose eldest daughter would marry the
Dauphin Charles. Louis would purchase Margaret of Anjou's freedom for
a further 50,000 écus. Edward's entourage, for their part, were laden with
presents and pensions. This agreement suited both parties. Edward IV,
once more secure on his throne, would have no further need of subsidies from Parliament, since the French pension would suffice for his
subsistence. Louis XI, holding him as an ally by the lure of money, could
devote himself entirely to dealing with Burgundy.

Was this indeed, as has been asserted, the real end of the Hundred
Years' War? It is permissible to doubt it. No peace had been concluded.
Edward IV had not renounced either the throne of France or the lost
provinces to which he could lay claim as the heir of the Plantagenets.
Finally he remained strongly established in Calais. His neutrality would
last only as long as it suited his interests. This became apparent as early
as January 1477, when the question of the Burgundian succession arose.
Urged on by his sister Margaret of York and then by Maximilian of
Austria, who had married Charles the Bold's heiress, and also disturbed
to find Louis XI, now master of Artois and Boulonnais, on the border of

his precious Calais, Edward IV was often tempted to renew the age-old struggle. To hold him back, Louis XI had to keep on promising him fresh advantages: the concession of prolonged truces, a promise to continue payment of the 'tribute' far beyond Edward's lifetime, the assignment of a large dowry to the young Elizabeth of York. Peace, only just preserved time and again, was almost definitely endangered when the settlement of the affairs of Burgundy by the Treaty of Arras (December 1482) involved the marriage of the Dauphin and Margaret of Austria. This repudiation of his daughter served Edward IV as a pretext for great military preparations which only his death halted, or rather suspended. For Richard of Gloucester, when he became King Richard III by a daring usurpation, was no better disposed than his brother towards Louis XI or towards his successor, the young Charles VIII. Moreover, when at length Henry Tudor put a full stop to the War of the Roses, there was still no settlement between England and France, which an uneasy system of truces kept in an atmosphere of mutual suspicion. As late as 1487 there was talk of a possible English landing in Guienne, and in 1489 English forces once more fought in Brittany.

But to pursue our story further would be playing on words. Though no peace had ratified its results, the Hundred Years' War was long since over. It was true that Calais did not become French again until 1553 and that for centuries longer the English sovereigns continued to bear the empty title of King of France. But these were belated survivals of no importance. When the Burgundian State was dismembered, a fresh factor in the history of Europe relegated the old Anglo-French dispute to the background. Henceforth, for two centuries, Valois and Habsburg were to contend for hegemony on the continent. Between them England under the Tudors played the role of a pendulum, sometimes swinging towards the Empire, sometimes towards France. Already there was a beginning of the policy of the balance of power in Europe, which was essential to England for winning overseas markets. Once the turning-point of the years 1477–82 was past, there was nothing left of the feudal war, or even the dynastic war whose ups-and-downs had filled so many years and made so many generations suffer. There was nothing left, it would seem, even of hatred between the two nations or suspicious public opinion, harder to uproot from men's hearts and minds. The mutual mistrust of which our own period quite recently had, once again, the most unhappy experience did not go back to Joan of Arc, as some people would have us believe, but only to Louis XIV; and even that is long ago now.

CHRONOLOGICAL TABLE
BIBLIOGRAPHICAL NOTE
INDEX

CHRONOLOGICAL TABLE OF CONTEMPORARY RULERS

ENGLAND	FRANCE	CASTILLE	BURGUNDY (Valois)	EMPIRE	PAPACY
Edward I 1272–1307	Philip IV 1285–1314			Albert I (Austria) 1297–1308	Boniface VIII 1294–1303 Benedict XI 1303–4
Edward II 1307–27	Louis X 1314–16 Philip V 1316–22 Charles IV 1322–8	Alfonso XII 1312–50		Henry VII (Lux.) 1308–13	Clement V 1305–14 John XXII 1316–34
Edward III 1327–77	Philip VI (Valois) 1328–50			Ludwig (Bavaria) 1314–46	Benedict XII 1334–42 Clement VI 1342–52
	John the Good 1350–64	Pedro the Cruel 1350–69	Philip the Bold 1364–1404	Charles IV (Lux.) 1346–78	Innocent VI 1352–62 Urban V 1362–70 Gregory XI 1370–8
Richard II 1377–99	Charles V 1364–80	Henry II (Trast.) 1369–99 John I 1379–90 Henry III 1390–1406		Wenceslas (Lux.) 1378–1400	Urban VI 1378–89 Clement VII 1378–94 Boniface IX 1389–1404 Benedict XIII 1394–1416 Innocent VII 1404–6 Gregory XII 1406–15
Henry IV (Lanc.) 1399–1413	Charles VI 1380–1422		John the Fearless 1404–1419	Ruprecht (Bavaria) 1400–11	
Henry V 1413–22 Henry VI 1422–61	Charles VII 1422–61	John II 1406–54	Philip the Good 1419–67	Sigismund (Lux.) 1411–37	Alexander V 1409–10 John XXIII 1410–15 Martin V 1415–31
				Albert II (Aust.) 1438–9 Frederick III (Aust.) 1440–93	Eugen IV 1431–47 Nicholas V 1447–55
Edward IV 1461–83	Louis XI 1461–83	Henry IV 1454–74	Charles the Bold 1467–77		Calixtus III 1455–8 Pius II 1458–64 Paul II 1464–71 Sixtus IV 1471–84

BIBLIOGRAPHICAL NOTE

IN THE following notes for further reading, no attempt has been made at completeness, and the mass of printed sources, chronicles and records has been deliberately omitted. The reader will find listed first the latest general histories dealing with the fourteenth and fifteenth centuries in Western Europe, then the most important or most recent monographs, together with notes on the points which still require detailed studies.

Few writers have attempted the parallel study of the two kingdoms of France and England at a time, however, when their histories were closely interrelated. Vols. VII and VIII of *The Cambridge Mediaeval History* (1932–6) contain chapters of varying value and detailed bibliographies. In *Histoire générale* ed. by G. GLOTZ, Vol. VI, part ii of *Histoire du Moyen Age*, by A. COVILLE (*L'Europe occidentale de 1328 à 1380*, 1941), is a mere summary, leaving England almost completely out of the picture. Vol. VII, part i, by J. CALMETTE and E. DÉPREZ, *La France et l'Angleterre en conflit* (1937), is more detailed, but not always reliable. One has to go back to earlier, and not yet outdated national histories, such as *Histoire de France*, ed. by E. LAVISSE: vol. IV, in two parts, by A. COVILLE (*Les premiers Valois et la Guerre de Cent Ans*, 1902) and Ch. PETIT-DUTAILLIS (*Charles VII, Louis XI et les premières années de Charles VIII*, 1904). Of similar age but more limited scope is the *Political History of England* ed. by W. HUNT and R. L. POOLE, in which T. F. TOUT deals with the period 1216–1399 (1905) and C. OMAN with 1399–1485 (1906). They will be superseded by two volumes of the *Oxford History of England*, yet unpublished, by G. BARRACLOUGH (The Fourteenth Century) and E. F. JACOB (The Fifteenth Century). A forthcoming Penguin Book, by A. R. MYERS, will deal with *The Later Middle Ages*, in 'The Pelican History of England', while E. PERROY hopes shortly to publish a more detailed account of *Fourteenth Century England*.

In *L'Europe Occidentale de 1270 à 1328* (Paris, 1940), being vol. VI, part i, of the *Histoire du Moyen Age* in *Histoire générale* ed. by G. GLOTZ, R. FAWTIER gives a lucid survey of early fourteenth-century conditions. For economic and demographic problems, add T. F. TOUT, *The Place of the Reign of Edward II in English History* (2nd ed., Manchester, 1936); Eileen POWER, *The Wool Trade in English Medieval History* (Oxford, 1941); H. LAURENT, *Un grand commerce d'exportation européen au Moyen Age. La draperie des Pays Bas en France et dans les pays méditerranéens* (Paris, 1935); J. DE STURLER, *Les relations politiques et les échanges commerciaux entre le douché de Brabant et l'Angeleterre au Moyen Age* (Paris, 1936); F. LOT, 'L'Etat des Paroisses et des Feux de 1328' (*Bibliothèque de l'Ecole des Chartes*, 1929); J. C. RUSSELL, *British Medieval Population* (Albuquerque, 1948).

The diplomatic history of the war has been written by E. DÉPREZ, *Les préliminaires de la Guerre de Cent Ans. La papauté, la France et l'Angleterre*

(Paris, 1902) and H. S. LUCAS, *The Low Countries and the Hundred Years War* (Ann Arbor, 1929). Fragments of an unfinished history of Philip VI of Valois, by J. VIARD, have appeared in periodicals, dealing with finances (*Revue des Questions Historiques*, 1888), the campaign of Flanders (*Bibl. de l'Ecole des Chartes*, 1922), the campaign of Crécy (*La Moyen Age*, 1926), the siege of Calais (*ibid.*, 1929), etc. The reign of Edward III has been somewhat neglected by historians. The best account is still to be found in T. F. TOUT, *Chapters in the Administrative History of Mediaeval England*, vols. III–V (Manchester, 1929–31); add *The English Government at Work, 1327–36*, ed. by J. F. WILLARD, W. A. MORRIS, J. R. STRAYER and W. H. DUNHAM (Cambridge, Mass., 1940–50, 3 vols.), and a forthcoming book by E. B. FRYDE, *Edward III's War Finances, 1336–40. Transactions in Wool and Credit Operations.* Several monographs deal with the Black Death in England, from A. GASQUET, *The Great Pestilence* (2nd ed., London, 1893), to G. G. COULTON, *The Black Death* (Cambridge, 1929), whereas in France the subject has been approached locally: R. BOUTRUCHE, *La crise d'une société. Seigneurs et Paysans du Bordelais pendant la Guerre de Cent Ans* (Paris, 1947).

Some aspects of John the Good's reign are dealt with by R. DELACHENAL, *Histoire de Charles V.*, vols. I and II (Paris, 1909). The more recent essay of J. TOURNEUR-AUMONT, *La bataille de Poitiers et la construction de la France* (Poitiers, 1940), is of little value. There exist a sketchy biography of *The Black Prince*, by R. L. D. PATTISON (London, 1910), and a more reliable one of *John of Gaunt* by S. ARMITAGE-SMITH (Westminster, 1904). Suzanne HONORÉ-DUVERGIER is preparing a history of Charles the Bad, King of Navarre. Several monographs retrace the activities of *routiers*, such as G. GUIGUE, *Les Tard-Venus en Lyonnais* (1886); J. MONICAT, *Les Grandes Compagnies en Velay* (1929), etc.

R. DELACHENAL, *Histoire de Charles V* (Paris, 1909–31, 5 vols.), gives a minute narrative of political and military history, but leaves out social, economic, and administrative questions. This last field has been explored by G. DUPONT-FERRIER, *Les officiers royaux des bailliages et sénéchaussées et les institutions monarchiques locales en France à la fin du Moyen Age* (1902); *Etudes sur les institutions financières de la France à la fin du Moyen Age* (1930–3, 3 vols.); *Nouvelles études . . .* (1936), dealing with the collection and administration of taxes, the *élections*, the Cour des Aides and Cour du Trésor ; H. JASSEMIN, *La Chambre des Comptes de Paris au XVe siècle* (1933); all give a good description of the administrative machinery, but say too little about its evolution.

To the last two decades of English history in the 14th century, A. STEEL, *Richard II* (Cambridge, 1940) is a good introduction. There are many studies on the Peasants Revolt of 1381, the most detailed being A. RÉVILLE, *Le soulèvement des travailleurs d'Angleterre* (Paris, 1899). E. PERROY, *L'Angleterre et le Grand Schisme d'Occident*, vol. I (1933), must be read in conjunction with N. VALOIS, *La France et le Grand Schisme d'Occident* (Paris, 1896–1904, 4 vols.). Both show the relations of ecclesiastical matters with the politics of the time.

The long and dreary reign of Charles VI has inspired several detailed but somewhat diffuse studies by L. MIROT, including *Les insurrections urbaines au début du règne de Charles VI* (Paris, 1906), and 'Une tentative d'invasion anglaise en Angleterre pendant la guerre de Cent Ans' (*Revue des Questions historiques*, 1915). It is to be hoped that the forthcoming book of M. REY on Charles VI's finances may throw new light on the Marmosets' government. Civil factions and quarrels between Princes are naturally to the front, but have been examined from the personal or political angle: J. D'AVOUT, *La querelle des Armagnacs et des Bourguignons* (1943), gives the facts and a bibliography; E. PETIT, *Histoire des ducs de Bourgogne de la maison de Valois*, vol. I (1909), stops at 1380; O. CARTELLIERI, *Geschichte der Herzöge von Burgund. I. Philipp der Kühne* (1910), is a mere summary, supplemented by *Beiträge zur Geschichte der Herzöge von Burgund* (Heidelberg, 1910–13). See also E. JARRY, *La vie politique de Louis de France, duc d'Orléans* (Paris, 1889), to which F. D. S. DARWIN, *Louis d'Orléans* (London, 1936), adds little, and A. COVILLE, *Jean Petit, La question du tyrannicide au commencement du XVe siècle* (Paris, 1932). The diplomatic implications are shown by M. DE BOÜARD, *La France et l'Italie au temps du Grand Schisme d'Occident* (Paris, 1936), and H. LAURENT and F. QUICKE, *La formation de l'Etat bourguignon. L'accession de la maison de Bourgogne aux duchés de Brabant et de Limbourg*, vol. I (Brussels, 1939), to which F. QUICKE, *Les Pays-Bas à la veille de la période bourguignonne, 1356–84* (Brussels, 1947), serves as an introduction.

The administration of the princes' appanages and the growth of their retinues are less well known, in spite of R. LACOUR, *Le Gouvernement de l'apanage de Jean, duc de Berry* (Paris, 1934), and of several essays, by B. POCQUET DU HAUT-JUSSÉ, on Burgundian finances, issued since 1937 in *Bibliothèque de l'Ecole des Chartes, Annales de Bourgogne*, and other periodicals. A still valuable picture of the breakdown of administration has been given by A. COVILLE, *Les Cabochiens et l'Ordonnance de 1413* (Paris, 1888).

On the Lancastrians, J. H. WYLIE, *History of England under the reign of Henry the Fourth* (London, 1884–98, 4 vols.), is discursive and out-of-date; add J. E. LLOYD, *Owen Glendower* (London, 1931). J. H. WYLIE and W. T. WAUGH, *The Reign of Henry the Fifth* (London and Cambridge, 1914–29, 3 vols.), and R. A. NEWHALL, *The English Conquest of Normandy* (Newhaven, Conn., 1924), are both very detailed. A short survey is given by E. F. JACOB, *Henry V and the Invasion of France* (London, 1947). The English administration of Normandy has been subjected to the examination of Miss B. J. ROWE in several articles (e.g. *English Historical Review*, 1926, 1931, 1932); R. DOUCET, 'Les finances anglaises en France à la fin de la Guerre de Cent Ans' (*Le Moyen Age*, 1926); P. LECACHEUX, *Rouen au temps de Jeanne d'Arc et pendant l'occupation anglaise* (Caen, 1931); H. DE FRONDEVILLE, *La vicomté d'Orbec pendant l'occupation anglaise* (Lisieux, 1936): R. A. NEWHALL, *Muster and Review* (Cambridge, Mass., 1940).

On the kingdom of Bourges, research is as yet less advanced. A very old *Histoire de Charles VII*, by G. DU FRESNE DE BEAUCOURT (Paris, 1881–91, 6 vols.), has been supplemented by monographs on military history, such as E. COSNEAU, *Le connétable de Richemont, Arthur de Bretagne* (Paris, 1886); J. DÉNIAU, *La Commune de Lyon et la guerre bourguignonne, 1417–35* (Lyon, 1936); A. BOSSUAT, *Perrinet Gressart et François de Suriennne, agents de l'Angleterre* (Paris, 1936).

As soon as one reaches Joan of Arc, the mass of books is overwhelming. Few of these are of any use to the historian. The over-critical *Vie de Jeanne d'Arc* by A. FRANCE (Paris, 1908, 2 vols.) has been answered by a more lyrical *Jeanne d'Arc* by G. HANOTAUX (Paris, 1911). In English, M. WALDMANN's *Joan of Arc* (London, 1935) is the most up-to-date, although perhaps less reliable than A. LANG's *The Maid of France* (London, 1908). One may be well advised to consult the *Procès de condamnation de Jeanne d'Arc*, edited with a French translation by P. CHAMPION (Paris, 1921, 2 vols.).

On Charles VII's reign after his coronation, the best known aspect is that dealing with the Ecorcheurs' pillagings, through monographs such as J. QUICHERAT, *Rodrigue de Villandrando* (Paris, 1879); H. COURTEAULT, *Gaston IV, comte de Foix* (Paris, 1895); Ch. SAMARAN, *La maison d'Armagnac au XVe siècle et les dernières luttes de la féodalité dans le Midi de la France* (Paris, 1908); or H. SURIREY DE SAINT-RÉMY, *Jean II, duc de Bourbon* (Paris, 1943). But there is no synthetic survey of the administrative reforms, the only valuable monograph being N. VALOIS, *Histoire de la Pragmatique Sanction et de son application sous Charles VII* (Paris, 1908). On agrarian reconstruction, local studies have been attempted, or programmes for research like A. LESORT, 'La reconstruction des églises après la Guerre de Cent Ans' (*Revue d'Histoire de l'Englise de France*, 1934). R. GANDILHON is preparing a monograph on Jacques Cœur, which is much needed. Dealing with the Princes' intrigues, L. D. V. OWEN, *The Connection between England and Burgundy during the first half of the fifteenth century* (Oxford, 1909), and M. THIBAULT, *La jeunesse de Louis XI* (Paris, 1907), may be useful. But the Burgundian State has naturally and rightly focussed attention: the short essay of P. BONENFANT, *Philippe le Bon* (Brussels, 1943), is a stimulating introduction to the subject.

Turning back to England, we must notice that the third and last Lancastrian reign has been very much neglected. K. H. VICKERS, *Humphrey, Duke of Gloucester* (London, 1907), is but a limited biography. Neither K. B. McFARLANE's thesis on Cardinal Henry Beaufort, nor S. B. CHRIMES's on Bedford have been published. One must read the last-named author's *English Constitutional Ideas in the 15th century* (Cambridge, 1936), and C. L. KINGSFORD, *Prejudice and Promise in 15th century England* (London, 1925). After 1450, one has the narrative of Cora L. SCOFIELD, *The Life and Reign of Edward the Fourth* (London, 1924, 2 vols.), which supplements the older monograph of C. W. OMAN, *Warwick the Kingmaker* (London, 1891). Social problems are dealt with by H. S. BENNETT, *The Pastons and their England* (London, 1932), and Sylvia L. THRUPP, *The Merchant Class of London, 1300–1500* (Chicago, 1948). Lastly the final phases of the war are explained by J. CALMETTE and G. PÉRINELLE, *Louis XI et l'Angleterre* (Paris, 1930).

INDEX

369